Praise for the InCryptid novels

"The only thing more fun than an October Daye book is an InCryptid book. Swift narrative, charm, great world-building . . . all the McGuire trademarks." —Charlaine Harris, #1 *New York Times*-bestselling author

"Seanan McGuire's *Discount Armageddon* is an urban fantasy triple threat—smart and sexy and funny. The Aeslin mice alone are worth the price of the book, so consider a cast of truly original characters, a plot where weird never overwhelms logic, and some serious kickass world-building as a bonus." —Tanya Huff, bestselling author of *The Wild Ways*

"McGuire's InCryptid series is one of the most reliably imaginative and well-told sci-fi series to be found, and she brings all her considerable talents to bear on *[Tricks for Free]*. . . . McGuire's heroine is a brave, resourceful and sarcastic delight, and her intrepid comrades are just the kind of supportive and snarky sidekicks she needs."
—*RT Book Reviews (top pick)*

"While *[Spelunking Through Hell]* veers noticeably from the urban fantasy of earlier volumes, taking place primarily in strange realms with almost no humans in sight, it still bears all the hallmarks of the InCryptid series: a clever protagonist, snarky banter, unusual creatures, and an entertaining blend of action, romance, and horror (the secret behind Alice's enduring youth and vitality is especially unsettling). At heart a love story, this entry delivers both a satisfying payoff for fans of the series and an intriguing expansion of its universe." —*Publishers Weekly*

"McGuire's characters are equal parts sass and sarcasm, set in an ever-expanding interdimensional world where Alice is on a journey highlighted by emotional chaos and roller-coaster pacing. Fans will be delighted by *[Spelunking Through Hell]*." —*Library Journal*

"*Discount Armageddon* is a quick-witted, sharp-edged look at what makes a monster monstrous, and at how closely our urban fantasy protagonists walk—or dance—that line. The pacing never lets up, and when the end comes, you're left wanting more. I can't wait for the next book!"
—C. E. Murphy, author of *Raven Calls*

BACKPACKING THROUGH BEDLAM

An InCryptid Novel

SEANAN McGUIRE

DAW BOOKS
New York

Cover illustration by Lee Moyer.

Cover design by Jeanette Tran and Adam Auerbach.

Edited by Sheila E. Gilbert.

DAW Book Collectors No. 1938.

DAW Books
An imprint of Astra Publishing House
dawbooks.com
DAW Books and its logo are registered trademarks of Astra Publishing House

Printed in the United States of America

Library of Congress Cataloging-in-Publication Data

Names: McGuire, Seanan, author.
Title: Backpacking through Bedlam / Seanan McGuire.
Description: First edition. | New York : DAW Books, 2023. | Series:
  Incryptid ; 12
Identifiers: LCCN 2022054304 (print) | LCCN 2022054305 (ebook) |
  ISBN 9780756418571 (Trade Paperback) | ISBN 9780756418588 (Ebook)
Classification: LCC PS3607.R36395 B33 2023 (print) | LCC PS3607.R36395
  (ebook) | DDC 813/.6—dc23
LC record available at https://lccn.loc.gov/2022054304
LC ebook record available at https://lccn.loc.gov/2022054305

First edition: March 2023
10 9 8 7 6 5 4 3 2

For Jennifer, who has never been anything but a rock to brace myself against, and for Grace. Thank you for helping me reopen a door that should never have been closed.

Price Family Tree

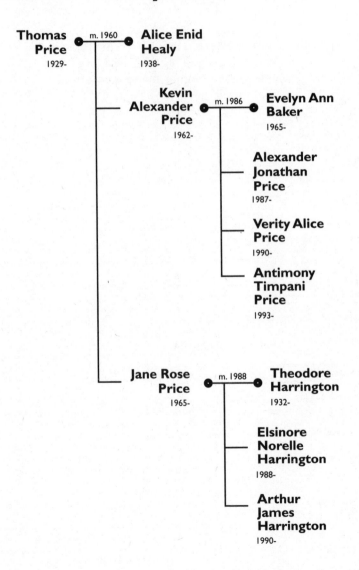

Thomas Price
1929-

m. 1960

Alice Enid Healy
1938-

Kevin Alexander Price
1962-

m. 1986

Evelyn Ann Baker
1965-

Alexander Jonathan Price
1987-

Verity Alice Price
1990-

Antimony Timpani Price
1993-

Jane Rose Price
1965-

m. 1988

Theodore Harrington
1932-

Elsinore Norelle Harrington
1988-

Arthur James Harrington
1990-

Baker Family Tree

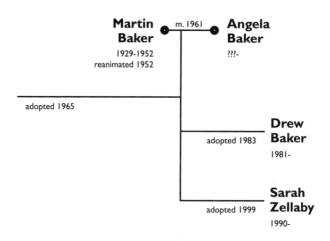

Martin Baker
m. 1961
Angela Baker

1929-1952
reanimated 1952

???-

adopted 1965

adopted 1983
Drew Baker
1981-

adopted 1999
Sarah Zellaby
1990-

AUTHOR'S NOTE

The InCryptid series is set in a world where parallel evolution and dimensional rifts have resulted in humans sharing the planet with multiple species of cryptid capable of passing for human, among many other differences and divergences. The COVID-19 pandemic has not happened in this version of reality, a decision I struggled with but ultimately decided best suited both the narrative and the series as a whole.

I am hoping people will understand the reasons for this departure from reality. But for right now, the integrity of this fictional world is better served by not including the pandemic.

Reunion, noun:

1. The state of being united again.

Reconciliation, noun:

1. An act of reconciling, as when former enemies agree to an amiable truce.

2. The process of making consistent or compatible.

3. See also "impossible."

Prologue

"Being born to the Covenant means there was never a moment when I chose this life. It was chosen for me, before my parents were born, and it was chosen for my children, if ever I had them. Alice was the first person I met who actually believed we all got to have a choice. She certainly did."

—Thomas Price

Just outside the Galway Woods, Buckley Township, Michigan

Sixty years ago

ALICE PRICE-HEALY, DAUGHTER OF Jonathan and Frances Healy, married to Thomas Price of the Covenant Prices for exactly one year, backed up until she was pressed against the side of the rotten old barn at the edge of the swamp, cursing herself for a fool the whole time. It wasn't an unusual occurrence, either the cursing or the foolishness, but the location was a bit out of the ordinary. Alice normally did the majority of her hunting and aimless wandering inside the Galway Woods, the forest of her childhood, where both her mother and grandmother had died.

(The fact that Enid had managed to make it all the way home before succumbing to the venom of the Bidi-taurabo-liaza didn't change the fact that she'd received the fatal bite while still inside the boundaries of the Galway. The forest had always done its best to protect the Healy women. Its best had never, not once, been enough.)

But today, oh. Today, Alice had been out doing the annual jackalope count—almost as many mature bucks in the colony this year there had been as last year, and that was a good thing, since the population was declining in most of the country—and she'd gotten off track on the way back, woolgathering about what she was going to do for dinner. It was her anniversary, after all. She ought to do something special. If she'd married anyone else, they'd be doing what Grandma and Grandpa had always done, putting on their Sunday clothes and heading into town for a meal at one of the nicer restaurants, the ones where they wouldn't even let a lady in if she wasn't wearing a decent skirt.

Sure, Buckley was small enough that they only had two places that nice, and she'd have been happier at the Red Angel or Bronson's *anyway*, but that didn't matter. Hell, if she'd married anyone else, they could have driven to Ann Arbor if they'd wanted to! Or they could have done like Mama and Daddy used to do, back when she'd been little and Mama had been alive to do anything with Daddy. Mama had never seen the point of fancy restaurants and putting on airs, called it a waste of time, money, and everything else a body had to waste. Fran had celebrated her wedding anniversaries in the shadow of the Galway Wood, sitting on a picnic blanket with her lovestruck husband and, after a few years, her continually active daughter, eating cold chicken sandwiches and laughing. That was probably what Alice remembered best about her mother. Her laughter, bright as a bell, and ringing all the time.

Well, her laughter, and what a damned good shot she'd been. Alice fumbled to reload her revolver, careful to keep her shoulders pressed against the barn. She could have used a damned good shot. Or a damned poor one. Anybody to help her get out of this stupid-ass predicament she'd gone and gotten herself into, letting herself wander without paying attention to where she was going until she had wandered straight into the swamp.

At least if she died out here, Thomas would know right away. Wouldn't that be a hell of an anniversary gift? "Sorry, sweetie, you're a widower now, but your deal with the crossroads is null and void and you can go wherever you want"? Maybe if she asked really nicely, Mary would help her stick around long enough to go by the house and deliver the news in person. Well, as much as the ghost of your dead wife suddenly appearing in the living room could be considered "in person." Really, it probably wasn't a good idea. She was pretty sure it could be taken as being intentionally cruel. "You weren't there to save me, so I *died*, and now you get to go outside, aren't you lucky."

And there she went, woolgathering again. Maybe it was time she admitted that being married to a man who couldn't even step far enough out the front door to join her on the porch was wearing on her.

Oh, she loved him. She had never loved anyone else half as much as she loved Thomas Price, and that was probably for the best, because some days she felt like she loved him so much it might kill her. Some days it felt like it was verging toward the dangerous kind of love, the kind her Daddy'd had for her Ma, the kind that had eaten him alive from the inside out after Fran had died.

She figured love was a lot like the swamp bromeliads. Good and healthy in the right ecosystem, but invasive and destructive if it got planted out of place. As long as she remembered the way love had swallowed her father, she thought she could keep her own love pruned back enough to stay healthy. At least, she hoped so. As long as Thomas didn't go dying on her or something ridiculous like that, she'd be fine. Probably.

As long as she didn't go and do something stupid like dying here, with her back up against a rotting old barn and no one else human for miles. She was outside of Cynthia's normal hunting range; the Huldra tended to take her prey a decent distance from the Angel, for the sake of keeping other predators from following her back to the bar, but even she didn't go this far looking for a snack. Desperately, Alice loaded bullets into the gun and tried to review the territories of every local cryptid she knew, from Sunny the boo hag to Earl the Loveland frogman. None of them intersected with this slice of the swamp. Backup wasn't coming.

Oh, someone would find her body . . . eventually.

That was assuming the swamp hags left any pieces of her to be found. They might not. Swamp hags ate a lot like hogs: they tore a carcass apart and swallowed every scrap. They were obligate carnivores, and if she'd been paying a lick of attention to her surroundings, she wouldn't have let herself drift into their territory.

Swamp hags were amphibians, like Loveland frogmen, but unlike Earl, they weren't intelligent beings or proper people. About as smart as the average frog, that was a swamp hag, but with the temperament of a wild boar and the slashing claws of a cougar. Size of a person, to boot, or bigger than a person if the person in question was someone like Alice, who had always been petite. She'd seen at least five of the slippery fucks before she ducked behind the barn.

At least their presence explained why the barn—and the associated dilapidated farmhouse—had been abandoned, despite being structurally sound enough to still be standing after years of neglect. Even in a place like Buckley, people mostly didn't like to live where man-sized amphibious monsters were likely to slide in through a window and eat the kids in the middle of the night. Alice slotted the last bullet into the chamber, snapping it shut, and rested the barrel of the gun lengthwise against her forehead in a brief semblance of prayer.

"Mama, if you could help me out with this, I'd surely appreciate it," she murmured.

Swamp hags hunted in colonies, if she remembered right—and years of working solo meant she *always* remembered right when it came to predators large enough to do her serious injury. For them to be as large as the ones she'd seen, this had to be an adult breeding colony, meaning she could be looking at, oh, twenty or thirty fully grown, hungry hags, as well as any of the little ones big enough to have arms and legs and claws and teeth, but not big enough to hunt on their own just yet.

There had always been a few swamp hags lurking around the edges of the swamp adjacent to the Galway, but never anything like this. She should have noticed them getting to this sort of population density, should have read it in the prey animals and the way the bloodworms had been getting scarcer and scarcer. But she'd been distracted with learning how to be a wife and navigating the surprisingly complex political network of the town, and she hadn't been paying proper attention.

She hadn't been paying proper attention, and now she was going to pay for it.

At least swamp hags were ambush predators rather than active hunters. They knew she couldn't get back to solid ground without running across the patches of marsh between her and safety. All they had to do was make themselves near to invisible in the muck and the mire, and as soon as she moved, they'd have her. That meant she could delay the inevitable by simply staying still. The only urgency was the time. The sun would be setting in an hour or so, and once it got dark, their hunting tactics would change. Once it got dark, they'd come for her, the same way they had probably come for the people who lived here, once upon a slaughterhouse.

Alice sighed, lowering the gun. There was something she could try, but it wasn't likely to work. It had been working less and less lately. Still, she closed her eyes for a moment, cursing herself for a fool for doing that when she was surrounded by unseen predators, and said, "Mary, I need you."

There was no sound or smell or sign that anything had changed, but still, Alice felt like the air had shifted, like something was different now than it had been a moment before. She opened her eyes, glancing to the side, and there was her babysitter, the long-dead, eternally teen-aged Mary Dunlavy, wearing the most recent iteration of her standard "I am a normal teenage girl, look how normal I am" outfit: knee-capper denim jeans and a black-and-yellow checkered top that Alice thought made her look a little bit like a taxicab from a movie. Her long white hair was held back by a yellow headband, and she had a quizzical expression on her face.

"Much as I appreciate the chance to catch up, Alice, I sort of figured you'd be at home, since it's your first wedding anniversary, not standing in the middle of the swamp surrounded by amphibious apex predators." Her tone matched her expression, more distant puzzlement than any sort of actual alarm.

Alice thought there must be something about being dead that made it harder for people to get really *upset*. She'd seen Mary do it a few times, and it was always alarming and strange. Most of the time, Mary answered every crisis with the same degree of faintly bewildered equanimity, like the world was just an unending series of small, interesting surprises that had no actual bearing on her continuing existence.

"I was *supposed* to be home by now," said Alice. "I went out to do the jackalope survey, and I got to thinking about dinner while I was walking back to the house, and I guess I got a little bit off track is all."

"You got so off track you wound up in the *swamp*?" Mary didn't sound like she believed her. That was fine. Alice wasn't certain she believed herself, either, and she'd been there. "Alice, you know this forest better than you know the back of your own hand. There's no way you got so distracted that you wound up here without meaning to. What's wrong?"

"You know, I'd really like to have a heart-to-heart with you about everything that's bothering me, but maybe not when we're about an hour away from me being torn to pieces by big weird amphibians who look like ladies for no good reason other than sometimes evolution's a real asshole, okay?" Alice shot her an exasperated look. "Any chance you can help me out of this?"

"Hold tight and I'll ask," said Mary, and disappeared.

Alice sighed again as she began scanning the marshy ground between her and the tree line for signs of swamp hags. Swamp hags didn't do tactics beyond the basic ones that instinct provided them with; they were basically big frogs, and if they had a little more in the way of clever than an ordinary frog, it was all down to them having bigger heads and bigger brains, which meant more space for thinking about things. But since they were still frogs, the things they were thinking about were generally food, safety, and whether or not it was safe to make more frogs.

So they wouldn't have chosen sophisticated hiding spots. And that would have been fine if they hadn't had just enough smart in them to wait until she was good and surrounded by marsh on all sides before they showed themselves.

How she'd been able to wander that far across the marsh without noticing was a little harder to understand. Sure, she usually managed to step where she needed to be stepping, and to avoid stepping where she shouldn't, but she hadn't been paying any attention to where she'd been going, and yet somehow that had translated to her not stepping in a single puddle or patch of mud deep enough to catch her attention. It didn't make any sense, which was why she didn't have any trouble believing it had happened.

The less sense something made, the less point there was in arguing with it.

Mary reappeared as abruptly as she had vanished, shaking her head. "Well, kiddo, looks like you're in luck," she said. "My employers have decided that in this instance, seeing you safely back to the woods counts as a standard part of babysitting duties. Follow me."

She began walking across the marsh, her feet never sinking into the wet ground, her shoes never getting muddy. Alice only hesitated a moment before she followed.

Mary had been one of the most trusted people in Alice's world since she was an infant in swaddling clothes, placed into the arms of a white-haired teenager by a mother who needed a little help. Fran hadn't known Mary was dead at the time, but the family had figured it out pretty quickly and, rather than firing the girl, had essentially adopted her. Every house needs a haunting, after all, and Mary was theirs.

But Mary wasn't *just* theirs, and never had been. Mary Dunlavy was a crossroads ghost, a dogsbody for the terrifying supernatural entity that brokered bargains for the unwise and the unwary, the desperate and the doomed. She couldn't do anything without their permission. When Alice had been young, that permission had been easy—Mary's babysitting duties were always allowed, unless the crossroads needed her elsewhere. And when Alice had been injured, anything that fell under the heading of nursing her back to health had been considered acceptable. Now, though . . .

Now, every request had to be run through the crossroads, and unless they said it was all right for Mary to do without a contract, Mary had to say no or offer to broker a bargain. Alice had never been particularly tempted to deal with the crossroads for her own benefit *before* Thomas made his own bargain, and now, having seen what they were doing to him, she was even less inclined to push when Mary said the crossroads didn't want her to do something.

She still didn't know the exact terms of Thomas's deal with the crossroads, only that it had involved her in some way, and when she died, if she died before he did, he would be freed from the arrangement and able to leave the house again. Maybe it was about time she pressed him to tell her the rest.

Drawing her second revolver and holding both at the ready, Alice began following Mary across the marsh.

Mary was following the safest route, her spectral nature keeping her from entirely noticing how wet it was. Alice wasn't quite so lucky. Her own special brand of uncomprehending good fortune didn't feel the need to step in when she was following a supposedly safe path, and so her very first step left her with one foot mired up to the ankle in muck. Alice scowled.

"I *liked* these shoes."

"Should have thought about that before you woolgathered yourself right into the swamp," said Mary, not looking back.

Alice shot an annoyed glance at her and kept following, pausing to yank her feet free of the mud every few steps.

They were halfway to the trees when two lumpy clumps of muddy, grassy earth rose up and reached for her, webbed hands hooked to grasp and tear. Alice shot them both, one in the forehead, one in the stomach, and they fell, more of the ground around them heaving as the other swamp hags smelled blood and prepared to attack.

"Alice?"

"Yeah?"

"Run."

Alice bolted for the trees, not looking back. Mary didn't, remaining visible and frozen in the middle of the swampy ground. She made a tempting target, even if she didn't have any actual flesh for them to devour, and with the scent of blood in the air, it was unlikely the swamp hags would realize she wasn't physical until they actually attacked her. Many prey animals froze when frightened. Mary's actions were perfectly understandable, if you were a creature with a brain the size of a swamp hag's.

So Alice ran, and Mary remained, and when the swamp hags

lunged for her, they passed through her insubstantial body, falling into the muck. Several of them turned their attention to the bodies of their fallen kin, beginning to devour them, while a few of the others turned toward Alice, gauging the distance between her and them.

Only three took off after the woman, the rest remaining to squabble over the meat and make ineffectual swipes at Mary. Mary rolled her eyes.

"Amateurs," she said, and vanished.

Alice was almost to the trees when Mary appeared in front of her, looking almost bored. "Three on your tail," she said, studying her nails. "Might want to get rid of them."

"Oh, for—" Alice swore under her breath as she whipped around and dug her heels into the swampy ground, firing three times. She didn't take the time to aim. It didn't seem to matter. All three bullets found their places, and three more swamp hags went down.

Mary watched this, hand dropping back to her side as her mouth fell slightly open. Even after years of dealing with Alice, the woman could still astonish her.

Does she even realize how impossible it is to do what she just did? she asked herself. *Everybody needs to* aim.

Everybody but Alice. When she'd been alive, Mary had believed humans were in charge of the whole world, with nothing to challenge them for their dominion. Dying had been a real eye-opener, in more ways than one. Humans were far from alone where intelligence was concerned; they might have the sheer numbers to put them at the top of the food chain, but lots and lots of other species, many of them humanoid enough to blend in, were also kicking around, looking for their place in the grand scheme of things.

Sometimes Mary suspected Alice had one or more of those "looks human enough to bring home to Mom, actually about as human as an opossum" folks kicking around somewhere back in her family line. Something like a jink or a mara or even a Fortuna, something that could bend luck to suit itself. It would explain a lot.

Panting, Alice turned and finished running for the trees, only stopping again once she was safely back on solid ground. "Thanks for the save, Mary. I'll write to Aldo and see if he wants to bring the boys this way for a frog hunt this summer." She grimaced at the thought of intentionally triggering a cull. Swamp hags were an important part of the ecosystem, but without any local predators, they would overrun their breeding grounds and start throwing the whole forest out of balance if they weren't culled. Didn't make killing them when they weren't an active danger fun.

"See that you do that," said Mary. "And pay *attention* when you're wandering around out here! Honestly, you know better than this."

"Guess I do," said Alice, holstering her guns. "Still, you came to my rescue."

"This time. What would you have done if the crossroads told me not to?"

Alice looked away.

Mary groaned. "You *can't* count on me the way you used to, Alice, you know that! Now get home before that husband of yours starts trying to summon me so he can ask where you are."

"I'm getting, I'm getting."

"And, Alice?"

"Yeah?"

Mary hesitated, her face going through the complicated series of small expressions that meant she was fighting against her own rules to say something she thought was going to matter. Finally, in a rushed tone, she said, "*Talk* to him. I know it goes against everything you think is natural, but you need to *talk* to him. Nothing gets better if you don't open your damn mouth. Okay?"

"Okay, Mary," said Alice, blinking. "I'll talk to him."

"Promise?"

"I promise," said Alice.

"Good girl," said Mary, and vanished, leaving Alice standing alone in the Galway Wood, near the edge of the swamp, the late afternoon light slanting through the leaves.

She turned, feeling out her location in the quality of the soil under her feet, and started in the direction that felt the most like home. She was quick, and nothing in the Galway that afternoon was hungry enough to get in her way. She made it home before the sun finished going down.

Thomas's silhouette was a dark blur in the kitchen window. Smiling, Alice broke into a run, on her way back to him once more.

One

"Best thing about that girl is how much she takes after her daddy. Worst thing is how much she takes after me."

—Frances Brown

A dimension that may or may not have a name, making bad choices, which is pretty much par for the course

Now, whatever that means

THE THING, WHATEVER IT was, had erupted from the ground in front of us in a writhing mass of tentacles, sort of like the world's largest sea anemone. They could have all been part of the same massive, subterranean beast, or they could have been unique individuals working in concert to ruin my day. With most of the thing still buried, I had no way of knowing, and at the moment, I had better things to worry about, like the fact that it was trying to kill us.

The part of me raised to respect nature and appreciate the need of all living things to participate in the great and glorious web of life wanted to know more. Wanted to get right up to the edge of the hole and look down, figure out the body plan and likely behaviors of the thing, determine whether we were dealing with one or many—begin the scientific process at its most basic. The part of me that has been surviving in hostile dimensions for half a century said that part was being bog-stupid, and we should shoot the thing until it stopped moving.

If there was something important here for us to learn, we could learn it from the corpse. Lots of naturalists have worked exclusively from dead things. It's a time-honored tradition, and you know what it gets us? A lot less dead naturalists, that's what.

Most of our ragged band of refugees had been smart enough to scatter when the ground started heaving like a cat trying to hork up a particularly difficult hairball. A few of the former Murray guards and some of Thomas's trained soldiers had formed a rough perimeter around the noncombatants, assorted polearms and other weapons lowered in a bristling wall of pointy pointy ouch ouch. I didn't begrudge them the attempt at creating a defensible position. Just showed they had marginally more common sense than the rest of us.

"The rest of us," in this case, was me, my husband, and my husband's semi-adopted daughter who he'd acquired during the fifty years we spent living in different dimensions. And it says something about the tentacle geyser in front of me that that sentence was *not* the weirdest thing about my day.

Or maybe it says something about my life. It can be difficult to tell sometimes.

The tentacles varied in diameter from about the size of a hose to bigger around than my torso. They waved threateningly, seeming to follow the vibration of our footsteps as they slapped at the ground. This wasn't as novel as it sounds. Lots of things that live underground use vibrations to hunt. They were dark pink, with an odd, leathery texture like an elephant's trunk, and probably meant whatever we were dealing with was the local equivalent of a mammal.

"Always nice to know what's about to eat you," I muttered, unholstering my mother's revolvers. One major downside of where the thing had emerged: if I chucked a grenade at it, a lot of people would get hurt, and I wasn't willing to dismiss them as collateral damage. Not after spending six months shepherding them across dimensions in a vain attempt to get them to someplace they could call home.

Well, this dimension was out of the running, if it was going to go sprouting tentacle fountains all over the damn place.

One of the tentacles snapped like a whip, almost brushing the front rank of guards. They gasped but held their ground, refusing to be intimidated. Okay, that was it. I stomped my foot as hard as I could, hoping the vibrations would make me seem like a better target. "Hey, *ugly*!"

That wasn't very nice of me. Maybe this thing was the most attractive bundle of tentacles in the whole dimension, and all the other bundles of tentacles wanted to come over to its horrifying underground lair for the local equivalent of coffee. But the thing was trying to hit my people, and I didn't like that.

Fortunately, I'd been right about the vibrations. The tentacles stopped lashing out at the guards and reoriented to lash out at me, leaving me to jump and dodge in to avoid being smacked upside the head. I didn't shoot. I wasn't entirely sure bullets would do me any good against this thing; I wanted to get more of it aboveground before I started trying to hurt it.

Thomas—the husband I mentioned before—shouted something. I glanced toward him, distracted. Only for a second. Maybe only half a second. It was long enough.

The next thrashing tentacle caught me square across the stomach and sent me flying backward, stopping only when my back found a convenient rock wall. I slammed into it hard enough to send my diaphragm into a spasm. Unable to catch my breath, I slid limply to the ground, where I blacked out.

So yeah. Just another normal day in paradise.

It was at least a *brief* loss of consciousness, since the scene was basically the same and my ears were still ringing when I woke up. My back ached, but not enough to indicate that I'd broken anything; at most, I might've cracked a rib and just not been able to feel it yet. That was fine. I don't think I have any ribs left that I *haven't* cracked at least once, and most of them are in the frequent-flier club.

The impact had also knocked my revolvers out of my hands, which was a much bigger problem than knocking the air out of my lungs: air is replaceable. My revolvers, which used to belong to my mother, are not. I shoved myself to a standing position, scanning the ground until I found them, and bolted forward. The tentacles were still flailing wildly, but I should be able to get to the guns before I got smacked again. If not, well. I bounce.

Thomas was shouting again, although I couldn't make out quite what he was saying. This time, I kept my eyes on my goal, refusing to let myself be distracted. If this thing wasn't going to back down, I was going to *make* it back down.

I don't know what it was about the run of dimensions we'd been in for the last few weeks, but they all seemed to think megafauna was an absolutely fabulous idea, yes, good, let's make more of it. When we got back to Ithaca, I was going to have a serious sit-down with Phoebe and Helen about what, exactly, they had been thinking when they said this was a good direction to find uninhabited worlds that might be suitable for our bottle universe refugees.

And this is all getting a bit confusing, so hey, let's pause in the middle of a pitched battle against a giant tentacle monster—or monsters, as the case might be—and agree on the basics. My name is Alice Enid Price-Healy. I spent fifty-five years as the unwitting hunting dog of a serpentine asshole who thought sending me in the wrong direction was morally acceptable, and my reward was finding the husband everyone had been trying to tell me was long since dead and buried. Turned out he was just fine, for values of "fine" that include "trapped in an inescapable bottle dimension, magically exhausting himself trying to keep the place from collapsing while he's still inside it." Since I'd been fine for a value of "fine" that meant "allowing myself to be regularly skinned alive in order to stay healthy enough to keep looking for my husband," I couldn't exactly get mad about the situation. Although I could certainly grumble about it whenever the opportunity arose.

See, fifty-five years ago, the bargain Thomas made with a horrifying supernatural entity we called "the crossroads" came due, and he was ripped away from the life we'd been building together and thrown across a few dozen dimensional barriers to wind up in that bottle dimension, which was actually the rotting, cast-off corpse of the world the crossroads originally came from, or something close to the world they originally came from—it's hard to be sure when you're talking about centuries of time and multiple dimensions of distance. He'd been too far away to get a message to me, and too trapped to make it home, and so I'd done the sensible thing, for certain definitions of "sensible," and gone charging after him.

We'd had two small children when that happened, and I'd passed them off to my best friend, Laura Campbell, with the promise that I'd be back as soon as I could. Well, I'd kept my word on that, it just turned out that "as soon as I could" was more than fifty years, thanks to the serpentine asshole I mentioned before.

Naga was a Professor of Extra-Dimensional Studies at the University of K'larth. We met when I was just a little kid. He'd been summoned by a group of snake cultists who'd believed he was their god and could grant them infinite power, and I'd been kidnapped as a sacrifice by the same group. Big mistake. Both parts, really. Naga wasn't a god, just a frustrated academic who didn't like cultists, and while I had a pissed-off mother with a big gun and a ghost babysitter, neither of whom was going to sit idly by while I got fed to a giant snake.

Naga and I survived that night. The snake cultists didn't. We'd stayed in touch while I was growing up, communicating through a mail system I didn't entirely understand but appreciated all the same.

There had been times, in the gap between coming home from college and my father's death, where Naga's letters had been all that kept me sane. So I'd trusted him. Of course I'd trusted him. He was my *friend*.

My friend who, as soon as he had the opportunity, started lying to me, intentionally steering me away from the path most likely to reunite me with my husband, keeping me from my children until they became adults with their own lives and their own children and no need or desire to have me around.

My friend, who let me spend fifty years thinking maybe everyone I loved was right when they told me I was chasing a ghost, that I was never going to find him because he wasn't out there anymore. My friend who—and this is the best part—convinced me to let him have me *skinned alive* over and over again so he could collect the magical membrane that adhered to my skin every time I pushed my way through the wall between dimensions.

Yeah. Great guy, Naga. I almost wish I hadn't let Thomas kill him. Only almost, and only because the more time I have to think about what he did to me—to us—the more I wish I'd been able to kill him myself.

But that's water under the temporal bridge. I went the direction Naga didn't want me going, and I found Thomas, just like I always said I was going to. Thanks to the wonders of magic, he was almost the same physical age he'd been when he vanished. I would have been happy married to a man in his nineties, but being able to skip that in favor of us both being young enough to survive getting *out* of the bottle dimension had been a bonus. So we were finally together, and we were going to get our happy ending, right? Right?

Wrong. So, so wrong. Because while he'd been locked in that bottle dimension, Thomas had essentially become a dynastic warlord, with a whole community of people who depended on him. All of them were either victims of their own crossroads bargains or descended from victims, and none of them deserved to be left behind to die there. Meaning that when we'd managed to get out, we'd done it with just over three hundred refugees in tow, and none of them had been equipped to strike out on their own.

Some friends of mine from Ithaca, Helen and Phoebe, had offered to give us a helping hand, in the form of supplies, various charms that would boost Thomas's natural ability to open doors between worlds, and a map that would help us get the ones who *could* go home back to their original dimensions, and find places where the ones who didn't have anywhere to go back *to* could settle down and figure out what they wanted to do with their lives. And that's what we'd been doing. Hence the megafauna parade and tentacle party.

We'd managed to shed nearly two hundred people during the trip, returning them to their homes or finding places where they wouldn't encroach on other intelligent life, and I was exhausted. With more than a hundred people left to resettle, it was starting to feel like this was another quest that was never going to end, and Thomas and I were never going to have a moment to ourselves.

"I got it!" shouted a female voice, heavy with a Maine accent, right before a human woman in her early twenties ran past me, a spear clutched in both hands. I snapped upright, gripping my guns, and watched her run. The tentacles between us weren't thrashing anymore; something seemed to be pinning them to the ground, where they strained against the unseen force.

I glanced to the side. There was Thomas, hands raised and face set in a grimace as he focused his sorcery on keeping the thing from hitting Sally. A small, unpleasant part of me pointed out that if he could do *that*, he could have been doing it before, but hadn't bothered when I'd been the one in danger. I shoved that part down as hard as I could. The fact that I'd been chasing a fairy tale ending for fifty years didn't mean anybody owed me one. It certainly didn't mean Thomas could be blamed for saving the girl who had become his daughter in all but literal blood rather than his still semi-unfamiliar wife.

It didn't. It couldn't. It was unfair of me to think that it did, and so I wasn't going to think that, no matter how hard circumstances tried to make me.

Sally leapt, spear held overhead in a classic javelineer's pose, and stabbed viciously downward. There was an offended bellow from the pit—the first sound we'd heard since the tentacles erupted from the ground—and they began to retreat, leaving Sally stumbling back from the edge of the hole, spear still clutched in both hands.

Panting, she turned to face me, a small, cocky smile on her face. "Thanks for the assist," she said, and strolled back toward where Thomas was standing. His hands weren't raised anymore. They were resting on his knees as he bent forward, panting slightly. Every dimension we went to had a different pneuma, and the pneuma was what fueled his magic.

Thomas is a sorcerer, a form of naturally occurring human witch who can tap into the pneuma of a world and use it to make the laws of physics sit, stay, roll over, and play dead. When we were together the first time, he mostly used it to move things from one place to another, start small fires, and occasionally keep me from falling out of bed when we got too enthusiastic. What's the point of being able to move things with your mind if you can't use it to keep your wife from bruising her ass on the floor, right?

Well, his time in the bottle dimension, where there was no native pneuma to draw on, had forced him to become a lot more innovative, and a lot more efficient about how he used power. Moving to a new dimension might throw him off-balance for a little bit, hence the panting, but once he recovered, he could do more with less than he had ever been able to accomplish before. Hence simple telekinesis becoming "I can restrain a whole-ass tentacle monster before it eats anybody." It was a pretty nice upgrade, all things considered.

The guards lowered their spears, turning to make reassuring noises to the other refugees as I holstered my pistols and cautiously approached the edge of the hole. Thomas watched me warily but didn't say anything. He knew better than to tell a Healy not to investigate a natural phenomenon.

I climbed the jagged mound in the earth, careful of my footing, and peered into the opening. A wide tunnel seemed to lead to the surface, and judging by the sides, it had been dug out by the creature we'd seen before. "Sally? Did you see what was down here?"

"Ayuh. Big round pink thing with a bunch of tentacles coming out around the edges."

"Uh-huh." That matched what I was seeing, and I didn't like it. I backed away from the hole, hands on my revolvers. "Thomas? We should be somewhere else now, if that's cool by you. Don't care whether it's on top of a big rock or in the next dimension on the list, but I'm going to say this is not a good place for people to settle. Also going to say I have a decent idea why there isn't any intelligent life around here."

"And why is that, dear?" There was a hard edge on the last word. He was annoyed. Well, that was nothing new. Not after the last six months.

"Because that was a giant star-nosed mole, or the local equivalent, and I don't think we want to be standing here when it burrows its way back," I said. "Poking it in the snout surprised it enough to make it leave, but that doesn't mean it's staying gone. Moles are carnivores. The ones back home eat grubs and worms, and are about the size of my hand. The ones here—"

"Would happily eat *us*, I'm sure," he concluded. He took a deep breath and pressed two fingers to the inside of his left wrist, as if he were taking his own pulse. Which maybe he was. I'm no sorcerer. Even after fifty years of playing hide-and-seek across dimensions, half of how it works is a mystery to me.

Not entirely because I didn't try to learn. Naga wasn't just taking my skin every time I came back to him for help: he was taking my *memories*, editing what I knew to make sure I'd keep being a good little dog and going where he wanted me. Eventually, I was sure, his pet Johrlac would have figured out a way to take Thomas and leave me running through the dimensions with no idea why. Johrlac are clever that way. There's a reason nobody likes them.

"I can't get us out of here just yet," he said finally, dropping his hand. "I'll need about another hour. Sally? Can you find us a route to the top of that rock?"

He gestured toward the low bluff I'd slammed into before. It was a semi-sheer rock face roughly eleven feet high—tall enough to keep us from attracting more moles, and also tall enough that half our party wouldn't possibly be able to climb it, even if we'd had a way of securely anchoring our ropes to the top. Some of them were old, and about a third were children. Isn't leading a group of interdimensional refugees to safety *fun*?

"I can do it," I said, as Sally said, "On it, boss," and took off running along the line of the rock, clearly scouting for a place where the climb would be easier. Her gait was uneven, unusually so, and after a beat, I realized she wasn't hurt, she was doing that on purpose.

"She's walking without rhythm so she won't attract the worm," I said, amused despite myself.

Thomas was approaching me, no longer winded, still clearly annoyed. I straightened, ignoring the twinge in my back.

"I could have found a way up," I said. "I have a lot more experience with scouting runs in parallel dimensions than Sally does." Sally was incredibly skilled at wilderness survival, even for a girl from small-town Maine, but then, she'd been stranded in a hostile bottle dimension full of people who wanted to kill her for the better part of a decade. I, on the other hand, was a bounty hunter feared across multiple dimensions and recognized in dozens more, who'd been skipping world to world for fifty years. There was no question which of us was better equipped to navigate unfamiliar terrain.

"Maybe so, but as she's not the one who got slammed into the side of a cliff five minutes ago, I thought it was better if I sent her off while I took care of *you*." He frowned, and I fought the urge to squirm. I always felt about two feet tall when he looked at me that way. "When are you going to learn that you're not indestructible anymore?"

"I was never indestructible," I protested. "I don't act like I am."

He didn't say a word. Just looked at me, raised an eyebrow, and waited.

The silence stretched between us until it became unbearable, and I blurted, "Okay, so maybe I got a little careless when it came to my personal safety, but if I couldn't patch myself up, Naga could do it for me, and anyway, it was all so I could keep looking for you."

The refugees were keeping their distance. They were smart enough to know when they didn't want to be in the middle of something. Hell, *I* was smart enough to know I didn't want to be in the middle of this, and yet here I was, stuck in a happy ending that involved a really annoying amount of yelling.

"Considering that I didn't ask you to come find me, I'd thank you to stop reminding me how much damage you did to yourself while you were trying!"

"Yeah, well, I didn't *ask* you to sell your soul to the crossroads for my sake, so I guess we're both going to be a little bit annoyed, okay?"

"Alice . . ." He sighed heavily. "I'm just asking you to please be careful. You can't receive magical healing right now. You might never be able to again. That means any injuries you get will have to heal the traditional way, and I don't want you to be hurt."

"Be careful."

"Yes. That's all I'm asking you to do."

"You're asking *me* to be careful, and you don't see anything wrong with that?"

Thomas hesitated for a moment. Then he grimaced, his own words finally catching up with him. "Alice, I didn't mean—"

"I think I have a pretty decent idea of what you meant. Try to keep your people from moving around too much. We wouldn't want to get another mole when Sally's not here to chase it away."

I turned and stalked in the opposite direction from Sally, hugging the rock wall as closely as I could without falling into a predictable gait. This time, I was the one who didn't look back.

Two

"Nothing wrong with having a temper. Oh, it can be inconvenient at times, and it's on you to learn how to manage it, but if you won't fight for yourself in this world, who's going to do the fighting for you?"

—Enid Healy

Storming off alone in an unfamiliar, megafauna-rich dimension, because that's a good idea

I STARTED TO COOL down before I reached the end of the rock, which looked about a hundred feet long in every direction, like a big skipping stone plopped down in the middle of an otherwise relatively flat plain. This was a very Earth-similar dimension, based on what we'd seen so far, which was why it had been such a surprise when the giant mole popped out of the ground. I was just glad it hadn't managed to chow down on anyone before it was driven away. Wouldn't want to make the local fauna sick.

Not that we would, most likely. Dimensions are laid out such that it's actually really difficult to force your way into a world completely hostile to your specific form of life. Oh, we were probably allergic to a lot of things in this dimension, and I wouldn't want to catch a cold here—I caught a cold on Ithaca once, and I had to avoid worlds with human populations for a good six months to keep myself from possibly starting a pandemic—but the base structure of our proteins was almost certainly safe for the local megafauna. Bad for us, good for them.

Of course, the opposite was also true, so if we had to set up camp here for a little while, we could always have a megafauna barbecue to help rebuild our strength.

Every dimension is different. I know I say that a lot, but that's because it's true, and it's not something that can be safely forgotten. Repetition is the key to retention. Every dimension is different, and that means every dimension deals with energy exchanges differently. Sometimes, we could shove our collective way through the pneuma of a new world, step through, and find Thomas, our resident taxi service, already prepared to go again. Other times, we'd arrive in a new place and he'd be so tapped out, he needed days to recover. His record so far, in both directions, was five minutes versus eight days. This world seemed likely to fall somewhere in the middle. Most of them do.

Sorcerers like Thomas seem to occur everywhere there's a pneuma, which is to say, everywhere that's capable of sustaining life. Not intelligent life: *life*, full stop. Oh, sure, maybe there are worlds that haven't progressed beyond single-celled organisms yet, but I'm sure even there, some of the protozoa have weird, inexplicable ways of speeding up their whatever the hell it is protozoa spend their time doing.

If we ran into a sorcerer mole, I was going to be annoyed, right after I got over being so intrigued that I nearly got myself killed. Hey, I know myself pretty well. I've had more than seventy years to get familiar with my quirks, and they include being way too interested in things that want to murder me. Sure, for a while there, my natural curiosity got overridden by the burning desire to find my missing husband, but now that I have him—and occasionally question why I wanted him in the first place—what I always thought of as "normal" is starting to reassert itself.

Thank God. I was pretty insufferable for a while there. Something about spending fifty years on a doomed quest messes with a lady's head.

The rock wall ended at a sharp, almost ninety-degree angle. I followed the turn, and found myself facing another long stretch of stone. This, at least, looked a little more eroded, and like we might be able to use it to boost the taller members of our company up to safety. Once they were on solid footing, they could help the rest up, and we could set up camp for however long we needed to be here.

Which hopefully wouldn't be too long. Sooner or later, some of the people we were supposed to be escorting to safety would stop panicking long enough to realize that for this place to sustain moles as big as the one we'd seen before, it would need to have something for those moles to *eat*. Moles do not live on menace and scaring the hell out of travelers alone. So what had our big, terrifying friend been eating?

Were we talking earthworms the size of anacondas, or beetles as big as Saint Bernards? Or both?

I'd be fine with the worms, honestly. Earthworms are pretty harmless. They eat things no one else wants, and they poop dirt. Hard to go wrong with earthworms. Beetles, on the other hand . . . some species of beetles are predatory.

Yeah, it was a leap from "megafauna mole" to "giant insects," but I've been to enough worlds with giant insects in them to have a pretty good idea of what kind of environment will spawn them, and this looked like a world where grubs the size of cows ate your shoes while you were trying to run away if ever I'd seen one.

At least it wasn't a giant spider world. I hate those. Giant spiders have absolutely *no* chill, and they can ruin everybody's day in a hurry.

The edge of the rock was rough, like it had been broken off too recently to have had time to erode. I trailed a hand along it as I walked, trying to puzzle out the geological forces at work. Maybe it had been pushed up from underground by something even bigger than the mole, or maybe it had been thrown here by some sort of an eruption. Erosion tends to be pretty consistent across dimensions with atmospheres, since there's only so far the laws of physics can bend before a world loses the ability to sustain human life.

About fifty feet from the corner, there was a crevice big enough for me to wedge a foot into. I peered carefully inside, reaching back to pull a glow stick out of my pack and cracking it before I moved any closer. The crack looked empty. Just to be sure, I tossed the glow stick into the crevice. It landed with a thump, and something that looked like a wood louse the size of a cat scuttled away.

Nothing else moved. I stood perfectly still, counting to twenty, and when *still* nothing else moved, I wedged my foot into the crack and boosted myself up, feeling around for a handhold on the stone above me. There were several cracks driven deep into the structure, and after a little readjusting, I was able to climb all the way to the top of the rock.

As I had hoped, it was smooth gray granite, dusted with patches of dirt but otherwise unremarkable. I dusted my hands against my knees and started walking across the stone toward where I'd left Thomas and the others. There was no sign of Sally. Maybe it was petty of me to hope that I'd managed to beat a girl young enough to be my grandkid, but I've never claimed not to be petty.

The sound of voices drifted up from below as I approached. I paused, slowing and intentionally softening my footsteps.

"—sign of her?"

That was Thomas, familiar British accent making the question sound more sophisticated than a simple location check. Even when I was mad at him, I would never get tired of hearing that voice. Just being *able* to hear it was a gift. When he'd disappeared, he hadn't been in a position to leave any recordings behind. Oh, I'd had the mice, but that wasn't the same. They could repeat his *words*, not the way he'd actually said things.

"None so far, boss." Sally had found her way back to the group without being eaten by anything, then. Good, I guess.

I didn't like the way I'd been reacting to her. I knew what a lot of people would say: that I was jealous of another woman spending so much time with the man I loved, but it wasn't that at all. Sally was Thomas's surrogate daughter if she was anything; she was definitely his family at this point, in an immutable, undeniable way. Plus she didn't like men like that, as she had been very careful to inform me on several occasions. Even if he hadn't been old enough to be her father's father, he would have been the wrong gender to catch her attention.

No, my irritation around Sally was entirely down to the fact that she and Thomas *knew* each other in a way he and I no longer really did. I'd had fifty years to figure out how to live without him, and yeah, getting him back had always been the goal, but on the occasions when I'd thought about what that was going to look like—rarer and rarer as time had gone on, and the mission had become more and more central to my relationship with the world—I'd never had a clear plan beyond "Thomas will come home and we'll go back to Buckley and everything will be normal again."

Only "normal" had never been an option, not for us, and it wasn't like our old normal was really something to aspire to. For one thing, "normal" had always meant "Thomas is trapped inside the house and can't go anywhere." On some level, I'd always known that getting him back would involve either fighting or deceiving the crossroads, and he'd be able to go outside again. I'd even been excited about that sometimes, imagining him playing catch with our son, back when Kevin had been young enough for that sort of thing, or teaching our daughter to ride a horse. But pleasant flights of fantasy about pastoral activities were not the same thing as facing the reality of a Thomas who could go anywhere he wanted.

For one thing, he could see how careless I was with my own safety, and he didn't like it. He hadn't liked it before we became a couple, but he hadn't been in any position to tell me what to do back then; I'd been someone else's responsibility. So while he'd occasionally grumbled about it, he'd never outright told me to be more careful. And then, once we'd been officially together, all my risks had been taken where he couldn't see them, and he'd been able to pretend they weren't happening. Which brought us to now, when he could actually watch me throwing myself bodily into danger, and he didn't approve. Not one bit.

But somehow, when *Sally* did it, it was fine. When *Sally* wanted to charge the monster without thinking twice, he didn't bat an eye. His standards were different when I was the one risking my life, and I didn't like it.

And yeah, I *was* jealous. I was jealous of the years she got with him while I was trying to convince myself he was still alive; I was jealous she knew him as he was now rather than trying to reconcile that person with her memories of the man he was back then. So it was safe to say I had some baggage, where Sally's relationship with Thomas was concerned.

Thomas sighed. I could picture him, glasses held between the first two fingers of his hand and palm across his eyes. "Of course not," he said. "Alice won't be seen if she doesn't want to be. Did you find a way for us to get everyone up top?"

"No," admitted Sally. "Did find a big hole, though. Bigger than the mole made. I don't think it's the only thing hunting around here."

"Well, isn't that delightful news," asked Thomas. "I can start telekinetically boosting people up, but if I have to draw on that much pneuma, it's going to delay our getting out of here by a day or more."

"And we don't know what comes out to hunt at night," said Sally. "I don't think that's a great idea."

Right. I'd been eavesdropping long enough. I picked my pace back up, stopping at the edge of the rock to look down at the group. "I found a way up," I said, giving no sign that I'd been listening.

The small cluster of mice standing on Thomas's shoulder cheered. There were four of them, each wearing a different livery. Leave it to the mice to have figured out Sally was family while Thomas was still trying to pretend that he wasn't planning to bring her home with us forever.

Thomas himself lifted his head, lowering his hand—across his eyes, as I'd predicted—and sliding his glasses back on before he offered me a wan, somewhat strained smile. Even with the tension around his eyes and the exhaustion in his posture, seeing him smile made me want to jump down from the rock, put my arms around him, and kiss him until I forgot why I'd stormed off in the first place.

The first thing that attracted me to Thomas Price was the fact that I knew I wasn't supposed to be attracted to him. He was Covenant; he couldn't be trusted. Oh, and my father hated him. Put together, those things made him the perfect man.

And then I got to spend time with him, got to know him, and figured out there was more to having a crush on someone—to falling in love with someone—than pissing off your parents. It didn't hurt that he was the best-looking man I'd ever seen, and while I've seen a lot more men since then, I stand by that assessment. Tall, with brown hair and blue eyes, cheekbones that could cut glass, and tattoos covering most of the skin from his collarbones down, but honestly, it was his hands that did it for me. Thomas's hands are long-fingered, quick and clever, and from the first time I saw them, I thought they'd been designed for holding me.

And he did. For years, he did. And then he left me, through no desire of his own, and I spent all the time between now and then just trying to get to a place where he could hold me again. It was all I'd ever wanted. I'd expected it to be enough. I didn't know what I was going to do if it wasn't.

"If you head along the rock that way," I pointed, "and go around the corner, there's a crack about twenty feet further on, with some good handholds above it. I tossed a glow stick in there, and saw a massive wood louse, but that was it. I don't think there's anything waiting for a quick snack. I can drop a rope over the side and help people up if they get to the crack."

"That would be lovely," he said, and moved closer, stretching his arms as far up as they would go while rising onto his tiptoes at the same time. Catching my cue, I dropped to my stomach, stretching my own arms toward his. By straining, we could brush our fingertips against each other. The mice promptly ran along his arm and onto mine, cheering as they made their way to my shoulder. Thomas stepped back again. "They were asking after you," he said, by way of explanation. "I thought you might like some company while we all get topside."

"Always glad to see the mice," I said, and pushed myself back to my feet, trying to ignore the tiny cheers as the mice grabbed hold of my hair to steady themselves. Their tiny claws dug into my skin, not hard enough to draw blood, and the sensation was familiar enough to bring a smile to my face.

Thomas answered my smile with one of his own, apparently taking my expression as a sign that I wasn't angry anymore. Well, maybe I wasn't. We had things to work on, but staying mad wouldn't do me any good. I waved down at him. "See you in a minute?"

"Certainly," he said. It would take time to get everyone moving, especially with the need to keep them pressed against the rock wall and stepping without falling into a rhythm, but at this point, we were all old hats at hurrying our little caravan along. Sally was already gesturing people into position. Thomas continued to watch me even as I backed up and turned to walk back the way I'd come, but he didn't ask me to stop, and in the end, I just kept moving.

Okay, so maybe being reunited with my true love after fifty years apart wasn't as easy or as much like a romance novel as I'd always hoped it was going to be, but I wasn't sorry I'd done it. I was sorry it had taken so much longer than it needed to, but even with our little frictions and sharp edges, having Thomas back in my life was the only thing I'd wanted for so long that I couldn't imagine being sorry to have found him.

Would it have been nice to have a reunion that didn't feature a massive band of cross-dimensional refugees? Sure. Would it have been even nicer if we'd been able to park most of them in one spot while we took the warriors and scouts with us for a quick, surgical search of available dimensions? Absolutely. Unfortunately, the amount of effort involved in keeping a door open for a large group, while immense, was less than the effort of opening a smaller door twice and then a third door for the aforementioned group. Plus not every universe touched on every other. We could go six or seven dimensions before we found a good place to drop people off, and trying to double back that far could have had serious consequences for Thomas's health—all assuming the local equivalent of the giant moles didn't come along and eat our people while they were waiting for us. No, efficiency and conserving our limited resources meant everyone came with us, much as it sucked. And it *did* suck.

The mice moved from my shoulder to my pack, where they began the Aeslin equivalent of Bible study, quietly discussing the day's events as they codified them into what would become formal scripture. Yes, Aeslin mice can be quiet. It doesn't come easily for them: their preferred volume is much closer to a shout than a whisper. But they're very small creatures in a very large world, and they know how to keep their voices down if it means not getting eaten.

It's always a treat when the Aeslin choose to communicate at something less than a shriek. According to my oldest granddaughter, Verity, I'm one of the few people they'll do that for. I'd say it's because they adore me, but really, it's because a lot of the places I went while I was looking for Thomas weren't very safe, and mice who didn't learn to keep quiet sometimes didn't make it back to the colony.

I regret every single one of them. The Aeslin trust us. That's why they worship us. And for them, dying in the service of their gods is something to aspire to. They don't usually martyr themselves, but every time I came home with an opening in my little traveling colony, there had been no shortage of volunteers to take the place of the mice I'd lost. And over time, the mice who'd managed to survive a trip or two started teaching the others the trick to it.

Half the Aeslin call me the Noisy Priestess. My clergy split when Thomas vanished, making me the only member of the family with two separate sets of rituals and catechisms. The other half of the mice call me the Pilgrim Priestess. I don't know whether the two branches will reunite when we get home, or whether they're going to stay as they are and found a *third* branch of my faith. I hope they'll reunite.

I'd like everyone to be reunited if they can be.

Thomas's clergy call him the God of Empty Rooms and Cold Regrets. They used to call him the God of Inconvenient Timing, but he didn't get a separate branch of the faith when they changed his name. I'm not sure whether I should feel flattered or he should feel cheated. As far as I can tell, neither is he.

We started this journey with a member from each branch of my faith, a member of his clergy, and a novice who had yet to declare for any specific set of sacred rituals. The first three have stayed the same—Aeslin rarely change faiths once they don their livery. The fourth, however, now calls herself the first Priest of the Conscripted Priestess, and has been since before we left Ithaca. Sally really made an impression when she gave the then-novice a piece of her waffle sandwich. The mice always recognize family when they see it.

Sally was going to have a lot more mice praising her name as soon as we got home, the lucky girl. At least she seemed to like them well enough, even if they were a little overwhelming when they all got going on one of their shared rituals. Wait until we got her back to Portland.

The thought of Sally meeting the rest of the colony was enough to make me smile. I was still smiling as I reached the edge of the rock and peered into the crack I'd used to boost myself up. My glow stick hadn't moved, making me think I was right about there being nothing down there but giant wood lice. Sure, they could be predatory in this dimension, but it seemed unlikely, and they hadn't attacked me before.

Climbing the side of the rock was as easy this time as it had been before, and nothing appeared to take a swipe at me. I shrugged off my pack when I reached the top, unzipping it to extract a length of rope and a railroad spike. Some people think toting railroad spikes around is a waste of carrying capacity, and to be fair, the things *are* pretty damn heavy. But I've encountered enough creatures with iron sensitivity to make me think that all those old stories about wicked fairies stealing kids probably have a root in reality. Not everyone who's managed dimensional travel uses it for good, or even for morally neutral acts. So railroad spikes are useful if you need to fend off certain types of unpleasant neighbor, plus they don't bend or break, and they make great mountain climbing anchors.

I tied the rope around the spike, then bent and hammered it into a crack in the top of the rock, dropping the bulk of the rope down along the side. Sure, I'd offer a hand up for anyone who needed it, but a nice climbing rope is nothing to sneeze at.

Straightening, I stepped back to wait.

Moving a hundred people is never fast. Doing it when half of them are children, elderly, or in poor physical shape is . . . well, it's just shy of glacial. I had plenty of time to study my surroundings while I waited.

Seen from my vantage point atop the rock, the land around us was almost uniformly flat but not level; there were small bumps and ridges, and some surprisingly deep grooves. I squinted at them, trying to understand their shape, before I realized what I was seeing fit well with the presence of the unusually jagged rock. This was a floodplain. Something about the local weather encouraged a form of flash floods, cutting channels in the soil and either eroding it enough to free rocks like this one or—given the depth of some of those channels—just plain washing them in from some other region.

It also explained the lack of trees. All the vegetation I could see was what I would have classified as a "grass" if I'd seen it on Earth, including something that looked a lot like bamboo, and something else with tall, fronded flowers that looked like horsetails and stood about twenty feet in the air. Mounds of earth similar to the one our mole had made dotted the landscape, pushed up through otherwise unbroken ground. There were no signs of civilization, or of anything I would recognize as a nomadic settlement.

That didn't necessarily mean anything. Even after all the time I've spent on the move, I have a human's innate prejudices, and that includes recognizing bipeds as intelligent before I recognize anything else. I could be looking at the central metropolis of the mole empire and simply be unable to recognize it for the majestic thing it truly was. It's a funny little twist of the brain that makes it hard for humans to look at things that don't stand on two legs and talk with one mouth and see them as people. I've been working on it for years. I figure I'll be working on it until the day I die.

The sound of voices snapped me out of my contemplation of the landscape, and I turned to see Thomas leading the others to my rope. Sally was some distance back, helping one of the older Murrays stay on her feet.

I moved to help as Thomas started boosting children up to me, one after another. People will have kids no matter where they are, if they have the biology necessary to do it, and the crossroads had only been throwing people from a few dozen worlds into their fancy killing jar. That meant a lot of compatible genes, and a lot of people decided to pass the time in the horrifying death world by getting it on. Mammals gonna mammal. Life wants to live, and for those of us with short life-spans and the capacity to reproduce, that means offspring. We live on in our descendants.

These descendants had been born on a world that wasn't dying only because it was technically already dead. Until we broke the killing jar and started our trek across the uninhabited dimensions of the multiverse, they had never known what it was to have enough food, water, or shelter. And in some ways, that was a good thing for us now. Oh, it's never a good thing for kids to be hungry, or dehydrated, or exposed. But they didn't complain when we asked them to walk miles under alien suns, and they didn't scream or cry when unspeakable monsters burst out of the earth. It was like parts of them had been deadened by the horrors they'd already faced.

Those parts were growing back, though, slowly but surely, keeping pace with the increasing roundness of their faces and the strength of their limbs. They had learned how to play even before we left Ithaca. Now, as I pulled them to the top of the rock, they glanced at me to see if I was worried about dangerous beasts, and when they saw no hint of caution in my face, they took off running, playing an elaborate game of chase and tag with rules only they seemed to know, rejoicing in the freedom to move without fear of dangers from below.

I smiled and helped the next children in the line along, freeing them to join the game.

After the children came the elderly, who promptly began dispersing themselves to stand sentry without being asked. They had belonged to different settlements and groups in the bottle dimension, but they had adjusted remarkably well to being one community, watching out for each other and prioritizing the health and safety of the group. They were going to be okay.

As long as we could keep them from being eaten by giant moles, that is.

After the elderly came Sally, and together, we helped the more delicate members of the company onto the rock, the amputees and the actively unwell, and the three pregnant women currently traveling with us. They murmured thanks and moved to join the others, and we turned to getting the rest of the group to safety.

Thomas was the last up. Thomas was always the one left guarding our rear, no matter how dire the situation; these people were his responsibility, and he wasn't willing to get himself to safety while they were still in danger. That, at least, was something I could understand, even if I didn't like it. Grasping the rope with both hands, he walked along the side of the rock, finding his footing with an ease born of long practice. Sally was already bending to help him the rest of the way, and I let her, retreating to pick up my pack.

"Alice," said Thomas, as soon as he was standing on his own again. "We need to have a conversation."

"Can it wait until we make camp?" I asked. "Assuming we're sleeping here tonight."

He and Sally exchanged one of those complicated tactical looks that I was coming to genuinely loathe. This might have been easier to deal with if I *had* been afraid she was sleeping with him. At least that's a situation we're culturally prepared for. This, though . . . there isn't a word for "I'm jealous you got to be my husband's right-hand woman for years while I was alone, and I don't like that you seem to know each other so well when I sometimes feel like he doesn't know me at all anymore." It's not envy, and it's not jealousy, and it's not anything I can articulate without sounding like I'm whining, and I hate it.

Believe me, if that word existed, I would have found it by now.

"We don't know what this dimension is like at night," said Thomas, finally, "but the same can be said for the next one on our list, and that one, we know, has intelligent inhabitants, which could make things even more difficult."

"Mmm-hmm," I said. The list Helen had given us before we left Ithaca ended with a run of possible settlement dimensions, and the next one down was one of the more promising. According to her notes, it was occupied by a species of intelligent felinoids who had previously made contact and interbred with Lilu. One of the larger groups of refugees, the Murrays, had Lilu blood; they might be able to find cultural commonalities that would make our next stop a good home for them.

If so, we could cut our group from a hundred to about twenty in one swoop, which would make the dimensional crossings faster, cleaner, and less exhausting for Thomas. We'd be able to get the rest of these people settled in a matter of months, if we could offload the remaining Murrays. Or maybe we'd get *really* lucky, and they'd all want to stay. We could be done in a matter of days, if luck was on our side.

"It would be safest if we stayed here," said Thomas. "We have a defensible location, and enough food to make it to morning without needing to go hunting or gathering."

"I don't like it," said Sally.

"Well, I do," I said, and moved to retrieve my railroad spike, wrapping the rope idly around my arm. "Get the word out, and we'll pitch camp before the sun goes down."

"We should still be careful," cautioned Thomas.

"There's that word again," I said dourly, and walked away.

Three

"First rule of dealing with Alice: never tell her to be careful. The more you tell her to be careful, the less she's going to be, because she hates it that much. I don't even think she does it on purpose. She's just stubborn by nature."

—Mary Dunlavy

Setting up a tent, alone, on top of a big rock in an unfamiliar dimension. Which is not a new occurrence, strange as that might seem

THERE'S A TRICK TO pitching a tent when you can't drive your tent-poles into anything, and weirdly enough, it comes down, again, to railroad spikes. Tying the ropes to the spikes can create enough of a counterweight to get the whole structure up and stable.

I'm an old hand when it comes to setting up camp. I got the tent I was hopefully going to be sharing with Thomas up by myself, in less than ten minutes, set the mice free to perform whatever rituals they thought would make the space safer for us to spend the night in, and went looking for people who needed help setting up their own shelter.

I found plenty. Most of these folks had never been expected to make their own decisions before our cross-dimensional march began, much less had the luxury of worrying about things like "something soft to sleep on" and "not getting rained out." They'd lived where their war-lords told them to, slept where their warlords told them to sleep, and used what they were given rather than putting anything together for themselves. Now that they were my responsibility—well, Thomas's re-sponsibility, but that made them half-mine as far as I was concerned—they were learning about those things, and they needed their hands held a lot of the time.

It wasn't long before a veritable tent city had sprung up on top of the rock. Children ran between makeshift shelters, shrieking and throwing balls of wadded-up fabric back and forth. They could find something to play with no matter where we were. I envied that about them. The sun was dipping lower in the sky, and campfires were starting to wink on like tiny stars as people settled in and started preparing their dinners.

And Thomas still hadn't come to find me.

Our tent was set up near the center of the cluster, and not by design; I would have preferred to be closer to the edge, where I could play sentry and be sure nothing was going to get to the children or the elderly without going through me first. But these people saw Thomas as their savior, and me as his beloved wife. They wanted to be close to us, which meant we would always wind up dead in the middle when something like this happened.

One more reason to be eager to get them wherever it was they were going to wind up. We'd never have any real privacy until we did.

I looked around the bustling encampment, trying to find any sign of him, and when I didn't, I shook my head, grabbed a lantern, and went back into the tent.

The mice had pulled a bunch of fabric scraps, sticks, and rocks into a rough circle and were putting on some sort of complicated pantomime. I stopped, blinking, as I reviewed the rituals I knew were normally performed around this time. Nothing sprang to mind. Finally, I asked, "What are you doing?"

"Priestess!" exalted one of my mice, and the other three joined in, all four of them cheering jubilantly at my return.

"Well, at least you're glad to see me." I hung my lantern from the hook on the central pole, filling the tent with a diffuse yellow glow. "So what's the ritual? I don't recognize it."

"This is the Holy Rite of A Spotter Is Better Than the Alternative, Priestess," said the mouse in Sally's livery. "It is a newer mystery but still considered essential to understanding the relationship between the Precise Priestess and her consort!"

So one of the rituals about Annie and her Sam, then. Huh. "Why's he not a god yet?" I asked.

"Priestess?"

"Sam's a good boy, and he's devoted to my granddaughter like a dog's devoted to a bone. He's not going anywhere any time soon. So why's he a consort and not a god?"

"When the clergy of the Precise Priestess did begin to discuss his deification, she did appear before them most wrathful, and say, lo, 'I

Want Him To Stick Around, You Meddling Rodents, and You Marrying Us Off Before He's Even Met My Siblings Won't Help.' This caused a Theological Debate among the colony, and we agreed that as each new god or priestess is either born to the family or Pledged to them, we could wait to decide his godhood until he had Pledged properly."

The other mice murmured agreement. I snorted.

"Glad to see that you can take feedback from the family," I said. "What about Sally?"

The mice looked perplexed. "The Conscripted Priestess has already been Pledged."

"I wonder if she's aware of that," said Thomas.

I turned, and he was standing behind me, just inside the tent, looking unsure, like he wasn't confident he'd be welcomed. I straightened, standing to meet him.

"Guess you found the tent," I said. "I put it up by myself. I was real *careful*."

"Alice—" he began.

"You *know* how I feel about that word," I snapped. "My father always told me to be careful."

"Because your father—and oh God, I can't believe I'm saying something that makes it sound like I agreed with him, about anything, ever, but—your father loved you, and he didn't want you getting hurt."

"Guess you found the wrong tent," I said, and moved to push past him to the exit.

He grabbed my shoulders before I made it more than a few steps.

"Alice, please," he said.

I turned until we were eye to eye, my jaw set in a stubborn line. He looked back at me, nowhere near so stubborn. His own expression was more one of raw confusion, discomfort and desire warring for possession of his face.

"I spent fifty years thinking I was never going to see you again," he said, miserably. "Fifty years imagining you alone, abandoned, hating me for leaving you . . . my only comfort was knowing that my deal with the crossroads precluded you making any deals of your own, and even that was a cold comfort, because it was possible the crossroads might declare my exile meant our agreement was fulfilled and they could do whatever they wanted. Fifty years of assassins wearing your face, coming to kill me because they could, because they'd been told it would wipe their own slates clean, sometimes just because they wanted to. Fifty *years* of missing you."

"I had fifty years of missing you too," I said, my own voice stiff.

"You had fifty years and a purpose," he said. "You were going to find me if it killed you. I didn't have that. I couldn't get out. You might as well have been dead, for all the chance there was of me seeing you again. And then, sweet miracle, you fell out of the sky into my own backyard! You were *there,* alive and still looking for me. You wanted to be with me, after everything. After all the bad decisions, after leaving you, you still wanted me."

"I still do," I said, almost in a whisper.

"I thought I was never going to see you again," he said, and took the hand off my left shoulder, moving to cup my cheek instead. Instinctively, I leaned into his touch. "Can you blame me for not wanting to see you hurt?"

"You don't tell Sally to be careful." It sounded petulant even to my own ears. I didn't pull away.

"Sally *is* careful, compared to you," he said. "She doesn't consider herself indestructible. She knows she can be hurt, and she knows that if she is, it could take her a long time to heal. When she throws herself at something, it's because she's already looked at the options and decided on the one that carries the least risk. She's being tactical."

"You're saying I'm not a tactical thinker?"

"No, darling, I'm saying you spent so long being able to bounce back from absolutely anything that you've forgotten what it means to have consequences for your actions. Your body can't handle magical healing right now."

"We didn't have magical healing back in Buckley."

"No, we didn't. Remember how much time you spent injured, or recovering? Remember how long you were too weak to go to the woods after the slime attacked you?"

I did, unfortunately. I turned my face away, hoping he wouldn't see the way I winced.

It was a futile hope. Thomas had always paid too much attention to the things I least wanted him to be paying attention to.

"I remember how hard it was on you, and how much you hated it." He ran his thumb along the line of my cheekbone, palm still cupping my face. "I remember how much I wanted to help, and how I wasn't allowed. I think it hurt us both, seeing you like that, and I'm sorry, but I never want to see you like that again. If that means reminding you that you're as mortal as the rest of us, I won't be able to help myself."

I turned my head to kiss his palm, then straightened, meeting his eyes again. "I don't like how you've started telling me what to do. I'm not one of your subjects. I don't take orders from you."

"And I'm sorry about that, too. Why don't we make an agreement, you and I? I'll do my best not to give orders—I'm unlearning the habit of autocracy, just like you're unlearning the habit of throwing yourself into danger like a woman who never expects to have backup again—and you'll do your best not to get hurt. You're the most precious thing in the world to me, Alice. That you were able to stay in one piece long enough to find me and bring me home is a miracle. Losing you now would be . . ." Thomas stopped and shook his head, finally pulling his hand away. "I can't even think about it. Please, for the sake of my heart, can you try?"

It all made too much sense when he put it that way. I looked at the wall of the tent and sighed. "I can try," I said, and looked back to him. "But you need to remember that I'm your wife, not one of your people to order around, and at this point, I have more experience with dimensional travel than you do."

Sure, my experience was full of unexpected holes, thanks to Naga's pet telepaths digging out whatever information he thought would be too inconvenient for me to have, but it was still *experience*. While Thomas had been in one hostile death world dimension for fifty years, I'd been running through hundreds of them, and I hadn't died. That sort of track record had to be good for something.

"All right," he said, and smiled. I hesitated, then smiled back. "May I kiss you?"

"Always," I said, and he wrapped his arms around me, bent me slightly backward, and kissed me.

Every time we kissed, it was like coming home. It was tempting to think that it had always been that way, and to be fair, I could remember some pretty scorching kisses from the years before his disappearance. The first time I'd come to his house to tell him how I felt, when I'd been absolutely sure I was going to be dead by the end of the week; the night he'd found me rinsing ghoul guts out of my hair in the downstairs bathroom and suggested we might do a better job of keeping our relationship from attracting the attention of the local gossips if we just went ahead and made it official; the night Kevin had been conceived. But there had been a lot of mundane, everyday kisses, too. More of those than the memorable ones, I was sure.

These days, though . . . absence makes the heart grow fonder, and fifty years had been enough time for my heart to go from "fond" to "absolutely obsessed." Every kiss was the best kiss anyone had shared since the invention of kissing, and made me regret how few opportunities we had for time alone while shepherding a large group of pan-dimensional refugees to their new home. He made my knees go weak and my pulse rate spike, and it was reassuring that I could still do the same to him. Thomas pulled back to study my face, eyes slightly glazed, like he was deliberating between painting my portrait and devouring me whole. I made a small, inquisitive noise and pressed my body against his, feeling the length of him like a promise of things we almost certainly wouldn't be able to do tonight.

As if summoned by the thought, someone clapped their hands outside the tent.

"Hey, boss?" called Sally. "Something that looks a lot like a giant bat just tried to take off with one of the kids. Think you might want to get out here."

Thomas sighed heavily, and leaned in to kiss me one more time, briefly, before he stepped back. "Duty calls," he said. "I love you."

Then he was gone, ducking out of the tent into the evening air. I stayed where I was for a long moment, panting and aching with the need for him to come back, shout "false alarm," and throw me to the floor. He didn't come back.

The mice cheered.

When I stepped out of the tent, the camp was virtually deserted. Fires still burned, lighting up the night in flickering orange, but the people were gone. I approached the nearest tent, sticking my head inside, and was met with the sight of four people—two adults, two children—huddled in the center. They all looked up as the fabric rustled, their eyes wide and alarmed, then slumped back down. One of the adults gestured for me to get out.

I got out.

There was no sign of Thomas or Sally. I still had my revolvers, and the knives inside my shirt, but nothing bigger than that; if this was a serious threat, I was a sitting duck. Hopefully, that meant we weren't dealing with anything major.

Something flew by overhead, flapping wings creating a heavy sound, like canvas snapping in the wind. I glanced up, but it was already gone. Right. Sally had said it was a giant bat. I just hoped it hadn't managed to carry anyone off before they all got under cover and out of the target environment. I kept walking, now turning to keep my eyes on the sky.

Bats are fast. They can strike almost before the eye can follow.

They're far from the fastest things in the multiverse, however, and after you've shot a striking snake before it could hit you, a bat just doesn't seem all that frightening. Besides, it might not be sure I was a good prey animal yet, and if it made another exploratory pass, I was going to put some holes in its wings.

I was so busy focusing on the sky that the hands grabbing my arm from the side caught me by surprise as Sally dragged me into the tent where she'd taken cover. I squawked, cutting the sound off as soon as I realized what was happening, and turned to glare at her.

"Sorry," she said, unrepentantly. "Boss is off making sure the kids're all under cover. He'll be pissed if I let you get carted off because you wanted to go big-game hunting with a peashooter."

"My guns are not *peashooters*," I objected.

"Bat the size of a horse? They might as well be." She shrugged. "If it's the nastiest thing we have to worry about tonight, we'll be fine. Boss just needs to get some sleep so he can refill his tank, and then we're off to the next world on the line."

"Where is he?"

Sally blinked. "I thought he was with you."

"You came to *our* tent and told him there was a problem," I said. "He left right away. Didn't you see him?"

"Yeah, but . . ." She paused. "Aw, fuck."

Still gripping her spear—which was part weapon, part security blanket, part teddy bear as far as she was concerned—Sally spun and ran out of the tent, leaving me behind. I was getting real tired of that. I sighed heavily, drew my revolvers, and followed.

The camp was quiet. The sound of leathery wings passed by again overhead, and I looked up, slow and easy. Bats hunt by sound. Because of that, they always know where you're going to be; they can echolocate your new location before you finish figuring out where it's going to be. Bats seem a lot like sorcery, when you get right down to it. I don't understand them, and I'm not sure anyone really does.

The night was otherwise silent. No birds or hunting predators; only the crackle of untended fires, the whistle of the wind across the plain, and the occasional beat of wings from overhead. The air was cool and pleasant. It would have been nice out, if not for the omnipresent threat of a giant flying rodent swooping down and taking off with me.

It was a shame this world didn't have any known intelligent inhabitants. I would have *loved* the chance to get my hands on a few biology textbooks, just to find out whether this was an "all megafauna, all the time" reality, or whether it just liked really, really big rodents.

Sally was right, though. At this size, my guns weren't going to do me a lot of good. They'd probably be able to convince the bat that I was too much trouble to eat, but they wouldn't knock it out of the sky. Still, that was something, and as a creature that ran entirely on instinct, it wasn't as likely to redouble its attack if I hurt it as a thinking creature would have been. I moved quickly, eyes on the sky, waiting for the bat to show itself.

It didn't do me the honor. Fucker.

Thomas could take care of himself. All sorcerers are elementalists at their core—that seems to be the main thing distinguishing them from all the other types of human witch—and Thomas's element was fire. If he'd been able to pull on this world's pneuma enough to pin down the mole, he could definitely pull on it enough to make a few sparks. Add that to the campfires burning everywhere, and well. If the bat attempted to mess with him, it would get to be the guest of honor at a very exclusive barbecue.

Problem: Thomas was our *only* sorcerer. None of the rest of us had any talent for channeling magical energy. I was blocked from even benefitting from the stuff, thanks to having been used as a channel for the spell that broke us out of the bottle dimension, nearly killing me in the process. (Thomas would contest the "nearly," since my heart stopped at one point and had to be shocked back into a normal rhythm. Thomas can be a little conservative sometimes.) If he used the pneuma he'd been able to draw from this dimension to set the bat on fire, we'd be stuck here longer before he could open another gateway, and we'd risk running into even *more* bats. Not good.

So no, we didn't want Thomas to be the one dealing with this if there was any possible alternative. I kept working my way through the camp, back to our tent—and more importantly, my pack.

With a flap of heavy leather wings, the bat soared into view. I opened fire immediately, and true to Sally's prediction, the thing kept flying. But it shrieked, the sound high-pitched enough to hurt my ears, and banked, heading back the other way. My bullets might only feel like beestings to something that size, but no one likes being stung by a bee.

"Thomas?" I pushed open the flap of our tent and stuck my head inside. No wayward husband. I hadn't really been expecting him; wherever he'd gone off to after getting separated from Sally, it wouldn't make sense for him to come right back here.

The mice were still in the middle of their ritual, tiny voices raised in celebration. They didn't even pause to mark my arrival, which meant they were probably at a delicate point in the recitation. I holstered my guns and moved to open my pack, digging quickly through its contents before finding what I needed and straightening up again.

"There's going to be a big boom in a few minutes," I said. "Don't get alarmed. It's just me doing my job."

The mice cheered and went back to what they'd been doing, my comment already dismissed. I smiled and let myself out of the tent. Sometimes it's nice when things stay predictable. Giant bats eat people; talking pantheistic rodents care more about religious rituals than they do about explosions; if I'm around, something's going to blow up.

No one else had emerged from their tents, all of them being somewhat smarter than that. I walked with my eyes on the sky, heading for the edge of the encampment. The farther I got from the fires, the darker it became. The sky was an unending blaze of stars above me, bright in that way that only preindustrial dimensions can ever manage. I was going to miss those skies once we were home for keeps. Not enough to make this trip last any longer than it absolutely had to, but still . . .

The first time I'd been able to catch my breath and look at a sky like that, I'd been in some unnamed backwater dimension two jumps from Ithaca, chasing down a bounty Naga had assigned to me. The man in question had robbed an important family back on his home world and somehow done a runner across dimensions, trying to disappear. Maybe that would have been allowed, except that he'd stolen some fairly important family heirlooms, and the people they actually belonged to wanted them back, along with a side order of punishment for the thief. They'd been paying Naga, and Naga hadn't been paying me, exactly, more letting me do him a favor in exchange for his continuing to fund my fruitless search for my husband.

Those memories were less comforting now than they'd been when I truly believed Naga was on my side, but they had been pleasant enough while they were happening. The bounties had given me something limited and achievable to focus on rather than spending all my time and energy thinking about the thing I *couldn't* seem to achieve, and the money Naga got for sending me on side trips funded more tattoos and more weapons for me to take with me when I got back on the main mission.

Only now I had to question every choice I'd made during those fifty years. Had I been hunting criminals, or had I been dragging innocent people and runaways to their dooms? Was I a bounty hunter or a hired thug? Either would explain the way some people reacted when they saw me, but only the first would help me sleep at night.

Still, I loved an untouched sky. I made it past the edge of the tent line, spread my arms, and began walking in a slow circle, eyes still turned upward. I wanted to attract attention, not be caught unawares. Just to up the ante, I started whistling, the sound low and carrying in the calm night air. Any hunter nearby wouldn't be able to resist.

Indeed, there was a flap of wings as the bat—or another like it, but hopefully the same one that had been stalking me before—began to loop lazily overhead. I amended my hopes. This was definitely the same bat. It was keeping its distance because I'd taught it I might be dangerous, but as I continued to walk and whistle, it swooped closer with each pass, clearly thinking I hadn't seen it.

That was good. I kept up my circles, waiting for it to work up the nerve to make an attack.

When it did, it was fast enough that it very nearly caught me off-guard. It went into a sharp dive, mouth open, arrowing straight toward me like it was going to swallow me in one bite, even though it wasn't quite large enough for that. It wasn't the primary hunting strategy employed by Earth bats, which usually preferred to snatch things out of the air, and I was briefly glad we were dealing with giant monster bats instead of giant monster *owls*. Owls come equipped with special feathers that let them fly without making a sound. We would have lost people before we knew what was going on, and more, this little tactic would have been suicidal, not slightly risky.

The bat dove. I hit the ground, yanking the pin from the grenade in my hand and tossing it straight into the bat's open mouth as I fell. Its jaw snapped shut, and I would have sworn it looked surprised by the offering, startled enough by my weird behavior not to go for a second immediate swoop.

It didn't spit the grenade out. That was good. I covered my head with my arms but didn't get off the ground or run, not wanting to make myself a better target.

Which was, naturally, when Sally and Thomas emerged from the tent line, saw me, and ran in my direction. "Alice!" shouted Thomas.

The bat wheeled and flew off closer to the two. Fucker was still looking for a meal. I couldn't blame it for that—instinct and all—but given the size of the explosive it had just swallowed, I didn't want it getting too near the tents. "Dammit," I muttered, rolling to my feet and waving my arms in the air as I hopped up and down. "Here! Over here! I'm defenseless and alone!"

The bat banked back around, clearly seeing me as the easier target. Good bat. Thomas stopped running, grabbing Sally's arm and pulling her to a halt along with him as he realized I was actually up to something. Better husband.

I stopped waving and ran *away* from the tents, as fast as I could.

I made it about ten feet before I felt the wind from the bat's approach on the back of my neck, and knew that if this grenade was a dud, I was about to have a big problem.

The grenade wasn't a dud.

I had a different problem. Namely, I had a massive bat less than a foot behind me when the grenade it had swallowed went off and the whole damned thing exploded, splashing bat guts and gore absolutely everywhere. The blast flung me forward to the rock. I managed to catch myself with my hands before gravity helped me catch myself with my face, and I lay there, as flat as I could make myself, while bat pattered down all around me in a thick, horrible rain.

When it finished falling, I rolled onto my back, spitting out a bit of muscle that had somehow managed to wind up in my mouth, and started laughing.

I was still laughing when Thomas and Sally reached me, Sally looking alarmed, Thomas looking resigned. He leaned down to offer me his hands, and I took them, letting him pull me to my feet. My boots slipped in the gore. I tightened my grip on Thomas, holding on until I was sure I wasn't going to just fall down if I let go. Once I had my footing back, I released him and wiped the bat out of my eyes.

"That was surprisingly fun," I said. "Think there are going to be any more of those things?"

"Try not to sound so happy about that idea, maybe," said Sally dryly.

"Ordinary bats live in colonies, although they generally hunt solo when not in a target rich environment," said Thomas. "This is not a place where a bat would normally expect to find a solid meal. I think tonight's guest was an opportunist more than anything else. We should set a watch, but chances are good that we won't have any more visitors."

"Great," I said. "Do we have enough water on hand for me to have a bath?"

Sally rolled her eyes. "Woman explodes a bat all the hell over herself, and wants a *bath*."

"Well, yes. There's blood in my hair." I smiled at her, aware of how distressing the expression would be with the gore covering my face. "It gets sticky."

"It's gross."

"You could have exploded the bat, if you're that interested in me staying clean."

"I can't even—" Sally threw her hands in the air, announced, "I'm going to go set watches," and stalked off back toward the tents, leaving me and Thomas alone with the remains of blasted bat.

I bent to retrieve one of the larger chunks, holding it up to show him. "Want a roast?"

Thomas laughed, and everything was going to be okay.

Four

"Every journey has an ending. Sometimes they're a new beginning at the same time. Sometimes they're just where things . . . stop."

—Juniper Campbell

Standing on a rock in an unfamiliar dimension, watching the sun come up

THANKS TO MY PROXIMITY to the explosion, I was the only one covered in inside-out bat, meaning we only had to find enough clean water for me. Thomas was conserving magic, and thus couldn't heat it at sorcerous speed, but everyone we approached was willing to let me set a pot on their campfire, especially once I started offering them pieces of fresh bat. It wasn't long before about a quarter of the camp was spit-roasting bat bits for dinner while I shampooed guts out of my hair, and everyone who hadn't received part of the first bat hoped that more of them would come along.

Luckily for my hair, our water supply, and Thomas's nerves, they didn't. None of the members of Sally's excellent watch spotted anything else in the sky above us, and the things they saw moving in the distance of the plains all stayed far enough away to be nothing more than dark smudges against the inky, star-streaked night. The hours passed peacefully, and I was able to rejoin Thomas in our tent for a few precious hours of being left alone.

I was getting way too accustomed to having him with me when I went to bed, the sound of his heartbeat as familiar now as it had been when we'd been together back in Buckley, young and foolish and convinced that we could overcome absolutely anything, as long as we stayed together. And maybe we hadn't been so wrong about that. After all, most of our problems seemed to come from us letting people keep us apart.

Thomas wrapped his arms around me and kissed the crown of my still-damp head, and if I had any bad dreams, I didn't remember them when I woke up. We rose to find the camp already halfway to being torn down, and sentries standing at the edge of the rock, watching anxiously as guinea pigs the size of elephants grazed in the tall grass of the plains below. I joined the watch briefly, shielding my eyes against the sun.

"Can't decide whether everything in this dimension is unreasonably large, or whether we're unreasonably small for this dimension," I said finally, turning away. Maybe we were the Aeslin mice here, too small to seem real to anything local. And maybe it wasn't our problem, because we weren't sticking around to play the residents of Lilliput.

Thomas came up behind me, sliding his arms around my waist and pressing a kiss to the side of my neck. I leaned back against him. "How are you feeling?"

"Better," he said. "I've tapped into this dimension's pneuma. I think I can get us out of here."

"You think, or you know? Because I have more grenades if we need to camp for another night."

He snorted and let me go, heading for a point toward the edge of the rock and producing a piece of chalk, starting to draw runes all over the stone at his feet. I helped a few people tear down their tents before joining him, and the crowd that had already begun to gather.

His runes were forming a rough oval that was probably meant to be a circle. I didn't say anything. The shape the runes formed didn't matter half as much as the runes themselves, which was a good thing, since the man couldn't draw a perfect circle to save his life, and I didn't want to find out that we *could* access dimensions that were antithetical to humanity by bending an angle slightly wrong.

When the last of the runes was drawn, he tucked the chalk into his pocket, stepped back, and raised his hands. That was all. There was no chanting, no mystical gesturing; just a heavily tattooed man standing with his hands up, like he wanted to frame the sunrise between them.

I don't think a sorcerer can control the sun. That's a bit arrogant, even for me. But Thomas's magic has always been most sympathetic to fire, and I had to assume that having a giant ball of flaming plasma rising right in front of him could only make it easier for him to grab hold of this world's pneuma and pull like he thought his life depended on it.

And maybe it did. All these crossings were starting to wear on him—as well they should. Dimensional membranes aren't designed for this sort of thing. There's a reason doors are usually opened by cults, groups of people working together who don't care if they burn out a few brains in the process. The Johrlac have a slightly more survivable process: they use complicated equations, again worked by multiple people—mathematicians, in their case, instead of cultists or sorcerers—and they still have fatalities. Dimensions like Ithaca, or Empusa, where trade with nearby worlds is common . . . aren't. They make up about one out of every fifty inhabited dimensions, and most of them don't last long.

Thomas's sorcery was *capable* of grabbing hold of a door and prying it open. With the charms he had from Helen to channel and shape his magic, he could even do it reliably and according to the map they'd given us. What he couldn't do was keep doing it forever. Sooner or later, he was going to burn himself out. Which was a big part of why we all had to travel together, and not count on him being in any shape to backtrack when we finally found a safe place for everyone to settle.

I just hoped he wouldn't hurt himself getting us there, and that we'd be someplace near Earth when he finally reached the point of exhaustion. I still had two of the beads I'd received from Naga, personal gateways that would be big enough for me, Thomas, and the mice, if it came down to that. But he wasn't going to let me leave Sally, and all my grumbling aside, I wasn't ready to abandon her. Even when we chafed on each other, she was growing on me. It just meant that when we finally *did* get home, we'd be staying put for a while.

Oh, we'd been planning to do that anyway, for a lot of very good reasons. I just didn't think we were going to have a choice.

Slowly, the air in front of Thomas turned translucent, like a very thin slice of tomato or watermelon or something else that was as much water as tissue. It looked almost bruised, in a way that seemed antithetical to the world around it. He raised his hands higher. The bruise clarified, until we were looking through a gateway into another world, one that had actual trees and no visible giant guinea pigs.

Thomas took a half-step back, hands still raised, and I fell in behind him, guns drawn, ready to interrupt anything that wanted to disrupt his concentration. Sally began to herd our charges through the gateway, moving them along as fast as she could. If he ever opened a door into an ambush, we'd be screwed, since our process didn't allow for much scouting. That was part of why we'd stuck so tightly to Helen's list. She might send us to worlds like this one, where the wildlife was more than happy to suck us down like bonbons, but she wouldn't intentionally send us into danger.

Ithaca is one of the more experienced dimensions when it comes to cross-world travel. Their economy is partially based on it, and they have the most sophisticated transit methods and maps I've ever seen. We could trust Ithacan directions—at least so far.

Sally followed the last of the refugees through, and I stepped in front of Thomas, breaking his line of sight on the portal. "Hey, babe," I said, as lightly as I could. "How about you drop that and come with me?"

He blinked, looking dazed, but didn't lower his hands. "Drop what?" he asked, voice a little slurred, like he'd been awake for three days without food or water.

"You'll see," I said. I reached up and took his hands, lacing my fingers through his. Then I stepped backward through the opening, pulling him with me.

To anyone watching on the other side, we stepped out of thin air. There was no visible doorway here: just a faint popping sound and the scent of char. Thomas blinked at me, still dazed, and shook his head vigorously from side to side as he let go of my hands. We both turned to see the new world in front of us.

According to Helen's notes, the locals called this place "Pteracercus," which seemed like a mouthful to me but wasn't my decision. They were preindustrial, living in eusocial colonies, and had previous experience with Lilu. They should be open to accepting some of our refugees. Maybe, if we were lucky and no one freaked out at the idea, all of them.

We could be going home soon. Best of all, this dimension was close enough to Earth that we'd be able to get back in two hops—Ithaca, then home.

Dimensions aren't all mashed together. They're more like hexes in a hive. Every dimension touches a *few* other dimensions, and half the trick of travel is learning the best routes between them. It can be difficult to look at two worlds that seem to be right on top of each other and be told that you have to go through six more if you want to cross from one to the other, but you get used to it. Helen's map had been designed to let us drop off as many of the survivors of the bottle dimension as possible before we reached this point.

And we still had so many that I was starting to despair of ever being finished. I sighed and tried to focus on the landscape around us rather than my frustrations.

We were in what looked like a low valley between a mountain range—several of which were actively smoking, because a volcano is always a good way to improve your day—and a forest wreathed in some sort of odd white cottony substance. Probably a local fungus, unless they grew the spiders *real* big around here. It was hard to tell for sure what color anything was, since the sky was a remarkable shade of persimmon, and the air smelled like some undefinable spice, something I almost recognized from the markets on Ithaca but couldn't quite name.

In the distance, what looked like a giant termite mound loomed, dominating the horizon. I frowned.

"Naturally occurring or the locals, do you think?"

"No idea," said Sally. "Haven't you been here before?"

"No good pathways off this world that I couldn't get to from Ithaca or Empusa," I said, with a small shake of my head. "I was focused on moving as fast as I could so I could cover the most ground. I knew Thomas wasn't this close to home. Helen had her people watching for him, too, after she found out what I was looking for, and she'd have noticed a human sorcerer cropping up in an adjacent. This is new ground."

"What do you think?" asked Thomas, putting his hands on my shoulders. "Do we risk it?"

I've always been blessed with weird, unpredictable luck. I inherited it from my mother, who everyone says was the same way. And yeah, sometimes it leads me into terrible danger, but most of the time, it means that if I trust my instincts, things will work out basically okay.

"Termites are usually pretty chill," I said. "If it's the locals, we're looking for them, and if it's termites, we could wind up worse places for the night, and we don't know how long the local days are, or what time it is here. I say we head for the mound." I paused. "And steer clear of the forest. It gives me the heebie-jeebies, and that usually means it's a good idea not to go that way."

"Right," said Thomas. He turned to Sally, giving her a sharp nod. She immediately moved to start gathering the group, readying them to move out.

It was less efficient than having Thomas give the orders directly, but it was what these people were accustomed to: back in the bottle world, he'd been playing all-powerful warlord, and he'd rarely given direct orders even to his own people. About half the folks traveling with us had belonged to other groups, and were more comfortable fighting and fearing him than listening to him. Oh, they did as they were told, because they wanted to survive, and it had only taken about an hour outside the bottle world to figure out that life with the undying wizard, his terrifying lieutenant, and his violently cheerful consort was better than life inside the bottle had ever been. Still didn't mean they wanted to talk to the man.

It seemed like a terribly isolated way to live. I couldn't judge too harshly, though; I hadn't been much better. For fifty years, I'd been forming social bonds only when I couldn't escape them, preferring to run free and unfettered in my unending quest for my missing husband.

Well, it was ending now. If we were lucky, it would end today, when we met the locals and they were willing to let our strays settle here. We were almost finished. We were almost, after all these years and all these miles, finally on the road home.

Distances can be deceiving. The termite mound had looked large and distant, maybe a day's walk, maybe more. After we'd gone what I estimated to be roughly three miles across the fields, I amended my estimates to "fucking massive" and "only about ten miles away." We kept moving.

Some of the children were hungry, and their parents fed them from their stores, not wanting to stop and forage for food in a strange place, and not with that unnerving, white-wrapped forest so close to hand. The individual trees were visible now, surprisingly Earth-like in form and array, and wrapped in sheets of gauzy white that looked way too much like webbing.

Maybe *this* was one of the giant spider dimensions. It would make sense to have two megafauna worlds stacked right on top of one another. Unlike prime-time science fiction shows, where every episode is an excuse to give the special effects team a new challenge and the fandom a new obsession, real dimensions tend to assemble in clusters of similarity. Find one dimension where the dominant life form has six limbs and has repurposed one of them into wings, find three more before you get back to something with a more quadrupedal floor plan. And so on.

(And yeah, sometimes I'm saying "dimension" when what I mean is "world," because not every world in a dimension can be accessed from every other dimension, and we're limited to the worlds we can reach when we're starting from Earth. Each dimension has as many worlds as ours does if not more, and for the most part, we can't use this form of travel to replace spaceships. Which is almost certainly for the best. If you start from Earth, every "dimension" is effectively represented by a single world, and if that sounds confusing, well. There's a reason Naga was a professor of making people understand how all this stuff works. He was also a traitorous, lying bastard, and I'm glad he's dead, but that doesn't mean the man wasn't wicked smart.)

I eyed the forest as we walked, hands on the grips of my guns, unable to keep from tensing every time I heard a sound. Since the mice were running quiet catechisms from my backpack, that meant I was basically tense all the time, which was a sadly familiar state. The children were staying remarkably quiet, but this many people will make a lot of noise even when they try not to.

As if triggered by that thought, some of the infants started to sniffle, then to outright wail. It should have seemed like a good thing. They were feeling healthy enough to cry. When all this started, they had been too weak and malnourished to do much more than cling to their caretakers and stare at the world. Now they cried and fussed and did all the other things I expected babies to do, and that was wonderful, that was amazing, that was exactly what we wanted from babies . . . only maybe not right now.

I fell back to pace Sally. "I haven't seen any wildlife, and it's making me nervous."

"Maybe we're scaring them off, what with being a big procession and all."

"Or maybe something ate everything that was worth eating."

Sally gave me a measuring look. "What are you thinking?"

I didn't want to say it out loud. Not only because speaking a thing into being can sometimes make it happen: because Thomas was still running a constant translation charm to keep us from being a traveling recreation of the Tower of Babel, and the last thing I wanted to do was spark a panic. I made a hopefully evocative gesture with my hands instead.

Sally blinked. Her eyes narrowed. "You really think so?"

"I think it would make sense after the land of giant rodents, and it would explain that forest."

"I'll go talk to the boss." And she sped up, moving through the crowd with practiced grace.

Adjusting to life on Earth was going to be difficult for Thomas.

Adjusting to life without the need to run from danger every five minutes was going to be hard for me. Both those things were likely to be borderline impossible for Sally. She'd been seventeen when she made her deal with the crossroads. She'd spent her adult life so far fighting to survive in a hostile, non-Earth world. Readjusting to running water and plentiful food and sleeping without setting guards was going to be real, real hard.

I looked forward to it. For all three of us. All we had to do was get there.

Some of our people were drifting closer to the tree line than I liked. I frowned and stopped walking. This wasn't just me being paranoid. This was me having common sense. What does a silent, cobweb-draped forest have in common with a trap?

Absolutely everything. Because it *is* a trap.

Something moved in the cottony shadows of the trees. It didn't move like a mammal. I stiffened, opening my mouth to yell.

I wasn't fast enough. I couldn't have *been* fast enough—nothing human could have. By the time I started to shout, the spider that had been stalking on the other side of the trees was lunging into the open, grabbing one of the men and dragging him, kicking and screaming, into the shadows. The people he'd been walking with stopped dead and stood there in open-mouthed, frozen terror.

I bolted toward them, drawing my revolvers. "Get out of the way!" I snapped. "Get to safety!" With a series of screams, they bolted back toward the group as I ducked into the shadows on the other side of the wood.

Under the trees, that cottony webbing was everywhere, sticky and all-enveloping. Nothing moved. I narrowed my eyes, peering into the shadows. The man the spider had taken was already gone, most likely dead before he understood what had happened to him. It occurred to me, abruptly, just how bad an idea it was to follow a giant spider into a nest of giant spiders. Were these spiders the solitary kind, or the kind that formed massive social units? Either way, I probably shouldn't be in here.

Aware of how exposed my position was, I took a step backward, just as I heard the distinctive, crinkling cellophane sound of flames off to one side. I glanced over. A sheet of fire was leaping along the spider-webbing, quickly consuming it. Any spiders in the area would be distracted for at least a little while. I spun around and bolted back into the open, nearly colliding with Sally.

She grabbed my arm, pulling me farther from the trees. "Don't give the boss heart attacks because you think it's funny," she snapped. "You okay?"

"I'm fine," I said, letting her pull me along. "I was trying to get that man back before something happened to him."

"You mean something worse than getting grabbed by a fuck-off enormous spider?" Sally let go of my arm. "Don't know what kind of places you've been hanging out, princess, but where I come from, a spider that big means somebody's dead."

"Where you come from, spiders that big only happen in horror movies," I said.

Thomas was trotting toward us, fingers still smoking. "Alice!"

I let him pull me into a rough embrace. Pushing me to arm's length, he ran his warm fingers down the length of my arms, clearly checking me over for injuries. He relaxed, marginally, when he didn't find any. "What were you *thinking*?"

"I was thinking I might be able to get that man back, and if there was one giant spider, there might be more," I said. "I was going to put a few bullets in 'em, convince them not to keep hunting us."

"I think the fire did that," said Sally, already walking away from us, heading back toward the group. They had clustered together some distance from the forest, staring at the fire. I glanced over at it. The flames had consumed all the nearby webbing, and were moving on to the webs atop the trees.

"You know, maybe we should keep moving." I looked back to Thomas, who was watching me anxiously.

"Why?"

"Because the spiders aren't going to sit back and burn, and they'll have to go *somewhere*," I said, just before spiders began boiling out of the forest. Spiders in all sizes, from roughly as big as a dog all the way up to a size I would have called "Sherman tank." They were moving fast, fleeing from the fire, and fortunately, they were frightened enough that they weren't stopping to look for lunch. They kept moving, pouring around us in a horrifying wave that seemed to go on for the better part of forever, spider after spider racing past us and into the forest on the other side of the plain where we'd been walking.

I stepped closer to Thomas, pressing myself against him, and held on. If we were going to get carried off by spiders, we were going together. This was not how I lost him again.

The spiders weren't infinite. After a horrible minute or two of racing bodies, they began to taper off, until it was only the largest and slowest of the spiders lumbering past us, the ones so big they barely seemed to realize we were there, much less recognize us as a potential source of food.

When the one the size of a small yacht strolled by with a seemingly total lack of urgency, I decided to hate this dimension with all my heart and soul. I shuddered, still holding on to Thomas, and he placed a hand on my back, trying to soothe me.

"Spiders should *not* be that big," I said.

"Not at home, but the rules are clearly different here."

He finally let me go, and everything was silent except for the crackle of flames engulfing the cobweb forest. "You frightened me," he said.

"I was trying to help."

"If those spiders had taken you, I don't know what I would have—"

"They were just following their nature." I glanced at the burning forest again. "Was that really a good-enough reason to take out their entire ecosystem?"

"They have other forests. They'll rebuild."

I frowned. Forests aren't interchangeable. But I also knew better than to argue when he looked that unhappy. I may not be great at being careful, but I'm pretty good at not pushing my luck. I stepped back, smiling at him.

"Let's keep moving."

Everyone was faster now that we had a fire to our back and an unknown number of singed, unhappy spiders in the forest to the side. They were also better about staying together, and all but the very smallest of the children had stopped crying, preferring to cling to their parents and stare mistrustingly at the world. I won't say it was a nice change—kids should feel safe to be kids—but it definitely made it easier to resume our progress toward the big termite mound in the distance.

We had traveled maybe another mile, maybe a little more, when we saw . . . things emerging from the mound. They came out of the side, near the top, and clinging to it before launching themselves into the air and flying toward us, or more accurately, toward the fire. They were insectile in shape, which made sense after the spiders and the termite mound, but didn't make them read as any friendlier to my mammalian eyes. Thomas took my hand, and I held on fast, both of us watching their approach.

They flew right by us initially, clearly scouting the flames, and I got a better look at them. Mantises. Praying mantises so large that they seemed like something out of a Godzilla flick, green and brown and terrible.

"One more world that doesn't believe in the square-cube law," I muttered.

"That explains why the forest went up quite so quickly," said Thomas.

The mantises, apparently having seen what they had come to see, were turning around and flying back toward us. I stiffened, letting go of Thomas's hand so I could rest my hands on my guns, ready to draw.

As the mantises drew closer, I saw they had some sort of complicated riding harness on their backs, occupied by bipeds approximately the size and shape of humans. I blinked, some of the tension leaving my shoulders. If these mantises were being ridden, they were less likely to attack us on sight.

Hopefully.

The mantises circled overhead, and some of the refugees we were escorting shrieked and drew closer together, clearly terrified. Sally gestured for them to keep calm, and I trotted in that direction, doing the same.

"Hey, be cool, be cool," I said. "We don't know they're hostile. Given where they came from, these may be the people we came here looking for."

No one looked all that convinced by my argument as, behind me, the first of the mantises touched down. I turned.

It was even bigger up close, unnervingly so, reminding some small, animal part of my mind that I was, in fact, just a little mammal, soft and very, very edible. It cocked its wedge-shaped head, studying me, and I swallowed hard.

A rope dropped from the side of the mantis. One of the riders—it had two, which was something of a relief, as it meant the second was remaining seated to control the mantis—slid to the ground. Sally, Thomas, and I arrayed ourselves between the rider and our people. We were a fragile line of defense, and one that would go down quickly if the mantis decided to attack, but we were better than nothing.

The rider was definitely bipedal, and could probably have passed for human under the right circumstances back at home. Their skin, however, was spotted in rosette markings, like a leopard's hide, and covered in fine, velvety fur. Their ears were pointed, and their eyes were a bright shade of yellow-green that would have looked more natural on a cat. No tail, though. Which was almost a pity. More people should have tails.

Their clothing was made of loose brown-and-gray cloth tied around their wrists and ankles to keep it from tangling with the reins while they were mounted. Their feet were bare. They moved with an easy grace, watching us warily. They were apparently unarmed, and once close enough, they raised their hands, palms outward, and spoke.

Thomas's translation spell caught their words. "Peace, strangers. Where do you travel?"

"We came from a world far from this one," said Thomas. "A friend said we might find refuge here for some of our number. We were heading toward the place from which you emerged. We hope to make it there before nightfall."

"The hunters in the dark will emerge when the sun goes down," said the rider. "They care not what world you travel from, or where you intend to go. You must make the passage quickly, or it will not be made at all. Do you know how their forest came to burn?"

"Er," said Thomas. "I'm afraid that was me. I was concerned for my wife's safety, and when I get worried, things sometimes catch fire."

The rider looked at him, then nodded. "We have seen similar things from travelers of your kind, in past. Our patriarch will welcome you."

"Patriarch?" I asked, warily. I was getting real tired of these extra-dimensional societies that organized themselves so the men were on top of the social order by default, leaving everyone else to scramble for a place beneath them.

"The eldest among us who remembers the coming of our most recent true Incubus," said the rider. Behind us in the crowd, a few of the Murrays gasped.

"We call them Lilu, and their presence among your kind is much of what brings us here," said Thomas. "May we continue?"

"Yes," said the rider. "We will send an escort, to be sure you make it to the mound in safety, and we will be grateful for your company at tonight's tables." They bowed, sketching a complex motion with one hand, before turning to head back to their mantis and shimmy up the rope, quick as anything.

They grasped and pulled the reins. The mantis launched itself into the air, the two behind it following, and the three began to circle overhead, escorting us toward the mound as promised. I glanced upward, unable to stop myself from feeling uneasy.

"Guess we're off to meet the Wizard," I muttered.

"In the jolly old land of Oz," agreed Sally.

Thomas took my hand, and we walked on.

Five

"An ally's an ally, no matter what they look for. Beggars can't be choosers, and unless you're in an absolutely superior position, neither can you."

—Alexander Healy

Sitting down to dinner inside a giant termite mound, and other sentences I've never considered before

THEIR PATRIARCH TURNED OUT to be a smiling man roughly Thomas's apparent age, with paler spots than most of the others, and who went by the unprepossessing name of "Kenneth." That was almost reassuring. Real-life cult leaders don't usually call themselves "Bloodfang the Consumer," but they also aren't generally content to go around being named "Kenneth."

True to Helen's notes, these people had interbred with a Lilu several years previous, and were happy to accept our genetically scrambled refugees. The Murrays and the others might not have a single dimension where they belonged without standing out, but this world was willing to have them, and most of them were glad to stay and settle, while the rest were at least ready to give it a chance. They'd been on the move long enough.

Besides, there was food here. A meaty stew I was willing to bet Sally didn't recognize as being insect-based, and which I was equally willing to bet none of them would *care* about being insect-based, since it was plentiful and good. Roast vegetables that didn't taste like anything on Earth, and even bread, which had a nutty aftertaste that told me they'd been using crickets for flour. So more livestock than agriculture, and very little of it mammalian in origin. That was fine. Our people could survive here.

Lilu genetics are unique, as far as anyone's been able to tell. They can reproduce with virtually anything, and they don't have allergies, making protein incompatibilities unheard of. And these people, who were coming from a similar starting tech level, would be able to assimilate into their society without making a ripple, replenishing their gene pool and answering the question of how people who no longer had a world and didn't belong to any single dominant species were going to survive.

We'd done it. We'd pulled three hundred people out of a dying bottle dimension, and we'd managed to find them a place where they could be safe. Happiness wasn't guaranteed, but then, happiness is never guaranteed.

Thomas and I sat together on a low cushion, watching as Sally compared spears with some of the locals, all of them very interested in one another's weapons. People were sitting everywhere in the vast lower chamber of the termite mound, and massive glowing grubs covered the ceiling, lighting things up almost as well as fire would have. They were absolutely necessary, since there were no windows. None of the lowest chambers had windows.

"The hunters in the dark can fit through the smallest spaces," said Kenneth, when I asked about the lack of windows. "They only dare try our walls so far, though; higher up, the steeds lie waiting, and are always willing to accept a meal which presents itself freely."

I paused, puzzling through that statement. "So the giant spiders would come in the windows if you had any, but they won't climb to the top of the mound or the mantises will eat them?"

Kenneth nodded. "Exactly so."

"Huh."

He smiled, the polite, bland smile of someone making nice with a guest who they hoped was going to leave soon, and drifted over to speak with a cluster of refugees. They laughed, agreeing with something he'd said.

Thomas's translation spell would leave with us when we went, and these people would have to learn to communicate the old-fashioned way, but looking around, it seemed like they'd be more than pleased to make the effort. The mound had a fairly large population of the spotted, semi-feline people, and our group had a reasonable number of striped, semi-feline people. I guess "semi-feline" was a not uncommon body form in the adjacent dimensions. The spotty ones seemed to be the original inhabitants; the less-spotty ones, like Kenneth, were direct descendants of the incubus who'd come to visit a few generations back.

Interestingly, he'd been traveling in the company of several Johrlac, and even more interestingly, according to Kenneth, we had just missed a similar group—where "just missed" meant "it happened about a year and a half ago," if I was doing the local time conversion correctly. No guarantees. But apparently, a group consisting of a Johrlac, an Incubus, and a couple of sorcerers had come crashing through, along with a fairly hefty chunk of masonry, and upset the spiders something awful before leaving again, taking their masonry with them.

It was hard to tell from Kenneth's descriptions, but it sure sounded like he was talking about a bunch of my grandkids. Which would be a pretty big coincidence, and just made me more sure that he was talking about people I knew. My family lives in the pause between "possible" and "probable," courtesy of Mom, and if it seemed too good to be true, it probably was. Maybe that's not how it works for anybody else. It's how things have always worked for me.

The visitors had been accompanied by a horrifying number of cuckoos, most of whom had been eaten by giant spiders or found dead in the fields after the group took their masonry and went home. Honestly, the whole thing was a little confusing, and I snuggled into Thomas as I tried to puzzle my way through it, finishing my stew and enjoying the somewhat novel sensation of having enough to eat while in a safe, enclosed place.

Thomas skimmed a hand across my hair, the sensation light enough to be barely present. I tilted my head back and looked at him; he smiled at me.

"I think we're nearly done," he said. "If all my people choose to stay here . . ."

"Then we head to Ithaca, tell Helen and Phoebe we're finished, and go back to Buckley to figure out what happens next," I said, agreeably. "I hope Sally likes the tailypo."

Thomas snorted. "Buckley is still up for discussion, and I hope the tailypo like *me*, since all the ones who knew me have long since passed away, and I don't particularly want a hostile conspiracy of lemurs in my living room."

"They're going to love you," I said. "Just like their ancestors did. Just like I do."

He leaned down and he kissed me, and I didn't care that we were in a room full of people, or that the ceiling was covered in giant bugs, or any of those things. All that mattered was here, and now, and the fact that after all this time, I had accomplished my goal. I got to have new goals now, ones that were maybe a little less straightforward but would almost certainly be healthier, or at least involve less gross physical trauma. I could go *home*, and it would *be* home, really home, not a waystation between me and the next leg of my wild goose chase. A little public kissing was nothing compared to that kind of relief.

Besides, it wasn't like we'd had a lot of privacy since leaving the bottle dimension, and as long as we were both fully clothed, there wasn't much we could do that would feel like crossing a line.

Sally plopped down next to me. I disengaged from kissing Thomas to twist and look at her.

"All done showing off your poking sticks?" I asked.

"Too many Lilu in one room," she said. "The smell is starting to make my head spin."

Lilu—incubi and succubi, in the more common usage—sweat pheromonal signals that make them almost irresistibly attractive to people with a compatible biology. It's never had much impact on the members of my direct family. I figure it's part and parcel of the ridiculous luck we all got from Mom. Sally and Thomas didn't have the same luxury, and while about half our company was part Lilu, we'd been traveling outside, where the open air could diffuse the signals.

That explained Thomas kissing me in front of other people. Not that he's been particularly shy about kissing me since we were reunited—we're both trying to make up for lost time. But he wasn't normally that casual about initiating. I adjusted my position, leaning against him as I focused on Sally.

"Does it feel like anyone's influencing you intentionally?"

She shook her head. "No, just general background noise. But there's enough women here who fit my standards that I'm starting to get a little flustered. I know we can't go outside without making ourselves targets for the giant spiders, but is there any place we could go to be a little less surrounded by people who might accidentally cause a massive consent violation?"

Most Lilu are very aware of the effect they have on other people, and take steps to keep themselves from influencing anyone by mistake. In this case, however, we had the Murrays, descendants of some not-very-nice people who hadn't been shy about using their natural talents to find mates once they landed in the bottle world. The modern Murrays were more restrained, and also had weaker powers of persuasion, thanks to the genetic contributions of their non-Lilu ancestors. That didn't mean they didn't walk around in a low-grade funk of supernatural Axe body spray at all times. And then there were the locals, who were just as far removed from their incubus ancestor, but were still sweating organic love potion. None of them had any good reason to have learned to control it, since Lilu can't easily affect other Lilu, and their pheromones don't affect close relatives on the non-Lilu side. Meaning that even the non-Lilu locals were safe due to other family ties, and this whole place was a sexy, sexy soup of inescapable perfumes.

"Good question," I said, and rose, pausing to kiss Thomas on the top of the head before I trotted toward Kenneth. He turned and blinked at me, somewhat nonplussed, although I didn't know whether he was thrown by my approach or general lack of deference. I'm not great at "unearned respect." It's not one of my big callings in life.

"Hey, bud," I said. "So we have a tiny problem."

"What would that be?"

"See, you lot are descended from that Incubus ancestor you're so proud of, and so are a lot of the folks we brought with us," I said. "Me, Thomas, and Sally, though, we're just human. No extra bits or bonuses. So the pheromones are getting to be sort of a lot, and we need to move to another room so we can breathe."

"You are free to go," he said, imperiously.

"And that would be the tiny problem. I don't want to wander into the stable and get eaten by one of your giant mantis friends or something, so we'll need someone to show us where we can safely go, and even more importantly than that, when we leave, the translation spell that's letting you all talk to each other so easily is going to go with us. Sorcerer, remember?" I shrugged, trying my best to look at least a little apologetic. I was afraid I didn't do a very good job. That's something else I've never been particularly good at. "Thought it would be polite to warn you that you're about to have a language barrier all up in here."

"We have navigated language barriers before," he said stiffly.

"Not like this. They speak about two dozen languages between them, and in some cases, the kids and parents don't actually know the same one. The dangers of raising your children under a translation spell. The kids speak English. The parents speak whatever was spoken back in their original dimensions, and they've never had reason to learn anything else."

Kenneth blinked slowly, finally looking as if he might actually understand.

"Anyway, the spell travels with Thomas, and we have to get out of here before something inappropriate happens, so if you could brace yourself and warn your people, that would be good." I smiled thinly. "Think of it as a test run for what's going to happen when we move on to the next dimension. Because we're not coming back here."

That wasn't entirely true. Thomas would probably want to come back eventually, to check on the people he'd been taking care of for decades. But I wouldn't be coming with him unless he wanted me to, and he definitely wouldn't be taking any of them back to Earth with him. There's taking in strays—something we're very, very good at— and then there's setting people up to be miserable, which we mostly try to avoid.

Kenneth nodded. "I will tell my people," he said, and moved to do just that.

I walked back to where I'd left Sally and Thomas. Sally was still sitting there, but Thomas was on the other side of the room, in quiet conversation with one of the Murray guards who'd always taken a local leadership position within the sub-group. I nodded toward him.

"Letting them know the plan?"

"Boss didn't want people to panic when they stopped making sense," said Sally. Her voice had taken on a nasal quality; she was talking without breathing through her nose. Smart girl. "Kenneth down?"

"I don't think he's *happy*, but he's going to send someone to see us to a room where we can be safe and breathe easier, and he knows the translation spell won't hold."

"Great." Sally sighed and looked up at me, seeming briefly, terribly young. She was in her early twenties, physically barely younger than me, but she'd been a kid when all this started. I offered her my hand.

She took it, pulling herself to her feet. I smiled encouragingly as I let go.

"Hey, we're almost done. Home soon. Home, and running water, and all the comforts of life on Earth. I mean, you'll be in the middle of nowhere, Michigan, but it's going to seem like paradise after these last few years."

Sally paused. Then, taking her hand carefully out of mine, she asked, "You're really willing to let me come live with you? I figured you and the boss would want to have some privacy once you got back."

Thomas was on his way back over to us, accompanied by two of Kenneth's guards. I raised a finger.

"Let's put a pin in that for just a second, while we get settled, but then I want to talk about it, so don't forget," I said. Then I turned to

Thomas, offering him a dazzlingly bright smile. "Okay, sweetheart, where are we going?"

Where we were going was another room, about half the size of the one we'd been in, with two walls taken up by rough-hewn bookshelves stocked with hand-stitched books, and a third covered by a sheet of slate, creating a primitive chalkboard. I walked toward it, studying the figures and formulae written there. It was clearly Johrlac math, designed to break the laws of physics and the laws of nature in the same delicate cut.

It was just as clearly Sarah's handwriting. She might as well have signed her name. I touched the chalkboard, smearing one of the numbers, and smiled over my shoulder at Thomas and Sally.

"We're going home," I said.

The guards who'd escorted us here murmured their regards and left, presumably returning to the chaos that must have overtaken the main room by now. "It's going to sound like the United Nations in there," said Sally, throwing herself down on a pile of heaped-up animal hides. Some of them looked mammalian, which was good; it increased the odds that our hosts were originally from around here, and not more invaders. After Naga and the situation on Empusa, I was a lot less well inclined toward intentionally invasive species.

"What makes you say that?" Thomas walked up and put his arms around my waist, looking at the chalkboard. "Have you mastered Johrlac dimensional calculus while I was away?"

"No, although I've learned how to recognize it." I twisted so I was facing him. "I say we're going home because we *are*, and because those other travelers Kenneth was talking about are ours. Sarah and Artie for sure, probably Annie and one of her friends. If Sarah's doing dimension-hopper math, she's gotten a lot more comfortable with herself since the last time I saw her. That's a good thing. Poor kid ties herself in knots over absolutely everything."

"You use all these words like they're supposed to mean something to me," said Sally. "What's dimensional calculus? And you used that word earlier—'Johrlac.' What does it mean?"

"Those are really two halves of the same question," said Thomas, letting go of me so he could turn to her. I managed, barely, not to glower. "The Johrlac are residents of a dimension called Johrlar. I've never been there. Alice?"

"Nope, me neither," I said. "They're a little xenophobic on Johrlar. Something about not wanting outsiders to taint their perfect hive mind."

"Hive . . . mind?"

"They're telepaths," said Thomas. "A true Johrlac lives in perfect harmony with their fellows, barely distinct from the minds around them."

"And if they're not a true Johrlac—if they're an individual or someone who likes to think for themselves—the rest of the hive doesn't consider them a Johrlac at all. We call the members of the species who aren't part of the hive 'cuckoos,' because they tend to infiltrate human spaces and change people's memories to make it like they've always been there. Sarah is technically a cuckoo, although if she's started doing Johrlac math, she may not be calling herself that anymore."

Sally blinked, clearly overwhelmed by the onslaught of information.

Thomas picked up the thread again: "Johrlac and cuckoos are the same species, divided by a manner of thinking, and they can both do amazing things. Including crossing dimensional boundaries without sorcery or drawing on the local pneuma in any way I've ever been able to verify. They use complicated hyperdimensional math that can bridge the gaps without any magical support."

"And they're not bound to linear distances the way we are," I said. "We literally *can't* jump straight from here to Earth. We have to go through at least one dimension that touches on both worlds. In this case, we're planning to use Ithaca, because we promised Helen and Phoebe we'd tell them when we were heading home, and because we know they're friendly there. But we could go in another direction if we wanted to, as long as we went somewhere that had a shared boundary with Earth. Johrlac don't need to do that. They just fill in the equation for the world they want, and then they go. I mean, it costs, sometimes."

"Costs?"

"I can't open a gateway large enough or difficult enough to kill myself," said Thomas. "Even if I wanted to, my magic would refuse the attempt. It's why I was unable to open a pathway out of the killing jar before Alice arrived draped in pneuma and willing to play battery for my endeavor. If I had needed to pull that much out of myself, I wouldn't have been able to. The spell would have fizzled before it killed me."

"Johrlac, though . . . they're not pulling *from* themselves, they're running math *through* themselves, and that works differently," I said. "So they can have an equation that's too big for the mathematician, and it can short out their brains. Sarah must have worked this spell correctly, or she'd be a corpse somewhere in the basement, and not gone along with whatever these nice folks mean by 'masonry.' And if she's doing dimensional math powerful enough to relocate buildings, she's doing pretty well."

"Sarah is the adopted granddaughter," said Sally, carefully.

"Adopted something or other," I agreed. "She's Kevin's wife's sister, but she's the same age as the grandkids, so she's functionally a granddaughter. I'd say you're going to like her, but I can't actually be sure about that. Sarah's pretty shy. She doesn't like most people, unless they're secretly comic books. Are you secretly a comic book?"

"I don't think so," said Sally. "I think I'd know if I were. Pretty sure I'm just a girl from Maine."

"About that," said Thomas. "When I came over in the other room, the two of you seemed to be discussing what was going to happen when we got back to Earth. I think we all have some assumptions. It might be good to clear them up now."

"I know . . ." Sally began, then hesitated, looking at her feet as she tried to sort through her words. Finally, she looked back up, and said, "I know you think families should stay together, and you have this idea about finding my parents when we get back, see if I can't go on home to them. But they're not . . . they're not like you. There's no way I could explain everything to them. For them, I disappeared and I probably died, and coming back now would just rip open all those old wounds and convince them I was a liar. James was always more family to me than they were."

Thomas blinked, taken aback.

"They acted like they couldn't be racist because they adopted a Korean kid," said Sally. "They never learned to *speak* Korean, or tried to make sure I kept any sort of connection to my heritage, or anything like that. It would have been work, and they'd already done all the work of adopting a needy foreign kid because their church told them it would be a good thing. They *hated* that I liked girls. Mom was in total denial. Said I'd get over it, and James and I would settle down and get married and have lots of happy babies. Dad said it was just a phase and everyone's confused when they're a kid. They didn't beat me. They made sure I had food and shoes, and they paid for me to go to cheer camp and they didn't get mad that my best friend was a boy, or when I went to senior prom with James. They were probably real upset when I disappeared. Only at least half of it was for show, because they knew they were *supposed* to be real upset when their only kid vanished. Either they're enjoying being childless, or they have a new kid in my room by now. Hoping that this time, they'll get a dutiful daughter instead of a screw-up."

I stepped away from Thomas. "You're not a screw-up. You stayed alive in a place that wanted you dead, and you're only the second person I've met who made their crossroads deal for a good reason. Thomas was the first."

He snorted. "Of course you'd think so."

"I mean, sure. If you hadn't done it, I'd be dead, and while I might have come back as a ghost, I probably wouldn't have, and the kids wouldn't have existed. I like the kids. I like the grandkids, too. They're a net benefit to the world. So yeah, I think your deal was made for a good reason. Sally, I don't know yet if her deal was a net benefit to the world, but since the boy she made it for is running around with the grandkids, I'm willing to bank on 'yes.' You are both saints who didn't deserve what the crossroads did to you, and when we get home, you can have cake."

"I miss cake," said Sally.

The mice, who had been riding quietly in my pack, cheered, ear-splittingly loud. We all winced.

"Do you still maintain a colony in Michigan?" asked Thomas.

I nodded. "I do."

"Very well, then. Sally, I shan't ask you to look for your family, only tell you that you're welcome to do so if you desire, and your penance for choosing to remain lost to them will be life with a full colony of Aeslin mice."

"The mice are pretty cool," she said, with a sideways smile. "They keep making religious rituals out of things I say and shit, and that's neat."

"It's neat now, when you have one priest," I said. "Once you have an entire clergy, you may think differently. Thomas? Does that mean you're okay with going back to Michigan?"

There were so many things we'd been putting off deciding, because we had so far to go before we'd be going home and needing to worry about them. Sally had always been something of a given, even if Thomas had believed there was some way she wouldn't be; she was his kid, even if he hadn't set out to adopt her, and I knew a familial bond when I saw one. And yeah, I might get frustrated sometimes, but I wasn't frustrated enough to try to separate them. I don't think I could ever be that frustrated.

But where we wound up after we got back to Earth . . . that had been up in the air. On the one hand, there was Michigan. Buckley Township, where we had the house and the tailypo and the Red Angel, and all the other things that would be at least somewhat familiar to the both of us. On the other hand, there was Portland, Oregon, where both our adult children and the majority of our grandchildren could be found. Thomas was just as focused on the importance of family as I was—more, maybe, since he'd never voluntarily run away from them. He wanted to get to know the kids. That meant being near them.

He smiled and reached out to push my hair back from one side of my face, tucking it behind my ear. "I want us to both be as comfortable as possible, and Sally, too. I want us to get accustomed to home. And if that means having some distance between you and the rest of the family, I'll still be closer than I've been in fifty years."

"Get a room," said Sally, rolling her eyes.

"We did, you just came with it," I snapped, and she laughed, and this was all falling together. Soon enough, this would all be over.

Six

"Children are mirrors of their parents. What they reflect is what you show them."

—Jonathan Healy

Getting ready to leave Pteracercus for Ithaca

TRUE TO WHAT I had guessed would happen when I saw our refugees with the locals, the ones I thought of as their leaders came to us in the morning, explaining their intent to stay in the halting, awkward manner of people who weren't sure whether or not they were about to cause offense. In the end, Thomas hugged a man who'd been one of his closest advisors, wished them luck in this new world, and came back to me and Sally with a smile on his face and a new lightness in his step.

After fifty years of keeping these people alive, he was responsible for no one but himself and his family, and most of his family was pretty self-sufficient. I slipped my hand into his, matching his smile with my own.

"Well?" I asked. "Can we get to Ithaca from here, or do we need to go back to where we started? Because I'll be honest, I could do without walking through the giant spider killing chute a second time."

Thomas responded by closing his eyes and taking a deep breath. When he opened them again, he sighed and pointed back the way we'd come. "I'm afraid the nearest crossing point is some distance that way. Perhaps we can request an escort?"

"If you're willing to ride, we can carry you as far as you have need," said Kenneth, looming up behind us in a way that was probably designed to be unnerving. It might have been, if I hadn't been aware that he was lurking back there. He wasn't as quiet as he thought he was. I guess you don't have to be, when you're the patriarch and no one argues with you about whether or not something is a good idea.

"Ride a giant praying mantis?" asked Sally, and perked right up, suddenly enthusiastic. "Sounds great! And like something I've never done before, which makes it *awesome*. Can we?"

It wasn't clear which of us she was asking. Thomas stepped in, saying, "If the offer is extended to all of us, then yes, of course we can. It's faster than walking, if nothing else. Alice?"

"I know how to ride," I said, trying to push aside the flicker of anxiety that said no, riding a giant flying bug was not the same thing as riding a horse, not the same thing at all. If Thomas was game, I could handle it. Besides, how bad could it actually be?

Bad. It could be very, very bad, as riding a mantis was nothing like riding a horse. There was no warning of motion before the giant insect was in the air, wings generating a backdraft almost strong enough to sweep us all off the saddle. I clung to the ropes securing me to the saddle as tightly as I could, trying to look like this wasn't the most upsetting thing I'd voluntarily subjected myself to in ages.

Sally whooped with delight behind me, thrusting one arm into the air as she held onto the anchor ropes with the other, and Thomas watched us both, looking mildly interested in the entire situation. Apparently, I was the only one who remembered the existence of gravity and its tendency to pop mammals like water balloons when we fall a far-enough distance. I glared at them both and kept hanging on.

Sally laughed at the look on my face, the wind whipping the sound away, if not quickly enough to keep me from hearing it. I glared at her. She laughed again, leaning in closer.

"So there's something that actually frightens the great Alice Price?" she asked. "That's good. I was starting to be afraid you were some sort of sophisticated robot or something, and now I think you might be a real person."

I glared harder. She grinned at me and leaned back in her rope harness, going back to punching the sky. At least one of us was having fun.

Thomas shot me a more sympathetic look, which I answered with a sickly smile. One of our grandkids, Verity, thinks gravity is a toy. She likes to play with it, push the boundaries and see just how much she can get away with, and generally give me heart attacks for her own amusement. I am a little more sensible than she is, which is a terrifying thought and makes me wonder how she's managed to survive to adulthood, given that gravity is the *only* thing I'm remotely sensible about. I fell out of a lot of trees when I was a kid, and broke more than a few bones. It left me with an exaggerated sense of caution.

Everyone else seemed to think this was safe enough, and so I forced myself, bit by bit, to unkink my shoulders. The ground zipped by beneath us at an incredible speed. The mantis couldn't be flying as fast as a commercial jet, but we were so exposed it felt faster.

Not that I've ever actually been on a plane, but I have to assume they have something a little more sophisticated than a rope harness to keep from losing passengers.

The mantis began gliding downward as we approached what looked like a demolition site, or the crater left by a large explosion. The trunks of crushed, shattered trees littered the ground, and the earth itself was torn up, like something large had been dropped from a great height. I blinked at the local who was steering our ride.

"What the hell happened here?"

"This is where our other visitors arrived," he said, bringing the mantis in for a landing. It landed without even a thump, beginning to wash its scythe-like forearms. The local twisted in his own harness, looking back at me. "We told you they brought their masonry with them. This is where it landed."

"So you're telling me they went full Dorothy and brought a *house*?" I began untying my harness. "Damn, Sarah, I didn't know you had it in you."

He blinked. "My name is not Sarah," he said, politely. "They call me Ciferol."

"Sounds pharmaceutical," I said. "Sally, Thomas, you ready to get off the big bug?"

"Can't we go for another ride first?" asked Sally plaintively. I turned to glare at her, and she laughed. "Yeah, I'm good to go."

"The channels feel cleaner here," said Thomas. "I should be able to open us a doorway to Ithaca with the pneuma I've already accumulated."

"Then we're good to go. Ciferol, thank you for your help. Can you drop the ropes so we can get down to the ground level?"

"Of course," he said, politely, and unhooked a bundle of knotted ropes from behind his position, tossing them so they dangled to the ground. More opportunities to fall a nice, long distance. Goodie. Falling is my *favorite* thing.

Falling is no one sensible's favorite thing, which means it's probably

Verity's favorite thing, and sometimes I think passing my genes on did no one any favors, even if I continue to hold up my descendants as proof that Thomas did the right thing by keeping me alive. I grabbed the rope, squirming into position to begin my descent.

"Tell your leader that you were of great help to us, and we appreciate it immensely," said Thomas. "We hope our people will be happy here with you."

"And if they're not, we'll be seeing you soon," said Sally, in an ominous tone. Ciferol shrank back in his rope harness. I laughed but didn't contradict her.

We weren't coming back here for a long, long time, if we ever did. Dimensional travel isn't meant to be undertaken with the sort of frequency that we'd been demonstrating since we left the bottle dimension. This was a special case. There was every chance, if we were lucky, that the three of us would never be leaving Earth again.

Well, maybe the occasional visit to Ithaca, to check in with Helen and Phoebe, but that wasn't *travel*, that was . . . being a good neighbor. More importantly, that was only one hop.

Helen thought that with the crossroads gone, Earth's pneuma would begin to recover from the damage that had been done to it, and sorcerers like Thomas would find themselves getting stronger. Opening a door as far as Ithaca wouldn't seem so unreasonable. If she was right, we could keep in touch with relative ease, and I truly hoped she was right. Thomas had gone from starvation in the bottle dimension to a constantly renewing supply of pneuma from a dozen dimensions, and I was suddenly worried that Earth would seem like a return to famine, rather than the feast it was.

Honestly, I was worried about a lot of things. Thinking about the future has never been my area of expertise. Hell, thinking beyond what I was going to do tomorrow has never been my strong suit. Reacting is my primary way of dealing with the world. Planning is for people who have more complex needs than "figure out what's for dinner," "kill the thing that's been killing Missus Norton's chickens," or "find your husband and bring him home while he still knows who you are."

Okay, so maybe my problems get sort of complex sometimes, but it's rarely the sort of complex that demands a lot of long-term planning. I shimmied down the rope, resolutely not looking down until my feet were firmly under me, then looked up to watch Thomas and Sally make their descent.

The mantis took off as soon as they were next to me, and the three of us were alone in a strange world, too far from the mound where the locals and our former followers were located to make it back before dark.

I wasn't sure I'd been happier since we left the bottle dimension. Sally and I fell in behind Thomas, one of us to either side of him, ready to muster a defense if anything went wrong.

He glanced at me. I smiled.

"Come on," I said. "Get us home."

This time, when he raised his hands, the bruised spot in the air clarified on a meadow dotted with tiny white flowers. A house stood in the distance, oddly Greek architecture with a modern sensibility that I couldn't have described if I'd been paid to do it, but recognized all the same. That's the thing about time periods. Sometimes you just have to know them when you see them. The spell, seeking the easiest option, had seized on the dimensional crossing circle Helen and Phoebe had on their property. We were finally going to wind up exactly where we wanted to be.

A light wind blew through the opening, smelling of wildflowers and herbs. I smiled. "Ithaca."

Sally looked less enthusiastic. Well, she'd only been there once, and then only in the process of passing through with our train of survivors. There'd been no time to linger or relax, which was a shame, since Ithaca is one of the nicer dimensions that I'm actually familiar with. The places Naga liked to send me were much more likely to fall under the heading of "horrifying murder world," and since Sally knew Ithaca was one of my regular stops, it made sense for her to be wary.

I gestured her through. She shook her head, gesturing for me to go first. I sighed.

"You know I don't go before Thomas does," I said. "I didn't spend this much time trying to find him to voluntarily go into another dimension without him."

Sally rolled her eyes. "Codependent much?"

"Ladies," said Thomas, sounding faintly strained. "If *one* of you could go through, I would very much appreciate it."

Sally shot me a dirty look and stepped through, onto the green, flower-speckled ground. I wondered, somewhat idly, whether she was going to step on the wrong flower and invoke Phoebe's wrath. Should probably have warned her about that. Oh, well.

I stepped in front of Thomas, breaking his line of sight on the portal, and took his hands in mine. "Come on, baby," I said. "Let's go home."

He blinked at me, dazed as he always was by holding a gateway—although not as dazed as he'd been when we had to hold it long enough to usher dozens of people through—and smiled as I tugged him through the opening and into another world.

Ithaca is not a preindustrial dimension, for all that it tries very, very hard to look like one. What it is is a dimension with incredibly strict ecological protection laws, which has always taken "we live in concert with the natural world" very seriously indeed.

The gateway closed, leaving us in the meadow. Sally was already on alert, scanning for threats that were unlikely to materialize this close to a residence. Helen says they have excellent perimeter fencing, and since I've never been attacked while I was at their house, I'm inclined to believe her.

Thomas wobbled, unsteady on his feet, and looked at me. "Are we safe?"

"We're safe," I assured him. "We're on Ithaca, you, me, and Sally, and all your people are settled where they can figure out their lives and what they want to do with them from here. You did it. We won."

"Oh, *good*," he said, closed his eyes, and collapsed.

There are a lot of ways people can collapse. Blood loss is one. Getting shot is another. This, though . . . this was boneless exhaustion, like a puppet whose strings had been cut. I lunged to catch him, not quite fast enough to grab anything more substantial than the wind left by his passing, and landed on my knees next to him, grabbing his arm to check for a pulse.

It was there, solid and a little faster than I liked. I looked over my shoulder to Sally, who was staring at us in open-mouthed shock.

"The house," I said, curtly. "Helen and Phoebe live there. Go tell them we're here, and Thomas has exhausted himself by pushing the dimensional crossings. We need help."

She didn't move. I narrowed my eyes.

"*Go!*" I snapped.

Sally turned on her heel and ran for the house, doubtless trampling dozens of Phoebe's precious flowers in her flight. I ignored her, focusing on Thomas.

He was still breathing, which was good. Collapses like this were familiar from my own time opening dimensional gates, when my body had cannibalized itself to try and let me go farther than I should have been able to. I'd never seen it happen to a sorcerer before, and I suddenly had to wonder whether he'd been intentionally overstating how

much pneuma he'd been able to draw from a few of the more dangerous worlds we'd passed through, in order to get us out of there just that
tiny bit faster than would have been possible otherwise.

If I had no sense of self-preservation when it came to him, it was
balanced out—and not necessarily in the best way—by his absolute
lack of self-preservation when it came to me. We might destroy each
other. We might be blissfully happy in our little house in Michigan.
Either way, we'd be together, and for both of us, that was what mattered.

When I'd pushed myself to this point, I used to handle it with glucose gel and electrolyte powders, both of which had run out half a
dozen dimensions ago, and which I hadn't been trying to restock, even
if it would have been remotely possible, because I'd had no idea they
might be needed. I positioned myself so I could pull his head into my
lap, leaning down to straighten his limbs. Wouldn't do to have him
wake up having strained something.

Thus, having reached the limit of my usefulness, I settled in to wait.

Sally came running back across the field, followed by two satyrs,
one carrying a wicker basket over her arm, neither hurrying half as
fast as Sally was. The taller of the two actually looked faintly amused,
like this was funny. I swallowed the urge to yell at her for that. Sally
had probably communicated the situation in a way that sounded entertaining, rather than the taller satyr finding the fact that Thomas
had collapsed in the first place somehow funny.

"Hoy, Odysseus!" called the taller satyr as they approached. "Broken your Penelope already? For shame. I expected you would be more
careful, all things considered."

"Thanks, Helen. You're very sweet." The other satyr laughed,
kneeling in the grass next to Thomas. Watching a woman with the
lower body of a goat kneel was a spectacle in and of itself. As a human, I find digitigrade anatomy unaccountably complicated. But they
probably feel the same about my weird-ass knees, and so it all works
out in the end.

I returned my attention to Helen as Phoebe unpacked the contents
of her basket, narrowing my eyes. "Is this exhaustion? Because it
looks like exhaustion to me, and I don't think I'll handle it very well
if it's anything else."

"Peace, Odysseus." Helen held up her hands, palms outward. "Give
Phoebe the time to work. As it's just the three of you, I'm assuming
your long journey is well complete?"

"All the survivors of the bottle dimension have been settled, either in their original worlds or in compatible communities," I said. "You need to update your maps. A few of those 'suitable' unoccupied dimensions turned out to have some pretty big inhabitants. Bats and moles large enough to eat people do not make for very good neighbors."

"You asked for places without intelligent people," said Helen. "You didn't ask for worlds incapable of supporting life."

Phoebe had produced a bottle of something pink and oddly sparkly, like it was laced with edible glitter, from inside her basket, and was tipping it against Thomas's lips, clearly encouraging him to drink. I glanced over and bit my lip.

Helen put her hand on my arm. "Peace," she said again. "Phoebe will help him to wake from this miscalculation, and you have no further travels from here, yes?"

"Only home," I said. "We're going home."

"The pneuma of your world has continued to recover," she said, approvingly. "I've taken glances at it when the connections were clear, and things are progressing in the right direction. Earth may be a healthy world again someday."

"That's cool," I said. "We're planning to stay there."

"Yes, you promised," said Helen.

Phoebe was still pressing her bottle to Thomas's lips. Finally, he coughed and swallowed, then began to drink in earnest, all without apparently waking up. I blinked, stroking his hair, then looked back to Helen in silent question. She sighed.

"He is exhausted. Had you no way of seeing that?"

"I can't see magic," I said. "Neither can Sally. He wasn't telling us how tired he was. He's been trying to keep things moving along. We were safe enough in that last dimension. If he'd *said* anything, to either of us, we could have stopped for a few days, given him time to rest up. But we were so close to home, and I think he wanted to get to the end as much as I did, so he didn't tell us anything was wrong. Is he going to be okay?"

The only acceptable answer was yes. Anything else and I was going to tear down the world to make it change. We'd come so far, fought for so long; this couldn't be the point where my luck—where *our* luck—gave out.

Phoebe returned her bottle to the basket, giving me a cold look. "You will allow us to open the gateway between here and your 'Earth,'" she said. "And you will allow us to give you a hamper to take with you, as I doubt your destination will be provisioned for your arrival."

"I keep cans and shelf-stable foods on hand, but the house is rural enough that I don't even trust the freezers when I'm going to be away for a long time," I said. One trip where the power had gone out almost as soon as I left the dimension had been enough to teach me that stockpiling meat was only a good idea when you could be there to make sure it actually stayed frozen. Some smells do not bear repeating. "Oh, and Cynthia from the Red Angel drops off a cake every Thursday, for the mice. But that's about it."

"A hamper," said Phoebe firmly. She stood, taking her basket with her. "And keep your handmaid close to you. She nearly trampled my cat's brush when she came running to the house."

Sally bristled at being called a handmaid, but I mustered a smile as I nodded to Phoebe, and said, "She'll stay here with us, I promise."

"He'll be fine," said Phoebe, taking pity. "No large workings for a fortnight, you understand? Anything that draws more pneuma than he can gather from the air stands the chance of doing him harm, and I feel you would prefer that not occur."

"I'll sit on him if I have to," I said firmly.

"Good." Phoebe leaned over to kiss Helen on the cheek. "Come to the house for the hamper, my leman, and set them on their way. I'll see ourselves alone this evening."

Sally blinked, looking surprised. Helen smiled a small, besotted smile after Phoebe as the other satyr walked away, then turned back to me.

Thomas was making little grumbling noises and shifting in my lap, although his eyes were still closed. I stroked his hair again, watching Helen.

"Well?" I asked. "Other than waiting for Thomas to wake up and Phoebe to deliver our lunch, is there anything else we need to do here?"

"Tell me, precisely, where you want your crossing to conclude," she said.

I took a deep breath.

"Buckley Township is located in Michigan, on the continent of North America . . ."

Seven

"Alice comes home. No matter how hard it is, no matter what it costs her, Alice comes home."

—Laura Campbell

Standing on a backcountry road in Buckley Township, Michigan, at long last

WHAT THE HELL IS wrong with that house?" demanded Sally, gesturing toward the old Parrish place with her spear, like she thought the house might be some sort of terrible monster she could square off against if she just tried hard enough.

The house did not oblige her by getting up to attack, but sat there in its horrifying splendor. I smiled.

"That, my friend, is home."

"Does it look like that on purpose?"

"No, we think it's cursed."

Sally blinked. "Cursed."

"Yup."

"But you live there, voluntarily."

"Semi."

The old Parrish place was a fairly classic example of middle-American farm architecture turned gothic and just a little menacing. The windows seemed to follow people as they moved, watching them with an oddly malicious expression. Houses shouldn't be able to look malicious, and yet this one did. Three stories tall, or maybe more, depending on the light, with a decrepit wraparound porch that was sturdier than it looked, thanks to both my own efforts and Cynthia keeping an eye on the place when I was out of town, and painted the leprous gray-green of rotting flesh, it was not the sort of place anyone should really be glad to see.

I had never been happier to see a house in my entire life. The porch swing was rocking gently back and forth, meaning our appearance had startled a few of the local tailypo, who liked to curl up there when there weren't any strangers around. Good. They needed to see us sooner than later. I hefted the hamper Phoebe had given us with one hand, my other arm still wrapped firmly around Thomas, keeping him from toppling over.

He'd woken up about ten minutes after Phoebe finished delivering her tincture, but had remained groggy and only half-present since then, with the bleary gaze and slightly slurred speech of a man who'd had far too much to drink. I was just grateful that Helen had been able to open her doorway this close to the house.

Thomas managed to stay on his feet as we crossed the street, and with Sally on his other side, we were able to make it up the porch. I eased him onto the porch swing as my backpack cheered uproariously, the mice rejoicing in their return to one of the places they recognized as home.

Sally watched warily as I shrugged out of my pack, putting both it and the hamper next to Thomas, and moved to the rail, where I put two fingers in my mouth and whistled, high and shrill and piercing. Sally winced.

"What, the mice aren't loud enough, you have to break my eardrums on your own?"

"Not quite," I said. The bushes rustled. "See, the man who lived here before us axe-murdered his entire family as a sacrifice to a swamp god he swore was talking to him. We've never been able to find any proof the swamp god existed, but most ghosts don't like the house, and it may be because of whatever convinced him he should make hamburger out of his wife and kids. The Covenant bought it sight unseen when they decided to banish Thomas to the hinterlands in order to get him out from underfoot."

The fact that they hadn't bothered to scout the area before sending Thomas here made it so much easier to convince their strike team that they'd wiped us all out, back when they finally came to clean up their little mess. That was, oh, forty-five years ago at this point, and the sting of it was still fresh. I whistled again. The rustling in the bushes got louder.

This time, I stepped back, not repeating my whistle, and gestured for Sally to keep quiet. She blinked but held her tongue. A few seconds later, half a dozen long-tailed, stripy bodies burst out of the bushes and swarmed onto the railing, chittering.

They looked like ring-tailed lemurs if they had been designed by someone trying to spin a toy line out of the idea of plush toys whose tails could double as boas, bondage devices, and rappelling lines. Their bodies were a little more than a foot and a half in length, while their tails hit five feet, easily. The smallest wrapped its tail defensively around itself, forming a cocoon of stacked stripy rings that covered its entire head. They had masks, like lemurs, or raccoons, and clever little hands, and all of them were staring at me.

"Sally, meet the tailypo," I said. The mice cheered. Sally stared.

"Tailypo," she said, finally. "Like the ghost story you tell on Girl Scout campouts. That tailypo?"

"I've heard the story, and they're nowhere near that vicious most of the time, although I don't recommend cutting their tails off to test the theory. Especially because the house conspiracy is mine, in that nebulous way that things which don't belong to you can be yours, and I'd be upset if someone hurt them."

Sally gave me a sidelong look. She seemed to have a near-infinite repertoire of ways to look at me like I'd just said something ridiculous. "Conspiracy?"

"It's the collective noun," I said. "A group of fish is a school, a group of geese is a gaggle, and a group of lemurs is a conspiracy."

"So they're lemurs?"

"Sort of. We call them the American lemur, and we're pretty sure they're primates—not a lot of good phylogeny when it comes to creatures science doesn't admit exist." One of the tailypo made a chirring sound. I whistled softly. "The tailypo got labeled folklore pretty early on in European colonization, and no one managed to convince the people who were putting things in 'real' or 'not real' boxes that they needed to be put in the 'real' one. Didn't help that the Covenant of St. George labeled them too ridiculous to exist, and did their best to make sure no one who saw a live one told anybody about it."

"Why? They're adorable."

The tailypo didn't speak English, so it was entirely my imagination that they looked pleased by Sally's praise. But it made *me* think better of her. "The Covenant started out fighting things that were a danger to humans," I said. "I mean, there's a good reason to be a dragon slayer when the dragons are trying to burn your village down on the regular, and nobody likes sharing their bay with a bunch of swamp hags. But they did such a good job that they ran out of real threats, and they were so convinced of their own necessity that rather than dissolving or pivoting to being a general public-service organization or something, they started focusing on anything they considered unnatural, or potentially dangerous in ways other than the physical. Why kill a tailypo? Because it's a silly thing. Evolutionarily, they don't make a lot of sense, and they make kids want to laugh and play dress-up with long tails of their own, and they can be pests. Better to get rid of them. Better to make sure people stay serious, and focused, and afraid of anything they didn't recognize. Like a raccoon with a super-long tail. Better to make the world a little simpler, because then it'll be a little easier to control."

I stuck my hand out to the largest of the tailypo while Sally was still trying to formulate an answer. "Key, please," I said.

The tailypo chirped.

"Key," I repeated, more firmly.

It—he, most likely, since the males tend to be about twice the size of the females—fell backward off the rail, vanishing into the bushes. I stayed where I was, my hand still outstretched, as he rustled around down there, then popped back up and pressed a dirty housekey into my palm. "Thank you."

"They speak English?"

"No, but they know a few words, like most animals." I turned to unlock the door. "That whole 'dude killed his family at the behest of a swamp god who he wasn't shy about describing to the locals' thing, followed by 'weird British dude moves to town, marries daughter of a family whose members have all died under mysterious circumstances, becomes a shut-in, disappears,' means local kids try to break in all the time, to show each other how brave they are. We're the least haunted haunted house in the county."

"Meaning you can't safely hide keys anywhere outside the house," said Sally thoughtfully.

"Got it in one," I agreed, pushing the door open and moving to lever Thomas out of the porch swing. He came accommodatingly enough, leaning on me like a man who no longer fully understood how to use his legs. "Go on in," I said, to Sally. "Nothing in there's gonna bite you—although the mice may yell a little, if they don't hide in the walls when they see a stranger."

Sally looked dubious, but went inside. No screams followed. Neither did cheers; the local Aeslin had clearly read her for a stranger. That was fine. They'd learn the truth soon enough.

Thomas propped against me and staggering along, I whistled under

my breath, and the tailypo poured through the door around my feet
as I half-carried him across the threshold.

Home.

Getting Thomas up the stairs in his current state was a no-go, so I
helped him to the couch, sweeping aside the nest the tailypo had made
of pillows and two of my grandmother's afghans as I lowered him to
the cushions. He made a small sound of protest, then sighed and rolled
onto his side, nestling down into the upholstery.

I went back outside to the porch to get my pack and the hamper.
Taking another deep breath of the Michigan air, I turned, went inside,
and focused on Sally. She was looking around the living room with
frank, unshielded curiosity. I didn't interrupt, trying instead to see it
through her eyes.

In many ways, the house was an extremely cluttered, if eclectic,
museum, with virtually everything still in the exact place it had been
on the night Thomas disappeared. I couldn't call it "tidy," because
stacks of books dotted the floor and leaned against the wall, far more
extensive than the room's overstuffed bookshelves could accommodate. There was the couch, two armchairs, and a coffee table; the former were softened by knit wool blankets in a rainbow of shades,
bristling with tailypo fur, and the coffee table still had magazines and
research notes on it from the mid-fifties.

A toybox near the front door provided a primary-color reminder
that we were parents once.

There was no dust. There were no cobwebs. If not for the tailypo
fur, it would have been easy to believe the place had been cleaned, if
not decluttered, only a few days before. The air smelled a little musty,
but that made sense, since the only regular occupants were a group of
wild animals and a colony of talking mice. Sally blinked, slowly, before she turned to me.

"You have a maid service that comes to the creepy murder house?"
she asked.

I almost laughed with relief to have her starting off with such a
mundane question. "Something like that," I said. "You've heard me
mention Cynthia? She runs the Red Angel, a sort of bar and gathering
house for our local humanoid cryptid population. You can find all
sorts drinking there. She's known me since I was a baby—knew my
mother before me. She's a skogsrå, one of the most common types of

Huldrafolk, and she always has younger staffers on hand who are willing to come over and keep the place tidy in exchange for a few extra dollars in their paychecks. She's got a key, of course. She's who I'll be calling about groceries as soon as we get settled."

"Why are you calling someone about groceries? Don't you want to go to the store?"

"I want us *all* to go to the store, so we can start getting the locals used to the idea that the Prices are coming home to Buckley. That means waiting for Thomas to be awake enough to come along, and getting our story straight before anyone starts asking questions."

"What's to get straight?"

"I know it's been a while since you had to deal with Earth and its annoying dependency on logic, but. The people in Buckley are used to me coming and going. They think I'm my own granddaughter at this point, which is probably less offensive to my actual children than the period where they thought I was Jane. I'd been pretty visibly pregnant before my disappearance, and she came out looking just like every other woman on my side of the family, so I never minded the confusion. She, on the other hand, minded a *lot*. Pretty sure she's never been willing to spend time in Buckley because she couldn't stand the idea that people already thought they knew Jane Price, and it wasn't her."

The thought made me more than a little sorry, and more than a little sad. I'd abandoned both my children. I'd let them both down. But somehow, the rift between me and my daughter had always been infinitely deeper than the rift between me and my son. Maybe it was because Kevin and I had those first few years together; maybe it was because he had more time with Laura before she also disappeared. Maybe it was just something about mothers and daughters. Whatever the reason, she didn't want to be mistaken for me, or for me to be mistaken for her.

"So if I'm my granddaughter, and I've brought my new husband back to occupy the family house with me, probably because I'm too much of a loser to wash up anyplace more urban or sophisticated, what are you?" I looked at her mildly. "You're pretty obviously not biologically mine, age aside. Thomas doesn't *look* old enough to have a daughter your age, and we'd both have needed to be barely out of high school when we adopted you for that to make sense."

"Cousin," said Sally, firmly. "I'll be a cousin. Never tell them whether I'm adopted. Genetics can be bizarre as hell sometimes, and it'll be a nicely distracting mystery to keep people from focusing on how intensely *weird* we are."

I laughed—actually laughed—at that, and kept laughing as a vast cry of "HAIL" rose up from behind the couch, followed by enthusiastic cheering. Sally jumped. I gestured toward the sound. "Remember, I told you we had a whole colony living here? Sally, meet the mice. Mice, meet Sally. She's your newest priestess."

The mice poured around the side of the couch in a furry tide, the members of my congregation racing up my legs, the members of Thomas's running up the arms of the couch and stopping to gaze at him with awe. Others, dressed in the livery of other family members or in novice colors, surrounded Sally and stared worshipfully up at her.

Sally squirmed. "Uh, a little help here?"

"There is no help for the Aeslin mice," I said. "You wanted to be family, and that means you get the full package, congregation and all. You think this is bad? The colony in Portland is three times this size. I only have about ninety mice living here."

"Forgive me, Priestess, but our numbers have increased," said one of the mice in my colors, politely.

"How much?"

"There are near to twice as many of us since the last time you inquired. The hunting has been excellent these past seasons."

"Cool." I turned back to Sally. "I have less than two hundred mice living here, mostly because their faith has been so sporadically renewed, what with me bopping all over the place looking for Thomas. Now that they have two Priestesses and a God in residence, they'll probably have more babies. I think we have the spacc in the attic for about five hundred without crowding or triggering a schism."

The mice around Sally cheered again.

"Usual rules apply to the new Priestess, guys," I said. "No one in her room while she's sleeping unless they're invited, no one watches her shower. If she wants to bring a date home, you make yourselves scarce until the stranger is gone, unless and until she makes a formal introduction."

"Yes, Priestess," chorused the mice.

One of the mice in Thomas's livery inched toward me on the back of the couch, ears flat and whiskers forward. "Priestess?" it squeaked.

"Yes?"

"Is this truly . . . is this . . ." The mouse's voice seemed to give out, and it fell silent, wringing its paws for several seconds before it glanced up again, and asked, "Is this truly the God of Inconvenient Timing? Has he been Returned to Us?"

"It is, and he has," I said, and held one of my hands up to the level of my shoulder, allowing the mice clustered there to step into my palm. I looked at them as I lowered my hand toward the couch. "He's home, and we're home, and we're going to be living here in Buckley at least for a while. If we leave, I think we're going to be leaving this place for good, and we'll take all of you along."

At Sally's feet, the novice who had adopted her as the newest symbol of the faith was enthusiastically telling the gathered mice the story of the Conscripted Priestess. Some of the other novices were starting to nod along in a way that told me we'd be seeing more of her livery soon enough. That was good. She could tell her mice her entire story, and we'd bring a few of them with us the next time we went to Portland. Soon enough, the whole main colony would know, and she'd never need to explain herself again if she didn't want to.

The mice on my hand jumped down onto the couch, followed by the rest who had swarmed me, all running to join the throng.

"The God of Inconvenient Timing is very tired," I said, to the colony as a whole. "He needs to rest. For the next three days, I invoke the Holy Bargain of For God's Sake, Alex, Make Those Damn Mice Stop Yelling While I Have A Hangover. Cheese and cake will be provided, and you may speak to any human who calls for you, but until the Bargain is concluded, you will leave the God alone."

Ever see a colony of hyper-intelligent pantheistic rodents look disappointed? I had, and yet it never failed to amuse me when it happened again.

"Is the Bargain invoked even now?" asked a mouse in the robes of Thomas's clergy.

"It is," I said, and even faster than they had appeared, the sea of mice vanished, scampering to their holes in the walls and leaving no sign that they had ever been there.

"I would think that was a hallucination if I'd had anything to drink today," said Sally.

"You knew about the mice," I said.

"Not that there were two hundred of them!"

"Oh, there's more than two hundred," I said. "Probably about seven or eight, currently."

"That is so many—"

"In the world." I sat down in one of the armchairs. Three of the lurking tailypo immediately claimed my lap.

Sally stared at me. "The whole world?"

"Aeslin mice are small and adorable and basically defenseless if you're much bigger than they are," I said. "The religion is biological for them. Some twist of their brain chemistry makes them see the divine in everything around them, and they latch on to things as the cores of their worship. This colony, and the ones in Portland—both my kids have their own, although Kevin's has been the main colony for decades—seized on my family a long time ago. They believe in *us*."

"That's . . . I knew they were religious. I don't think anyone who's been around them for more than five minutes could miss that." Sally sat abruptly, cross-legged on the floor, resting her cheek against the shaft of her spear. "I just thought they had a choice."

"They do, really. Colonies will schism when they get to be too big for their habitat. The ones who leave find something new to worship, and they don't regret leaving what they're basically genetically programmed to regard as having been a false faith. So they don't have a choice about believing in *something*. They absolutely have a choice about believing in *us*. We know there's a responsibility in being the chosen idol of an Aeslin congregation, and we try, as a family, to live up to it. Plus, as you've already experienced, their definition of 'family' can be pretty broad. As soon as they decided you were a Priestess, that was it. You were stuck. You can't be de-deified now, even if you wanted to be."

"So what would happen if I left?"

"Like, left-left? Walked away from the family and the mice and never came back?"

She nodded. I considered.

"Well, they have a concept of death." Memories of my grandparents' congregations, and my father's, swam through my mind. "They know when one of their holy figures dies, and they deal with it in their own way. But they'd remember you forever. The mice here still perform rituals dedicated to my great-grandparents. And they never forget anything."

"That seems sad."

"I guess it is, in a way," I agreed. "But it means nothing's ever lost, and even when your family is far away, they're always at least a little bit with you."

"Sorcerers used to use them as living spellbooks," said Thomas. "They would teach their magic to their mice, and the mice would preserve it, so that even if something happened to the original sorcerer, the magic would endure. They kept paper ledgers as well, but a spellbook that couldn't be stolen, couldn't be confiscated, and could run under its own power if challenged? That was something special." He sighed, long and slow and tired. "I had time to wonder, while we were locked in that abysmal place, whether the scarcity of Aeslin might not have been in some way orchestrated by our common enemy. The crossroads hated sorcerers so."

"Thomas!" I pushed myself out of the chair, spilling tailypo in all directions, and hurried to the couch. His eyes were still closed, his head tilted toward the ceiling. Kneeling, I smoothed his hair away from his forehead, leaving my hand resting there when the gesture was finished. "How are you feeling?"

"As if I've run a marathon with neither food nor water, and no prizes waiting at the end."

"But there *was* a prize waiting at the end of this marathon," I said, as encouragingly as I could manage. "We're home."

"Home?"

"Buckley. Your place." I laughed. "We still have my family home, but it's being rented out right now, and I never actually moved back there."

He opened his eyes, finally, and blinked at me. "Why not? You always complained about how far we were from the woods."

"Far?" asked Sally. "Did the woods move while you were away? Because that tree line is like five feet from the rear of the house."

"It's fifty yards, almost exactly," I said. "Far enough that the roots don't reach. The house where I grew up is only slightly closer, but the way the fields are laid out, some of the more ambitious trees have roots that make it all the way to the house. It's nice to know they're there. But no, silly, I didn't want to leave our house just so I could be closer to the trees. Moving would have meant admitting this was going to take more than a few months, and by the time I had to face that, moving would have taken too much time. And I couldn't explain it to the tailypo, and it would have felt like giving up. Like I was admitting I'd never be able to bring you home."

"Alice . . ." He began to push himself up. I shifted my hand to his chest, pushing him gently down.

"It's okay. Stay on the couch. I'm going to call Cynthia, let her know we're home, and ask her to send someone over with whatever's for dinner at the Angel tonight. Phoebe's hamper is lovely, but we need something more filling than baklava and jam. I'm sure Cynthia will be thrilled to know I finally found you and won't be crashing through her windows anymore."

"I'm fine," he protested, before yawning broadly and nestling deeper into the couch. "I'm just going to rest my eyes for . . . a second . . ."

"Sure thing, sweetie." I kissed his forehead and stood, turning to Sally. "Keep an eye on him, okay? If he wants to get up to do anything more strenuous than using the bathroom, call me."

"Where are you going?"

"Phone's in the kitchen," I said. "It's an antique, but it works. So where I'm going is to arrange for dinner, and make sure there's nothing dead and rotting in the fridge. And then I'm going to come back, and eventually he's going to wake up, and we'll give you the house tour together so we can all take showers—the hot water's surprisingly good in this old place, courtesy of our son replacing the hot water heater every few years out of some weird sense of filial duty—and you can find yourself a bed. But first, there will be dinner. And we will enjoy the fact that we're in a place where nothing's trying to kill us, and tomorrow I will introduce you to the Galway Wood."

Eight

"The relationship between Alice Healy and the Galway Wood is inexplicable and strange. Someday I'll understand what it means, assuming she hasn't already buried me there."

—Thomas Price

The old Parrish place, Buckley Township, Michigan

THE PHONE WAS ABSOLUTELY an antique. I'm not up on modern technology by any measure, and even I knew it was ancient. I cradled the receiver between my cheek and shoulder as I dialed, then moved to check the fridge. I didn't usually leave things there to rot when I went traveling, but "usually" is not the same as "never."

The phone rang four times before there was a click and a familiar voice said, "You've reached the Red Angel, this is Cynthia speaking, how can I help you?"

"Cyn, it's Alice," I said.

"You're back!"

"We are," I confirmed. "And I was hoping whatever you had on for dinner would stretch a little farther."

"You could have just come to the bar, you know. No one here's going to run screaming from the sight of a human."

"Not so much an option yet." There was nothing in the fridge except for a few bottles of beer and some ancient condiments. I was pretty sure the mustard was old enough to vote. "Oh, and if you have someone who could go on a grocery run tomorrow, the cupboards are bare over here."

"Yeah, I've got a girl who can make the run for you, as long as you tip well. How long are you planning to stay?"

"Maybe you're not listening to me," I said. "We're *back*. We're staying. For good."

"'We' being you and the mice?"

"No." She was the first person I was going to tell with words, the first person who'd known him before everything went to hell. This call had been essential, and had felt like a good idea when I made it, but suddenly my tongue was dry as cotton in my mouth, and the next words fought me, refusing to come without a fight. "We being me, Thomas, and the stray Thomas picked up along the way. Her name's Sally and she's human, but she's essentially his adopted daughter and the mice have already deified her."

Cynthia gasped, the sound short and sharp. I could hear her fingers tighten around the receiver, the plastic groaning under the force of her grasp. "You *found* him? Alice, you found Thomas? You brought him home?"

"That, or I found a doppelganger so good that he could fool me completely." Wouldn't that be a fun turn of events, given how concerned he'd been about me being an imposter? But no. He knew too much. He knew *me*. He was the real deal.

Cynthia made a weird choking sound that I realized after a moment was laughter. Oddly strained, but laughter all the same. "You ridiculous . . . Okay. So you found him, he's alive, and you're at the Parrish Place, yeah?"

"Three people," I repeated. "No dietary restrictions I know of. Oh, and if whoever you send to the grocery store could grab us a sheet cake, the mice are sort of worked up right now, and they'd really appreciate it."

"Are you sure *you're* not a doppelganger? Alice Price, offering store-bought cake?"

"I'm going to need to clean this kitchen to the bolts before I feel like I can bake here, and that's not happening until I've had half a dozen showers," I said. "The mice can deal with substandard baked goods for a few days."

"Got it. Oh, and Alice?"

"Yeah?"

"Welcome home."

She was laughing again as she hung up, sounding like she was teetering on the very edge of hysteria. I looked at the phone, thinking about all the other calls I needed to make, all the big, important, inescapable calls . . . and then I set the receiver gently back in the cradle.

Only one of those calls needed to happen tonight, and it wasn't going to involve a phone. In fact, I'd probably take the phone off the hook before I made it, to keep everyone else who was immediately going to try checking in from getting through.

Of course, that might trigger a panic and cause all of them to descend on Buckley before I was ready, but would that be worse than putting off talking to the one other person who'd been there since the beginning? I didn't know. Why did everything have to be so complicated all of a sudden?

I closed the fridge, resting my forehead against the cool metal. For fifty years, my life had been incredibly simple. Go: search: fail: heal: repeat. I'd been following a very straightforward set of commands, searching for a man who might or might not be out there to find, letting the situation provide whatever complications I was going to need to deal with. And now we were back in the real world, where things were complex and tangled and didn't follow straight, predictable lines. Two kids, six grandkids, two ghosts, and an unknown number of allies, most of whom wouldn't have been born yet when Thomas disappeared, but who knew me well enough to want to check in. Once they learned we were here, things were going to get very complicated for a while.

But this was what I'd wanted. This was what I'd been searching for. And exhausted and overwhelmed as I was right now, I wouldn't change a thing, because he was home. With me, in Buckley. We were both still ourselves, bar a little—or a lot—of trauma, and some telepathic tinkering with my head that we might never have all the details on. We were home.

That would have to make up for everything else.

I straightened, pushed my hair away from my face with both hands, and put on a sunny smile before heading back to the living room. Sally was still sitting on the floor. Thomas was still apparently unconscious on the couch. I walked over to the armchair I'd been seated in before, shooed two tailypo out of it, and settled again. They hopped down to the floor, then back into the chair, where they curled in my lap. That was fine. That was normal, surreal as that might seem.

The tailypo are not in any way domesticated; they're wild animals that have decided to den in a human house, mostly because decades ago, I managed to trick Thomas into playing animal hospital for an injured one, and they're smart enough to remember when they've got a good thing going. They know what they want and they know what they like, and they're reasonably well behaved as long as you don't try to make them do anything they really don't want to do. Like stay out of my lap.

"Cynthia's going to send someone by with dinner, and she's got someone else who's going to go by the grocery store for us tomorrow morning, meaning we'll be able to cook and keep ourselves alive while we recover enough to want to deal with the locals."

"Are the locals that bad?"

"Eh." I wobbled a hand in midair. "Typical small-town stuff. Everyone knows everybody else, and even though I'm officially a local, I've been scarce enough since I assumed this particular identity that people have questions. There's going to be an adjustment period, and that's why it's so important for us to have our stories straight before we start interacting with them. Whoever Cyn sends with the groceries will be a cryptid. Dragon princess, probably, since she usually has a few of them on staff, or a gorgon, or someone else who can pass for human long enough to do the shopping. Species doesn't matter. What matters is that everyone on her staff knows my deal, they know Thomas's deal, even if he's an urban legend more than a person to them, and they won't ask any really stupid questions, or try to catch us out in logical contradictions that make us sound like we're secretly international jewel thieves or something."

"We provide . . . leverage," said Sally, in the ponderous tone of someone who was quoting something. Then she cackled, clearly delighted with herself.

I blinked slowly. "Okay, whatever that means. Anyway, food soon, house tour when Thomas is awake, then showers."

"And in the meantime, you can tell me who the players are."

I raised an eyebrow. "The players?"

"You keep mentioning people like you think I'm not joining this show in the middle of the season. Like this Cynthia who's bringing us dinner. You said she's a 'Huldrafolk'? What the hell is a Huldrafolk? What's a dragon princess, for that matter? Cryptids are things like Nessie and the Mothman, not things that go down to the Hannaford's to buy milk and eggs."

"Guessing that's a grocery store, and um, wow. You've been cool enough about everything, and I found you in a weird murder dimension, that I guess I forgot you wouldn't have grown up with all this stuff. You want me to start at the beginning?"

Sally nodded vigorously. "Please."

"Okay. How much do you know about the Covenant of St. George?"

"You and the boss have both mentioned them, and neither of you likes them much, and you said earlier that they started out by killing dangerous things but moved on to killing things like the tailypo. Explain it like I don't even know that much. I promise not to get offended by you talking to me like I'm five."

"Right. Okay, so centuries ago, dragons were fucking things up for people, and—"

"Hold on. Hold on." Sally held up her one hand, motioning for me to stop. "You're already assuming something there. Dragons are *real?*"

"*Were* real, mostly. They're not extinct, but they're so close that a few bad days could take them out. It's complicated. But once, they had the kind of numbers you really don't want a massive apex predator to have. Once, they ate people, and burned down houses, and generally made themselves unpopular. So the Covenant formed to make them stop. An organization of monster-hunters dedicated to the idea that humans deserved to survive, and to be safe." I sighed. "It wasn't a bad idea in the beginning. They were even pretty cool for their time. They let women join. They didn't care about race or religion. They just cared that you were human and wanted humanity to endure."

"So what happened?"

"They won." I shrugged. "And like any underdog who wins when they didn't think it was possible, they started getting full of themselves. They decided it wasn't good enough to protect humanity, they had to *eradicate* the dragons. Then they had to do the same to anything else they didn't like or understand, or that they thought might be dangerous. I don't know when religion came into it—it wasn't there in the beginning; someone found a way to graft it on later and make it stick—but some clever asshole decided they were going to redefine their mission as wiping out anything that hadn't been on Noah's Ark. So if it wasn't mentioned in the Bible, it was out. With a little creative interpretation, of course, since the Bible mentions unicorns, dragons, and all manner of other things the Covenant decided they had the right to slaughter."

Sally made a face. "They don't sound like very nice people."

"Not so much. Again, maybe they were in the beginning, but once they were on top, they got more and more determined to stay there, and they became more and more willing to kill anything that got in their way. Eventually, they were too good at their own jobs, and they killed so many of the 'monsters' that everyone else decided the monsters had never been real in the first place, and the Covenant started losing power. Success drove them underground, and that made them bitter, so they got even more aggressive about hunting down and killing innocent creatures.

"You asked what a cryptid was. Well, technically, a cryptid is any living organism whose existence has yet to be proven by science. So all your neighbors back in the bottle dimension, Helen and Phoebe in Ithaca, everything we saw during our road trip, all cryptids—or they would be if they came here. Since most of them are staying in their home dimensions, they get to be just people there."

Sally nodded. "So some cryptids are things like the tailypo or the mice, and others are *people*?"

"Don't let the mice hear you implying they're not people; they learned a great lecture on sapience from one of my grandkids, and they can repeat it word for word. Which they will, with great enthusiasm, until they decide you've actually listened. We use 'people' as a label for anything that can reason for itself. So some people are bipeds, like humans, and some of them look *enough* like humans that they can hide in plain sight. Some of them are roughly human-shaped, but can't pass unless they have cover or some sort of a disguise. And some aren't bipedal at all. Dragons were people. They were just people in positions of power who didn't see *humans* as people. And that's been the problem since the beginning. When someone looks around and decides they get to make that call, things always go bad."

"Like how the Covenant kills cryptids."

"Yes."

"And you know so much about the Covenant because . . . ?"

"My grandparents were members," I said. "So was Thomas. The Covenant sent him to Buckley to keep an eye on my family, because we were 'dangerous traitors' who might decide to share their secrets. As if anyone would believe us."

Sally blinked. "Your family belonged to the Covenant."

"Thomas, too, in case you missed that part. And yeah. They were enthusiastic members of the 'Earth is for humans and humans only, and anything humans don't like deserves to die' club, until they weren't, and then they came here." I waved a hand, airily. "I'm simplifying, of course. You'll get the whole story when it won't be completely overwhelming."

"Because *this* isn't overwhelming?"

"No, this is the short version. My grandparents quit the Covenant because they figured out it was bullshit, left England, moved to the middle of nowhere to raise a family, and that might have been the end of it, except the Covenant is made up of paranoid bastards, and they sent Thomas to spy on us. He showed up when I was sixteen, and he was the most incredible man I'd ever met." I couldn't stop my voice from turning a little dreamy at the end.

Sally made a face. "Okay, ew, border of too much information and 'I don't want to think about my father figure's sex life.'"

"You're gonna meet our kids eventually."

"Still. You could have adopted."

I smiled at her. "You're remarkably weird for someone who's been through as much as you have."

"Pot, kettle."

"Right. So I met Thomas, fell in love with Thomas, convinced myself I would never have a future with Thomas, went into the woods trying to find the thing that killed my grandmother, got bitten by a super-venomous sort-of-snake, nearly died. Thomas, meanwhile, met me, fell in love with me, told himself he wasn't in love with me because we'd never have a future, then sold himself to the crossroads to save my life. Oh, and then he didn't tell me he'd done that, the fucker, so I went off to college and didn't come back for years. We were kind of a disaster. The kind where the authorities sift the ashes and make politely unhappy noises about how there were no survivors."

Sally looked thoughtfully at Thomas. "He's different when you're around. Calmer, somehow. Less like he wants to fight the whole world. He also yells more. I think you're a disaster, but you're good for each other at the same time."

"I hope so, because it's going to be a while before I let him out of my sight." I stroked one of the tailypo curled in my lap. "His deal with the crossroads was brutal. It didn't take him right away. For whatever reason, they decided to play with their food. First he got locked inside the Buckley town limits. Then he got locked inside his house. I know this sounds fake, but it was a different time. We had telephones, and we had the mail, and he had no reliable way of using either one."

Sally blinked. "How's that?"

"Telephones used to go through an exchange. You'd dial, and then the operator would connect you to the number you were trying to reach. I think they phased out the humans in most big cities by 1950 or so, but here, they hung on for another decade. I was an unmarried woman ten years his junior, and he was a foreigner who had taken to his home with some unknown illness. If he'd tried to call me, even if my father had allowed me to take the call, the operator would have stayed on the line hoping for some juicy gossip."

"You're right," said Sally. "That sounds fake. But I'll allow it."

"So he couldn't call me, and I couldn't call him without risking damage to my reputation. And I was angry, because he didn't tell me about his deal right away. He didn't want me to feel like I owed him for saving my life. So I thought he was cutting me off for no reason, like he was punishing me for getting hurt. And I went off to school, and he stayed here, locked inside this house." I waved my hands. "Maybe he'll want me to reclaim my family home once he's had some time to get his footing back. It's a year-to-year lease, we'd have to wait twelve months at the absolute most before we could move. Or maybe he'll feel the way I do, like the good times we had here outweigh the bad parts."

"So you couldn't call each other. What about the mail?" asked Sally.

"My father didn't like Thomas. Thought he had come to Buckley to abduct me, drag me back to Britain, and force me to join the Covenant against my will, and he refused to see that I was always going to be my mother's daughter, and I was never going to turn into the mild-mannered, accommodating princess he wanted. So he 'helpfully' agreed to mail Thomas's letters, and they never reached me, and my letters to him never reached *him*, and we both thought we'd been abandoned. For years."

"How the fuck did you wind up married?"

I laughed. I couldn't help myself. "Long, *long* story. Wasps killed my father, I thought they were going to kill me too, I didn't want to die without banging the man I'd been in love with since I was a teenager, so I came here to screw him senseless before I made my last stand. I did, and then I did, and I didn't die, courtesy of the mice, and I came back and he dug the wasp eggs out of my back, and then I just never left." I gave him an unabashedly fond look. "I never left. He told me about the terms of his deal eventually, and then I married him, and yelled at him a lot for thinking I'd have been willing to do that out of obligation, and we got five years of happily ever after before the crossroads took him away from me. Oh, and he quit the Covenant. Right around the time he sold his soul. Guess he didn't want to risk them showing up and finding out how weird things were getting around here."

"Okay," said Sally. "But what about—"

The doorbell rang.

I stood, scattering tailypo in all directions. Sally rose from the floor, her grasp on her spear shifting from casual to anticipatory. I glanced back at her. "No stabbing," I said. "We are currently in a no-stabbing phase of our lives. I'll let you know if that changes." She scowled at me, but lowered her spear.

I opened the door.

The redhead on the porch would have looked perfectly normal in any crowd, as long as she wasn't expected to remove the overstuffed down jacket encasing her arms, shoulders, and back in a puffy layer so thick that the actual shape of her was all but obscured. She had a large foil pan in her hands, a paper bag perched on the top. She blinked at the sight of me, and blinked again as she looked past me into the house.

"You were serious," she said, sounding faintly awestruck.

I smiled. "Hi, Cynthia," I said. "Come on in. Don't mind the mess; we just got back. The mice are on time-out, so they're not going to swarm you."

"That's good to know," she said, and stepped inside moving with an incredible lightness. She looked Sally up and down, clearly taking her measure, and barely glanced at the couch before heading for the kitchen.

The very tip of her tail dangled under the hem of her skirt, only visible once she had turned her back to us. I wasn't sure Sally would even notice it, since she'd never dealt with a Huldra before. I followed after Cynthia.

"Is that all?" I asked.

She set her pan on the counter, removing the bag before unsealing the lid. "Dinner tonight is barbequed spare ribs—from a few of the dire boars that wander around near the swamp, not from anything you wouldn't want to eat—with baked beans and cornbread. I'll swing by at closing with peach cobbler, but it won't be ready for hours yet."

A tailypo scampered up to investigate what she was doing. She dipped a hand into her coat pocket, producing a hard-boiled egg and forking it over. The ring-tailed pest chirped and ran off with its prize, taking up a place atop the china hutch and shoving the egg into its mouth as fast as it could physically manage.

"Oh, now you've done it, they'll all be coming in here to beg for treats," I said. "But seriously, Cynthia, what's going on? You seem pissed."

"What's going on is that you've been on an impossible mission for fifty years, and I've supported and encouraged you, because I've always known it was futile." Her voice was low and tightly controlled. She glanced from the tray of ribs and beans to me, eyes flashing. "I've always been here. Patient and kind and keeping things on an even keel, and never telling you what a terrible idea this was, but Alice, that doesn't mean it wasn't a terrible idea."

I stared at her. Cynthia shook her head, and continued.

"You bring *that man* here, back to Buckley? Back to the place where my mother's trees are growing? Where *your* trees are growing? I thought your happy ending would be eventually coming home and marrying the Galway like the widow you were, not hauling a dead man out of the grave. The Covenant's been sniffing around the edges of this continent since your damn granddaughter went on live TV and declared a fucking *war*. More than sniffing around on the coasts. They just haven't made it this far inland yet. You really think they're not watching this place, now that they know they didn't manage to kill off your whole family? You really think they're not going to *notice* him? You've put us all in danger, Alice, so you could play house again."

"I thought you'd be happy," I said, voice small. "He was . . . You were his friend. You've been my friend. You made sure the mice and the tailypo were fed while I was gone. You . . . you took care of me."

"I was hoping if I took care of things long enough, you'd come to your senses, not do the impossible," she said, turning to face me. "If you've put this town in danger, if you've put my people in danger, I don't know that I'll be able to forgive you."

"I'm not calling the Covenant, and neither is Thomas," I said. "Sally's new to all this, but she's not going to do it either."

"See that you don't," she said. "You'll have groceries in the morning, and cobbler when I get off shift. I'll make a social call in a few days, when I've had time to calm down and we're not all dead."

"I appreciate it," I said, somewhat stiffly. I'd been expecting a joyous reunion, not a borderline accusation that I was putting the entire township in danger by doing what I'd always been very open about trying to do. This was only a surprise because apparently even Cynthia, who had been my ally since the beginning, hadn't been able to believe I was going to accomplish it.

Finding out that people don't have any faith in you sucks. You'd think I'd be used to it by now, but apparently not.

"Have you called your family yet?" she asked, with less open accusation in her tone.

"Getting here wiped Thomas out," I said. "He's been sleeping since we got home, which is part of why I don't want to go shopping on my own. That, and I'll need to get the truck out of storage and make sure it runs without catching fire or something before I can haul more than I can carry, and I'm planning to be here for a while. I want to *bake*."

"You and your Bundt cakes," said Cynthia, sounding almost fond.

"There's nothing wrong with a quality Bundt cake," I said. "I'll call Kevin and Jane once Thomas is ready to deal with company, because you know they'll be here as soon as they can catch a flight."

"That's part of what I'm afraid of. You called that babysitter of yours?"

"I don't think she's been my babysitter for a long time, and no. Once she knows, she'll tell the others, and then everyone will know, and we're back to 'I'd like Thomas to be awake and able to say he doesn't mind before I call a family reunion down on his head.'"

Cynthia nodded slowly. "You're being smarter about this than I expected you to be."

"Yeah, well, I'm not a kid anymore." I shrugged. "I had to figure out how to plan before I punched a while ago."

"Not so I've seen."

"You've seen me when I was catching my breath," I said. "I'm not catching my breath anymore. I'm home. There's a real difference."

"Okay. Maybe you're not going to cock this up completely. I'll have hope, anyway." Cynthia offered me a pale smile, then turned and walked away. I followed her to the living room, watching her offer Sally a brief nod before heading to the door.

Sally, standing and clutching her spear, didn't say anything or introduce herself as Cynthia stepped outside.

"I'll see you later, Cyn," I said. "Hopefully Thomas is awake when you come back with the cobbler. You can meet Sally after we've both had a chance to shower."

"Remember what we talked about," said Cynthia, and shut the door.

I snorted. "She can make anything sound dire." I turned back to Sally. "There's food if you're hungry, although it'll keep if you're not. It's a little early for dinner, and we haven't used the dining room in decades. I know it's going to be clean. That doesn't mean it's in any condition to host a sit-down meal. We're probably eating on the couch, and that means waiting for himself to wake up and share it."

Sally blinked, still staring at the door. "That woman . . ." she said, and stopped, clearly unsure how to continue.

"Yes?" I prompted.

"That woman had a *tail*," she said. "An actual *tail*. It moved. When she walked, it moved. She wasn't just a furry. What the actual fuck?"

"You're going to have to get used to people with tails," I said. "One of the grandkids is dating a fūri, and he has a tail when he's not playing human. Which seems to be most of the time, since fūri don't have 'look like a hairless biped' as a default form. He looks human *enough* that it's not as weird as it could be, which is a good thing, since her sister would never stop tormenting her if she could spin their relationship into being something kinky." I paused. "Honestly, Verity probably does that anyway. I didn't have any siblings, and watching the two of them interact makes me sort of happy about that. Verity is not kind to her younger sister."

"But . . . a *tail*," said Sally. "On her body. How does that make anatomical sense?"

"I mean, it probably makes more sense than humans evolving *not* to have them, given the way our spines work, but we have books you can read, if you're that interested in cryptid anatomy. When she comes back with dessert, if she's less cranky, I'll try to get her to take her jacket off. That's really going to blow your mind."

"Why?"

"Huldra are . . . honestly, no one's quite sure what Huldra are. They don't tend to leave bodies when they die, and that makes autopsies impossible. They come in three primary types. One turns to stone upon death. One basically melts into water, and one literally takes root and becomes a grove of trees. All three kinds, though, have hollow backs, and are sanguivores."

"I feel like I'm going to be unhappy when I learn what that word means."

"It means they live on blood, Sally," said Thomas from the couch, his voice raspy from his impromptu nap, but clear all the same. "Vampire bats are sanguivores. So are mosquitoes. Huldra are the largest and most sophisticated sanguivores in the world."

"They're *vampires*?" Sally gave me a disbelieving look, before switching it over to Thomas.

"Not in the way you're thinking, but it's a close-enough term," said Thomas. "They feed on blood. They're as much vegetable as animal, but as Alice said, we don't fully understand their biology. The world is full of mysteries, and we should be grateful, as a world completely understood is a world with little enchantment left to offer." He lifted a hand, resting it on his forehead. "And on that note—can anyone solve the mystery of where I am right now?"

"We're home, honey," I said, walking over and bending down to brush a kiss against his fingers. He opened his eyes and smiled blearily up at me. "How are you feeling?"

"Exhausted. Home, meaning . . . ?"

"Buckley."

"Ah. That explains the lumps in the couch."

I paused, frowning. "We already had this conversation," I said. "You woke up, explained the Aeslin mice to Sally, and went back to sleep. You asked why I never moved back to the house where I grew up, so I could be closer to the woods."

"And *I* asked how it was possible to be closer to the woods, since those trees are practically knocking on the back door already."

"You really don't remember?"

Thomas shook his head, eyes still open, and began pushing himself into a sitting position. I stepped quickly away, giving him the space to move. "I'm afraid not," he said, apologetically. "I've never attempted that many dimensional transits in close succession before, and I'm afraid I've tapped my reserves a bit more than I expected to. It doesn't help that they won't refill as quickly now that we're back on Earth."

"Helen said the pneuma had continued to recover in the absence of the crossroads," I said. "The world's getting better."

"Yes, but a creature in the process of healing doesn't necessarily have strength to spare," he said. "I can feel the ambient magic of the world, and I'll rebuild my own over the next weeks, but it's not the endless wellspring it was in some of the dimensions we passed through. It's going to take time."

"Good thing we're staying here, then," I said. "If we want to go to Portland, we'll call the routewitches for a ride, like normal people."

"What the hell's a routewitch?" asked Sally.

"Okay, like seriously weird people who want to get to Oregon," I amended. "I'd say we'd fly, but we need to go to Vegas first, get some new identities for the two of you. I wouldn't even try to take you on a Greyhound right now."

"Vegas?" asked Thomas.

"We have some new allies you need to meet," I said. "The current family forger is Big Al, a Jink living in Sin City. He can set us up with papers for you and Sally. Things that won't set off alarms in some ancient government database somewhere that thinks your visa expired fifty years ago and Sally needs to be returned to her parents."

"Oh," said Sally.

"Getting him to set Thomas up may be a challenge, but it won't be

worse than anything else we've done recently, so we'll be fine."
Thomas gave me a puzzled look. "His family got caught in a Covenant
purge. He *hates* the Covenant. Helping a traitor will probably appeal
to him, after we convince him you're not some sort of deep-cover
agent."

"Things are real complicated around you people," said Sally.

Thomas took my arm, pulling himself to his feet, and smiled beatifically. "Yes," he said. "Isn't it wonderful?"

Nine

"Take care of yourself, then your family, then the rest of
the world. That's the order that doesn't break your heart."
—Frances Brown

The old Parrish place, Buckley Township, Michigan

THE HOT WATER HELD out long enough for all three of us to shower—
even though that shower lasted more than half an hour in Thomas's case. I guess fifty years without running water leaves a man feeling
pretty filthy. I dropped towels outside the door and kept myself busy
changing the sheets on our bed and getting one of the guest rooms
ready for Sally.

Cynthia and her people had kept the house clean enough to be livable, but there's a gap between "livable" and "comfortable" that
needed to be addressed. When the Covenant had been shopping for a
place to shove their prodigal son, they'd been looking for something
that fit a narrow list of requirements: location, affordability, and avail-
ability. They'd never looked at size, which was why a single bachelor
had been shoved into a three-story house with seven bedrooms.

There was a time when I'd dreamt of filling them all, turning this
house into the sort of vibrant, loving place I remembered from my
early childhood, when Mama had been alive and Daddy had been
brittle but unbroken. Those dreams were past, but the bedrooms remained. I left Kevin's room untouched, and walked past the nursery
we had prepared for Jane, opening the room we'd used for the Guc-
ciards when they came to visit.

It was spotless if unwelcoming, with a queen-sized bed, a large
wardrobe, and a window looking out on the Galway. Best view in
Buckley. I stripped the bed, remade it with fresh sheets, and left the
door open as an invitation.

Sally was still in the shower. I walked back to the bathroom and rapped lightly on the door.

"You drown in there?" I called.

"Shampoo is *magic!*" she yelled back.

Right. Not dead. I smiled. "Wait until you remember what conditioner is," I said. "I've got a room ready for you; it's the open door down the hall. Come out when you're done."

"Got it!" The water didn't stop. Well, I did say the water heater was good, and if she wanted to risk getting frozen when the heat ran out, that was her decision. I couldn't blame her. I've seen real magic, people pulling things out of thin air, doors between dimensions, things that should have been impossible. Very few of them have truly been able to compare to the miracle that is indoor plumbing.

I walked back down the hall to the bedroom I shared with Thomas, only feeling a little guilty about the fact that I had yet to call Mary and tell her we were home. She'd understand. Or she wouldn't, and we'd deal with it. Either way.

I pushed open the door to find Thomas standing next to the remade bed, buttoning the cuffs of a shirt that still fit him as well as it had fifty years before. He looked up as I stepped inside, offering me a smile that made my heart drop toward my knees. I closed the door behind me.

"Hi," I said.

"Alice, did you throw *anything* away?" he asked.

I shrugged. "Some dynamite that had gotten too unstable for me to think it was a good idea to carry it. Pretty much everything in the kitchen. You do *not* want to look in the fridge right now. But if it wasn't perishable? No. You were coming home. You couldn't give me permission to get rid of things, and I wasn't going to mess around with them."

"Oh, sweetheart." He stepped toward me, reaching for my hands. I let him take them. "I was trying to save you when I sold myself to the crossroads. Not condemn you."

"You didn't," I protested. "This has been awful, and I won't pretend it's the life I thought I was going to have, but I wouldn't change it if you told me I could. We have a family. We have each other. And when I felt myself snapping under the strain, I ran. I didn't stay where I was and turn into my father. I won. I kept not giving up on you, on us, I kept your things and I kept the lights on and I kept looking."

Thomas nodded as he listened.

"I kept looking because I knew you had to be out there for me to find, and then I *found* you, I found you, I brought you home, and home's still here. The woods are still here, the Angel's still open, everything we need is here. The kids are adults now, so I can't pretend nothing's changed, but we made it. You saved me."

"And now you've saved me as well." He let go of one of my hands, reaching up to trace the outline of my mouth with his thumb. "Not for the first time, either. I begin to feel I may be behind on my salvations."

"Don't be ridiculous," I said, and leaned in, and kissed him.

He let go of my other hand immediately, sliding his arms around my waist as I pressed against him. I slid my own arms around his shoulders, linking my hands together behind his neck, and we held each other up that way, two people standing together in their bedroom, in their own home, for the first time in fifty years.

His stomach growled.

I laughed as I stepped away, and he gave me a half-ashamed look. "My apologies," he said. "I think I'll be somewhat subject to the demands of the flesh for the next little while, as I adjust to the absence of constant danger."

"Cynthia seems to think that's not going to last," I said. "Verity flicked the Covenant in the nose a few years back, and they've been a lot more active since then. We may have more danger to worry about soon."

"Danger before dinner?"

"Hope not."

"Then let's go down."

Sally was on the stairs, dressed in the same filthy clothes, rumpling her hair with one of the towels I'd left on her bed. I looked at her and nodded. "We'll take you shopping as soon as we can," I said. "Until then, I'll loan you a nightgown after dinner, and we can put your things through the washer."

"I don't know how I'm going to handle having more than one pair of socks," said Sally, looking critically at her currently bare feet. "What's the normal number of pairs for someone my age?"

"Asking the wrong people," I said amiably. "Come on. Ribs and beans in the kitchen."

"Food," breathed Sally, and sped up, Thomas and I following close behind.

The tailypo had ignored the foil tray of ribs and beans in favor of ripping open the paper bag Cynthia had brought in at the same time, stealing the cornbread and what looked like a half dozen or so hard-boiled eggs. They were perched atop the kitchen counters, munching happily away, shells and all. They chirped at us when we entered, and some of the younger ones shifted their postures defensively, blocking off our access to the food. I proceeded to the cabinet where the plates were kept.

"Thomas, spoons are where they've always been," I said. "Think you can get out something to serve with?"

He didn't respond. I turned, three plates in my hands, and blinked at him.

Tears were running down his cheeks, unhampered by any attempts to stop them. He sniffled when he saw me looking, swiping them ineffectively away.

"I'm sorry," he said. "I don't remember where the spoons are kept. I'm . . . This is all happening, isn't it? This is really where we are, in Buckley, and the mice are absent for some perfectly understandable, perfectly explicable reason, and we're home. We're actually home. I won't have to leave you again. The crossroads are dead."

"We're home." I put the plates on the counter and crossed to him, taking his shoulders while Sally watched in worried silence. "We're really here, we're really all together, and the mice are giving us some space because I asked them nicely and they have enough adjustments to make to the scripture that they're probably relieved to have some time where they don't need to worry about us. I promise you, this is happening. We're all here. Even Sally."

"Hi, boss," said Sally, raising one hand in a small, anxious wave.

I let go of Thomas's shoulders, moving to open the drawer where the silverware was kept. Like everything else, it was clean if unused, scrubbed free of tarnish by Cynthia's helpful staffers. Asking her how much she'd charge to keep the place from crumbling into dust was officially one of the smarter things I'd ever done.

"Let's eat," I said. "We'll all feel better after we eat."

Tears still rolling down his cheeks, Thomas nodded and took the serving spoon from my hand, turning to the tray of ribs and beans. Sally followed, and in short order, we all had plates and were returning to the living room. True to my prediction, the couch was looking like the best place to eat, as it didn't require me to reopen the dining room before I'd had a chance to go through the whole house. Most of the tailypo followed us, clutching the remains of their stolen cornbread as they fanned out and distributed themselves around the room.

It was comfortable, and oddly domestic. Everything about it was ordinary, the sort of night I could easily imagine us having a thousand times over, one meal after another, one quiet recovery from the previous day at a time. I could get used to this.

The doorbell rang.

All of us turned to look toward the door. Sally's hands tensed, as if she had just realized she wasn't carrying her spear. "Is it that Cynthia lady again?" she asked, voice low. "She rang the bell last time."

"Unlikely." I put my plate aside. "It's not as late as it feels. She's probably still at the bar. The dinner rush won't even have hit yet." Not that the Angel ever had anything as optimistic as a "rush." Mostly it had a dinner trickle, as befit an establishment that intentionally didn't court the business of the dominant species.

"Should we go to the kitchen while you answer that, since the locals are accustomed to you?" asked Thomas.

"No," I said. "They'll need to get used to both of you eventually."

The bell rang again.

"I'm coming," I snapped, and stood, heading for the door. I paused when I got there, looking back at the two of them. Something about this felt wrong, like it should have been impossible for anyone to interrupt our evening uninvited.

But then, how often does trouble wait for an invite?

I reached for the doorknob. I opened the door.

The girl on the porch had her hands shoved into the pockets of a denim jacket two sizes too large for her, swamping her relatively delicate frame. The rest of her clothes fit better—a white shirt under a buttoned red plaid flannel, denim jeans, and battered sneakers that looked like they'd seen a few hundred miles of road. Her hair was short, dark blonde and windswept, the kind of careless cut I'd seen on more than a few girls my granddaughter's age. She looked modern and timeless all at once, a gawky Tinkerbell who had never left Neverland behind.

I blinked. Then, slowly, I smiled. "Took you long enough."

"Had to find a ride," she said, rolling her shoulders in a denim-clad shrug. "Also wasn't completely sure what the message I got meant, so it took me a while to get a straight answer out of the boss."

"Since when is anyone the boss of you?"

"Oh, a lot has changed around here, starting with the management." She took her hands out of her pockets and spread her arms.

"But you finally look like you're older than I am, which I appreciate, and I can tell you haven't called the babysitter. So can I claim my hug, as first dead girl on the scene?"

"Always," I said, and stepped forward, wrapping my arms around her.

Hugging Rose Marshall is an experience. For one thing, even though Mary has always been a solid and predictable presence in my life, I knew Rose when she was alive, and so I know she's dead in a way that doesn't apply to most other ghosts. Part of me expects her to be insubstantial in some way. Which she never is, because she doesn't instigate a hug unless she's wearing a coat borrowed from one of the living; the rules of her specific kind of haunting mean that when she's got a coat, she's effectively alive until she takes it off or the sun comes up, whichever happens first. So she gives good, firm, lasting hugs.

She was wearing some sort of perfume that smelled like baby powder and lavender. I inhaled it as I let her go. "It's good to see you, Rose. What the fuck are you doing here?"

"Oh, see, your granddaughter went and slaughtered the crossroads—sort of, it's complicated and it kind of gives me a headache if I think about it for too long, but 'killed' is less confusing than 'bent time so they never existed, even though we're still dealing with the aftershocks of all their bullshit power plays'—and I got sucked into the power struggle that followed. Bobby's gone, there's a new boss running the twilight, and I'm not strictly a road ghost anymore, even though I can slum it when I want to." She spread her arms again, displaying the coat. "I wanted to be off-duty tonight, so I did this the old-fashioned way. Cocked my thumb, flagged down a passing route-witch, talked them out of a coat and a ride, and now I'm here until dawn or the boss calls, whichever happens first. I'm hoping for dawn. It's been a while since I had a night off, and I could use the break. Hey, do I smell ribs?"

"You do." I stepped aside so she could go into the house. "Cynthia dropped off dinner, and we have a hamper of baked goods from Ithaca. Cyn'll be by in a few hours with dessert. She always brings enough for the mice to eat, too, so you should be fine."

"Cool." Rose slipped past me into the living room, and I turned to watch her greet the others.

Sally was staring, a rib lifted halfway to her mouth. Seeing a teenage girl strolling in like she owned the place had to be disconcerting, and it was about to get worse.

Rose grinned, showing what felt like every tooth in her head. "Ey,

Mr. Tommy in the *house*! I thought I felt more than one of you shoving your way through. Who's the kid?"

Sally blinked, lowering her rib back to the plate. "I'm older than you."

"That'd be a neat trick, since from where I'm standing you're human, twilight all the way, not midnight or starlight or anything else, and that means you *can't* be older than I am. Even Alice has cobwebs of things she was never meant to know clinging to her. Nothing wrong with being young. You only get the shot once, no matter what you look like."

"Hello, Rose," said Thomas, with a mild smile. "What are you doing here?"

"Like I told the lady, I came the old-fashioned way, one cocked thumb at a time. But I did have a little bit of an ulterior motive, I'll admit that much. Alice, where's the ribs?"

"Kitchen," I said. "You want me to prep you a plate?" As a hitchhiking ghost, Rose could only taste food when one of the living gave it to her.

To my surprise, she waved her hand, brushing me off. "No, I'm good," she said. "You can ritually give it to me when I get back. Bring the kid up to speed, and then I'll get you the rest of the way once I have pig on a plate."

She walked out of the living room, vanishing into the kitchen, where I heard her cheerfully greet the tailypo.

"I didn't call her," I said, shutting the door before I returned to the couch and retrieved my dinner. "I swear."

"If you were going to call one of the family ghosts, it wouldn't be this one," said Thomas, eyes on the kitchen doorway. "Rose is pleasant, but she's never been as useful as your sitter."

We were both avoiding her name. With Mary, naming her could be construed as calling for her, and if Rose had managed to pick up on our arrival, odds were good Mary had done the same and was just giving us a chance to catch our breath. She's always been the politer of the family ghosts.

Sally leaned over to prod me in the shoulder. "Hey," she hissed. "You tell me what's going on and you tell me right now."

"Rose is a hitchhiking ghost," I said. "She doesn't technically haunt the family, but we were in high school together, and she took enough of a shine to me that she stuck around. At this point, she likes us, and she has a thing about keeping ties to the land of the living whenever possible."

"Good footnote," said Rose, emerging from the kitchen to offer me her plate. It was mostly rib, with some beans, and a piece of cornbread she had apparently managed to snatch back from the tailypo. "About as close to accurate as could be expected after everything you've missed, really. Hi. I'm Rose. I was originally what we call a road ghost—the ghost of someone who died on or around the road, and wound up bound to it in the afterlife. That's changed a bit since the crossroads died, but there's no point in getting into it now."

"Oh," said Sally. "You're really a ghost?"

"Yup," said Rose. "Also nope, anymore. Scoot over." That was all the warning she gave before she dropped herself to the couch between me and Sally, forcing Sally to scoot or have a lapful of Rose. Thomas watched this with bland amusement, like he couldn't think of any better way to spend his evening. "It is the very definition of long stories, but I'll try to be brief about it, because everybody's got shit to be doing right now. Antimony made a deal with the crossroads to save the life of her boyfriend, which seems to be a bit of a family tradition at this point, and when they came to collect, she didn't want to do what they asked, so she went for 'murder' as the next best thing to obedience. She is *so* your granddaughter, Alice."

"What did the crossroads ask her to do?" asked Thomas.

Rose smiled at him. "It's good to see you again, Tommy. You always did cut right to the chase. The crossroads wanted Annie to play killer for hire. Take out this snotty little sorcerer in a town called New Gravesend, in Maine."

"That's where I'm from," said Sally.

"Huh, funny coincidence." Rose shot me a glance, making it clear that she didn't think it was a coincidence at all. "Annie went to New Gravesend, met the sorcerer, decided she didn't want to kill him, picked a fight with the crossroads instead. Like you do. Somehow, she found a way to bend time and stop them from ever existing, and I don't understand it, it gives me a headache, so please don't ask me to explain. If you really want to comprehend a massive metaphysical 'fuck off and die,' you can ask her yourself the next time you see her. My involvement has been more in the aftermath. Turns out the crossroads did a lot of passive regulation in the twilight, and when they went away, everything got all topsy-turvy and screwed-up for a while."

"The twilight?" asked Sally, blankly.

"The place human ghosts go when they haven't moved on but aren't currently haunting anything," said Rose. "It's where we are most of the time. Only with the crossroads gone, being there was sort of like being in a low-budget horror movie from hell, and it took a while for the aftershocks to settle."

Thomas frowned. "That sounds unsettling."

"It was *miserable*. But we got through it, and I got to see Bobby go down for good." Rose smiled a feral smile and seemed to remember her dinner in the same moment, turning to me and making a little 'gimme' gesture with her hands.

"I, the living, give this food to you, the dead, freely and without constraint," I said, handing the plate to her.

"You always make that sound so dire," said Rose. She picked up a rib, gesturing with it. "Asshole chased me for fifty years, and I saw him dragged to hell. Maybe not literally, but close enough for me. Guess it's a season for people getting the things they've been wanting for fifty years."

"Bobby?" asked Sally.

"The man who killed her," said Thomas. "He'd made a much less altruistic bargain with the crossroads than either of us. Why do I feel like that isn't the end of your 'long story,' Rose?"

"Because you're smarter than your wife?" Rose suggested. I wrinkled my nose, and she grinned at me. "See, in the process of getting all this shit sorted out, I kinda attracted the attention of a few gods."

"Gods?" asked Sally. Her voice was getting increasingly blank as she asked her questions, like we were trending deeper and deeper into ridiculousness.

"Yup," said Rose. "Persephone, the Ocean Lady, and the anima mundi, to be specific."

"I've only heard of one of those," said Sally. "Persephone's the Greek goddess of the dead, right?"

"Sort of," said Rose. "She's our Lady of the Dead, she's consort to Hades, and she loves us. I've been under her protection for a while. The Ocean Lady is the twilight manifestation of the Old Atlantic Highway. She's aware and intelligent—and very, very divine—but she doesn't talk much, unless she does it through her routewitches. I would have been one of hers, if I'd lived. And the anima mundi is the living soul of the Earth. They're what the crossroads displaced when everything first went wrong, and as soon as it became so that the crossroads had never existed, the anima mundi reasserted themselves."

Thomas nodded, clearly following this better than the rest of us. "Divine intervention is never without its costs."

"Yeah, well, it would have been nice if someone could have pointed that out while I was racking up what turned out to be a pretty hefty bill," said Rose. "I'm a Fury now. I serve my triad, and they send me where things need to be set right."

"Do we need 'setting right,' Rose?" asked Thomas.

"Only in that the anima mundi feels sorrow for all the people who were betrayed by crossroads bargains, and would see you settled and safe now that you've returned home, but would very much prefer you not go gallivanting for a while," she said. "They're still recovering from centuries of nonexistence. They're weak. And having travelers punching holes in them all the time isn't going to help them get stronger. So on that level, I guess I'm here on business, to ask you nicely not to hurt my boss. And on another level, I felt Alice come home, and it's been a while, so I figured I should make sure she knows what's what. And on a third level, it really felt like she wasn't alone."

"Yes, I'm home," said Thomas. "You can tell your employers I have no intention of leaving again anytime soon; I left only because the crossroads gave me no choice in the matter, and now that I'm here, I feel that traveling again would be to invoke the wrath of my lovely wife. It's been some time since we were together, but I remember her wrath as considerable."

"That's good," said Rose. "Have you spoken to anyone human since you got back? Obviously you've been in touch with Cynthia, or she wouldn't be feeding you, but have you called your kids?"

"No," I admitted. "I wanted to give us a few hours to catch our breath before we started causing problems again."

To my surprise, Rose nodded, expression implying that this was the smartest answer I could have given. "That's good too," she said. "Things have been hectic for the living, what with the war and all, but—"

"Hold on," interjected Thomas. "The war?"

Rose blinked at him. "Of course," she said. "You wouldn't have heard. The Covenant has formally declared war on your family. They're focusing on the coasts right now, looking for weaknesses, but they'll be pushing inland soon, and sending more strike teams."

I dropped the rib I'd been idly gnawing on. It landed in my baked beans, splattering them all over Rose's denim-clad leg. She looked at the mess, raising her eyebrows.

"Well, now, that's going to take forever to clean up," she said, mildly. "Oh, wait, no, it's not, because as soon as I leave here, I'm going to turn insubstantial and it's going to fall right through pretty phantom me. You telling me you didn't know we were at war either?"

I shook my head. "You know I've been otherwise occupied."

"Please. You were there when Very-very, Quite Contrary, decided to go on national television and tell the Covenant to come at me, bro. You were *in the building.* You can't honestly be surprised that they've decided to come at her." Rose looked at me for a moment, then frowned. "Or maybe you can be. Maybe you've been out of the normal flow of things for so long that you've forgotten how cause and effect work." She ducked her head, redirecting her attention to her plate, and to the process of shoveling as much of the food into her mouth as possible before we kicked her out.

"War," I said, softly, and looked across Rose and Sally to Thomas, who was watching with quiet resignation. The Covenant had been sniffing around the edges of the continent when I left on my last trip, but it hadn't been anywhere near actual war. "I swear we haven't been at war the whole time you were gone," I said. "Things have been pretty quiet here. I mean, there have been incidents—"

"Like the time the Covenant shot up your windows," said Rose casually.

I shot her a venomous glare. "Yes, like that."

"Excuse me?" said Thomas. "The Covenant did what to your what?"

Rose cackled. "Oh, Alice. You went and got the boy back, but you didn't tell the boy what kind of naughtiness you'd been up to in the interim. You're going to have a lot of explaining to do before you head off to do something stupid and heroic."

"Is it always like this?" asked Sally plaintively.

"No, sometimes it gets weird," said Rose.

The doorbell rang. I turned and glared at it. I was getting real tired of interruptions.

No one else was moving, so I sighed and said, "I'll get it," as I set my plate aside and pushed myself off the couch. Cynthia was waiting on the porch, a covered casserole dish in her hands. She looked past me into the house, then back to my face.

"House properly haunted?" she asked.

I stepped aside so she could enter. "Not the ghost I expected to start with, but the one I got. That dessert?"

"Yup. Groceries will be here in the morning." She moved past me, smiling at the couch—but only the one end of it, I noted. She still wasn't allowing her eyes to settle on Thomas. "Hey, Rose. Long time no irritate."

"Don't worry, I'm in town now, I can make up for it," said Rose, and laughed. "Good beans."

"Thanks." Cynthia turned as I was closing the door, passing the cobbler into my hands. "There's no ice cream. I'd apologize, but naughty cryptozoologists barely even deserve any dessert, much less ice cream. Can you get dishes?"

"They're in the kitchen." The cobbler smelled heavenly. For someone who didn't eat much solid food, Cynthia was amazingly skilled at the sort of hearty, filling Americana that kept diners and roadside dives like hers in business. Even more impressive, most of her customers didn't eat that sort of thing: she'd learned specifically for her rare human patrons, and to be able to convince the county health board that she was running a perfectly ordinary, if somewhat remote, dive bar.

I went to get plates and utensils. By the time I returned, Cynthia was settled in the armchair I'd been fighting the tailypo for all afternoon, her coat folded over her lap and her tail wrapped around her ankle. Sally was doing a remarkable job of trying not to stare. Not that she was going to succeed. Sure, we all agreed that Rose was a ghost, but she hadn't done anything *ghostly* yet. Cynthia was the first visibly inhuman intelligent being Sally had encountered on Earth. It was understandable for her to be a little overwhelmed.

"Rose tells me she was getting you up to speed on recent events," said Cynthia, without preamble. "You going to do your duty?"

I set the plates, silverware, and cobbler down on the coffee table, frowning at her. "What duty is that?"

"Get rid of the Covenant."

I laughed. "I don't know what kind of superpowers you think I have, but Thomas is the sorcerer here, not me," I said. "There aren't enough knives in the world to get rid of the Covenant. I should know. I've tried."

"We're not asking you to wipe them out, pleasant an outcome as that would be," said Rose, scooping cobbler onto her plate. "Just get them out of North America, or at least away from the East Coast. They've been harassing the routewitches. The Ocean Lady doesn't like it when things harass the routewitches."

I frowned at her. "I thought you were here to check in on us, as a friend."

"I am."

"But the first thing you did was tell us not to go traveling, because the anima mundi doesn't like having holes punched in the membrane between dimensions."

"Mmm-hmmm." Rose popped a bite of cobbler into her mouth, swallowing before she said, "This is amazing, as always, Cyn."

"Always glad to delight the dead," said Cynthia mildly.

"And now you're telling me the Ocean Lady wants the Covenant gone, and I didn't give you that cobbler, so how can you taste it?"

"Oh, that." Rose looked at her plate like it had betrayed her, heaving a put-upon sigh. "I always forget. I'm a Fury now. Different rules. And I really *did* start your way because I wanted to see if you'd actually fetched Tommy home with you. I was halfway here when the anima mundi called, told me I had to make sure you were staying put for a while, and dropped me back into the daylight, where my next pickup was a routewitch with a message from the Lady. At which point this was very much a work visit."

"If anyone's going to get them out of New York, it's the two greatest traitors of the last century showing up and providing a distraction," said Cynthia. "Just don't lead them back here. We have enough to worry about."

"How are we supposed to get to New York?" I asked. "We don't have a vehicle or legal identification for Thomas and Sally. We need to rest, recover, and head for Las Vegas, to make sure they exist on paper."

"The Ocean Lady is asking you for a favor," said Rose. "You really think she won't supply you with transport to wherever it is you need to go? You say you'll do this for her, you'll have a car ready first thing in the morning."

I looked to Thomas. He shrugged. It had been too long since he'd been a part of the playing field; he didn't know whether this was the right thing to do or not.

Of course not. I looked back to Rose.

"Where is everyone?" I asked. "Right now. Our family. Where are they?"

Rose took another bite of cobbler. "Immediate or extended?"

"Immediate."

"Let's see. Kevin and Jane are in Portland, with Evie and Ted. Elsie's home right now, and so's her brother."

"Artie being home is nothing new."

"Did I say his name was Artie?" Rose managed to make the question ominous and mild at the same time. "He's home, either way. Annie's there with Sam and James. They want to stay out of the line of fire for right now, and Portland's far enough from the current battlefield. Alex, Shelby, and Charlotte are in Ohio with Angela, Martin, and the flock of little cuckoos Angela's trying to rehabilitate. And Verity, Dominic, and Olivia are in New York with Sarah and Mary, trying to hold off the Covenant. I'm pretty sure Mary's hair would be going white, if it hadn't turned white when she died. No one likes to be a babysitter in a war zone."

I bit my lip, looking at Thomas again. Our family was scattered across the continent, and the ones in New York needed us most right now.

He met my eyes and nodded. "Well, then, Rose, I believe you can tell your Ocean Lady we'll be heading for New York in the morning."

"Does that mean no groceries?" asked Cynthia.

"Yeah, for now, but we'll still need that cake, since the colony will be mostly staying here," I said. "There's one more thing you could do for me?"

Cynthia looked wary. "What's that?"

I indicated Sally with a sweep of my hand. "She has no clothes she's not currently wearing, and that's going to get unpleasant fast. Is there anyone working at the bar right now who might be able to help her out?"

Cynthia's wariness melted into an almost-feral grin, and Sally started to look nervous. I leaned over to scoop some cobbler onto a plate.

So much for taking some time to rest and recover. At least it wouldn't be boring.

Ten

"If family's in trouble, I don't care if the damn house is on
fire. You get out there, and you help them. That's what
keeps us worthy of being a part of a family. Being willing
to help when they need us."

—Enid Healy

The old Parrish place, Buckley Township, Michigan

FORTUNATELY, SALLY'S DEPARTURE FROM Earth had been recent
enough that she knew what a Walmart was, and while Buckley is
too small to have anything like that within town limits, it's only about
a forty-five-minute drive to Gaylord, where there's a Walmart Super-
center that—best luck yet—stays open until midnight. Even more fortunately, keeping the house accounts paid for all these years has meant
keeping me vaguely up to date, on a financial level. I prefer to use cash
when possible, and mostly squirrel it away under the couch cushions.
Sally had been handed five hundred dollars and instructions to come
back with as much of a wardrobe as she could assemble, plus whatever
else caught her eye, plus ice cream if they passed a drive-through.

Cynthia was driving her. My only real regret about the evening was
that I couldn't go with them to watch the fireworks. But I was doing
something much more important. I was sitting on the edge of the bed
I hadn't slept in for years, sharpening one of my knives on a small
whetstone while Thomas dug through his wardrobe, studying clothing
he hadn't seen for decades. It was oddly domestic, and might even
have been relaxing, if we hadn't been gearing up to head for New York
first thing in the morning.

Rose had promised to come with whoever came to pick us up, at
least to make the handoff and reassure us that we were with the right

driver, which meant we'd be riding with someone who knew the situation, and not someone who'd just been drafted into driving some weirdoes to another state.

That was nice.

"Alice?"

I looked up from my knife. Thomas was watching me, a tie in one hand, a kukri in the other. "Yes, dear?"

"What was that Rose was saying before, about the windows getting shot out?"

"Oh." I waved my knife airily, then studied the edge as I said, "It was nothing. It happened about two years after you vanished. The Covenant didn't know you were gone, of course, but they knew about our marriage, and they knew we'd had at least one kid. They wanted him."

"What in the world could they possibly have wanted with a five-year-old?" Thomas asked. "They're sticky. All the time. It's the purpose of five-year-olds."

I lowered my knife so I could stare at him. Thomas blinked, raising his eyebrows.

"What? He was three when I disappeared, he would have been five and, hence, sticky. Why would the Covenant have wanted him?"

"Blood charms?" I waved the knife again, before setting it beside me on the bed. "The ones keeping the Covenant out of the Price family accounts? Your banker in London passed away, by the way, although he gave his client list to his son. He's been handling things for the last twenty years."

Thomas had left a banker's key, attuned to the family account, with his man in London. If someone the blood charms recognized as a Price wrote and asked for money, the key could be used to authorize a withdrawal in the requested amount. It was a complicated piece of magic. As I lacked the ability to recreate it, and had never seen a way it could apply to my search for my missing husband, I'd left it pretty much alone. It kept the money safe from the Covenant. Kevin could make withdrawals, which meant he could give me money to pay the bills for this old place without putting a financial strain on himself or the family. That was all that really mattered.

"We weren't *that* wealthy," Thomas objected. "Coming to America and abducting a child to get at a few pounds seems excessive, even for the Covenant."

I made a noncommittal sound. I'd never seen the account balances— it wasn't allowed, even for the widow, when the key wouldn't work on my word—but Kevin had been paying maintenance and upkeep on this place since he turned fifteen. Prior to that, I'd been burning through my own meager savings and depending on the kindness of every ally I had to keep the roof from caving in. The rent from my childhood home had helped, as had the fact that even people who'd hated my dad still thought well of my mother. Frances Brown made friends everywhere she went, from the day she was born until the day she died.

Point was, I knew what it cost to keep the house going, and Kevin had funded it for the better part of fifty years. Whatever number we were talking about here, it was definitely more than "a few pounds."

"They really tried . . . Oh, *Alice.*" Thomas suddenly seemed to realize his response had been more analytical than was necessarily appropriate when talking about an incident that had involved armed Covenant soldiers attempting to abduct our child. "What happened?"

"Well," I began. "It took me a while to wrap my head around the idea that you were actually gone, even with Mary trying her best to convince me the crossroads weren't going to give you back." I realized midway through the sentence that I'd said Mary's name aloud, and winced, waiting for her to appear. When she didn't, I relaxed and continued.

"The bills kept coming in, of course, and I didn't know what you'd had the time to pay before you vanished, so I went through your office. I'm sorry!" I help my hands up before he could say anything. "I couldn't risk the power being cut off while I was away, and I was just starting to experiment with ideas to get out of this dimension and look for you, and the more I could handle before it became a problem, the better."

Thomas took my hands as he sat on the bed, lacing our fingers together and tugging them down, until our joined hands were resting in his lap. He looked at me gravely. "I'm not your father, Alice, to protect my office from my *wife* the way a wolf protects its kill from scavengers." His voice was gentle. "You know you've always been welcome anywhere I am. If I asked for privacy at times, it was because I was working on elemental spells that could have harmed us both if disrupted."

"I know, I know," I said, looking down at our hands. "I know. You never told me to keep out. I did that on my own. Yell at a person enough times, they stop doing whatever it is that gets them yelled at, I guess. Even if the person who did the yelling is gone. I'm sorry."

"You don't have to apologize to me. Not ever."

"Oh, I'm sure I'll think of *something* I need to apologize for," I said, and smiled, trying to look coy.

Either I missed the mark or he was more concerned about the Covenant's attempt to abduct Kevin than I'd realized, because his expression didn't waver. "What happened? What does my office have to do with anything?"

"Oh. That." I took a deep breath. "Like I said, I wanted to make sure everything was in order, so I went through your office . . ."

The first six months after Thomas disappeared had been the hardest of my life. Everything reminded me of him. The house, the Red Angel, the streets of Buckley, the library, the children. Everything except the woods. The Galway was still my sanctuary, and the trees loved me the way they always had. If anything, they might be glad he was gone.

From anyone or anything else, I would have resented that potential joy in my misery. From the Galway, which had never liked him in the first place, it was only natural, and proof that at least something was still the way it was supposed to be.

Like Kevin, Jane had been born at home, eased into the world by Laura and Mary, with Cynthia and Basilia Kalakos assisting. Having a sanguivore on hand meant I didn't get blood all over the rug, and Basilia was not only a trained midwife, her paralytic gaze worked remarkably well as a painkiller. Better than I would have received at the hospital, that's for sure.

With Basilia's help, I was able to sleep through more than half of my labor, coming back to consciousness only when she allowed the effect to wear off so I could push. The first person to hold my shrieking, squalling little girl was Mary, the dead girl who'd practically raised me, and that seemed only right, just like the absence of my daughter's father seemed entirely wrong.

But it was temporary. It was only temporary. I was going to find him, I was going to bring him home, and we were going to be a family. We *were*.

After Kevin was born, Laura had stayed for two weeks, giving me time to adjust and recover, while Thomas learned what was going to be expected of him and the baby figured out how to nurse. Despite not having—or wanting—children of her own, Laura seemed to have a natural gift with infants. I'd been expecting the same two weeks this time, before Laura left me with Mary and the babies and went back to the carnival to resume her own life. But it had been six months, and she hadn't left me yet.

Jane spent most of her time shrieking, but she stopped crying the second she was in Laura's arms, hiccupping and looking around with huge blue eyes, or simply sliding into sleep. Either way, giving Laura the baby was sometimes the only way to make the screaming stop. Part of me wanted to be ecstatic about that, to see it as a sign Laura was going to stay forever, that I'd get to have my best friend with me while I raised my babies. She could have one of the downstairs bedrooms, and Thomas would be thrilled when he got home.

Another, larger part of me, saw her ongoing presence as a silent criticism. Better than anyone—even better than Mary—Laura knew how close I was to falling apart. I'd gone almost three days without eating, and over a week without bathing, before she'd shown up to check on me and the progress of my pregnancy. Jane had been born the day after Laura's arrival. The fear that I'd slide back into depression had to be enormous, and if I did that, the babies could die. Cynthia and Mary would do their best, but they both had other things to worry about.

Which was why, six months almost to the day since a rip in the world swallowed my husband whole, I was in his office, going through the papers on his desk, looking for any financial paperwork or banking information that could help to keep us from losing the house.

Instead, I found was a small stack of letters. One was addressed to Nicholas Cunningham at Penton Hall, in England. Others went to Australia, Hawaii, Japan—places I'd only heard of, never been, but which I knew Thomas had visited before he came to Buckley.

And the last was addressed to me.

I sat on the floor of his office, staring at the envelope. It wasn't sealed. He'd been expecting me to find this; he'd been expecting me to read it, and he was sparing me the agony of deciding whether or not to rip open something he'd sealed. I'm not normally precious about envelopes, but the idea of destroying something he'd touched . . . right now, it was too much.

Gingerly, as if I was afraid it might bite me, I eased the envelope open and pulled out the letter he'd folded neatly inside.

His handwriting was elegant and precise, the result of years of careful tutelage under the watchful eye of the Covenant matrons, of whom he rarely spoke, and never without an uneasy expression. Just seeing it made my eyes blur with tears. I wiped them dry, and started to read.

My dearest Alice—

I know your aversion to entering my office, even if I've never encouraged it. If you're reading this, I'm gone. I hope it will help you, at least a little, to know that I've held out far longer than I thought would be possible; this is the eighth such iteration of this letter I've composed. You can find the others in my bottom drawer, if you desire to read them. Perhaps it will be too much like salting an unhealed wound, or perhaps it will be the salve needed to help you heal. There's never been a time for us when a lack of letters would have made the situation better, after all.

I laughed, choking back tears, and kept on reading.

We knew when we began our time together that it was limited. I was a man with a terminal illness, and you were the angel of mercy who chose to love me anyway. Our marriage has been one of the truest joys of my life, and I am honored every day that you chose me for your husband, and not any one of the men who could have given you a better, more stable life. I love you, Alice Price. Please, no matter how far away you are from me, don't allow yourself to forget that. I will always love you, for however long I live.

If our marriage was a blessing, then our children are a miracle. The Price line lives on in them, and they will have access to our family accounts in England once they grow old enough to make financial requests. Instructions are written in the black book in the top drawer of my dresser, along with the number for my banker and the current key. It must be held in the hand, near enough to taste blood, when any withdrawals are authorized. It's barbaric, I know, but without it, the Covenant would have emptied the accounts the day they sent me here, and even the small comforts I have been able to afford our family would have been denied. The blood charms protecting the family fortune were spun by my great-great-great-grandfather, Bancroft Price, whom

I suspect of having been a sorcerer in his own right. They will hold, and more, they will render Kevin untraceable. So long as he holds the key, the Covenant will be unable to follow any funds to his location. The same will hold true for Jane, should they decide between themselves that she would be better suited to balancing the family accounts.

It was never my intention that any of you should struggle, nor want for anything, simply because I cannot be there to provide. And before you let your pride win out and tell me where to stuff my concern for money, please remember that I would be taking care of you if I were there with you. I swore to care for you until the end of our days. Even if my days are over, allow me that privilege. I beg.

You may, if you prefer, open my other letters and read their contents before sending them, but I would prefer they be sent, and in my own handwriting, if at all possible. Most are to old friends and allies, to tell them I am no longer available to respond to their correspondence. They've been expecting this for some time now. They won't be surprised, although some may send you condolences over the next few months.

The one which has, I'm sure, confused you most dearly is addressed to Nicholas Cunningham, of Penton Hall. He is second-in-command of the Covenant, and the highest-ranking likely to subject himself to a communication from a disgraced exile. He is a reasonable man, as much as a man who has dedicated his life to fighting monsters who wish only to be left alone can be considered to be. He was among the group which decided I should be sent to Michigan to watch you and your family rather than put to death for my crimes against the Covenant. I believe he will listen.

I am not telling him of my disappearance, or of your vulnerability in my absence. I am not saying anything that could encourage the Covenant to come to our home or endanger our family. I am simply making him aware of a threat to humanity which has been thus far overlooked, and needs to be addressed.

The Cuckoos, Alice. Loath as I am to share any information with them, the Covenant must know more about the Cuckoos than your grandfather was able to share with them. That we have managed to overlook them for this long only underlines how dangerous they truly are. Humanity cannot be left defenceless against them. And who knows? Perhaps, if we provide the

Covenant with an enemy worthy of fighting, they will learn to leave the rest of the world alone.

It is a small hope. It is the only hope we have remaining. They no longer count my name among their number: perhaps, with this, they will no longer list us as dangerous enough to watch. Perhaps this is how I can finally protect you.

I love you, Alice. I have loved you since before I knew you, and I think I was always going to love you, whether I came to Buckley or not. You are my heart and my home, and I am so sorry to leave you.

> *With all my love,*
> Thomas

I could barely see through my tears by the time I reached the end of the letter, but I still managed to fold it and tuck it back into the envelope. I put it aside, proud of the fact that my hands weren't shaking, and flipped through the others one more time, taking quiet note of the precision with which he'd written their addresses. All had a return address, except for the one to Penton Hall.

The Covenant had purchased this house for him, back before he tendered his resignation, of course. He had probably assumed they knew where he lived.

Moving slowly, like I was afraid anything faster would break me into a million pieces, I levered myself off the floor and went back to the living room, to take Jane for a feeding and tell Laura I hadn't found the account books but had found something that might be even more important, at least in the short term.

The plan, sketchy as it was, was that she would stay in the house with the children for the next few months, while I went to the route-witches and petitioned them for aid. We'd already determined that umbramancy wasn't going to be the answer. I needed access to the living dimensions surrounding our own, the ones Naga had told me stories about, not to the lands of the dead. And unless I wanted to experience a katabasis, Orpheus-style, going to the lands of the dead wasn't going to do me any good, anyway.

The crossroads had ripped a hole in space to take my husband. There was no way they wouldn't have left a body to torture me if they'd killed him. So he wasn't *in* the lands of the dead, and that meant going to some pretty dark places, looking for some pretty shady solutions.

It wasn't a quest for children. Thankfully, Laura was willing to take care of them until I came back.

I'd heard her the night before, talking to Mary in the kitchen when they both thought I was asleep, exhausted from the combined stresses of grief and trying to keep two small children, one too young to do much more than hold her head up for short periods of time, alive. "You know this might be forever," Mary had said. "She might not come back for a very long time. She might not come back at all. Are you prepared for that?"

"Alice always comes back to me." Laura had managed to make a statement of absolute faith sound perfectly reasonable, like she was remarking on the weather. "If she's alive, she'll come back. She just has to find Thomas before she can stay."

"Have you been reading futures?"

"You know I wouldn't tell you if I had." Laura's voice had been almost chiding. "That monstrosity you call an employer would interfere if they thought Alice was going to succeed, and you'd try even harder to keep her here if you thought she was going to fail. Alice needs this. If she doesn't at least try to bring him home, she won't be Alice anymore. I'd rather she be Alice and far away than something broken and fading in the corner, but here. You remember Jonathan."

"I do," Mary had admitted. "You don't think she would . . . ?"

"I don't know. Did you think he would?"

I had withdrawn then, reassured and stung in equal measure. Reassured because Laura understood why I had to go; stung because the woman who'd been my best friend since we were both children thought I could turn as cruel and brittle as my father if I didn't get my way. Was she wrong? Not necessarily. But that doesn't mean I'd wanted her to *think* it.

And then it had been a new day, and I'd agreed to go into Thomas's office to make sure our affairs were in order. After finding the letters, I went upstairs and dressed for the field, denim and flannel and sturdy boots, before coming downstairs, kissing Jane on the cheek and giving Laura a hug, and announcing, "I have to go into town. Thomas left some letters I really ought to mail, and I think I'm going to go check on a possible routewitch that Cynthia flagged for me."

Laura stepped back and looked at me gravely for a long moment before she nodded, and said, "I didn't think you'd make it this long. I love you, Ally. Try to remember that, and try to come home to us."

"I always do," I said, and the finality of the click the door made when I closed it behind me only sounded a little bit like my father hissing "liar."

That routewitch was a bust, but he knew the address of a cunning woman who directed me to a coven of would-be snake cultists who'd never managed to summon anything larger than a headache, and even that lead went away when I pointed out that they might be better off conducting their rituals in a space with slightly better ventilation. I was in Tennessee by then, and Rose found me shivering outside a diner, trying to decide between spending my last two dollars on bus fare or breakfast.

For a moment, she almost looked disappointed. Then she said, in that slippery way of hers, that someone named Apple wanted to see me, and so I needed to get into the next car she flagged down.

Apple turned out to be the Queen of the North American Route-witches, which was not a thing I'd even known existed before she sat down with me at a truck stop table, a plate of pancakes in front of her and a whole gang of bikers arrayed behind her, ready to defend her honor if I tried to present any sort of threat. She was yet another eternal teenage girl—between her, Rose, and Mary, I was starting to feel like being allowed to finish puberty was something unusual—dainty and dark-haired, with the practiced smile of a lifetime politician. She was older than she looked. I could tell that even before she opened her mouth, and she spoke with the voice of someone much older and wearier.

"The answers you're looking for won't be found among my route-witches, or at the crossroads, Alice Price," she said. "You should still be able to find some, if you look hard enough. My Lady says the way is open, for the careless and the clever, and I think She means you. But you'll have to be quick and you'll have to be unrelenting, and you need to leave my routewitches alone. They can't help you. It's time for you to go home. Everything you're looking for is there, in the last place you expected to find it. You have your own problems knocking on the door, and if you don't handle them, they're going to handle the rest of us."

Disagreeing with her seemed like a terrible idea. After our meeting-slash-interrogation was over, she instructed one of her bikers to drive me back to Buckley, and he agreed without hesitation, loading me into the sidecar of his motorcycle and taking off down the highway as the sun was beginning to rise. It would have been picturesque, if it hadn't felt so much like a failure.

And then I was standing on my own front porch, and somehow it had been more than two years since the last time I'd been there, and when

I rang the doorbell, Laura answered, flour in her hair and cake batter on her cheek, and stared at me for a long moment before she said, "It's about time," burst into tears, and pulled me into an embrace that seemed to last forever.

It didn't, of course. It only lasted until a toddler with big blue eyes and curly white-blonde hair pulled into pigtails on either side of her head came up and grabbed Laura's leg, shoving herself neatly between us. I let go immediately, stepping back and looking down, and Laura took that opportunity to scoop Jane off the floor and hold her up so I could see her, so she could see me.

"Look, Janey!" she cooed. "It's Mama!"

"Hi," said Jane, voice a little-girl lisp. Then, hopefully, "Andy, cookie?"

"Just don't tell the mice," said Laura, and set her down again. "Go wait in the kitchen, sweetheart. We'll be right there."

Content with this, Jane turned and toddled off, not saying anything more. It wasn't much of a reunion, and it wasn't until much later that I realized how little I felt, seeing my daughter for the first time in over two years.

I started to step back. Laura grabbed my wrist before I could go anywhere. "No, you don't," she said, and dragged me inside.

Everything looked exactly the same, and everything was different. Thomas's books were still all over the living room, and a pair of tailypo were curled atop the tallest bookshelf, their tails balled around themselves until they looked like plush dolls. Kevin's toys were strewn across the floor, along with some brightly colored pieces I didn't recognize but which I assumed belonged to Jane. She looked good. Healthy, well-fed, not traumatized at all by my absence. That was a good thing.

Laura waited until we were away from the door before she turned and asked, "So, are you here because of the Covenant, or because you're ready to come home?"

"Am I here because of *what*?"

Her face fell. "Oh," she said. "I see."

Then she explained, and I saw too.

Those letters I sent had notified the world that Thomas was gone, and warned his allies we might need a little extra help. That was good. But they had also informed the Covenant about a threat to humanity large enough to make a happily exiled former member reopen contact. Honestly, I'd been a little skeptical of Thomas's hope that telling them more about the cuckoos would accomplish what he thought it would, or that it was necessary enough to risk drawing their attention.

My grandfather had believed the cuckoos had been around for centuries, maybe since the dawn of human history, preying on us, setting up their unnecessarily elaborate murder plans and taking out whole communities, all while staying undetected, thanks to being psychic assholes who could literally write themselves out of people's memories. We might never have known they existed, if not for my mother being somehow naturally resistant to their powers. We still didn't know why that was, or whether I had inherited any of her natural resistance.

Thomas had been being practical by telling the Covenant what little we'd managed to learn about the cuckoos since my grandfather's death. He'd been trying to protect our family when he did it, but he'd also been trying to keep humanity safer in a world where most of the other true monsters had already been destroyed. Now that attempt was coming back to bite us all.

According to Laura, a Covenant operative had come to the house the week before, a woman named Veronica Bell, who had claimed to be a distant cousin of Thomas's mother, and asked to speak with him. When Laura had told her Thomas wasn't available, she had switched her attention to the children, specifically Kevin, who had come up to show her the fricken he'd caught behind the house. Mrs. Bell had apparently cooed at him, told him he was a very clever boy to already be destroying monstrous things, and tried to take him away with her, telling Laura it was for the best for the boy to be with civilized family.

Laura had disagreed, vigorously, and managed to expel Mrs. Bell from the house by way of the wards she'd constructed since my departure. Umbramancer work can be remarkably delicate, when they have time to set it up, and she'd been given two years.

If the Covenant had moved faster, the story might have unfolded differently. "The only thing I can figure is that they didn't want to come for Kevin until he was old enough to be useful to them," she said, bluntly. "Useful, and toilet-trained. Can't imagine taking a toddler in diapers on a transatlantic flight would be very fun for anybody."

"And they definitely came for Kevin? Not to talk to Thomas about the cuckoos?"

"If they'd come a year ago, maybe. Now? I think they'd be willing to take Jane, but they came for one of the children." Laura had looked at me levelly. "That Bell woman said that as it was clear Thomas was not going to come back and do his duty by the family name, someone else would have to come and continue the name. Oh, and unlock the Price assets for 'proper' use."

"I swear, I'd sign those accounts over myself if I had the authority, and let the Covenant choke on it," I'd muttered. "How's Cynthia?"

"The Angel's locked down, has been since Bell came to town. According to Mary, she's got a whole team with her. A dozen Covenant operatives, all of them ready to close in. I don't know what they're waiting for."

"I do, if you were able to push their lead agent out of the house. They know we have some sort of extra-natural protection in place, and that means they also know they won't be able to just stroll inside. They're preparing for a show of force. If you asked me to lay a wager, I'd say they've been waiting for either me or Thomas or both to put in an appearance, so they could take us out and be sure we wouldn't follow them. They're going to have to answer your refusal with violence. It's the only thing that makes sense."

"None of this makes sense." Laura looked at me with impotent fury. "It's been two *years*, Alice. Have you even found a way out of this dimension?"

"Not yet. But I'm getting closer. The answer's out there. If I can just get hold of Naga, I'm sure he'll be able to help me. I'm sorry." I met her eyes without flinching, because I really *wasn't* sorry. After everything we'd been through, everything I'd put and was putting my family through, I wasn't actually sorry. "It's going to be a little longer."

"Well, I can't stay here any longer." She narrowed her own eyes, looking for all the world like she wanted to stare me down. "I'm happy to keep watching the kids as long as you need me to, Ally, but I can't keep doing it in Buckley. I've been in one place for too long already. The ghosts are starting to find me. I need to get back to the carnival."

As an umbramancer, Laura was even more exposed to haunting than an ordinary road witch. Routewitches and ambulomancers have their share of fans among the dead, but it's the umbramancers who get the brunt of their attention. Why does it work that way? Hell if I know. I just know it does, and Laura had been trying to dodge the dead for as long as I had known her, which had made summers fun when we were kids and my best friend and my babysitter were effectively at war with one another. It had taken Laura years to be even a little bit comfortable with Mary, and Mary didn't mean any harm. Random ghosts were likely to be less friendly.

"You're ready to go home, then?"

She nodded. "It's time. I can take any of the mice who want to go with me, so they don't lose track of the kids, but . . . we won't be here when you come looking, Alice. After you find Thomas, you'll have to find us."

I think there was a choice in that moment. A chance to say "no, I'm done, I'm tired of wild-goose chases, I want my children and my family and I'll come to the carnival with you, my mother started there, let me end there." And I won't look back now and pretend not to have been tempted. I was tired. I was more than tired; I was defeated. The endless futility of my search for answers was beating me down, and I didn't know how much more I had in me. That moment was a turning point. It was an opportunity to turn my back on what I was becoming and choose what I had always meant to be.

I bit my lip. I opened my mouth to answer. I never got the chance. The Covenant strike team that had surrounded the house after their lookouts saw me go inside opened fire.

Why that exact moment? I didn't know, and I still don't. I can recount the past, but I can't guess why things happened, only explain how they did. Laura and I were in the living room; Jane was in the kitchen. Kevin was upstairs, although I didn't know that, and maybe that's the answer to what I would have said if I'd actually had a chance to reply to Laura's offer. I was home with my children, yet I hadn't asked about my son at all. I hadn't asked if he was okay, or whether I could see him. I was physically there, but I was still very far away, and I wasn't coming back any time soon.

The first bullet went through the front window, shattering it cleanly. The tailypo woke up, chittering in surprise as they jumped off the bookshelf and huddled under the coffee table, removing themselves from the line of fire. I pulled the gun from inside my jacket, snapping, "Get the kids," to Laura.

She nodded and ran for the stairs, racing up them as the second bullet came through the window. I dropped to a crouch, working my way over to peer outside.

There was a ring of people surrounding the house. It looked like there were about fifteen of them, which would have been an insultingly low number if it hadn't been such a relief. I was a terrible mother. I wasn't pretending to be anything else. That didn't mean I wanted somebody shooting at me and my kids. Especially not some Covenant asshole who had probably figured out a way to make their bullets hurt extra just so they could make the traitors suffer.

At the center of the line was a tall, whipcord-thin woman with devastatingly sharp cheekbones. It was absolutely believable that she was related to Thomas; they looked similar enough for me to see it. She smiled when the curtain twitched, motioning for the shooters around her to stand down before cupping her hands around her mouth.

"Mrs. Price!" she called. "I don't believe we've been introduced. I'm your husband's aunt, Veronica Bell, and I'm here to collect my nephew."

I was pretty sure "nephew" wasn't the term for what Kevin was to her, but like hell was she getting anywhere near him. I grimaced and shot out the window on the other side of the room, hoping to give her the wrong idea about my current location.

She shook her head, expression turning disappointed. "Oh, Mrs. Price. I thought better of you."

That made one of us. We were isolated enough that no one was going to come to see what was going on out here; if the neighbors heard the gunfire, they'd assume someone was taking a few deer out of season, and leave it at that. You don't live long in Buckley if you're overly curious about things that don't concern you, like people shooting up the house of the town outcasts.

Staying low, I crossed the room to the kitchen doorway, where I lay down on the floor and hissed, "I call for counsel."

"Here, Priestess," said a small, shaky voice from behind a crack in the baseboard. It was rare for an Aeslin mouse to be so subdued, or so obviously afraid. "How may we Serve?"

"I need twenty volunteers," I said, a plan coming together with blazing rapidity. It was stupid. It was quite possibly suicidal. It was going to give Laura and the kids the time to get away from here. "They will be lauded and honored above all others in my service—but they have to be *volunteers*, and they need to realize they may not be coming back. No novices who think this is how they earn their vestments, you understand?"

"Yes, Priestess," said the mouse, and went silent, save for the skittering sound that meant it was moving away from me, into the walls.

I stayed where I was. I was still there when a small foot nudged my shoulder, and I tilted my head back to meet the guileless blue eyes of my daughter.

"Where's Andy?" she asked, sounding almost bored.

"Andy?—oh, *Auntie*."

"Andy," she repeated, now annoyed. "Where?"

"She's upstairs, sweetpea," I said. "We're playing the floor game now. Want to play the floor game with me?"

She gave me a mistrustful look. "Cookie."

Oh, for . . . "You can have a cookie after we play," I said, almost desperately. "You can have *two* cookies."

This seemed to satisfy her. She sat down next to my head, barely missing my ear. "Good."

That was when the shooting started again.

This time, they didn't stop with blowing out the front window. This time, they kept going until the air smelled like cordite and my ears were ringing so loudly that I could barely hear Jane wailing. I rolled over. She was uninjured but terrified, clinging to the leg of a nearby chair. She had gone for the chair, and not for me, when she was afraid. That should probably have hurt my feelings. In the moment, it felt like a blessing, since it meant I wouldn't need to peel her off of me before I could react.

"Laura?" I called. "Are you okay?"

"They're shooting for adults, not kids," she called down the stairs. "They're not aiming low. So I'm fine as long as I don't try to come down the stairs and they aren't actually inside the house."

"I think they want to be sure we're incapacitated before they come in."

"That sounds like a nice way of saying 'dead.' Tell me you have a plan."

"I have a plan."

"Tell me you have a plan like you're not lying."

"I *have* a plan." Something skittered inside the wall. I rolled over, putting my hand in front of the hole in the baseboard. "I'm ready for you."

The mice started running out of the hole and up my arm, one after the other, until I had the requested twenty volunteers on my chest and shoulders, watching me with tiny, earnest eyes. I explained what I wanted them to do, and they listened as intently as they could until I was done. Then they ran away, as I rolled over and began to crab-crawl away from the still-wailing Jane, heading for the back door.

The mice were faster than I was. I was almost there when one jumped onto my shoulder and squeaked, "Sixteen Enemies surround the Home, Priestess!"

"Good," I said. Sixteen was too many, but sixteen, I could handle. Sixteen meant my count hadn't been that badly off. "How many are outside the back door?"

"Two."

"Better." I pushed myself into a low crouch and walked to the door without straightening. Pressing myself to the wall, I eased the door open and peered out.

Two Covenant agents stood in the field behind the house, a good fifteen feet from the door, their attention turned toward the front yard, where Veronica was probably giving further instructions. I eased the door closed again.

"You know what to do?" I asked the mouse.

It nodded. "Yes, Priestess."

"Then tell the others it's time."

The mouse was gone in a flash, racing for the living room. I stayed where I was, one hand on the doorknob, and listened as shouting began outside the house. Not just shouting: familiar shouting.

Two things everyone who spends any time around the Aeslin mice quickly learns: they can be louder than should be physically possible, and they never forget anything they hear. That includes accents. If you know *where* someone is from, but not what they actually sound like, a yelling Aeslin mouse can do a remarkably good job of impersonating them.

The mice ran for the bushes, getting under cover, and began to shout from all sides, some in Thomas's perfect Penton pronunciation, others in Grandpa's softer Scots-border accent, or Grandma's Cornwall. They set up an incredible cacophony, and the Covenant answered with gunfire, all directed of it at the bushes.

The Covenant was so focused on the noise that the two out back didn't notice when I opened the door all the way, or when I stepped onto the porch. I shot them, one after the other, and retreated back inside. Jane was still wailing. I looked frantically around, finally spotting the cookie jar on a counter. Scurrying across the kitchen, I grabbed it and took out a handful of cookies, shoving one into her mouth and handing her the others.

She chewed, eyes very wide and bright with tears.

"I need you to play the quiet game now," I said, voice low and probably unnervingly intense for someone as small as she was. She stared at me, and didn't stop eating her cookie.

That would have to be good enough. The Covenant was still shooting outside, although none of them were currently shooting *at* the house, which was a start. I stepped out of the kitchen, hissing, "Laura, come on," toward the stairs.

"What did you do?" she asked, finally descending, arms full of Kevin. He wailed when he saw me, reaching for me with open hands. I gave him the rest of the cookies and he slumped against Laura, looking puzzled.

"The mice are providing a distraction," I said. "The back door's clear. You can take the kids and run for the Galway. It doesn't mind you. If it doesn't already know Jane, it should. I bet it's going to love her. It loves all the Healy girls."

"Our things . . . ?"

"After the Covenant's sure they've killed us all, you can come back for them." I gestured toward the door. "Between your wards and Thomas's, I'm pretty sure they can't burn the place down, even if they try. They may get through the front door, but they won't get much further. The traps Thomas left will see to that."

Laura looked at me for a long moment, silent and solemn. Then she nodded, turned, and scooped Jane off the floor before she ran out the back door with the children in her arms, not looking back.

The gunfire from the front of the house continued. I wanted to re-load and start shooting. I didn't dare. If I killed them all, the Covenant would just send more; that was how they operated. I needed them to believe they'd won, somehow. I needed them to go away and give up.

Walking back into the living room, I slumped onto the couch, let-ting my head loll. "Mary, if you've ever cared about me, I could really use you right about now," I said.

"This is a fine pickle," said my babysitter, the cushion next to me sinking under the weight of her as she settled on the couch. "How are you getting out of it?"

"Covenant knows I'm here," I said. "They know the kids are here. I think they know Laura's here. So they're expecting two women and two children. I know you can carry dead things through the lands of the dead. Can you get me some corpses?"

Mary paused. "You want me to raid the local morgue?" she asked, finally, sounding horrified and intrigued.

"I don't care if it's local. Local might not be for the best. I need bodies, Mary, bodies that won't be missed and won't be identified. And I need the Covenant to think they gunned us all down when they attacked the house, so I need them before they realize they've been tricked."

Mary disappeared. I closed my eyes. Either she was coming back with the bodies or she wasn't, and if she wasn't, this wasn't going to work. The gunfire outside was starting to taper off, and I was starting to think it might be curtains for me when she popped back in, one arm wrapped around the ribs of a blonde woman with a bullet hole in the middle of her forehead. She didn't look anything like me, but if some-one didn't *know* me, she might have been enough to fool them, especially because of the whole "corpse" thing. As a general rule, living people don't like looking closely at corpses.

Mary shoved her toward me and vanished as the woman fell limply to the floor, cold and dead and nameless. I looked at her and wished I could feel anything beyond faint relief.

Mary reappeared with a dark-haired woman who could pass for Laura, and who had been shot through the throat, and then again with two children, both riddled with bullet holes. Them, I couldn't look at directly. Them, I had to turn my eyes away from. Them, she didn't drop, but settled on the far end of the couch.

Then she turned to me, eyes cold. "Never ask me to do anything like that again," she said, voice like a crypt door slamming closed.

"The crossroads didn't—"

"The crossroads can go *hang*," she snapped. "This protects you and it protects the babies *you* abandoned, so the crossroads can't stop me, but don't you ever, ever ask me to steal bodies for you again. The fact that I *can* doesn't mean I *should*. Do you understand?"

It was so rare for Mary to be truly mad at me—usually it was the other way around—that for a moment, all I could do was blink at her. Then I nodded and stood, pulling a knife from inside my shirt. She frowned.

"What are you doing?"

"That's the one thing we don't have: blood splatter. These people weren't killed here." I ran the knife down the side of my arm, careful to avoid the major veins, and swung around, holding my arm up so the blood splashed out in a wide arc. Some of it splattered against Mary, bright against her pale skin, before it fell through her and hit the floor. She blinked at me.

"I can't decide whether that's clever or self-destructive," she said.

"It won't hold up to any real forensic analysis, but it has to be good enough either way." I glanced to the kitchen. "I need to go. Can you stick around and haunt the place, make sure they don't stay here too long or get past the living room?"

"For now," said Mary, and vanished.

That would do: I wasn't getting anything better. I turned and ran, trusting the wards would hold, that the blood would be enough, that the lie would be believed. It was a thin hope, pinned on a flimsy deception. We would have to get lucky a dozen times for it to work.

But getting lucky is sort of the basis of my life, and if I couldn't count on that, what could I count on? So I ran, away from the house, toward the woods that had always been my sanctuary. I was still bleeding; I'd leave a trail the Covenant could follow, if they had dogs or tracking spells. I couldn't go looking for Laura and the kids; I'd only put them in danger. So when I hit the edge of the woods, I paused, looking in all directions, and then took off along the tree line, away from the Red Angel, heading for the deeper woods.

I'd ran for what felt like the better part of an hour—long enough for the bleeding to slow and stop as the wound on my arm clotted over, although it still threatened to start bleeding again if I moved it too much—before the ground turned marshy underfoot, and I realized I'd gotten turned around somewhere in the trees. I was coming up on the lakeside, well away from the Red Angel but still very close to the water.

The trees thinned ahead of me, giving way to a clearing dominated by a decrepit old barn that looked like it hadn't been occupied in decades. I slowed and angled toward it, intending to take shelter and give myself a chance to catch my breath. Cover could only benefit me if I was being potentially pursued by hostile Covenant assassins.

The barn door wasn't locked. It creaked ominously as I pushed it open, the wood swollen with moisture and smelling of damp rot. Inside, the farming equipment had long been removed or scavenged. Good thing, too, since this wasn't good farming land. Why had someone bothered to build a barn all the way out here?

Maybe out here hadn't been "all the way" when they did it. The Galway didn't move as much as some forests, being made up largely of slow-growing trees, but it *did* move, and given time, it would reclaim whatever was taken from it. Someone could have logged enough space to start a small farm, thinking they'd grow it into a larger one, and found themselves unable to handle the distance from Buckley proper, abandoning the land when they realized how hard it was going to be to be so isolated. Maybe there was a house the same age as the barn a little deeper into the trees. Given how far I'd traveled and how close I was to the swamp, maybe it was the house I'd found after the jackalope census, the one that basically belonged to the swamp hags now.

Whatever the reason, the barn was here, solid and still stable, even if it was rotting, and the walls were intact enough to provide cover for as long as I wanted to rest. I could wait until the sun went down. The Covenant people wouldn't be able to navigate the woods after dark the way I could, and by that point Laura would be well away from here with the kids.

I'd be safe until then.

With that thought firmly in mind, I started walking across the barn, heading for a mound of half-rotten straw on the other side. If it wasn't full of rats, it would be someplace to sit for a while.

I was almost there when the floor gave way beneath me with a rotten cracking sound and dumped me into the darkness.

The impact of the fall knocked me out cold. I came to in the basement of the barn with a ringing head and only the faintest traces of sunset filtering through the hole above me. I'd been unconscious for hours, and getting out of the hole was going to be a challenge, especially since it wasn't like I'd stopped to grab a flashlight when I fled the house.

"Fuck," I muttered, pushing to my feet. The wood around the edge of the hole was as rotten as the rest; jumping and pulling myself up wasn't going to work. Well, if there was a basement, there had to be a door somewhere. I turned to start looking for it, and kicked a piece of wood. The clatter it made as it rolled across the floor caught my attention. I looked down.

I was in the middle of a summoning circle. One that I recognized, if only vaguely. I froze, trying to sort through the fragments of memory clouding my mind. They came with the distant taste of chocolate, for some reason, and the feeling of having escaped some terrible trap. I blinked, still trying to make them come together, until, with a snap, they all fell into place.

Of course. This was where I'd been taken when the snake cultists kidnapped me as a sacrifice to the god they were intending to summon, the god who had turned out to be my adopted Uncle Naga. Which meant . . .

I squinted through the gloom. This summoning circle had been drawn specifically to reach Naga's dimension. He'd been able to come through several times since then, opening the doorways himself, but every time I'd contacted him, it had been with the aid of either Thomas or Laura's mother, my Aunt Juniper. I didn't have the magic to do it on my own.

These cultists somehow had.

I pulled a knife without even really thinking about it, reopening the wound in my arm and bleeding onto the circle. Rather than wiping the ancient lines away, it seemed to feed them. They swelled and strengthened, beginning to glow, and I cut myself again, releasing even more blood.

Blood loss is not good for humans, and I was starting to feel dizzy by the time the glow in the lines brightened to the point where I could actually see the filthy basement around me. I sank to the floor, bowing my head.

"Naga, I don't know if you can hear me, but they summoned you this way once, and I'm hoping I can use it to reach you again," I said. My tongue felt heavy in my mouth. "It's Alice. I'm alone and I'm scared, and the crossroads took Thomas. Please. I have to find him. I have to bring him home. I'll do anything you ask me to. Please, if you can hear me, please come and get me. Please, I have to find my husband so I can put my family back together. Our children need their father. Please."

I closed my eyes, and passed out before my head hit the ground.

Eleven

"Everything wants to survive. Even dead things. We
enjoy existing as much as anybody else does."
—Mary Dunlavy

**The old Parrish place, Buckley Township, Michigan,
back in the present**

—AND WHEN I WOKE up, I was in Empusa," I said. "Naga had heard
me calling, and sent some of his grad students to fetch me before I
could die of blood loss. They put me back together, and he agreed to
help me look for you. I don't know he was lying. Maybe he wasn't;
maybe he really intended to help, in the beginning, before he realized
how much money he could make by letting me search fruitlessly
forever."

"Alice . . ." Thomas sat down next to me on the bed, reaching over
to take my hand in his. "You could have *died*."

"Sure. The Covenant could have shot me, or I could have bled out
in the barn." I shrugged. "But I didn't. I got lucky. Mary chucked a
couple of my grenades out the front door, took out about half the
Covenant team, and then screamed real big and stopped moving.
When the survivors came in, they found the bodies in the living room,
and the wards kept them from going any deeper into the house. And
they decided, pragmatically enough, that they'd killed us all. I think
it helped that the Galway did *not* want them here, and you know how
creepy my forest can be when it gets cranky."

"To my eternal chagrin, I am aware," he said.

"So they set fire to the place and went back to England to tell the
people in charge that the Price vaults were locked forever, and we'd
probably be having this conversation in a different house if Laura

hadn't carried the kids to the Red Angel and told Cynthia what was going on. Cynthia mobilized the clientele who'd been hiding from the Covenant there with her, and they were able to put out the fire before it did much damage. This old place didn't want to burn."

Thomas stared at me. "So you woke up in a different dimension while the Covenant was trying to burn down the house, and Laura was running around with our children, and you kept *going*?"

I blinked at him. "I mean, yeah. I was already *in* a different dimension, and I finally had someone who was willing and able to help me start looking for you properly. I wasn't going to turn back before I had what I was looking for."

Thomas started to laugh, slowly leaning forward until his forehead was pressed against mine. He squeezed my fingers, hard.

"I am never, never letting you out of my sight again," he said.

"That's good, because I didn't spend fifty years looking for you to get ditched."

"I mean it. I'm not supposed to follow you around all the time—and eventually it's going to start getting on your nerves—but clearly, when I leave, you do some of the most incredibly self-destructive things I've ever heard suggested." He closed his eyes, not pulling away, and I took that moment to just *look* at him.

Maybe it's because I loved him for so long before I was allowed to do it openly, or maybe I became a giant sap once I found someone who was actually willing to love me back, but I've always loved just looking at him, and fifty years had given my memory plenty of time to slip. I needed to fill all the little details back in, all the tiny pieces of him that I'd been losing this without even realizing it. Bit by bit, the erosion of time had been wearing him smooth in my mind, turning him into some sort of polished ideal that I could adore but couldn't really love, not like this. Not like it was a stone in my stomach, something I'd swallowed but could never digest, something that was nonetheless a part of me forever.

He took a deep, shaking breath, opened his eyes, and pulled back enough to look at me gravely. "Promise me," he said. "Promise me if something happens to me in New York, if things go badly, you won't do this to yourself again."

"How could I?" I shrugged. "It's not like you can make another deal with the crossroads, since our lovely granddaughter went and killed them so dead they never existed in the first place."

"Yes, but if I died, you have far too many routes by which to access the afterlife."

I snorted. "Mary wouldn't help me before, what makes you think she'd help me now?"

"She's right, I wouldn't," said Mary, from the other side of the room. I grimaced. She must have seen it, because I could hear the smirk in her voice as she continued. "You really thought you could tell a long-ass story, mention me by name a dozen times, and not have me hear you eventually?"

"No." I reclaimed my hands and leaned back, using them to prop myself up as I shot a smile at my former babysitter and permanent personal haunting. "Hi, Mary."

"Hi," she said, barely looking at me at all. Her eyes—as always, the color of a winter sky above a hundred miles of empty highway, impossible and sepulchral—stayed fixed on Thomas. The ghost looked like she was seeing a ghost, and the irony of that was almost enough to distract me from how disconcertingly modern her clothing was, jeans and a T-shirt with the logo of a band I'd never heard of splashed across the front. She wasn't *my* babysitter anymore. She hadn't been for a long, long time.

Even the dead will grow and change, if you give them enough time.

Thomas twisted around and stared back for several seconds, before a slow grin split his features and he stood, taking a step toward her. "Mary Dunlavy," he said. "It's been too damn long."

"Tommy," she said, with a little hiccup. "You actually . . . I mean, she actually . . . You didn't die." She blinked, and her eyes were very bright. Could the dead cry? I couldn't remember ever having seen it happen, but maybe it was possible. I no longer put anything past our resident ghosts. "You didn't die."

"No, Mary, I didn't." Thomas kept smiling at her. "Sometimes I wished I had, but I didn't, and Alice found me, because she's still the most stubborn creature in creation, and that's partly down to you. So thank you."

"That girl was stubborn from the moment she was born," said Mary. "I didn't have anything to do with it." Then she stepped forward, very quickly, and threw her arms around his chest, hugging him hard.

I barely heard her whisper, "I thought I'd killed you."

Thomas didn't miss it either. He wrapped his arms around her in return, smile fading into an expression of regretful understanding, and just held her.

I slid off the bed, moving to stand beside them, and didn't say anything. Mary had been carrying her guilt for a long time, and I hadn't exactly helped with that, since I'd blamed her with everything I had in the immediate wake of his disappearance. Sure, she'd been doing her job, and sure, I'd always known the crossroads came first where she was concerned. It was her tie to them that allowed her to emulate the living so well, with none of the rules about how and when she could appear that controlled Rose, and without them, she would have faded into whatever came for ghosts when their hauntings ended.

And none of that had mattered to me, because when she'd come to collect him, she'd done it in the middle of the night. She hadn't given me the chance to say goodbye. And so I'd blamed her, and kept on blaming her even as she'd moved away from me to take care of my children, and my grandchildren, and all the sprawling offshoots of a family that had been doing perfectly well without me.

I'd almost forgotten she'd been his friend almost as long as I had. I'd introduced them when Thomas was worried his new house might be haunted—and if I was being honest, I'd introduced him because I was already developing a crush on the man, and Mary had been the only authority figure in my world who I'd trusted to give him a half-way fair shake. She didn't care that he was Covenant. She only cared that he was too old for me, and that my father hated him, which would have been a problem even if she hadn't been reasonably sure it was at the root of my attraction.

But they'd been friends even without me, forming their own strange sort of fellowship, one that centered around surviving the strangeness of Buckley, even if "surviving" wasn't quite the word where Mary was concerned, and trying to make sure I did the same. There had even been a time, which I wasn't particularly proud of now, when I'd been afraid the two of them were going to fall in love and leave me behind.

Instead, we'd all left each other, Thomas by being thrown into another dimension against his will, me by running away, Mary by continuing to be the person she'd always been and taking care of the children when their parents couldn't.

Thomas held her tightly until she started trying to disengage, and then he let her go, watching as she stepped back to a reasonable distance.

"I want to know everything," she said. "Not right now, but . . . everything."

"I can say the same to you," he said. "The crossroads are gone. How are you still here?"

"Alice," said Mary, rolling her shoulders in an easy shrug. "And the kids. I mean, really, I should be blaming Fran for being willing to hand her daughter to a dead girl, but I think the blame is shared."

Thomas and I both looked at her blankly. Mary smiled.

"I had two jobs, where most crossroads ghosts only get one," she said. "I served the crossroads, and I took care of the Healys. Fran got in early enough and wrapped me tight enough in Alice's life that the metaphysics shifted somewhere along the way, and when Annie got rid of the crossroads, I still had a job to do. I'm a Phantom Babysitter now. I haunt the family. That's what my afterlife looks like. Just you assholes, from here until eternity."

I laughed. I couldn't help it. Mary eyed me.

"Something funny?"

"We get to *keep* you," I said. "Forever. That's amazing."

Her smile grew slowly. "Yeah. It kinda is. Now, do you two want to tell me what the hell is going on here?"

"I found him," I said. "Alive."

"That much is pretty obvious, Alice."

"Yeah, but everyone told me it wasn't possible, so I'm going to be smug about it for a while," I said. "I found him, I brought him home, and now we're going to live happily ever after. With a little stop-off in New York to deal with the Covenant incursion Rose says is going on."

Mary looked at me oddly. "You're going to New York?" she asked. "You know Kevin and Jane aren't there, right?"

"We do," said Thomas. "While I am very eager for that reunion and introduction, and am quite sure Sally would rather be reunited with James than do much of anything else, it seems rather more pressing that we contend with my former associates."

"Plus Rose says her bosses want us there," I interjected.

Mary nodded, her focus still mostly on Thomas. "Wow, fifty years wherever the hell the crossroads put you haven't changed you one little bit, have they?" she asked, almost amused. "And cool. Just wanted to be sure. We could use the help, honestly. We've been sheltering in place there for weeks, and—" She stopped, cocking her head sharply to the side like she was listening to something the rest of us couldn't hear. "And I have to get back. Tommy, welcome home. You have no idea how happy I am to see you. Alice, I hope you're staying put this time, since you don't have anything left to look for." She finished with a stern look that made it clear what the answer she wanted was.

Fortunately, it was the one I was prepared to give. "I'm staying in this dimension for the foreseeable future," I assured her. "Thomas is here. That's all I've ever needed for a place to feel like home."

"You're both going to have a lot of work to do, but I'm genuinely glad you're finally going to start doing it," she said, and disappeared, as abruptly as a light switch flipping off.

I turned to Thomas, a small smile on my face. "Well, Verity will know we're coming, at least," I said. "Think Cynthia will be back soon with Sally and Sally's new wardrobe?"

"And the cake, one hopes, since otherwise we're likely to cause a riot when we inform the colony that we're already planning to depart."

I made a sour face, and he laughed. Normal was never going to be what it had been before he disappeared. We were fifty years too late for that. But we were going to find out what normal meant for us now, and we were going to be happy there.

I had faith.

Cynthia's peach cobbler was just as good cold as it had been hot, if somewhat texturally different. I leaned against Thomas on the couch, my feet tucked underneath me, and munched my way steadily through the sweet mixture of pastry crumble, fruit, and sugar while he did much the same with a plate of ribs. Neither of us had bothered reheating the food. The luxury of fresh food from a dimension where everything had evolved to be complementary to our biology, if not always compatible, was more than enough. If the food had been hot, it might have been overwhelming.

On some level, I was almost glad we were plunging straight into another crisis. Sure, I said I wanted time for us to take things easy and get to know each other as people again, but I was also afraid of it. We'd both changed so much over the course of the last fifty years. The people we'd been were gone, casualties of the passage of time, and we couldn't get back to them if we tried. It wasn't possible.

And I was a little bit afraid that if we had nothing external to fight against, we'd wind up trying anyway. That was the last thing I wanted.

Besides, he was going to need time to reacclimate to life on Earth, without constant life-threatening peril around every corner. Maybe a little light peril would help with that. And he needed to start meeting the grandkids, anyway. I was sure he was going to adore them—but it was probably a good idea to start with someone *other* than Antimony, who was likely to immediately tie him to a chair and demand he become her personal Merlin, which would create a certain amount of pressure before he was necessarily ready for it. She needed to learn. He needed to breathe.

Family is complicated. Peach cobbler, on the other hand, is refreshingly simple, and I kept shoveling it into my mouth with the single-minded devotion of someone who has learned through long and painful experience that when you *can* eat, you *should* eat, always. A full stomach is a blessing not frequently afforded by a universe that's more interested in chaos than it is in comfort.

We were still eating when the front door swung open and Sally stepped inside, looking faintly stunned, her arms overloaded with bags. Cynthia was close behind her, carrying more bags, as well as a half-sheet cake with white icing and pink and yellow frosting roses in the corners.

"Success?" inquired Thomas.

"Little miss here had a panic attack in the candy aisle when she realized we were surrounded by honest-to- Iðunn humans, and had to be taken to the bathroom until she stopped shaking," said Cynthia. "But yes, success. We got everything you asked us to get."

"Walmart is a corporate parasite that crushes small businesses and reduces commercial diversity by out-competing everything around it, but they sell socks," said Sally. I could see the strain under her flippancy. I set my cobbler aside and uncurled from the couch, moving to take some of the bags. "And underwear, and bras, and jeans, and shoes. I don't think I've ever owned this much clothing."

"We also got snacks for the road trip you're about to leave on, since groceries would be pointless right now." Cynthia put the cake on the coffee table before setting her share of the bags down on the floor. "We swung through McDonald's on the way home. Your girl can *put away* some chicken nuggets. I think she's half honey mustard by weight."

"Did you bring us any fries?" I asked.

"No," said Sally. "They're no good cold, and they would have been cold by the time we got home."

"Fair enough. Want to see a magic trick?"

"Sure," said Sally dubiously.

"That's my cue to get out of here," said Cynthia. "Alice, I'm keeping the change. I'll apply it to your grocery bill. If you call the Angel when you're on the way back, I'll make sure everything's stocked up and ready before you get here."

"Appreciate it," I said, and watched as she walked quickly to the door and let herself out. Cynthia had seen this before. She was smart to get clear before things got loud.

Turning back to the living room, I clapped my hands. "The Holy Bargain of For God's Sake, Alex, Make Those Damn Mice Stop Yelling While I Have A Hangover is still in effect," I said, loudly and sternly. "But as always within the bounds of this bargain, offerings must be made. You are invited for cake, in the living room, providing you keep the cheering to a minimum and take your portion away with haste. Is the bargain satisfactory?"

There was a long pause, long enough to make me think maybe they were sulking and I was talking to the walls for no real reason. Then, from all sides, came a resounding cry of "HAIL!"

Sally winced. "I thought you told them to keep the cheering to the minimum."

"That *was* the minimum," I said, as mice streamed out of the baseboards and swarmed the cake like locusts covering a farmer's field, ripping off chunks of sponge and frosting and racing away with them, vanishing into the baseboards. I watched with a small, indulgent smile. A full colony of Aeslin mice gathering food is an impressive sight. "Cake is a literal religious experience, and they're very excited about it. The fact that they're not singing a song in honor of the cake, the baker, the farmers who grew the ingredients, *that's* them showing restraint."

Sally blinked. "They worship . . . cake."

"No, they worship *us*. The cake is just a fulfillment of the promise made to them by Great-Great-Grandma Beth when she found them in her chicken coop."

Sally's expression turned dubious. "How many generations of your family am I going to be expected to memorize? Ballpark figure, if you could."

"Your family too now, Sally," said Thomas with amusement. He had been watching the Ceremony of Cake without getting involved, perhaps not wanting to test the bounds of the Holy Bargain that was keeping him from being swarmed like a sheet cake himself. Now that more than half the mice were gone, it must have felt a little safer to speak. "We'll be presenting you to the town as a cousin, and I do believe those new identities Alice mentioned arranging in Las Vegas would list you as a relation."

"With your permission," I said, as Sally shot me a sharp look. "I mean, we've already established that you don't want to go back to Maine, and Thomas seems pretty set on keeping you; if we can make that true on paper, we make things a lot easier on all of us in the future. So I guess you're experiencing the adoption equivalent of getting drafted, if that makes sense."

"I guess I am," said Sally. She didn't look displeased about it. "I guess you weren't kidding."

"How could we be kidding?" I asked, and picked up a few of the bags. "The mice adore you. Thomas adores you. I mostly don't want to push you down a well. That means you're on a par with how I feel about most of the rest of the family, and we're keeping you as long as you want to be kept."

"And if you want to go to college, or go off somewhere and start a life with fewer talking rodents and random assaults by monster-hunters, we can help with that," said Thomas. "Alice tells me the family accounts are still intact. We don't want for money."

"This is so weird," muttered Sally. She looked at me. "There a reason you're stealing my underwear?"

"I figured I'd put it in your room," I said. "Unless you really wanted to haul it all yourself?"

". . . you can help," Sally allowed, sounding only slightly overwhelmed. I picked up two more bags. She did the same, and we began the process of getting everything upstairs while Thomas continued to watch the mice denude their offering of cake.

Sally set to unpacking her things, and then Thomas joined me upstairs so we could do the reverse, packing clothes and weapons for the trip ahead. He discouraged me from bringing too many grenades, saying mildly that while he was not averse to some recreational violence, he would prefer I not blow my own limbs off while I was recovering from my delusions of indestructibility. I encouraged him to bring more shirts than he thought he'd need, glad once again that I had never thrown anything away; he might be out of style, but at least he wouldn't have to wear anything that was actively bloodstained for very long.

All in all, it was a soothing process, and we finished and went to bed shortly before midnight, home, safe, and back in a world we almost understood.

That night, Thomas and I slept in our own room, together, with no refugee camp outside for us to defend and a closed door between us and his adopted adult daughter, who had still been sorting through her purchases in her room, which she seemed to be starting to believe was actually hers, when we went to bed. The mice had whisked away our dinner leftovers along with their cake, carrying them off to feed the parts of the colony who weren't as free to scavenge on their own—the infants and the elders. The bones had been given to the tailypo. Our house was an ecosystem, as it had always been before, and while the exact balance of residents might have changed, it felt like home for the first time in decades.

To my mild surprise, neither of us felt like being any more intimate than the inherent closeness of curling up against each other in a space that had always belonged to just the two of us, where the rest of the world had somehow managed never to truly intrude. I slept the deep, cleansing sleep that normally followed a fever, the kind of sleep that had been so common when I was a kid that I had barely noticed it slipping away.

I woke up to early-morning light streaming around the edges of the curtains and the feeling of a hand stroking my hair. I lifted my head, which had been resting on Thomas's chest, and looked up to find him half-propped on the pillows, smiling at me.

"Good morning," he said.

"Hey," I said, and smiled drowsily back. "Sun's up and we're still here."

"Not for long," he said. "I believe what woke me was the sound of someone honking a horn outside. You were far too deeply asleep to notice."

"I felt safe," I said, and stretched, scooting slightly away from him to do so. "Not the most common thing, so when it happens, I tend to just let myself have it."

"I intend to make you feel safe a great deal more often," he said solemnly. I smiled at him. He leaned over and kissed me. "We're home now. We'll be safe from now on."

"After we go drive your former co-workers out of New York," I said. "Not thrilled about that part. I was excited about having time and privacy."

"We have both right now," he said, and reached for me. My smile grew as I let him gather me close, and for a little while, the urgency of everything else didn't matter. We were here. We were home, and we still had each other, despite the impossibility of that fact.

We won.

When we finally pulled apart, I kissed him before rolling over to get my feet on the floor, stretching again in the process. "I could definitely get used to that as a way to start the morning."

"I intend to see to it that you do," said Thomas, sitting up on his side of the bed. He paused then, a quizzical look on his face. "I thought the bed I had in the bottle dimension was a reasonable approximation of this one; it seems I was wrong."

"Wait until we get one that's less than fifty years old," I said.

He smiled at me. "Temptress."

"Temptress calls first shower," I said. "You can go wake Sally. Or ask the mice to do it, but realize that if you do, they may decide they're allowed to start badgering you."

He was still laughing when I left the room and made my way down the hall to lock myself in the bathroom. There would be time for shared showers later, when an unfamiliar routewitch wasn't about to be honking outside the house. We didn't have any neighbors for them to bother, but still, if we were going to get on the road before lunch, we couldn't get too distracted.

It normally takes about thirteen hours to drive from Buckley to Manhattan, depending on traffic and stops. With a routewitch behind the wheel, it could take six or sixteen, depending on their current relationship to the road. Since the Ocean Lady wanted us to get our butts over there and take care of the Covenant, I was willing to bet this was going to be an unreasonably swift trip, one marked with an absence of construction zones or speed traps. But I've been wrong before.

Sally was in the front room when we came downstairs, a mouse on her open palm. Her attention was focused on the tiny creature, which was earnestly reciting one of the rituals associated with Mary. There were plenty of those. "Ready to go?" I asked.

Sally looked up, almost startled, before giving a single sharp nod and setting the mouse down on the couch. "All packed," she said, standing. "You expect we're coming back here?"

"We always do," I said, reaching back to put a hand on Thomas's arm.

The words felt hollow. We'd just managed to get here; leaving already felt like an admission of some kind of failure, like we should have been able to find a way to stay put at least long enough to cook a proper dinner and start falling into a routine. Sadly, the world has never been that accommodating. We'd be back. We always came back.

We had to.

Thomas took my hand in his, clearly seeing my discomfort, and asked, "Has either of you called the mice?"

Sally blinked. "I was just talking to one . . ."

"Yeah, but did you tell them we were leaving?" I asked. She shook her head, and I snorted. "Right. Clergy! Mine, and those representing the Conscripted Priestess and the God of Inconvenient Timing!"

As I'd expected, there wasn't even a pause before several small heads poked out of a hole in the wall. The mice might be constrained by the Holy Bargain, but they were still going to be stalking us through the house as long as we were here, soaking up every scrap of liturgy they could get.

"We're leaving," I informed the mice. "Not for very long, hopefully, but we should see the Arboreal Priestess while we're away. Please choose representatives from the appropriate clergies to accompany us."

The mice popped back into the wall, their disappearance followed by the sound of violent squeaking. I waited patiently, and less than thirty seconds later, five mice emerged: representatives of our four branches of the faith, and one of the senior members of the local branch of Verity's clergy. They ran across the room and up my leg, grabbing onto my backpack and getting themselves settled.

"To the rest of you, stay safe, and please don't pick any fights with the tailypo before we get back," I said.

There was no immediate reply, but the air in the room shifted slightly as more mice ran down the walls, coming to watch us go.

"That Holy Bargain packs a punch," said Thomas, voice low.

"It does, which is part of why we only invoke it when we absolutely have to," I agreed, and made for the front door, Sally and Thomas close behind.

I opened it to reveal a green sedan parked in the driveway. The driver was waiting inside, assuming there *was* a driver, and the Ocean Lady hadn't sent us some sort of phantom coach or something. Sally and Thomas filed out behind me, and I locked the door, tucking the key into my pocket.

"We'll get you keys of your own cut as soon as we get home," I promised them, and started down the steps toward the car.

It felt odd to be taking the key with me rather than hiding it or giving it back to the tailypo. One more brick in the wall of "we are home, we are staying" that I was trying to build. I'd given up on carrying a key through adjoining dimensions after I lost the tenth one, preferring to trust that I'd be able to get inside when I got home.

The car window rolled down as we approached, and the driver—a broad-shouldered Black man in a red flannel shirt over a white tank top, leaned over to address our group.

"Y'all my fare?" he asked.

"That depends on who sent you and where you think we're going," I replied.

"Lady sent me, says you lot need to be tossed out in Manhattan, near the Meatpacking District," he said, accent a blend of New Jersey twang and something broader and less defined. He'd been driving a while, then, long enough to blunt the edges of whatever he'd originally sounded like. "Sound about right?"

"Right name, right city, although I didn't know the neighborhood," I said. "I thought Rose was going to be coming with you?"

"Lady sent her on a job."

Which, if what she'd said before was accurate, meant she couldn't say no. right. I leaned over to extend my hand through the open window. "Alice Price-Healy."

The routewitch's eyes widened as he took my hand and shook, respectfully. "Lady said I'd be driving friends, but didn't say she meant *dangerous* friends," he said. "I'm Darius. I serve the Queen of the Routewitches in the shadow of the Ocean Lady. I'll get you where you're going."

"Good. I appreciate it." I reclaimed my hand and straightened as Thomas stepped forward.

"Thomas Price," he said, then at me. "Did you want . . . ?"

"No, sweetie," I said. "You take the front." He hadn't been in a car in fifty years. If he wanted to ride shotgun, I wasn't going to argue with him about it. It wasn't like I could help the driver with directions or anything like that.

Looking almost giddy, Thomas moved past me to open the front passenger door and slide into the car, settling his valise between his feet. None of us were carrying enough clothing for any sort of long stay, but we were armed, and I've learned that if I have the weapons I need, everything else is pretty much negotiable.

"And you are, miss?" asked Darius, looking to Sally, who was frowning as she worked something over in her head. Sally looked back at him, a line between her eyebrows as she kept working at whatever was distracting her. Then she smiled, bright as the sun that was still inching upward in the sky.

"Sally Price," she said.

Darius nodded, obviously taking this in stride. I glanced at Sally and smiled as she blushed and looked away. Too late now; she'd said it out loud. She had been acquired.

We piled into the back, arranging our bags and road snacks

between us, my pack on top to avoid squashing the mice. They were keeping low and quiet in the presence of a stranger, but that wouldn't last once they realized he was a routewitch; the Aeslin had a tendency to reveal themselves at inopportune times when they felt like it was safe to do so.

"We'll need to stop for breakfast, if you don't mind," Thomas said apologetically to Darius. "There isn't much food in the house as yet, and our dinner leftovers didn't survive their encounter with the local wildlife."

"No trouble," said Darius. He tilted his head back, smiling at me and Sally in the rearview mirror. "You ladies all right back there?"

"We fit," I said. "Sally hasn't been in a car for about ten years, and Thomas hasn't been in one for fifty."

"He looks good for his age, then," said Darius, and laughed, a rich, rolling laugh that filled the car almost as pervasively as the smell of the pine tree air freshener hanging from the mirror. "Well, then, here we go. McDonalds all right with you?"

"I would do crimes for a McMuffin," said Sally, almost reverently.

"Luckily, you won't have to," said Darius, and started the car.

Sally didn't have to do crimes *for* a McMuffin, but she put four of them away so quickly that I thought she might have done crimes *to* a Mc-Muffin by the time she was done. Sadly for her and fortunately for my sanity, the milkshake machine was broken. The mice had yet to show themselves, but Darius only looked at me curiously in the rearview mirror as I tucked three hash browns and two Sausage McMuffins into my bag, settling to eat my own breakfast while the mice silently devoured theirs.

Thomas, meanwhile, had an expression of almost orgasmic relief on his face as he sipped his first cup of coffee in fifty years. It was probably a good thing it was crappy fast-food coffee; if we'd managed to get him the quality stuff, he might have expired on the spot. I hadn't spent half a century hunting for him to lose him to a pot of Kona.

Darius turned off the highway once we'd all been fed, sliding easily onto a frontage road, and that was where the fun of riding with a routewitch really began. He drove like he'd been following these specific roads every day of his life, steering around potholes and avoiding construction areas with a local's learned ease. He never slowed, save for when he approached a red light or a stop sign, and he never broke any traffic laws I could see. And even with all that being true, we were halfway across Pennsylvania before it even approached lunchtime.

Sally leaned forward. "Fun as this tour of the backroads of America has been, are we going to stop for lunch?" she asked. "I thought we'd have stopped to get gas by now."

"You need the bathroom?" Darius asked. "We can stop if you need the bathroom. Seemed like you had enough snacks back there, didn't need to hit a service station. This sweet girl can run another three days on the fuel she's got in her tank, and I don't really feel like having steak for dinner tonight."

He caressed his dashboard with a proprietary hand, and the timbre of the engine's purring changed for a moment, like an animal being stroked by a beloved human. I put a hand on Sally's arm before she could ask what he meant about the steak, giving her a small but pointed shake of my head. She didn't want to know. Not while we were still in the car.

Maybe it's the result of spending so much of my youth around Cynthia, but I know a sanguivore when I see one, and I didn't think Sally was quite ready to deal with the idea that she'd been riding around inside of a vehicular vampire.

"Yes, I need the bathroom," said Sally sourly.

Darius smiled. "Of course," he said, and turned at the next intersection, pulling into a neon-decked truck stop parking lot. Sally was out of the car almost before it stopped rolling, flipping a wave over her shoulder at us as she booked for the main building. Darius leaned back in his seat, turning off the engine.

"Either of you needs to go, you should," he said. "I don't plan to stop again before we hit the city."

"That'll make this a what, four-hour drive?" I asked.

"About that." His smiled was radiant. "I don't believe in wasting time when the Lady asks me to do something."

I wanted to ask a lot of questions about how a highway could ask him to do anything, much less ask him to hop in his vampire car and drive a bunch of strangers to what seemed like a remarkably specific location. Under the circumstances, it didn't seem quite politic. I undid my seatbelt.

"I'm going to head in and hit the ladies' room," I said. "You two have fun out here." I shifted my attention to my bag. "And you be good while I'm inside."

My bag didn't respond. The mice were still in hiding mode, then. Darius gave me an odd look but didn't say anything. I guess when you're a witch of the living road serving a goddess who's also a highway, you learn not to ask too many questions.

The air was cool and crisp and smelled of diesel and frying potatoes, that particular mix that screams "truck stop" all over the country. I stretched my arms up over my head as I walked away, enjoying the late-morning sun, the cool air on my skin, and the fact that I was walking *away* from Thomas, not running frantically toward him, trying to keep convincing myself over and over again that I wasn't wasting my life on a fruitless quest for something I'd never find. It was weird not to be scared all the time. We were heading into what Rose called a war, but compared to the last fifty years of my life, it felt like a vacation.

I wasn't sure I'd ever had one of those. The doors slid open at my approach, and I stepped inside, scanning for the bathrooms. They were on the other side of the wide, open room, set up as a sort of pseudo-food court, with the usual assortment of halfhearted options hawking their wares in direct visual and olfactory competition with each other. Sally was standing in front of the Sbarro, staring at the glass case of cheap, over-cheesed pizza like she hadn't seen food in years. I drifted over toward her.

"Bathroom's this way," I said.

"Pizza," she said, sounding distracted. I wasn't entirely sure she was responding to me, so much as just . . . talking when she thought someone might be able to hear her. "I forgot about pizza."

"Well, we're going to New York, and they have some of the best pizza in the country," I said. "Every kind of pizza you can think of."

Sally turned to look at me, shaking her head a little, like she was coming out of a daze. "I'm lactose intolerant," she said.

"Vegan cheese exists, if that's what floats your boat," I said. "And Lactaid. Did you make it to the bathroom before you got caught in the siren song of the pepperoni?"

She shook her head. I smiled.

"It's always hard to reintegrate once I've been on the road for a while," I said. "After my first long trip, I ate my body weight in chocolate, threw up, and then did it again, because I'd forgotten how much I loved the stuff until it was in front of me again. It's gonna be okay."

"Really?"

"Really-really. You're a Price now, and we take care of our own. And we do *not* allow our own to eat lousy fast-food pizza after going without for ten years."

Sally laughed, and kept laughing as we walked to the bathroom. There were a lot of adjustments ahead, for all of us, but I was increasingly sure that we were going to weather them just fine.

Darius started the car as soon as Sally and I got back in and fastened our belts, and we pulled out of the truck-stop parking lot a little faster than we'd pulled in.

"Something wrong?" I asked.

"We're on a timetable, and I don't want to be late," he said.

I blinked. Thomas, however, got there first. "A timetable? For what?" he asked.

"The Lady didn't say. She just wants you in New York before three, and I do what she tells me."

"Wait," said Sally. "I know my geography pretty well. That's not possible."

Darius laughed. "First time?"

"Sally didn't know what a routewitch was before yesterday," I said. "Let's play nice with the new kid."

"Ah," he said, in sudden understanding. "Well, Sally, is there anything you need to know? We've got a few hours yet before we get where we're going."

"I still don't know what a routewitch is," said Sally sourly. "I asked, and you all kept talking and ignored me."

Thomas winced. "I'm sorry," he said, looking stung. "I didn't mean to ignore your question."

"A routewitch is a human person with a natural connection to the road," said Darius. "If someone's connection is strong enough, they may be able to use it to do magic, mostly associated with travel. I'm one of the best there is at subtly bending distance. I can cover a hundred miles of real space in three miles of road space if I'm in the zone and have my baby with me." He caressed the car again.

"Okay, *what* is with the car?" I asked.

"She doesn't run on gas, if that's what you're asking. She's a special model. Rolled off the assembly line and straight onto the Ocean Lady, where we made a few modifications. She won't even start for anyone but me, and for me, she'll drive until she falls apart." Darius leaned back in his seat, taking his hands off the wheel. The car didn't swerve even a little, just kept rolling straight and easy down the center of the lane. "I'm honestly extraneous here, except that she wouldn't be able to go as far, as fast without me here to act as a sort of bonus battery. We boost each other."

"But how is that possible?" asked Sally. "The laws of physics aren't negotiable."

Darius laughed, and the sound was loud and joyous as he set his hands back on the wheel. "Sure they are. There's no law that's not negotiable, if you know how to get your shoulder against it and push. Speed limits only apply if you respect them. Try telling a sylph about conservation of mass, or a jink about probability."

"She doesn't know what those things are yet," said Thomas. "I don't know how much the Ocean Lady told you about my situation . . . ?"

"Not much. You're not her problem, except right now, when your people are bothering her routewitches. We have a lot of folks in the New York area, and even if we didn't, those Covenant assholes are like mold. Once they take root, they spread until they've covered everything. This is *her* place, *her* continent. She's a new god, but she's big on the idea that she has to protect what's hers if she wants to be worthy of the title. So she wants them gone." Darius glanced at Thomas. "So she just told me I'd be picking you up, and it would be doing her a favor, and would also keep that little Fury she's gone and helped to empower off my back for a while. Anything that gets me in good with the divine is cool by me. Apple, though. Apple told me more than that."

"Wait." I leaned forward, straining against the limits of my seatbelt as I put as much of myself as possible into the front seat. "*Apple* is still in charge?"

"Queen of the North American Routewitches, from Utqiagvik to Florida City. All our roads are hers to have and protect, and will be until she passes her crown."

"She was queen fifty years ago," I said. "And she was like *twelve*."

"She's seventeen," said Darius. "She didn't have access to good food for over a year before she found her way to the Lady, and it stunted her growth. She's been Queen since 1944, and she's not going to step down until the road is kinder. The Lady loves her. I'm not as old as she is, but I can't imagine a better Queen. And she told me that you, Mr. Price, had made a bargain with the crossroads."

"I did," Thomas allowed. "It seemed like the best choice remaining to me when it happened, and I still don't regret it. Not even after everything that followed."

"You're close to unique that way," said Darius. "Not just in that—the Queen doesn't speak well of petitioners. Says they're greedy and shortsighted, and deserve whatever punishment they receive. She speaks well of you."

Sally, who had made a bargain of her own, for reasons just as good as Thomas's, squirmed in her seat, but didn't say anything. Sometimes there's nothing you *can* say.

"Queen says your granddaughter wouldn't exist if you hadn't made that deal, and she's the one who untangled the crossroads from our arteries, kicked them out of this reality. The Ocean Lady owes your family a debt of gratitude for what you did for us."

I blinked. The idea of a god owing us a favor was daunting, if reasonable enough.

"Regardless of the divinities in play," said Thomas firmly, "I made my bargain and was sent into exile for my trouble. Sally did much the same. She's been fighting by my side for the last decade, and while her bargain was as compassionately made as my own, she had less idea of what she was doing. I had the benefits of a Covenant education and a long acquaintance with a crossroads ghost. She had an untrained sorcerer reading from his mother's journals and trying to make sense of a world he was barely brushing up against. This is her first true encounter with the forces humanity shares this world with. Try not to invoke things she knows only as children's stories. We don't want to overwhelm her."

"I'm not a child," snapped Sally. "I won't get overwhelmed."

"If we tried to tell you everything at once, yes, you would," said Thomas. "Any rational person would. Covenant training begins when children are young and malleable enough to accept whatever they're told, and it includes breaks for them to stare at the walls and panic when needed as they begin to understand how complicated the world really is. We'll tell you everything as it becomes relevant, I promise. It may just take some time."

"That's the most rational thing I've ever heard a sorcerer say," said Darius. Glancing at Sally in the rearview mirror, he explained, "My kind don't care much for his kind. Our magic is sort of like a house that's run off solar power. We generate it and we draw it from a willing source. It's very self-contained and self-renewing. His kind, they take it from the world around them without asking."

"But that's an ethical debate for another time," said Thomas.

"What do you know about the Covenant in New York?" I asked.

"I know they announced themselves by burning down a burlesque club that had the bad luck to be owned by a bogeyman," he said.

"I heard about that," I said. "My oldest granddaughter worked there, and she was helping the locals recover from the fire when I left to find Thomas."

"That's a start," he said. "Things have gotten worse since then."

"Worse" was something of an understatement. After burning down the Freakshow, the Covenant had started hunting the cryptids of New York, beginning with the ones who, like the bogeymen, had been hiding in plain sight. Bakeries, dry cleaners, nail salons, all targeted and destroyed. People died. The Freakshow had been lucky: the waheela they had on staff had smelled the accelerant and been able to evacuate the place before it went up. There had been no casualties.

None of the other businesses had gotten off so lightly, and after several years of unrelenting attacks, people had started abandoning their homes, moving away from everything they'd always known. And that was when the Covenant had expanded their attacks further outside the city, to New Jersey and other neighboring states. They were sending regular patrols into the Pine Barrens, tormenting and slaughtering the cryptids who lived there, and chasing the sasquatch and boo hag populations toward the Canadian border.

And through all of this, the human population had been kept in peaceful ignorance. The Covenant's desire to go unseen was probably saving more lives than we could count. As long as they were trying to stay under the radar, they'd restrict themselves to small fires and the occasional abduction. If things came out in the open, all bets would be off. They'd love the chance to reestablish themselves as a vital line of defense for the human race, protecting humanity from the "monsters" that lurked in every shadow. They just needed the right opportunity to come forward. Which meant Verity's television appearance had probably done more damage than any of us had known at the time.

According to Darius, people were still debating whether her final fight had been CGI or practical effects, and since the latter was winning, the argument had begun to pivot toward whether it had been faked at all. If enough people came down on the side of "a giant snake really came through the stage and ate some dancers, giant snakes are real, we're all in a lot of trouble," the Covenant would have their opening.

For the moment, most of the cryptids remaining in the city were staying as out of sight as possible while still keeping their jobs and roofs over their heads. The cryptid hospital in Manhattan, St. Giles, had also managed to stay open thus far, thanks to being literally underground and protected by basically every intelligent cryptid in the area. None of them wanted to see their only chance for species-appropriate treatment go away. The real issue was the dragons.

The dragons who kept their Nest in Manhattan couldn't evacuate with the rest of the cryptids. Literally *couldn't*, since the last known adult male of their species was under the city. I blinked when Darius reminded me of that fact, unsure when it had become common-enough knowledge that a random routewitch would know about it. Adult male dragons were bigger than buses, and while they *could* move under their own power, they mostly preferred not to, building themselves large lairs and surrounding themselves with wives who would happily feed them and keep them company.

That may seem lazy by human standards, but it's really more like the queen bee of a hive trading freedom for a life of pampering and luxury. Even the oldest, largest male dragon could still protect his wives, and would do so with force, fire, and fury. They were the reason the Covenant had been founded in the first place, in part due to an unpleasant cultural misunderstanding: female dragons looked exactly like human women. It was a great piece of mimicry when what you wanted was to blend into the population of the fast-breeding mammals near you, but it was a terrible one when you didn't want those same mammals to fall in love with you and try to spirit you away to be their brides.

Basically, a lot of medieval assholes couldn't take "no" for an answer, and spun stories about dragons kidnapping princesses to encourage populations to rise up against them. Not every dragon was a nice person. According to the histories, a lot of them were assholes in their own right, and were perfectly happy to lay waste to the local human settlements. It didn't really matter that they couldn't fly. When a giant fire-breathing reptile storms down from the mountains and torches your house, you don't stop to say "that would have been more impressive if you'd been in the air." You scream, you char, and you die. So the Covenant had come together to make the dragons stop.

They didn't *know* there was a male dragon in Manhattan, but they were starting to suspect. People had been careless with the news, spreading it to dragon enclaves around the world, letting the women know there was a male in the world again, and more, the female dragons of Manhattan—called "princesses" by people who hadn't known any better—weren't leaving, implying that they had something to protect. The Covenant had apparently started focusing their attention on suspected dragon princesses, snatching them whenever they could, trying to confirm the rumors, trying to find their way to the ultimate prize for an organization of dragon-hunters that had long since run out of dragons to fight.

Things could have been worse, but they could have been a hell of a lot better, and they were on the cusp of turning even uglier.

We were silent as Darius finished his explanation and turned off his latest frontage road, suddenly, impossibly driving onto the Queensboro Bridge. "Almost there," he said, more subdued than he'd been before he started telling us what was actually going on. The Covenant wasn't targeting routewitches yet, but that would come soon enough. When they ran out of "monsters" to destroy, they would move on to the humans who had the audacity to tangle with powers the Covenant thought should be reserved for them alone. A witch was fine when they were working for the "forces of good." Not so when they were just trying to live their lives and not be told what to do by monster-hunting bigots.

I patted my bag reassuringly, trying to comfort the still-silent Aeslin mice. The Covenant is much of why my family's colonies are among the last in the world, if not *the* last. They didn't like talking rodents so blatantly harmless that no one could quite figure out why they were considered unnatural, and they disliked the fact that Aeslin generally refused to lie even more. If an Aeslin mouse saw you kill someone, they told people about it. If they saw you commit a crime, they told people about that, too.

Really, it was a miracle I got away with as much as I did when I was younger, given the combination of my father's paranoia and the resident colony of Aeslin mice.

"Thanks for the ride," I said.

"Wish you hadn't needed it. I wouldn't be anywhere near New York if the Lady hadn't asked, and I'll probably wind up taking a few of the locals out of town when I go. Call it a fare for the favor of the road. The Lady doesn't want the world to lose any more backroads or byways than it already has."

Sally was goggling out the windows, staring at a city she might or might not have seen as a kid, when she'd been growing up in Maine, but that she'd definitely seen on television and in movies. Something familiar and human that was absolutely still here. Thomas was doing something similar, although a bit more discreetly. They were reentering the world like comets plummeting toward the ground. I just hoped we'd have slightly more survivors.

Manhattan looked largely like I remembered it. The stores that were still open were different ones, and there were more "For Rent" signs in the windows than I would have expected, but the city itself, the bones of it, were the same as they had always been. It was reassuring, in its urbanized way, and I clung to that impression of familiarity as Darius pulled up to the curb.

"You're here," he said.

"'Here' being?"

"Don't ask me. This is where the Lady said I needed to take you, and I don't know anything more than that. Other than this is where you get out of my car, since I'm not taking you back and risking pissing her off."

"Fair enough." I shrugged and unbuckled my belt, reaching for the door.

Sally caught my wrist. I turned to look at her.

"Yeah?"

"What do you mean, 'fair enough'?" she demanded. "He wants to dump us out on a random street corner, and you're *okay* with that?"

"He's doing what a god told him to do. I don't think arguing gets us very far." I shook off her grasp and got out of the car, taking my first breath of Manhattan air.

As always, it smelled of frying onions and cooling asphalt, the construction and cooking that were always happening in the city coming to greet yet another tourist. I snagged my bag and slung it over my shoulder, stepping up onto the sidewalk to wait for the others. Thomas followed a moment later, his own bag in one hand, and came to stand beside me. Sally looked sullen as she emerged from the car, shooting a sour glance back at Darius.

He rolled his window down, nodding to us. "If you need a ride back, I'm sure the Lady will let me know," he said. "I'm one of the best she has for this kind of distance. You folks stay safe, all right?"

"We'll do our best," I said, looking around. The street wasn't particularly crowded; not too unusual for this time of day. Workers on their lunch break and other fast-walking people went about their business, along with a few hustlers, and a small gaggle of what I presumed were tourists, but that was all. We were here. Time to start blending in.

Which might be something of a challenge when we were just standing here looking like scruffy backpackers getting ready to spend a year wandering around Europe, but I've done stranger.

Darius nodded, rolled up his window, and pulled away from the curb, vanishing down the street faster than should have been possible, leaving us alone.

Twelve

"You can run, you can hide, but your family will always find you. Stop seeing that as a bad thing. It has nothing to do with blood."

—Juniper Campbell

Standing on a random street in Manhattan, with no real idea where to go from here

SALLY MOVED UNTIL SHE was practically standing on top of Thomas and me, and I realized she was almost shaking. Bands of marauders and giant monsters were inside her comfort zone. Big human cities weren't. Not anymore.

"It'll be okay," I said, trying to sound reassuring. "We wouldn't be here if there weren't a reason."

"Trust Alice when she says things like that," advised Thomas. "She's run her entire life on a policy of 'Well, now that I'm here, might as well see what happens,' and while I won't say it's always been easy, it's certainly worked so far."

I wrinkled my nose at him, then turned a slow circle, gawking like the tourist I was.

This was a wide two-way street with multiple lanes, a commercial block with office buildings and storefronts stretching from corner to corner. From where we were standing, I could see at least three small convenience stores, a supermarket, a shoe store, and a shop that appeared to be selling nothing but fancy cupcakes. Anyplace but New York, I would have assumed I was wrong about that last one. No one can make a living on cupcakes alone.

"Okay," I said, coming to a stop. "Nothing immediately jumping out at me. Which means it's time for Mary."

"Time for Mary?" asked Sally blankly.

"Yeah," I explained. "It's time to say Mary's name over and over until she hears me, which she always does, and shows up to tell me what we're doing wrong. Mary doesn't like it when I annoy her this way. She told me once that it was like someone going up to a hotel desk and ringing the little bell over and over and over again."

"But Mary's a super common name," said Sally. "Wouldn't the bell just keep ringing all the time?"

"No," said Mary, behind her. I hadn't even seen her appear. Sally whipped around, eyes wide. I covered my smile with my hand. It was nice to see somebody else on the receiving end of that trick for a change. "It only works when the person saying it is family. You could have said the name a million times before you called yourself a Price, and I never would have heard you. Now, it's just a little muffled. The sound'll get stronger the longer you're one of mine. When Jane got married, I could barely hear Ted at all. Now he's as loud as the rest of these assholes. I didn't hear Tommy until Kevin was born." She shot a smile my way.

I answered it. "Hey, Mary. You know why they dropped us off here?"

"Because this is where you needed to be," she said, and beckoned for us to follow her as she turned toward the nearest of the convenience stores. The smallest, dirtiest one, naturally.

Sally balked, wrinkling her nose. "What could you possibly want to buy in *there*?" she demanded.

Mary gave her a curious look. "You have something against candy and toilet paper?"

"When it's being sold out of a shop that looks like it's been collecting grime since my grandparents were in grade school? Yeah. That place isn't filthy. Filth is too good for it."

"I'll tell Pris," said Mary. "She'll be thrilled to hear how well the camouflage is working."

The bell over the door was as crappy as the rest of the place; it didn't chime so much as make a dull clunking sound when Mary opened the door, stepping inside and leaving the rest of us with little choice but to follow. I stepped into the gloom, squinting at the understocked, dust-covered shelves. Only one of the overhead lights was working, and it flickered and buzzed unpleasantly. The blonde woman behind the cash register didn't look up from her magazine.

She was the only attractive thing about this place, devastatingly gorgeous, with the sort of cheekbones a sculptor would kill to create. I blinked, raising an eyebrow. Thomas got there first.

"Are we approaching the Manhattan Nest?" he asked politely.

The woman finally glanced up, just a flicker of interest before her eyes snapped back to her magazine. She grunted.

"We are," said Mary. "I hope you remember how to show respect and not get your face burnt off. New girl, you just follow these two's lead. They may not know what the Internet is, but they know how dragon politics work."

"I have an AOL account," I said, stung.

Mary snorted. "Hey, Pris, the new girl"—she gestured to Sally—"thinks the place looks like it needs to be condemned."

The woman—Pris—glanced up again, focusing on Sally with some interest. "You really think so?"

"Uh, yeah," said Sally.

"That's so *sweet* thank you!" She paused then, expression hardening slightly. "You human?"

"Yes," said Sally.

"Huh." The woman looked back to her magazine, dismissing us once more. Mary laughed as she led us to a door labeled EMPLOYEES ONLY. The sign was written on a sheet of plain cardboard in thick black marker, and held up by strips of duct tape.

"Classy," I said.

"Yup," Mary agreed. "We have nothing but the best accommodations here." Opening the door required undoing three locks, one of which must have had a magical component, since whatever Mary did to open it made Thomas's eyes widen in surprise.

On the other side of the door was a short, featureless hall lit by two bare bulbs, ending at a second door. Mary started down it, pausing and looking back at the three of us when we were halfway to the end.

"I know you wouldn't have come here on your own," she said. "I really do appreciate the fact that you're willing to jump right into things, even if we didn't give you as much of a choice as you would have liked. But I need you to promise you're not going to freak out when you see what's through here."

"You have my word," said Thomas gravely.

"You're not the one I'm worried about." Mary gave me a pointed look.

I sighed. "Okay, I get it, I've been gone for like three years," I said. "I'm not going to freak out at whatever you have to show us."

"More like five years, when you add it all together, and I'm still going to hold you to that," she said, and finished walking to the second door. It wasn't locked, and opened to reveal a tiny, boxed-in courtyard with several doors along one wall but no obvious street access. There was a stretch of sky high overhead, implying that this space had originally been more accessible. That was less immediately attention-grabbing than the small swarm of little blonde girls who were playing a complicated game with a red rubber ball and what looked a lot like a Komodo dragon the size of a large dog. All of them stopped when they saw us, going motionless. The ball bounced twice before rolling to a stop against one of the walls. That snapped the Komodo out of its stillness. It scurried in front of the girls, who clustered behind it as it opened its wings and hissed at us.

Opened its . . . wings?

"Mary," I said, voice very low. "Is that a young male dragon?"

"Liam just turned five," said Mary, as fondly as she would have mentioned any other child who occasionally fell under her care. More loudly, she added, "Liam, these are the friends I told you were coming. I appreciate you defending your sisters, but it's okay, I promise."

The dragon—Liam—furled his wings and gave us a mistrustful look before herding the girls to the other side of the courtyard, well away from the lot of us. It would have been funny, if he hadn't been so intensely serious about it, glancing back at us almost constantly.

"Verity told me they'd found a male dragon, and that meant the dragon princesses would start having little boys again," I said, voice still low. "I just never thought I'd get to see one."

Thomas didn't say anything, and his eyes were suspiciously bright as Mary turned toward one of the doors on the other side of the courtyard. I touched his shoulder, concerned, and he reached up to take my hand, offering me a weak smile.

Then Mary opened the door and the three of us followed her through, leaving the children behind.

Based on size and general construction, the room she led us into had started its existence as a slaughterhouse—it could easily have qualified as a warehouse, or a ballroom for people who liked to throw really unnerving balls. The heavy iron chains that had been used to suspend cuts of meat still hung from the ceiling, ending in sturdy hooks. The floor was plain polished wood, and the walls, while they had been painted a cheery shade of yellow with cream trim, were clearly bare brick under that thin layer of home improvement. A catwalk ran all the way around the second floor, with plain metal stairs connecting it to the space where we were standing. The ceiling was at least twenty feet up, and the only windows were high ones, set along the very top of the walls. Most of the sun was coming in through the large skylights in the ceiling itself. All in all, it was a stark, austere space.

The people who were clearly living here had done their best, using secondhand furniture and DIY partitions to create a variety of sectioned-off areas in the open space, little living rooms boxed off by freestanding bookshelves, tiny fairylands of bright rubber blocks and cheerful dinosaur rugs. The exposed walls were softened by hanging rugs and tattered tapestries, or covered up by more bookshelves. It was an industrial environment. It was also a *populated* one.

And then there were the people themselves. I had never seen this many dragon princesses in one place: there were at least twenty adults, and as many little girls, filling the designated play areas with noise and laughter. There were five more of the large lizards that I now recognized as the males of the species, and given what the species had been through, that alone was an embarrassment of riches.

There were non-dragons in the crowd as well: several people whose grayish skin marked them as bogeymen, an Inuit woman in a remarkably frilly black-and-pink dress sitting on the lap of a Japanese man who had his arms looped loosely around her waist, and a pair of dark-skinned men who were working in a makeshift kitchen area, remarkable mostly because of the cloud of bees that danced and wove around their heads. I didn't stare. Thomas, eyes still damp and a bit too bright, didn't stare. Sally, though . . .

Sally was getting a crash course in the fact that humans had never actually been the only sapient species on the planet, despite having always been told they were. It had to be jarring. I had trouble, sometimes, remembering just how jarring that sort of thing could be, since I'd grown up in this world, despite my father doing his level best to push me out of it. Discoveries like hers had never been a revelation for me.

"This used to be the primary Nest for the Manhattan dragons," said Mary. "It's sort of a refugee camp now. Has been since the Freak-show burned."

"When did that happen, exactly?" asked Thomas.

Mary looked at him steadily. "Two thousand and fifteen. They torched the place, then left for a while, thinking they'd pulled off their goals. They came back. They haven't gone away since."

To his credit, he didn't flinch. "And what year is it now?"

"Two thousand twenty-two," said a new voice, from the other side of the room. I turned, breaking into a wide smile at the sight of a familiar face.

Even after five years away—I'd last been home in twenty seventeen, right after we'd sent Antimony off to go undercover with the Covenant—Verity looked essentially the same. Still short, still blonde, still built like someone who'd been dancing and doing gymnastics every minute since she'd figured out how to walk. She had what Thomas used to call "the Carew look," a certain shape to her face and features that made it clear to anyone who saw us together that we were related, even if it wasn't always quite as clear precisely how.

She was wearing jeans and an ombre sweater that faded from pink to orange, lingering on peach, and she looked somewhat warily at the three of us as she approached.

"You've aged," she said, focusing on me as the most familiar face in the bunch. "I didn't know you knew how to do that."

"I kind of got out of the habit for a while, but I've decided to start again, for the sake of the people who love me," I said.

"Uh-huh. Who are your friends?"

Kevin would have told the rest of the family about our brief appearance in the kitchen in Portland. Even if he hadn't wanted to, the mice would have passed the news along to the other clergies in no time, and then there would have been no hiding it. We're not a family that keeps secrets well. She had to know. And still, she wasn't looking directly at Thomas.

"My friends . . . All right. This is going to be awkward every time I have to do it, so we might as well get on with it." I stepped a bit to the side, putting myself between them, and took a deep breath. "Verity Price, meet your grandfather, Thomas."

Sally didn't protest her omission. She was more than smart enough to see that this wasn't something she wanted to be in the middle of.

The mice that had been riding quietly in my bag up until this point lost their ability to be quiet when they heard an introduction happening, and announced their presence with a resounding "HAIL!" before quieting down again, the better to observe and record.

Verity didn't react to the mice. She just shifted her gaze, slowly, to focus directly on Thomas. She tilted her head very slightly to the side, then looked back to me.

"Are you sure?"

I blinked. "What?"

"I asked, are you sure? Because anyone who knows you knows that you've been looking for him for the last fifty years, and it would be easy as anything to set up an imposter."

I fought back the urge to laugh. "Believe it or not, he had basically the same reaction when I showed up. Thought I was an assassin sent to impersonate his wife and get close enough to kill him."

"How'd you convince him you weren't?"

"I beat the living crap out of him."

Sally made a small sound of protest. Thomas took his eyes off of Verity for the first time since she'd entered the room, looking at me.

"Now, dear, I wouldn't characterize it precisely like that," he said. "I believe the beating was mutual."

"And while I don't recommend hitting your partner, it was the only way we were going to resolve that particular conflict," I said. "I convinced him, and he convinced me at the same time."

"If she hadn't convinced me by telegraphing her punches the way she always has, she would have when she helped to break us out of the bottle dimension where we'd been trapped," said Thomas. "She's truly Alice."

"And he's truly Thomas," I said. "I'm not a telepath, but the level of closeness we experienced during that working—he's the real thing, Very. I found him. I told you your grandfather was still alive out there for me to find, and I found him, and I brought him home. Would you like to meet him?"

"Yes," she said, in a very small voice. "And after that, I've got someone I'd like to introduce you to."

"All right." I beckoned her closer, waiting until she had stepped up next to me before I put a hand on her shoulder and turned to Thomas as if making a formal presentation. "Thomas Price, may I introduce you to your granddaughter, Verity De Luca-Price." I glanced at her. "That's right, isn't it?"

"It's Price-De Luca, actually," she said, voice still small, eyes locked on Thomas. "Are you really my grandfather?"

"You look so much like your grandmother," he said, and took a half-step closer before he apparently thought better of it and kept his distance, hands still fixed at his sides. "I am . . . I am truly overjoyed to have the opportunity to meet you. I'm sorry I've been gone for so long."

"So were we," she said, and smiled at him for the first time, wide and open and entirely earnest. "What do I call you?"

"I . . ." Thomas glanced to me, eyes wide. "I don't know. Kevin had barely mastered 'Pa' when I disappeared, and I've never had the chance to figure out what you'd all be calling me."

"Well, she's Grandma." Verity nodded toward me. "Weird as that sometimes is, when she looks younger than me. Which she still does, by the way, and it's *annoying.*"

"Not by as much as I have sometimes," I said.

"And she will *not* be doing that anymore," said Thomas. "The person who had been assisting her in staying static is no longer with us."

"Cool," said Verity. "If she's Grandma, I guess that makes you Grandpa."

That was when the mice couldn't hold it in any longer. "HAIL!" they shouted. "HAIL THE TITLING OF THE GRANDPARENTS!"

"My colony's in the walls, if you want to let yours go and start the liturgical exchange," said Verity. "Mary, can you let Dom know that it's safe for him to come out now?"

Mary nodded and disappeared. I raised an eyebrow.

"Safe?"

"I wanted to wait until I was sure I believed you'd actually found Grandpa and not just shown up with a strange man claiming to be your husband," said Verity. She finally turned her attention to Sally. "Instead, you have a strange woman. Kumiho?"

"Human," I said. "Verity, meet Sally. Your new . . . aunt? Jane's your aunt, so I guess 'aunt' is the right word. Meet your new aunt."

"Hi," said Sally, giving a little wave.

Verity stared at her, and then at me. "Explain."

"Made a deal with the crossroads, got chucked into the same place as the boss over here"—Sally hooked a thumb at Thomas—"don't really feel like I can go back to where I was, so your grandparents have sort of forcibly adopted me."

"She already has a branch of clergy forming," I said, setting my bag on the floor so the mice could emerge and run for the nearest wall. Several people watched them go. No one interfered. I guess the continued existence of Aeslin mice was no longer a surprise to the folks who were actually living with a colony. "They call her the Conscripted Priestess."

"So we have the Conscripted Priestess and the Stolen God," said Verity, with some amusement. At my sidelong look, she explained, "Antimony went out and acquired a new brother when we left her unsupervised. She's set enough on keeping him that she got backdated adoption papers shoved through by Uncle Al."

"Family just keeps growing," I said.

"That's true," she agreed, and turned as a door on the far wall opened, smiling at the man who stepped through. He was short by most people's standards, even mine, which left him well matched to Verity, standing only a few inches taller than she was, and had the sturdy build of someone who'd been physically active every day of his life. His hair was dark, his eyes were brown, and his arms were full of squirming, brown-haired toddler wearing a corduroy jumper. Mary was close behind them, and shut the door once she was through.

"You remember Dominic, right, Grandma?" she asked, as the man approached. He wasn't paying any attention to me at all. His eyes were locked on Thomas, like he expected to be attacked at any moment.

Thomas, for his part, blinked at him, looking faintly nonplussed. I nudged him with my elbow. "I told you Verity was the granddaughter who'd married a defector from the Covenant," I said.

"You did," he agreed. "I'm sorry. I wasn't expecting . . . I'm sorry. De Luca, yes?"

Dominic nodded. "Yes, sir, it was," he said. "It's Price now. The only person who still carries the name of an extinct family line is my lovely wife, who insists it should not be forgotten. I'm a bit exhausted by trying to argue with her on the matter."

"Carew women have that effect," Thomas agreed, and Dominic laughed, still visibly nervous even as some of the tension dissipated.

The toddler in his arms squirmed harder, kicking at his midriff. "Down, Daddy," they said. "Down."

I turned my attention to the child. "Is this . . . ?"

"Yes," said Verity. "Olive, stop squirming, don't kick your father, and say hello to your grandmother."

The child turned wide blue eyes on me, blinking several times as they took my measure. Then, with another kick, they proclaimed, "Not Gramma! *Down!*"

"Sorry," said Verity, moving to take the fighting child away from her husband. "She's only met Grandma Evie, and I don't think she realized she got to have more than one of you."

"Not a surprising thing to be confused about," I said. Something Mary had said much, much earlier suddenly clicked, and I smiled at the child. "I suppose this is Olivia?"

"Yes, it is." Verity bounced the girl against her hip, trying to calm her. "She's stubborn as anything. Possibly the most stubborn person I've ever met."

Dominic coughed and shook his head, signaling that his daughter wasn't the most stubborn person *he* had ever met. I hid my smile behind my hand.

"Hello, Olivia," said Thomas solemnly. She turned her head to study him. "Your mother is correct. Alice is your great-grandmother. Your Grandpa Kevin's mother. I'm your great-grandfather, and it's very nice to meet you."

"I swear, this family needs a flowchart," said Sally.

Verity laughed and gave in to Olivia's squirming, bending to release her. The little girl paused long enough to give me and Thomas one last speculative look before racing off to join one of the clusters of children her own age, throwing herself into a knot of dragons and dragon princesses with gleeful abandon and no sign that she cared whether or not her playmates were human.

Verity straightened. "This parenting stuff is hard," she said. "I think it'd be hard even without the Covenant trying to kill us all. As it is, I'm constantly afraid they're going to find us, or that they'll get their hands on Olivia somehow."

Remembering the Covenant coming for Kevin, I said, "I know, sweetheart. I'm so sorry you're having to carry all of this."

Verity's façade of stoicism crumpled, and she rushed into my arms. I wrapped them tight around her, pulling her into an embrace.

"I'm sorry." I kissed the top of her head. "I'm so sorry."

"This is all my fault," she whispered.

I looked at Thomas, then at Dominic, waiting for one of them to tell me how to answer that. Dominic looked away. Thomas, on the other hand, moved closer, setting a hand on her shoulder.

"I could say the same," he said. She lifted her head enough to frown at him. "I didn't just leave the Covenant, I offended them. I turned down a good place and a good marriage to run off into the hinterlands with the descendant of traitors, and I denied them things they wanted. The insult of my departure, they could have forgiven. The offense of my survival—and worse, my happiness—was too much for them. They've been looking for an excuse to come after any descendants I may have left behind ever since."

"They tried to come for your dad when he was only a little older than Olive there," I reminded her. "Maybe you attracted their attention most recently, but this is on all of us, not just on you."

"I've been trying to tell her that, but she's not big on listening to her old babysitter," said Mary.

Verity straightened, wiping tears from her cheeks as she tossed a smirk in Mary's direction. "Let's be honest here, I'm not big on listening to anyone," she said. "But we'd be absolutely lost without you. I don't know how anyone raises a child without a full-time nanny on hand."

"Shelby was *not* delighted when you announced your pregnancy," said Mary. "She wasn't ready to give me up yet. And you won't be, either, when your turn comes."

"Annie's already said she's not going to have any kids, Elsie isn't dating right now, and I don't think we need to worry about Sarah," said Verity. "Shelby says she wants to stop at one until the war is over, which I think is wise. So unless the new girl already counts as family enough that you'd have to leave me to take care of her, I think I'm in the clear for now."

"Okay, wow, leave me out of whatever weird baby lottery thing you people are running here," said Sally, putting her hands up. "I, also, am not seeing anyone, having been trapped in a horrifying parallel dimension for the last twelve years, and even if I were, an unintentional pregnancy would be very unlikely to result, as I am an entire lesbian, and most trans women don't have high sperm counts unless they're *trying* to make a baby. Which any girlfriend of mine would not be doing with me if she knew what was good for her."

"Good," said Verity. "So see, Mary, you're going to be with us for a good long time."

Mary rolled her eyes but didn't look displeased.

"Are we staying here with you?" I asked. "Not that it's not lovely to stand around and chat, but Rose seemed to think we needed to get here sooner than later. We don't have papers for these two yet, and we haven't called Kevin or Jane."

"Oh!" said Verity. "Yes. You will be. We have a room all set up for . . . well, for two of you. We didn't know about Sally. Sorry, Sally."

"I'm the surprise younger aunt you never asked for," said Sally, sounding unbothered. "As long as I can get pizza and a pillow, and maybe a polearm if this is really going to be a war, I'm good."

"Oh, I have polearms," said Verity, brightly. "If you want to—"

Mary cleared her throat.

"—come and see them later on, after we get everyone settled in, that would be great," Verity finished, pivoting smoothly. She smiled at Mary. Mary didn't smile back.

"Sally can share our room," said Thomas.

Verity looked to me for confirmation. I nodded. Sure, privacy would have been nice, but it wasn't like I was going to be getting frisky in a building full of unfamiliar cryptids, at least one of my grand-daughters, and my newly met great-granddaughter. Given those fac-tors, privacy could honestly wait a little while.

"This way," said Verity, and beckoned for us to come with her as she made for another of the doors.

We followed.

Thirteen

"Family are the people who, at the end of the day, will find you a bed and welcome you home."

—Alexander Healy

In a repurposed slaughterhouse, surrounded by dragons and descendants

VERITY LED US TO a hall lined with glass-fronted doors. I assumed the rooms behind them had originally been the slaughterhouse offices, back when this place housed a functional business rather than a Nest of dragons and their allies. Paper had been taped across the glass, creating a fragile sort of privacy, but a few stood ajar, showing small rooms hastily converted into sleeping quarters. None of them were very personalized: this was a refuge, not a home.

"Sorry for the makeshift housing," said Verity. "We initially moved in here after the Freakshow burned down. Got a good deal from the dragons, and it only got better when they realized that this was going to keep happening for a while."

"Good . . . deal . . . What?" Sally looked to me and Thomas for an explanation.

She looked so baffled that I explained as we walked, "Dragons need gold to stay healthy. It's a biological requirement for them. That's part of why they used to come into conflict with humans, back in the day. A dragon's Nest is basically a bank with no tellers and no alarm systems, if you can get into it while the dragon's out scavenging for dinner. Since humans invented capitalism, dragons need money if they want gold these days. Which is why most of them have a reputation for being greedy penny-pinchers who will take the shirt off your back if you let them."

"This used to be the main Nest," said Verity. "Before we . . . well, before. It was standing empty after the dragons moved out. They didn't sell it because they thought they might want to bring their male children here when they got a little older, let them see the sky before they were shipped off to their eventual home enclaves. With the Covenant around, the next generation of dragons is probably going to spend most of their lives in caves for their own protection."

Thomas grimaced. "Even without the Covenant," he said. "If we're ever going to acclimate humanity to the idea that we're not alone in this world, it would be better to start with something nonthreatening, like the sylphs, rather than going straight to fire-breathing reptiles the size of city buses."

"Yeah, we've been there, and it didn't work out," said Verity. "So we moved all the employees from the Freakshow in here, and started getting settled. Then it became clear the Covenant was happy to play war of attrition with us, and the dragons started moving the boys up to join us."

"Why?" asked Sally. "If they were all underground before, isn't this less defensible?"

Verity didn't answer. The cold truth was that moving the children to the aboveground facility made sense if the dragons and their allies were trying to make sure some of the baby boys would survive if the adult male was found and destroyed. Having male dragons at all changed everything for their species, which could continue to reproduce parthenogenetically for an indeterminate period of time but couldn't make males without having one in the first place. They lost genetic diversity with every generation that was effectively cloned from the one before.

Verity's discovery of the male dragon under Manhattan had changed everything. And now the dragon princesses faced the possibility of losing him. Making sure their sons weren't in the same place as their father was probably the smartest thing they could have done.

"Anyway, there aren't many humans here, but we have two Madhura running the kitchenette, and it's still pretty safe to go for takeout if you're careful about it or go with Sarah," said Verity, stopping at one of the closed doors. "We have to watch ourselves, always, and we don't come back here through the front door unless we've secured the block."

"Did we put you all in danger today by showing up the way we did?" I asked.

"Mary wouldn't have brought you in if you had," she said, reassuringly, and opened the door to reveal the square, barren room on the other side. A queen-sized air mattress was shoved into one corner, and there was a desk and a dresser, both clearly from IKEA. Verity flicked the light on. It didn't make the room look any less industrial, but it did reveal the hole cut into the baseboard next to the dresser, allowing the mice a clear path into the room. Verity saw me looking, and smiled.

"The dragons didn't like us making modifications that could impact the eventual sale price of the building, but we had to if we wanted the mice to stop chewing their way out of the walls," she said. "This was faster, and it's easier to repair when we finally get to leave."

"This isn't open warfare," said Thomas. "How are we meant to help you?"

"I don't know," said Verity, sounding briefly exhausted. "But at this point, anything is going to be better than what we have going on. Standoffs are only fun in the movies."

"Do you know what kind of forces they have here?" asked Thomas.

Verity looked at him solemnly. "We don't have a full roster. The only person who *might* have been able to give us a better sense of the shape of things is Antimony, and she's been confined to Portland until this is over. Too many current field agents met her while she was undercover at Penton Hall, and they know Timpani Brown is a traitor. They'd be able to follow her right back to us."

That must have been Annie's alias while she was infiltrating the Covenant. I nodded, listening intently.

"Dominic and I have been laying as low as we can, mostly focusing on evacuations and support, for a bunch of reasons. Olivia's one of them. Turns out it's a lot harder to make myself jump off a building when I'm seven months pregnant." She rubbed the back of her neck with one hand, looking faintly ashamed of herself. "I'm still getting back up to my normal levels of disregard for my own safety."

Thomas shot me a look, while Sally snorted.

"Gosh, I never thought a death wish would be genetic," she said. "So you're doing support. Why does that mean you can't give us a head count?"

"Because we've been limited in what we can learn while still keeping off their radar, which is still our primary concern. Dominic and I were here the last time the Covenant showed up, and Sarah hurt herself pretty badly putting the whammy on their field team to make them think we were dead," she said bluntly. "Part of it involved convincing them I wasn't *really* a Price, I was some sort of hired impersonator. I damaged that false memory when I went and fought a Titanoboa on live television. They may have been having flashes of knowing things were wrong before they even got here, because one of the first things they did when they arrived was start rooting out cuckoo nests, since they knew, on some level, that mind control was a danger."

"So?" I prompted.

"So if any of them see us clearly enough to make a solid ID, that mental block may collapse completely," said Verity. "Meaning Sarah would have hurt herself for nothing, and they'd know they didn't just have another traitor on their hands, they had one who was working with one or more cuckoos. Right now, they think Dominic's dead. They're running protocols and processes he knows, and he can warn people when the Covenant is likely to be moving into their area. They find out he's alive . . ."

"They find out he's alive and they change everything," I concluded grimly. "Good reason."

"Plus right now, they're not profiling random blonde humans and attacking the ones who fit on the theory that they might be me," added Verity. "Based on what Dominic and Antimony know about their tech, we think they're using some sort of heat scanner to pick out nonhumans when they're looking for targets. Honestly, if we had half their tools for detecting cryptids, outreach would be *so* much easier. But right now, you can walk down the street and you'll be fine. If they figure out Dominic is alive and I'm the woman who was with him when he 'died,' too many innocent people could be at risk. We're minimizing casualties."

"Where's Sarah?" I asked abruptly.

"This time of day, probably Starbucks," said Verity. "She goes for coffee in the afternoon. She's the only one of us who can be absolutely sure of being safe. The Covenant still hasn't figured out how to track cuckoos, especially not if they're following human rules of behavior. They can carry anti-telepathy charms, but those can't help them differentiate cuckoos from humans with similar coloration, and New York has plenty of pale, dark-haired people."

"Their heat scanners don't find cuckoos?"

"Cuckoos run about eight degrees cooler than the average human. Most nonhuman bipeds run six to twelve degrees *higher*. At least for right now, the Covenant is looking for the hot people—and even if they weren't, their odds of finding a single cuckoo in the city would be less than one in a million. Most of the cuckoos in North America vanished a little over five years ago, when they tried to open a dimensional door and skip town. They didn't survive the process. Sarah may be the last cuckoo left in New York, and for once, that's not because of anything the Covenant did. So she gets the occasional break from being shut up in here with all the local minds she's actively attuned to, and we get coffee delivered once a day." Verity shrugged broadly. "It helps. Not enough, but . . . it helps."

"Right," I said.

"The dragons are focused on protecting the Nest, the bogeymen are focused on trying to batten down the hatches and hold the sewers, and all the other cryptid communities are doing their best to close their doors against the outside world. So we're not getting a lot of reports from the locals about the Covenant's movements. We know they're actively hunting all the time; they've caught a lot of the solitaries, and they keep patrolling every night, looking for anything 'deviant.' We've confirmed the existence of at least three field teams. There may be a fourth, or it may be members of the other three coming together in their off time to enjoy their favorite hobby, wrecking the lives of innocent cryptids."

"So that's what, twenty people?"

"Somewhere around that." Verity looked at me, letting me glimpse the naked fear in her eyes. "If you're thinking 'Twenty's easy, I carry twenty knives all the time,' stop. They're *dangerous*, Grandma. They travel in groups, they're trained killers, and they're *cruel*. They don't fight fair. They don't particularly care about collateral damage, as long as they can kill the people they think of as monsters. Most of the city doesn't know we're at war. Sure. That's how the Covenant *works*. They move in the shadows, they pretend ignorance is bliss and what you don't know can't hurt you, and they kill, and they kill, and they keep killing, because as long as they keep their heads down while they're doing it, people just write the deaths off as background noise!

"You haven't *been* here, Grandma, you haven't tried to comfort the people who've just lost spouses, or parents, or children. You haven't watched people trying to cope with the deaths of their loved ones when no one else seems to care. We may not have tanks rolling down Broadway, but this is war, and it only ends when the Covenant can say nothing inhuman is left alive in Manhattan. And when they do *that*, they start heading out into other places, to cleanse *those*, too! There's at least twenty of them, we don't know all their names, we don't know most of their faces, but they're here, and they're killing people, and we need them to stop. *I* need them to stop. And I need you to figure out

how you're going to make that happen, because my people are pretty
damn tired of dying."

She took a deep breath before turning toward the door. "I'll let you
get settled in. Come out when you're ready. Istas will show you around
the warehouse and make sure you know the escape routes and house
rules. Sally, it's nice to meet you. Grandma, it's nice to see you again.
Grandpa . . ." She hesitated, apparently not sure what she was supposed to say. The silence stretched like a piece of chewing gum, getting longer and longer and more and more fragile. Finally, she shook
her head, and said, "I'm glad you're not dead after all. And I'm glad
all of you are here. Really. We need the hands."

Then she was gone, leaving us alone in a situation that was very big,
very complex, and very not designed to be handled by my usual brute-
force methodology. Which explained why it was grinding her down
the way it clearly was. Of all my descendants, Verity was the most like
me in temperament. A problem she couldn't punch into submission
was a bit outside her comfort zone.

It wasn't much closer to my own comfort zone. Thomas was fifty
years out of time, Sally knew nothing about the cryptid world, and I
was joining a fight where knives and hitting weren't likely to be the
solution.

Wasn't this going to be fun.

I sat heavily on the edge of the bed, which sank a bit beneath me, revealing its origins as a piece of camping gear hastily press-ganged into
service as bedroom furniture, and bent forward, dropping my head
into my hands.

The bed rose as someone sat down next to me, and Thomas put a
hand on the small of my back.

"I feel rather as if I've just been dropped into the middle of a the-
atrical production with no program and no notes on what happened
during the first two acts," he said, sounding surprisingly unruffled.

I lifted my head, eyeing him suspiciously. "You're not upset?"

"Oh, I'm so upset that I'm astonished I can still draw breath," he
said, in a reassuring tone. "I left our infant son, and now his daughter
is old enough to have a child the age he was the last time I saw him."

"That wasn't him in the kitchen?" asked Sally.

I felt Thomas turn his attention in her direction. "I suppose it was,
but I have trouble wrapping my head around that fact. I've mostly

been cleaving to the idea that it proves he's still alive, and not dwelling on all the reality of what his age means. Alice was a surprise but not a shock. She still looks almost like she did when I had to leave her behind. I would have loved her no matter what. I still didn't have to make any major mental adjustments to look at her and see my wife. Looking at a grown man and seeing my son is a more difficult feat. Looking at a grown woman with a daughter of her own and a De Luca by her side—a De Luca! Now there's a family I never thought to see turn traitor— Well. That all takes a bit more adjustment."

I uncovered my face and sat up, looking at her. "I haven't missed nearly as much time as Thomas has—or as you have—but five years is a bigger jump forward than I usually make. I vanish for a year, maybe two. Not five. Not long enough for my granddaughter to get pregnant and have a daughter of her own, and probably decide I was dead. She's not going to evacuate. Even with a baby, there's no way we convince her to leave this city to its own ends, not when she feels responsible for what's happening."

"So your whole family's like this?" Sally asked.

I considered for a moment. "They're all different," I said finally. "But pretty much, yeah. I ran out on my children when they were too small to understand why it was happening. They couldn't tell me not to go. They couldn't come with me. All they could do was stay behind. And somehow that led to them growing up with this incredible determination never to leave family behind again. Verity is what she was raised to be, and she was raised by the people I broke, so I know where her cracked bits are. Yeah, they're all like this, to one degree or another. I haven't seen most of them in . . . well, in five years longer than I thought I had."

I barked a sharp laugh that threatened to become a sob, and Thomas shifted his hand from the small of my back to my shoulder, drawing me closer. I took another deep breath, looking for serenity. Looking for stability. Looking for anything other than the bone-deep exhaustion that threatened to rise up and overwhelm me.

"Think someone in this place has a sleeping bag I can borrow?" Sally asked. "No offense, and I trust you two not to get frisky while I'm in here, but I'm not sharing a bed with two people I'm not banging."

"Were you this picky in the bottle dimension?" I asked, halfway amused despite myself.

"Nope," said Sally. "Didn't have the luxury of pickiness when we were all huddling together for body heat, or when we couldn't spare the water for bathing more than once a month. You learn to put up with a lot. And you know what else you learn?"

"What?" Now the amusement was complete.

"You learn not to dwell on shit. The thing that tries to kill you today will try to kill you again tomorrow, and all you're going to do if you sit around thinking about it is give yourself an ulcer. I'm back in the real world."

"Technically, all worlds are real—" Thomas began.

"The *real world*," Sally repeated, more firmly. "I am in the place pizza comes from, I am almost certainly going to get to stab some people, I have clean socks, and you're intending to keep me, meaning I don't have to try to figure out how I'm going to explain any of this bullshit to the Hendersons. I loved them, I did, and they tried their best to love me, but they adopted me because their church told them Jesus wanted them to, and then I turned out to be gay and weird and not very interested in their version of God, and so they were already falling out of the habit of loving me when I vanished. I'm sure it was a relief to everyone but James when I went away. And if I spent all my time sitting around dwelling on that, I'd scream forever, so instead, I'm going to go get some damn *pizza*. Anyone coming with me?"

"I am." I stood. "Verity can't risk being seen, but if the Covenant spots me, they won't recognize me. Even if they do, they won't believe it. They may catch the Carew look. That's fine. Let them come after me, just as long as we don't lead them back here."

"Is this one of those situations where I would make things worse by insisting on coming with you?" Thomas asked.

I hesitated. "Actually . . . maybe."

He raised an eyebrow. "Do tell."

"One woman who looks kinda like she might be a Carew, but maybe not, walking with a Korean woman? Not that suspicious. A Carew and a Price, on the other hand . . ."

"They still hate us that much," said Thomas, and sighed. "I'll stay here, then, and get a better sense of the lay of the land."

"Good plan." I turned to Sally. "Ready for your pizza?"

Verity was in the main room, talking quietly with a cluster of dragons. She turned when Sally and I emerged. I waved her over, causing her to scowl briefly before she half-walked, half-trotted toward us.

"What is it?" she asked.

"Sally wants pizza, so we were going to go for a walk before we figure out how to take down the Covenant. What's the protocol for leaving the building?"

"Go out through the convenience store, try not to look suspicious while you're doing it, and call for Mary to meet you on the sidewalk and let you back in," said Verity. "If she doesn't show up within a few minutes, keep walking, and do a few circuits of the block before you try calling her again. If she doesn't come after the third time, take a walk. Get at least a mile away, then call her again. I'm guessing you don't have phones?"

We both shook our heads. Verity sighed.

"Okay, we'll add that to the list for tomorrow. Right now, it's just Mary for access for you. Or Sarah, if you see her, but you can't count on that. I really wish you wouldn't just wander off."

"But you're not telling us not to go."

"You're my *grandmother*. Do you think I could make that stick?"

I considered for a moment, then shook my head. "Not really. But I'm armed, we're both paranoid, and I want to get a vague sense of the atmosphere out there."

"All right," she said, reluctantly. "Just be as careful as you reasonably can, okay? I don't want to deal with Grandpa getting widowed when the two of you *just* got into the same place again."

I sighed. "I know I can be a little crabby sometimes, but I'm more careful than you people give me credit for. Even if I continue to hate that word and everything it stands for."

"Less talking, more pizza," said Sally.

"You heard her," I said. "Who am I to stand between a woman and her burning need for pizza? I even promise to do my best not to wander into traffic because I got distracted by all the shiny lights of civilization."

"You better," said Verity. "I want you all to meet Dr. Morrow while you're in town, but I'd like it to be a meet-and-greet, not an emergency surgery. I think you'll like him—and he's not going to ask questions about paperwork or insurance once he knows you're with me."

I lifted my eyebrows as I nodded approvingly. After everything we'd been through during our interdimensional travels, all three of us were overdue for a physical, and Verity was smart enough to recognize that. "Got it: save the car crash for after we've met your pet doctor. Ally?"

"Caladrius."

"Damn, you found a Caladrius?" They're almost extinct. Have

been for centuries. Something about the combination of being something that can be slaughtered for useful resources, and looking *almost*
human while being obviously *not* human annoyed the Covenant. The
fact that the almost-human thing they look like happened to align
pretty well with the modern church's depiction of angels probably
didn't help.

Probably.

"Two, actually," she said. "They're at St. Giles, and they'll be
thrilled to meet you."

"Great. You get all that, Sally?"

"Nope," said Sally. "There's so much, I'm not really getting much
of anything beyond 'If I promise to look both ways before crossing the
street, I can have pizza.'"

"That works for me," I said, and leaned over to give Verity a quick
hug before I started back toward the door we'd arrived through.

As before, it was unguarded, and the door wasn't locked, easily
letting us back out into the little courtyard. The dragon kids weren't
bouncing their ball anymore, having traded it in for piling themselves
into a heap of golden heads, almost like a hoard, with the long, reptil-
ian form of the young male curled proudly on top. They were giggling
sleepily, obviously pleased with themselves. I paused long enough to
look at them before heading on, Sally close behind me.

"The thing to remember about dragons," I said, once we were in
the short, private hallway to the convenience store, "is they look human, but they're not. They're people, and they deserve respect and
dignity, but they're not *human* people."

"Meaning . . . ?"

"Meaning those kids were probably following some deep-seated
instinctual pattern. I've seen adult dragons form piles like that my
whole life. Not normally with the big scaly one on top, but still, often
enough that I figure it's not something they *choose* to do so much as
something they'll just find themselves doing from time to time. And
it's perfectly normal."

"What . . . How does that . . . If that's a boy, and those are girls, how
does that even *work*?"

"Humans have an incredibly low degree of sexual dimorphism," I
said, and opened the door to the convenience store. "It's why we can
share sweaters and shoes and knives and such. Dragons have a very
high degree of sexual dimorphism. Enough so that for a long time, we
thought they were two separate species."

The convenience store was empty save for Pris, who was now

engrossed in a romance novel, barely seeming to pay attention to the shop she was supposed to be watching. She looked up when the door swung closed behind Sally and me, and got up with an exaggerated sound of irritation to cross over and lock the door.

"We'll hopefully be back soon," I informed her.

She scoffed but otherwise didn't acknowledge that I'd said anything at all. She walked back to her stool and sat heavily, retrieving her book from where she'd placed it face-down on the counter.

"Great customer service," said Sally.

I shrugged. "Cut her a break. She's dealing with some pretty heavy bullshit from the dominant species right now, and that means we're as likely to be enemies as allies, even after we've been vetted."

One corner of the dragon's mouth tugged upward in what might have been a quickly smothered smile. She still didn't look at us. I waved anyway as I left the store, Sally on my heels, and stepped into the balmy New York afternoon.

"Pizza?"

Sally's request was plaintive, and made my stomach grumble.

"We're in New York," I said. "No matter which way we go, there's going to be pizza within a block or two. So pick a direction, and we'll go that way."

Sally turned a slow circle before pointing in the direction that seemed to have the most people heading in it. "There," she said.

"Cool." I started walking.

Letting her pick the direction served two purposes. First, this way she was less likely to get mad at me if we had to walk more than a block for pizza. Second, living with weird-ass luck like mine has meant learning how to *manage* weird-ass luck like mine. If I'd picked the direction, we would probably have walked straight into a Covenant patrol, and I wasn't in the mood to deal with that just now. We'd have to face them eventually, but we could do it on the other side of pepperoni.

Sally huffed when we hit the end of the first block with no pizza in sight, only to light up like a Christmas tree when we saw the dollar-slice storefront halfway down the next block. I put a hand on her arm.

"Buddy system while we're outside," I said. "We stay together, got me?"

Sally sighed. "Yes, *Mom*."

"If you're going to call me that, we should probably be consistent about it, just so we don't confuse people more than we're already going to."

She turned and blinked at me, then snorted and kept walking. The smell of pizza was starting to drift down the sidewalk, washing everything else away. Hard to smell the city when you have a nose full of basil and melted cheese.

Inside, it was the sort of narrow, boxy space that New York specializes in, with a tiny waiting area and a counter running from one side of the room to the other. The guy behind the register looked like he'd been half-asleep before we arrived, probably due to the afternoon lull: there were only a couple of other patrons standing at the counter, eating slices off of paper plates. Sally ignored them. All her attention was on the glass case of pizza options.

They were pretty straightforward, generic, even: pepperoni, mushroom, plain cheese, and an "everything" pizza that was missing at least fifteen toppings I could think of off the top of my head. She was still staring at them like they were the most beautiful things she'd ever seen.

The clerk looked at us, disinterested. "What can I get you?"

"How many slices in a large pizza?"

"Eight."

I glanced at Sally. She was still staring at the pizza slices.

"Can I get a large pizza *box* with two slices of each kind you have in the case right now?"

The clerk shrugged, then nodded. He was a clerk at a dollar-slice place in Manhattan. He'd heard way stranger requests. "I'll have to charge you for a large pie."

Despite the name of the store, the slices were two-fifty each, rather than a dollar, although a sign on the case indicated that today's dollar slice was ham and pineapple—maybe explaining why that flavor was conspicuously absent. "That's fine. How much?"

"Twenty-two."

A two-dollar surcharge for a large pizza box seemed like a small price to pay. I fished twenty-five dollars out of my pocket and dropped it on the counter between us. "That sounds great."

He pulled a box from under the counter and began sliding slices deftly into it, creating a patchwork pizza in less time than it would have taken me to open the case. "You want me to heat this up for you?"

"If it's not too much trouble." Sally shot me a wounded look. I was keeping her away from the pizza. I patted her reassuringly on the shoulder. "This way it's nice and hot when you get it. I saw a drugstore back the way we came. We can stop and get you some Lactaid before you eat your body weight in cheese."

The clerk laughed, sliding our boxed pizza into an open oven that must have been more electric than contains-actual-fire. "You want a soda or anything with that?"

"No, just the pizza will be fine."

"Here you go." He pulled the pizza out of the oven, put the box on the counter, and pushed it toward us. "Have a nice day."

I handed the box to Sally before she could grab it and start cackling. "You, too."

Outside on the street, Sally glared at the closed box. "Lactaid is good for not getting horrible stomachaches and gas."

"Yes," I agreed, starting back toward the Nest.

"But not having it yet is bad for being able to eat pizza."

"If it's safe for us to go back inside right now, we can eat in our room. If it's not, we'll find a park or something and you can eat outside. This is New York. They have benches." Or they used to, anyway. It had been a few years since I'd been for a visit. My work didn't usually take me to big human cities.

The question of whether benches still existed kept me occupied as we walked, until we pulled up level with the drug store I'd seen before. "Can I wait out here?" asked Sally.

"Why?"

"Because I'm holding a whole-ass pizza, and I'd rather avoid jostling it more than I have to?"

I considered this, and decided Sally probably wasn't in any danger of attracting Covenant attention by standing outside a CVS for five minutes in broad daylight. This was New York. People loitered here all the time. "Okay. I'll be right back."

The drugstore was laid out the way drugstores have been for my entire lifetime, and finding Sally's Lactaid wasn't hard. I stopped off at the large cooler, snagging three bottles of cold Coca-Cola, then got into line to check out.

Things cost more than I was used to. Just those four items took more of my remaining cash than I liked, and I made a silent note to get more when I could, taking my paper sack from the clerk and heading back out of the store to the sidewalk.

Where Sally was not.

I blinked, very slowly, then turned in a slow circle.

She was gone.

Fourteen

"Raising daughters isn't hard. Just put locks on all the doors and windows, and never take your eyes off them."
—Jonathan Healy

On a sidewalk in Manhattan, trying to figure out how I'm going to explain this to Thomas

I TURNED AROUND AGAIN. Sally persisted in being gone.

There was no pizza on the sidewalk. If she'd been taken, it had been quick and clean enough that she hadn't dropped the box, which was probably a good indicator for her survival. I still didn't like it. I considered the virtues of yelling her name, and just as quickly abandoned them. Standing in a public place yelling is only the right choice if the goal is attracting as much attention as humanly possible. I didn't want that. So instead, I tucked the bag under my arm and stepped back from the curb, leaning up against the wall outside the drugstore like I was waiting for a friend.

"Hey, Mary, if you could swing by, that'd be great," I said, glad there was no one around to see me talking to the air. Sometimes it's better if no one catches you talking to yourself.

Mary came around the corner about ten seconds later, walking straight toward me. She didn't hurry or call my name, or anything else that might have attracted unwanted attention. Mary has always been even more dedicated to avoiding attention than I try to be. Her hair can make it hard for her, but she still likes to try.

"Hey!" she chirped, raising one hand in a wave once she was close enough that she didn't need to raise her voice. It looked just like any teenage girl spotting a friend. I spared a moment to admire how much better she'd gotten at playing "normal" over the years. When I was a kid, her impersonation of the living had left a lot to be desired. Now, if I didn't know better, I could almost believe it. "What's up?"

Once she was next to me, she lowered her voice and said, "I know Very told you to call before you came back, but she meant when you were back on the block. Unless you've seen something?"

"Nope," I said. "Sally was waiting outside with the pizza while I ducked into the drug store. She's not armed, as far as I know. I came back out, and she was gone. Pizza's gone, too, so if she was attacked, it was fast and the people who did it were dedicated to the idea that they didn't want to attract attention."

"Sarah just got back to the Nest, and she didn't see any Covenant nearby," said Mary. "Neither did I. The coast's been clear for most of the day. That's great for us, potentially terrible for whoever they're targeting instead."

"Since if we're not taking it in the teeth, someone is," I concluded. "I was only inside for about five minutes."

"That's a long time, in an abduction."

"I know. You said you could hear Sally, but she was a little muffled. Is she family enough for you to find her?"

Mary frowned. "That's a good question, actually. Adoptions are new ground for me, but whenever one of your weirdoes has gone off and gotten married, your spouses have eventually come into view, and I hear Thomas or Evelyn just as clearly as I hear you. James was muffled at first, but I can hear him perfectly well now. Poor kid's been through a lot." She closed her eyes, letting her chin drift toward her chest for several seconds before she opened them again and looked up at me. "Huh. She's not far from here, and she's not dead."

"That's a start," I said, relieved. Mary's ability to know where we were at all times had always been a tricky thing. When the crossroads were around, she'd been required to put them first, and that meant not helping directly without making a bargain—not generally something we wanted to consider for anything less than a life-or-death situation. And she wouldn't help find someone who'd asked to be left alone, which I'd learned by the time I started high school, and gleefully exploited to keep my father from tracking me down every fifteen minutes.

Sally didn't know to tell the family ghost not to tell us where she was. Mary couldn't see Sally's surroundings or anything like that, not without popping into the room and leaving me alone, but hopefully she could help me find her myself.

"Can you get us there?"

Mary hesitated before she nodded.

"Okay. Next question: can you let Verity know that Sally and I have been sidetracked a little, but it's no big deal, and we'll be there as soon as we can?"

Her eyebrows raised. "You want me to lie?"

"No, I want you to keep her from thinking something's wrong."

"Something *is* wrong."

"And if we don't keep her from realizing that, Thomas is going to come storming out to look for us, and then we'll have to deal with Thomas when he thinks someone he cares about is in danger. That's never been a fun time." Thomas had been more than willing to break laws, bones, and social norms when he thought I was in danger. If he thought Sally was in danger . . .

I was his wife and he knew I could handle myself in the "real world." Sally was effectively the first daughter he'd been allowed to keep and care for. I had no idea how many things he'd be happy to set on fire for her sake. I didn't want to find out the hard way.

Mary sighed, then said, "I'll be right back," and walked briskly around the corner, going back the way she had come. I remained where I was, leaning up against the drugstore wall and pulling the first Coke out of my bag. I was going to need the sugar to get through whatever happened next.

The formula for Coke has changed several times since nineteen sixty-five. I considered that as I sipped the fizzy brown liquid. I'd been drinking Coke on and off across the decades, and while every change had been a surprise, none of them had really been a shock. Watching Thomas experience the scope of them all at once was going to be hilarious.

If you can't treat your time-displaced husband as a comedy generator, who can you treat that way?

I watched the street while I drank my soda, looking for any sign that something out of the ordinary had happened here. I didn't know modern New York well enough to know whether the amount of traffic I was seeing was normal or not.

It would have been easy enough for someone to pull up, grab Sally, and take off with her, if she hadn't fought back. If she'd decided to get into the pizza before I came out with the Lactaid, her guard might have been down, but if that had been the case, why hadn't she dropped the box? Unless she had been lured away somehow, but that raised an even-bigger question: who would want to grab her? I had thought Sally would be safe because there was no way the Covenant could connect her with us yet, but what if it had been someone else? There were ways to make all this make sense. I just needed to find them.

I was still silently scanning the street when Mary came back around the corner. "Verity knows we're going to be a while, and she's telling Thomas not to worry," she said, voice low. "But if anything goes wrong, I'm going for backup immediately. You get that, right? This is not going to turn into some sort of ridiculous last-stand situation where you die because you don't want to call for backup. I wouldn't put up with it if Verity weren't already stretched so thin."

"I'm here to make things easier, not start trouble," I said, and pushed away from the wall. "Which way are we going?"

Mary turned a slow circle, then pointed. "That way."

We started walking.

I finished my Coke and tucked the empty back into the bag before passing it to Mary. She shot me a quizzical look. I flexed my hands.

"Unless you've changed tactics a lot, you're not a physical fighter," I said. "Hopefully I won't have to be, but if we have to extract Sally by force, I need my hands free."

Mary grimaced. "I wish that didn't make sense," she said. "Fine, I'll carry your stuff. But you could ask."

"Sorry."

She led us to a subway entrance, and we descended into the warm, urine-scented air. A group of transit police lounged against one of the station walls. They gave us the slow, lazy looks of people who knew they were in positions of unquestionable authority over everyone around them, and I barely managed not to bristle. Mary gave me an odd look. I shook my head.

"I don't like apex predators, that's all," I said. "Keep going."

"We'll need to get you a MetroCard," she said, and started toward a bank of machines, which had presumably replaced human ticket-sellers at some point. To my confusion, she walked past the first rank of them, not stopping until she reached the larger, darker-colored machines at the back.

"The little guys don't take cash," she explained, catching my expression. "Since you don't have a credit card yet—you don't have a credit card, right?"

"Right," I said.

"Since you don't have a credit card yet, we need a machine that takes cash."

"I thought you could use cash to pay for anything," I said, digging in my pocket for the remains of the money I'd squirreled away earlier.

"Technically, you can," she said. "As long as there's one machine that takes quarters, they can say that phasing out the majority of the cash machines isn't a classist attack on people who don't have stable jobs and the ability to maintain plastic money. Do *not* mention it to Antimony, she can rant for about an hour before she stops to catch her breath."

"Still passionate about everything that catches her attention?"

Mary laughed. "You have no idea." She looked at the crumpled bills in my hand—maybe thirty dollars, all told—and sighed. "May as well put it all on the card. You'll wind up using it if you're here for more than a few days, and a working MetroCard is never a bad investment."

"I literally have no idea what you're saying most of the time, and am just going along with whatever you tell me to do," I told her, feeding the money into the machine.

Mary laughed, only a little bitterly, as she leaned past me and punched a series of buttons on the screen. "I wish you'd been that accommodating when you were a kid."

"No, you don't." The machine whirred and spat out a small yellow rectangle. I pulled it loose. It wasn't flimsy like I would have expected, being made of some material that felt like it was halfway between a photograph and a piece of cardstock.

"Don't bend that, don't lose it," Mary said. "You'll need it to get into the subway." She dipped a hand into her pocket and produced a card of her own.

I blinked at it. She laughed.

"These things die every day," she said. "Finding the ghost of a Metro-Card isn't hard at all."

"I do not want to think about the theological implications of that," I said, and followed her to the turnstile, where we swiped our cards and proceeded deeper into the subway.

Apart from the machines, nothing had really changed since the last time I was here. The other passengers were disinterested in dealing with strangers; they sat well clear of us and stared off into space, or read their books or scrolled their phones with the laser focus of people who desperately wanted to be left alone. The transit police prowled through it all like hyenas looking for a weak antelope to bring down, and the trains arrived with a screech of brakes and a great rushing of exhaust and air. The smell was better than it used to be, but that wasn't hard.

Mary was leading the way, and for once, I was more than content to follow. She waited as several trains passed us by, before tugging me onto the 1 train heading for 34th Street. I looked at her curiously. She shrugged, and said, "Pretty sure she's in Koreatown."

"I don't know where that is." Or why Sally would have gone there, or what could have possessed her to take off the way she had, stealing the whole pizza and leaving me with nothing to tell Thomas.

"Don't worry. I do."

We didn't talk after that, staying silent for the nearly twenty-minute subway ride, until she rose, and I followed, and we disembarked into a station that looked both nothing and exactly like the first one. Manhattan subway stations have that feel to them. Every one of them is unique, designed to stand out in some way from its fellows, but the essential function of the space, and the endless passage of commuters, inevitably wears it all down to the industrial bones of the system. Gray concrete and dingy tile abound.

Mary led the way up a long, uneven stairway to the street, and when we emerged into the open air, no one gave us a second look. Unless we did something blatantly touristy, we'd never stand out, and even if we started gawking and pointing, we were close enough to the theater district that I couldn't imagine tourists were uncommon here. Mary didn't hesitate as she ploughed through the crowds and straight ahead, barely looking left or right. I grabbed her arm before she could walk into traffic, and she gave me a betrayed look.

"What?" she asked. "I'm going to Sally."

"Yes, and I'll die if I walk in front of a crosstown bus," I said. "So please remember that you have someone with you who isn't immune to traffic, okay?"

"Fine," said Mary, sullenly, and stayed on the curb until the light turned and gave us permission to walk.

When she started up again, she was moving even faster, forcing me to almost jog to keep up. It was fast enough that I didn't have the breath to ask her where we were going.

We whipped around a corner, and she made a beeline for a residential door crammed in between a loading dock and an accounting firm, the sort of tiny place that had a hand-painted sign in the window and probably got ninety percent of its business through direct referral. The sign was written in English and Korean, reflecting the character of the neighborhood around us. Most of the businesses I could see had similarly bilingual signs.

Mary tried the knob on the door and, finding it locked, turned to me. "She's in there," she said.

I eyed the door. It was metal, either steel or aluminum, with a pretty solid lock. Worse, it opened outward.

"I can't open that," I said. "Can you walk through and open it from the inside?"

"I can, but it might attract attention, so I thought I'd see if we could do it the living way first."

"Oh, because standing on a street out in the open, picking a lock, is way easier to overlook."

Mary rolled her eyes. "You don't have to be sarcastic," she said, and walked through the door, vanishing. A moment later, the interior door swung open and Mary undid the latch on the security door, pushing it far enough out for me to grab hold of the edge. "I know it's a talent of yours, but it's still impolite."

"Civility, absolutely my primary concern right now," I said, and stepped inside.

The hallway on the other side was narrow and dingy, and smelled distantly of a dozen unidentified fried things, all of which were probably delicious before they withered into the ghosts of meals past. Apartment doors lined the walls to either side. Mary walked ahead of me, head cocked, until she suddenly stopped, attention fixed on one door.

No way forward but through. I looked at her, exchanged a nod, and turned back to the door, raising one hand to knock briskly. Seconds ticked by. No one answered.

Well. That was going to be a problem.

I looked at Mary, eyebrows raised. "You sure this is the right place?"

"She's in there," she confirmed.

Right. I turned back to the door, took a step back, raised my foot, and slammed it into the door directly above the knob. The door shuddered but didn't give. I kicked it again, harder this time, and was rewarded by seeing it swing inward, the lock snapped in two.

Exterior doors are usually harder to kick down. Interior doors, especially in residential apartments, tend to be flimsy things, barely better than cardboard.

The room on the other side was small, square, and meticulously clean. It looked like the storage space for a rock-and-gem shop, the walls lined with geodes in a dozen shades of purple, rose, and gold.

Small tables held more, and the largest crystals sat directly on the floor, quartz spires jutting toward the ceiling. A small cluster of women occupied the center of the room, surrounding the velvet couch where Sally sat, her wrists and ankles zip-tied together, a furious expression on her face. She shot a furious glance at the door as it opened, only thawing a little when she saw me standing there.

The women followed her gaze, frowning in near-unison. I amended my first impression from "possibly not human" to "almost certainly not human," because they were all virtually identical. They could have been septuplets, pretty, Asian, young, and female, dressed in simple, well-worn clothes as meticulously clean as the room around them. Their hems had been patched in several places; I could see the worn spots along their seams. Frugal, inhuman, surrounded by precious minerals . . . right.

"Excuse me, ladies, but I believe my pizza has been misdelivered," I said, and stepped into the room.

The women fell back, none of them reaching for weapons or moving as if to defend themselves. This was weird. Sally, on the other hand, perked up, sitting taller on the couch.

"Alice," she said, with visible relief. She looked past me, and frowned. "Where's the boss?"

"Oh, I don't know, I thought you might like to ever be allowed out of his sight again, so I didn't tell him you'd been snatched the second I turned my back on you," I said. "If these nice ladies want to let you go, and maybe explain what the hell they thought they were doing in the first place, we might be able to leave without horrible violence."

One of the nice ladies threw a chunk of quartz at my head. I ducked, letting it hit the wall, and sighed as I straightened. "Or it could be time for the horrible violence."

The other women mostly looked dismayed as the one who'd thrown the rock grabbed a quartz spire and rushed for me. None of them had done anything they deserved to be shot for, yet, and so I stopped her with a kick to the chest, knocking her off balance and causing her to drop the quartz at the same time. She staggered. Before she could recover her balance, I grabbed her by the arm and yanked her against me, spinning her around so that her back was pressed to my chest. I let go of her arm and locked my own around her throat, pinning her in place, not quite cutting off her air.

"I'm not opposed to horrible violence, as a rule, but you seem like perfectly nice ladies, apart from the abduction of my adopted step-daughter, so maybe this is where you back down."

The woman I was holding tried to thrash. I put more pressure against her throat, and she stopped. Not a trained combatant, then. I could think of six ways to break my own hold, and most of them would have left me at a disadvantage.

"How'd they take you?" I asked.

Sally sighed. "Needle to the arm. Stung, then everything got blurry. Then I was in a van, and my pizza was gone." Her expression turned sour. "I really wanted that pizza."

"Well, if they've lost it, I have the Lactaid now, and by the way, you're not going anywhere unsupervised ever again."

"Going to be hard when I want to date."

"So we just make sure you date someone I approve of as proper supervision."

The women I wasn't in the process of choking out were starting to look more and more confused. One of them stepped forward, frowning at me.

"You know the representative of our cousins?" she asked.

I blinked. "This is genuinely outside my usual wheelhouse. Sally, you know these women?"

"I don't know any of my biological family, and that includes your cousins," she snapped, eyes on the woman who had spoken. "I'm not anybody's representative here."

"Sorry, miss, I think you have your familial relationships wrong," I said, as politely as I could manage. "If you'd just give her back, now . . ."

"But we saw her leave the Westerner's Nest!" protested one of the other women. "They allowed her inside! They allowed *you* inside, and you match them, gold and blue! They would never have allowed her inside if she weren't representing our cousins!"

Oh. Oh, no. This was starting to make sense. I loosened my hold on the woman who'd attacked me, looking at the quartz placed all around the room with new eyes. There was so much of it, and of course the most impressive pieces had managed to catch my attention first, but most of it was nowhere near as eye-catching. There were cardboard boxes of broken spires under the little tables and on the bottom shelves of the display cases, and even a few jars of what I guessed was probably quartz dust.

I turned my attention back to the woman who'd spoken first. "I know you," I said, trying to keep my tone respectful. "I know what you are, and I am so, so sorry."

Her face fell for a moment before snapping back into a mask of stern disapproval. "Why are you sorry? Our bloodline is as strong as any other. We never needed fire to hold our territory."

"No, you didn't," I agreed. "And I'm sorry because Sally's presence doesn't mean what you think it does. You have to have realized by now that she's as human as my friend and I."

"I'm not technically human anymore," said Mary amiably. I had almost forgotten she was there. "Side effect of being dead. I still qualify as a person, but when you're taking the census of humanity, I get shunted into a footnote."

The women were looking more and more confused. The one who seemed to have elected herself their spokesperson scowled.

"Of course we realize the girl is human. They still allowed her to enter their Nest. She *must* be affiliated with our cousins."

"She's not, though. She's mine," I said, almost apologetically. "My name's Alice Price."

The change in their demeanors was immediate. All of them looked panicked, and the one I was holding started to squirm for the first time, forcing me to tighten my hold if I didn't want her to break free.

"Price?" hissed their spokeswoman. "As in, a servant of the humans' foul Covenant?"

"Not for a few generations now." I let go of the woman, shoving her away from me. She staggered, nearly falling down, and ducked behind the others while she caught her breath. "We're more into conservation these days. We've been working with the dragons to help them navigate the current situation in the city. Am I guessing correctly that you're yong?"

The spokeswoman narrowed her eyes. "Do not speak our name," she snapped.

"Fine. Korean dragons, then, if you'd prefer it."

She stood up straighter, still glaring. "We are a Clutch of same," she said. "We stand for what has been destroyed."

"Well, right now, you stand as kidnappers and wasters of pizza, and I'd like Sally back, if you don't mind terribly."

"They let her *inside*."

"That seems to be where I'm losing you." I didn't know how much the yong knew about the situation with the dragons, but given how open a secret William had become since Verity discovered him, I was reasonably sure they had some idea what was going on. I took a deep breath. "I'm guessing you've been watching the Nest because you know they found a male."

"*Their* extinction is delayed while ours yet looms, and by what right? They were the ones who failed to contain the danger in its infancy, when it might still have been stopped from traveling to our lands and slaughtering our husbands," snapped the spokeswoman. "If anyone deserves to find a mate for their Clutch, it's us."

"I'm sure every breed of dragon left in the world feels that way," I said. "I know a laidly worm who would give anything to find a male of her species. She's living with the European dragons in Southern California, helping them negotiate the purchase of a husband for their Nest." I paused. "Laidly worms are a lot closer to European dragons than yong are. If she can't share a mate with the dragons around her, you couldn't either."

"But they could give us *access* to him," said the spokeswoman, sounding frustrated. "He might be able to answer our questions, might be able to . . . If a male of *their* breed has survived, who's to say others haven't done the same? Who's to say one of *our* men doesn't lie dreaming in the deep caverns of the earth, waiting for his wives to come and wake him?"

"Oh my fucking—this is because you want to get *laid*? By a *dude*?" Sally was feeling better. She bucked against her bonds, trying to break free of the zip ties. It was a futile effort. I admired it all the same. "Heterosexuality is not a legal requirement! You can be a perfectly happy lesbian if you just give it a try!"

"Many of our number take comfort in the arms of their kin," said the spokeswoman. "Unless you suggest we lie with humans . . . the thought is repulsive. Mammals stink of their primate origins. We are above them in all ways."

"European dragons don't get into relationships with humans," I said, pulling a knife from my belt. "I guess Korean dragons don't either."

"The thought is repulsive," the spokeswoman repeated. "To sully ourselves by . . . No. Better to live celibate, and raise our daughters to do the same."

Sally looked deeply confused. "I think we have a different definition of the word 'celibate' here," she said.

"Again, knowing more about European dragon biology than Korean, I'm guessing a bit, but the European kind reproduce parthenogenetically in the absence of males," I said, holding up the knife for the clustered yong to see before gesturing toward Sally with my free hand. "You mind if I take my kid back? Because we're pretty attached to her, and I don't want this to get uglier than it already has."

It made sense that the other types of dragon, upon hearing William existed, would start asking questions about where they could get their own handy-dandy species-saver of a boyfriend, and most of them wouldn't be in Osana's position. She lived with the dragons. She shared their Nest. She knew they weren't hiding any secret knowledge about a hidden laidly worm drake.

I would have felt bad for the yong, if they hadn't announced themselves by abducting Sally and generally behaving like bad neighbors.

When none of them moved to stop me, I eased my way toward the couch and sat down next to Sally, bending to cut the zip tie on her ankles first. Freeing her hands wouldn't do much good if she'd been disarmed, and while the yong might have made some big mistakes in grabbing her, I didn't think they'd be quite stupid enough to let her keep anything that looked like a weapon.

Also, I had no idea what weapons Sally did or didn't carry when she didn't have her beloved spear. I'd have to talk to her about that. A lady should never be out in public without at least four knives, and preferably a few more innovative items.

"Partheno-what?" asked Sally.

"The females get pregnant whether or not they've had sex with a male," I said, and cut her hands free.

Sally stared at me as she rubbed her wrists, clearly equal parts fascinated and appalled. "So what, like a whole species that operates on virgin birth?"

"Several species, when you take them all together, and yeah, pretty much," I said. "The Covenant killed the males for the crime of being big-ass lizards who stood out and had the potential to raze entire settlements in a fit of pique. The females got away because they looked enough like us to be ignored."

I looked back to the yong spokeswoman. She wasn't glaring anymore. If anything, she was looking lost, standing where she was, the others arrayed behind her like they thought she could somehow provide them with cover.

"I'll speak to the current Nestmother and see if she can arrange a meeting for you," I said. "But I'm not making any promises. She may say no; William may not know anything. Either way, kidnapping is not the way to get what you want. Do you understand me? I realize you're desperate, and I know you're scared, and if you touch any one of us again, none of that's going to matter, because I'm going to make sure you don't do it a third time."

"Your *Covenant*"—the yong spokeswoman all but spat the name—"is in our city. They stalk our streets, they take whoever they find. Does your prohibition against abductions apply to them as well?"

"I don't get to tell the Covenant what to do, or this would be a very different world," I said. "Wish I did, absolutely do not. But I'm here to make them go away if it can possibly be done. Stop getting in the way."

Something inside her seemed to snap when I said that. She sagged, sinking inward on herself, and the other yong hurried to hold her up, all of them watching us unhappily.

"Where's Sally's pizza?"

"We disposed of it," said one of the other yong. "We intended to feed our cousin's representative properly, once she was done protesting our relationship and claiming not to know what we were."

"Sorry you got the wrong girl," said Sally, standing and moving so that she was as close to me as possible without actually making contact. She was still rubbing her wrists. They must have tied them tighter than was good for human circulation. I shot them a short, sharp look, and they had the good manners to look chagrined, although that might have had something to do with the knife I was still holding.

"Is this a good place to find you?" I asked.

The spokeswoman nodded. "This is our home." She looked to the door, lip curling slightly as she added, "But it will need some repairs, unless you're a carpenter as well as a homewrecker."

"Nope," I said. "I break things, I don't repair them, as a general rule. Call it payment for the pizza and kidnapping. I'll be back if I'm able to arrange a meeting for you. Sally, you ready to go?"

"Yeah," she said, and glared at the yong as she followed me to the door, where Mary was waiting.

Together, the three of us made our way out of the building, where Mary looked at Sally, sighed, and said, "Think you can manage not to get kidnapped again? I need to get back, the baby's having a meltdown about not wanting to take a nap."

"I'll do my best," said Sally solemnly.

"And I can manage navigating the subway," I said.

"Good." Mary vanished.

"So what happened?" I asked, as we started walking.

Sally glanced anxiously around. "Isn't it dangerous to talk about this stuff . . . you know, out in the open?"

"Don't give away anyone else's secrets, don't say addresses out loud, especially not when there might be vulnerable people there, but talking, in general? That's fine. Humans are notoriously bad at listening. It's a side effect of being the dominant species for too long. We're so complacent that whenever we hear something that doesn't fit into the way we know the world works, we tend to ignore it."

"Oh." Sally looked down at the sidewalk. "As soon as you went inside, they pulled up in a van, and they surrounded me, talking loudly about how nice it was to see me again, how much they'd missed me, how it wasn't safe for me to be out on my own, all sorts of stuff that didn't make any sense. I was trying to figure out how to tell them they had the wrong girl when there was a needle in my arm and everything got fuzzy and weird. I woke up in that apartment."

"That tracks." If anyone had seen Sally getting snatched, they might have called the police, but seeing two young Asian women helping a third into a van probably wouldn't have raised any alarms, and given there had been no one there when we arrived, I was willing to say that her abduction had gone frustratingly unnoticed. "One question, though: if they were so sure you were working for a group of theirs, why bother to knock you out before putting you in their van?"

"They kept asking me questions in Korean, and they switched to English when they realized I couldn't understand," said Sally. She shrugged. "I didn't answer them. I think they were starting to get a little annoyed with me before you showed up. Is this sort of thing going to happen often? Because I can't say I'm a fan."

"Word," I said, agreeably, and together, we descended into the subway.

Fifteen

"Holding on too hard is a fine strategy if you don't mind potentially losing everything."

—Laura Campbell

Manhattan, heading toward a former slaughterhouse filled with dragons, so a pretty normal day, really

THE SUBWAY RIDE WAS easy and uneventful, once we figured out how to swipe my card twice to get us on the train and which direction that train needed to be going. "Uptown" and "Downtown" were intuitive for the locals, not so much for us. We got off when we reached the Meatpacking District, and I led Sally back to street level, my sack of Lactaid and now-warm Coke tucked underneath my arm.

"I don't think we have enough money for a second pizza, but we can grab you a slice if you'd like," I offered.

Sally sighed. "Do I come off like a wimp if I say that at this point, I just want to lock myself in a bathroom and have a nice, ordinary panic attack where no one can see me falling apart? I'm freaked out and exhausted."

"Of course not," I said. "Let's get you home."

We walked all the way to the grungy convenience store that served as an entrance, stopping outside to lean against the wall, where I muttered, "Hey, Mary, if you could come and let us in, that would be real cool."

"How long do we wait?"

"Give it about five minutes. That should be long enough for her to extricate herself from putting Olivia down for her nap, and not long enough to make anyone suspicious about us hanging around out here." I pulled one of the warm Cokes out of the bag and passed it to Sally. "Drink this if you need something to do with your hands."

Sally sniffled, twisting off the cap. "You don't have to be so nice to me, you know."

"Kinda do, though, since my husband adopted you while I wasn't looking, which makes you my family, too. And massively effective skin-care regimens aside, we both know you're young enough to be my *granddaughter*, so 'daughter' is only a stretch when we're talking to normal people." I shrugged, brick wall scratchy against my skin. "I fucked up having kids of my own. If Thomas wants to give it a go, I'm not going to get in the way, and that means I *do* have to be nice to you, if only so we're not all miserable all the time."

Sally looked at me as she took a sip of warm Coke, eyes wary. Finally, she said, "You mean that."

"Life's too short to go around saying things I don't mean."

"Says the twenty-year-old octogenarian."

"I said life was *short*, not that life was *logical*."

Sally was still laughing when Mary came rushing out of the convenience store and grabbed me by the wrist. "Verity needs you," she said, pulling me sharply toward her.

Sally stopped laughing.

I dug my heels in and pulled my arm out of Mary's grasp before she could pull me *into* the door, which she hadn't bothered to open on her way out of the store. "You're forgetting to stay solid," I said, voice sharper than I meant it to be. "What's going on?"

"We'll explain everything once you're inside," said Mary, and beckoned for us to follow as she ducked back through the door, still not bothering to open it.

"See?" I said to Sally, as I opened the door and followed Mary into the convenience store. "People don't pay attention. We've been at the top of the food chain for too long. We got complacent."

"Stop talking and come on," said Mary, grabbing my arm to haul me along. She felt only half-substantial, like a cloud of thick, icy fog. I blinked. While walking through walls and doors and the like was pretty standard procedure for her, and something she was more than happy to do when asked, she was usually either fully solid or fully intangible, not hanging out in whatever weird in-between state she was presently occupying.

She tried to undo the locks on the door. Her hands went right through them. She swore, trying again, with the same effect.

"Mary," I said, voice as level as I could make it despite the swelling panic, "you need to focus. Think about the kids. Think about *me*. We need you solid."

She shot me a desperate glance, and I realized the dragon who'd been behind the counter every other time we'd come through here was gone. We were alone.

Mary took a deep breath and tried for the locks again, this time undoing them with the normal amount of resistance. She shoved the door open and rushed through. We followed her.

"Is she going to explain?" asked Sally.

"Eventually."

The short hall was empty. The courtyard was similarly deserted, save for the red rubber ball, which had rolled to a stop in one corner. Somehow, that was the most unnerving thing of all: seeing that ball abandoned, bereft of the children who had been playing with it.

Mary gave me one last, despairing look, and opened the door into the slaughterhouse. We followed her through.

The semi-reassuring hum that meant a Johrlac who was already attuned to my mind was on the premises kicked in as soon as I was inside, and I looked around the chaos that the slaughterhouse had become, scanning for a familiar black-haired figure. I didn't see her.

What I *did* see was several dozen dragons, adults and children, all of them shouting at one another like they thought they could somehow yell the world back into making sense. The Inuit woman I'd seen before was pacing, a lacy parasol over one shoulder and a fierce glower on her face; she had been joined by the man whose lap she had been sitting in. He was following a few steps behind her, looking worried.

Verity and Dominic were at the center of one of the clusters of dragons, both talking rapidly, although I couldn't hear them over the din. Dominic had Olivia against his hip and was bouncing her as if he could distract her from the fact that all the adults were yelling. Mary flickered out, reappearing next to him and taking the toddler out of his arms. She was always solid when there was a small child involved. Her sometimes-erratic relationship with physical reality didn't struggle that much.

Dominic promptly turned in our direction, touching Verity on the elbow to get her attention. She straightened, and the two of them walked away from their conversational partners, heading toward us at a fast clip. Some of the dragons stopped yelling to watch them go, and more than a few glares were cast in our direction.

Okay, this wasn't good. And maybe that was stating the obvious, but it's never once been a positive thing when I come back from a shopping trip to find the world cast into chaos. I crossed my arms and frowned at the pair of them.

Verity stopped a few feet away, sighing and dragging one hand through her short blonde hair. The gesture caused it to stick out in all directions, like a startled hedgehog.

"Grandma," she said. "We have a problem."

"Got that from the yelling," I said. "Where's Thomas?"

"That's not—"

"I swear to God, Verity, I love you more than I love myself, but I just spent fifty years looking for that man, and if you think I'm going to be okay with stepping into this much of a cacophony and not knowing where he is, you don't know me very well." I glared at her. "So I *know* you weren't about to tell me his location wasn't important."

"I was—" she began, before catching herself and admitting, "I was about to say it wasn't important. You got me. I promise, he's safe. I just need to talk to you."

"About what? What the hell is going on?"

"You left," said Dominic. "You didn't return, for much longer than your errand could explain. Sarah came back with the coffee and said she hadn't picked up any traces of you during her walk. And about that time, Cara was supposed to be showing up with a group of children."

That was a new name. I presumed "Cara" was either another dragon or an ally; either way, it wasn't as important as the fact that she apparently hadn't shown up. "How was she transporting them?"

"Dry-cleaning van full of cheap old rugs," said Verity. "We have a few underground access points to William's cavern. Park there, load the kids into the back, pile blankets over them in case the van gets pulled over, and then drive them to the pickup spot. We roll the boys inside the rugs, then carry them in that way while the girls walk."

"Uh-huh. And are you using the same routes regularly?"

"We're not *amateurs*, Grandma. We've been rotating through eight different routes, and we never do a pickup run the same time twice. This was routine. It should have gone off without a hitch."

"Except that it didn't." I shook my head. "Sally and I were late because we got nabbed by a Clutch of yong who knew you had boys in here. They don't want one—wrong species, it wouldn't help them with their genetic bottlenecking—but they want access to William—"

"Absolutely not," snapped a nearby dragon. She had clearly been listening in, and just as clearly wasn't sorry about it. She shook her head, expression a twisted mask of disapproval. "Our husband is not some sideshow attraction to be shared with every cryptid who expresses an interest."

"They're a sister species whose continued existence may depend on them finding a male of their own," I said, soothingly. "If there's any chance William knows something about where any surviving yong males might be hiding, they deserve to know."

"We've asked him about other Western dragons, and about laidly worms, but we haven't asked about yong, long, or Tatsu," Verity admitted, slowly. "I knew there were some clusters of their females left, but it hasn't been a priority, with everything else that's been going on."

"Well, it's a priority for *them*," I said. "Regardless, they knew this was your Nest, and they knew where the door was, well enough that they were watching and followed us when we came out. You've been being careful. 'Careful' doesn't mean 'flawless.' If the yong could find you, who else could?"

"Humans can't tell us apart," said the dragon who'd objected to the idea of giving the yong access to William. "They could never have figured out which one was Cara."

So Cara was a dragon: got it. "And have you been counting on that?" I asked, even as Verity turned to stare at her. "Very, how much of your operation security has been down to the dragons?"

"About half," she admitted. "People are usually more careful when their children are involved."

"Says the woman who strapped our daughter to her chest and leapt off several buildings before I could stop her," grumbled Dominic.

I decided to ignore that. "Say the Covenant has been watching this place, whether because they had reason to suspect something was happening here, or because it's in a range they're surveilling for cryptid activity in general," I said. "It's easy to fall into the trap of thinking that it only matters if they see me or Verity, because of that 'Carew look' that Thomas likes to go on about. But we're not the only ones here. It's a little odd to have this many blonde women who look like sisters living in the same place. Even if they didn't know for sure whether or not you were human—even if they hadn't been using their little temperature scanners—there are ways of telling people apart, no matter how similar they look. Even cuckoos have distinguishing features. Sure, most humans can't tell dragons apart facially, but do you all have the exact same hairstyle? Because I'm looking around this room, and I can tell you with reasonable certainty that you don't. I could tell you apart, and I've been here less than a day."

The dragon looked flustered. I turned my attention back to Verity. "I'm guessing this Cara never showed up."

"No." Verity shook her head. "She's missing, along with five of the little boys and three of the little girls."

How many male dragons did they have? It seemed rude to ask, under the circumstances, but we were definitely going to have a discussion about birth rates when this was over. "So I'm guessing all the yelling is because of the missing kids, and nothing else has gone wrong?"

"Some of them were sure the two of you had to be involved, and are threatening to have all the humans and human-lovers expelled," said Verity. "Grandpa is trying to talk down the people in charge, since they're *really* sure he must be involved."

"They've never trusted me," said Dominic. "For them, once Covenant is always Covenant, and he's a figure out of their bedtime stories. Some of them believe Mr. Price carried the Covenant to these shores in the first place."

"Uh, our family was already here when Thomas showed up. We had a two-generation head start on him," I said, while Verity elbowed him lightly.

"He's your grandfather-in-law," she said. "You don't have to call him 'Mr. Price.'"

"I would be uncomfortable with that degree of familiarity when I've just met the man," said Dominic, voice going stiff. "He may be a traitor, but his research is still taught in the Covenant. He was a trailblazer in his time, and his rank upon leaving the organization was higher than my own. He deserves my respect."

"He deserves your respect, and my support," I said. "Verity, if he's trying to convince people of his innocence, I should be there. Where is he?"

"You're just going to make things worse, Grandma."

"I can be diplomatic."

She snorted, then caught herself. "Oh. You're serious."

I scowled at her. "I *can*. Now where, exactly, is your grandfather?"

She sighed. "Through here," she said, and motioned for me to follow her to a door.

Sally followed me, and we left the chaos behind us.

Well, we left *that* chaos behind us, anyway. There was more chaos on the other side of the door, in the form of a variety of angry cryptids, all of them yelling at once, and several more frantic dragons looking for somewhere to direct their furious energy. Verity brushed by them all with soft apologies, and Sally and I followed along behind, and for a moment, it looked like we might actually go unchallenged.

Then a skinny woman with grayish skin stepped in front of us, putting her hands up to signal Verity to stop. "Come on, Verity, you know better," she said. "This is not a meeting for humans."

"But it's a meeting *about* a human, and I have evidence that supports his innocence," she said, indicating me and Sally. "They came back. They didn't sell us out to the Covenant. They wouldn't have bothered coming back here if they'd been expecting this sort of a welcome. Come on, Kitty, you know me, and you know my family. Did you really think my grandfather was somehow behind this?"

"Your grandfather is an urban legend as much as he's a man," said the bogeyman who had stopped her, whose name was apparently Kitty. Kitty gave me a wary, sidelong look at the same time. "If anyone could betray us and tell his own wife to walk right back through the doors into the hornet's nest, it would be him. He already betrayed the people who raised him."

"If you mean the Covenant, he knew he was going to betray them from the moment he grew into his sorcery and started setting things on fire," I said. "And it's pretty clear he wasn't unusual for the Price bloodline. Even if sorcery doesn't show in every generation, they put so many protections on the family fortune that it's a miracle *anyone* can get to that money. They were expecting one or another of their descendants to wind up on the outside eventually, and they took what steps they could to make sure whoever it was would be okay when that happened. I, on the other hand, have never betrayed anyone, and if you don't want me to demonstrate exactly how poorly I think of you casting aspersions on my husband, you'll let us into the room."

Kitty frowned. "And this would be . . . ?"

"Alice Price," I said, voice flat. "Verity's grandmother."

"And I'm Sally," said Sally, helpfully. "Alice's stepdaughter. Sort of. It's complicated, I think I've been adopted. I haven't betrayed anybody, either, if that's something we're worried about all of a sudden."

Kitty blinked, looking at me with new respect—and no small amount of fear. You don't get rid of a reputation like mine just by deciding you're going to retire and be a good citizen from now on, no matter how much I might wish the world worked that way.

"So, since it sounds like you have my husband behind that door, it would be awesome if you could let us through of your own free will, before I have to make you let us in *against* your will," I said, almost cheerfully, and with a visible swallow, Kitty stepped aside and let us pass.

Verity moved to put herself ahead of me again, maybe concerned that I was going to stab the next person who got in my way, and pushed the door open, revealing a room almost identical to the office we were going to be using as our "bedroom" for the duration, save for the absence of the bed and the inclusion of a folding table. Several dragons were standing around it, all of them attempting to interrogate Thomas at the same time. Thomas, for his part, was looking at them calmly, with no sign that he was disturbed in the slightest by their behavior, hands folded neatly behind his back.

Verity pulled in a small, sharp breath. I gave her a curious look. She shook her head. "Annie stands just like that when she's mad at us," she said, voice low. "I just didn't expect that kind of family resemblance."

"It's like we're related or something," I said.

The telepathic hum had gotten louder as we worked our way deeper into the building, and in this room, it was so loud that I almost couldn't focus on anything else. I frowned, looking around the room, but saw no sign of Sarah. What I did see was a bunch of highly upset dragons who seemed to have decided that blaming Thomas for all their problems, back to the dawn of time, was going to make those problems go away.

If I still couldn't see Sarah, she was actively shielding herself as hard as she could. I did inherit some of my mother's resistance to Johrlac influence, which meant that for her to stay unseen, she had to really be focusing on her shields. She was upset, probably because everyone else was upset, and it's hard for telepaths to avoid that sort of thing.

No way was I going to stand by while these people upset my granddaughter and blamed my husband for things that weren't his fault. I stepped over to his side, close enough that our shoulders were brushing, and smiled a bright, unnerving smile at the dragons around the table. "Hi," I said, voice bright and a little vacant, the way it had been when I was a children's librarian who didn't want to worry anyone. "It looks like you've started without me. Oopsie. I'm Alice, this nice gentleman's wife, and he's not a traitor, and we're not the ones who led the Covenant to your doorstep. You did that just fine on your own by making speciesist assumptions about humans, which is a reasonable thing to do, since we're kind of awful sometimes, but works against you when you never take other factors into account."

The dragons looked at me blankly.

"Humans are primates. It's part of why we have such a wide range of facial diversity across the species; we evolved from animals that form strong social bonds, need to be able to avoid accidentally impregnating a direct descendant, and tend to travel in groups. We recognize each other almost purely visually, with no dependence on scent cues or psychic signals. That means even closely related humans will have some morphological differences, to help us tell each other apart. Dragons aren't all identical, but your differences are more subtle than ours, so sometimes we can be assholes and mistake you for one another. And then you assume we're incapable of telling you apart. But humans will even figure out ways of telling cuckoos apart, if you give us enough time, and the Covenant team that's been watching the area has had plenty of time."

"Then how do you explain them attacking just as you arrived?" demanded one of the dragons.

I shrugged. "Shitty coincidence? The universe trying to make sure everything happens at once so we don't get too comfortable trying to deal with it? The Covenant being smart enough to move when they saw an opportunity? *If* they saw us show up—and that's a big 'if,' but that doesn't mean it didn't happen—then they may have thought this was their best shot at acting without attracting the attention of the whole Nest."

"Why?" asked another dragon.

"I don't know!" I threw my hands up. "I can't speak for the Covenant. I was never a member. I've never been in one of their strongholds. But I know they're reasonably clever people, or they wouldn't have been able to keep causing problems for this long, and they would be aware that new people coming into an established group almost always leads to a period of adjustment. Strike during that period, and your chances are better than if you wait for things to stabilize. One thing's for sure: you've all been complacent and arrogant."

"I don't like your tone," said the first dragon.

"Well, *I* don't like the fact that one of the first things Verity said to me was that the Covenant could use temperature sensors to pick you out of a crowd, and you're all clustered here in a target-rich environment, and there's no possible way the Covenant hasn't flagged at least one of you coming or going. They haven't attacked because they don't know Verity and Dominic are in here, and because someone let slip about your husband. They must be hoping you'll lead them to him."

The dragons looked collectively horrified. Finally, in a stiff tone, one of them said, "That's a wild accusation."

"Is it? Because I just met a group of yong who knew you had a male of your species somewhere in this city, but not exactly where. And the dragons in Los Angeles know about him. It was the biggest secret possible. You can't be blamed for not keeping it perfectly."

The dragons muttered but didn't say anything. I took that as a good sign.

"Look," I said. "They probably think they could wipe you out whenever they wanted. Sometimes the thing to do with a nest of vipers is to leave it alone, since at least then you know where they *are*. You can always come back and clean it up when the time is right. Your husband, though? He's a much bigger, better target. They're trying to find their way to him. They've probably been watching for weeks to see how you're getting the kids in and out of here, and today was just the day they decided to strike." I didn't know much about how route-witches viewed time, but if they could bend it like they did distance, even a little bit, the timing of this attack explained why Apple had been in such a hurry to get us out here.

A little warning would have been nice.

"Cara will never talk," said one of the dragons, hotly.

"Can you say the same about the kids?" I asked. When none of them said anything, I asked, "Does this Cara do the pickup runs very often?"

"She's our primary driver," said another dragon.

"Okay," I said. "Look, we know the Covenant has been looking for you. It's pretty clear at this point that they know about William, or they know that people *believe* in William, and they've been hunting for dragons. That part isn't conjecture. We know that's happening. So if they've been trying to find dragons, what makes you think having identical physiognomy was going to be enough to keep you anonymous and safe here? Sure, they can't tell you by your faces, but they can recognize you by your hair. By your favorite jacket. By your *shoes*."

Hair is actually a lot more important than most people want to think it is. Mine had always served me as a form of camouflage, long and tidy when I was playing the good little children's librarian, short and styled with a literal knife when I was trying to convince the universe that I was a badass bounty hunter who could handle anything it wanted to throw at me. Maybe it's the shallow human in me, but if I can put the right costume on, I can play the role.

"Sally and I were snatched by a group of yong when we went out for pizza." So much for not letting Thomas know what had happened. Out of the corner of my eye, I saw him turn to stare at me. "Okay, well, Sally was snatched, Mary and I tracked her down." Good thing she'd already declared herself family and hence trackable through phantom means. "They were watching the door before we got here. When they saw Sally, they assumed she was the representative for a different Clutch of yong who'd been allowed access to your Nest for some reason, and they didn't approve."

"If you were going to let me in, they thought you should be letting them in, too," said Sally. "They kinda sucked."

The dragons were getting visibly upset. "They shouldn't have been poking around here," said one of them, sharply. "They had no right to take you."

Several of the dragons nodded, and it was clear where their thoughts were trending. I decided to cut this off before they could get all the way around to declaring some sort of draconic feud against the local yong Clutch. As badly off as European dragons tended to be in the modern, human-dominated world, all the other kinds have come off even worse, which is sort of funny when you consider that it was European dragons who inspired the creation of the Covenant in the first place.

Sometimes the world puts a concerted effort into not being fair.

I turned my attention on the dragon who'd spoken. "Look. I don't think the yong are working with the Covenant, but I think the Covenant saw them create a potentially serious diversion by snatching someone who'd come out of your shop, and so they moved while they thought there was a chance the people here might be distracted. They may have used the yong to serve their own ends. That doesn't make the yong traitors to the rest of the cryptid world."

"I'm sure you're unsurprised to hear that I agree with Alice," said Thomas. "In this case, it's not because of her tactical analysis of the situation, but because of my own experiences with my former employers. They'll have changed some of their tactics in the last fifty years, absolutely, but they won't have changed them enough to voluntarily work with *any* sort of dragon, whatever their origins. All of your myriad breeds are ranked among their greatest monsters."

Mary stepped through the door behind us, tapping Verity on the shoulder and murmuring something in her ear. Verity paled as she nodded, then turned to follow Mary out of the room. Oh, that probably wasn't good. Anything that couldn't be discussed in front of the people who seemed to be our hosts . . . not great. I kept my eyes on the dragons, standing in steady support of Thomas.

Several of the dragons looked around when they heard Verity pull the door shut behind her. I snapped my fingers.

"Hey," I said. "We're the problem in front of you. We're the ones you're debating whether or not to trust. I'm assuming that if you come down on the wrong side of things, we get tossed out of here?"

Awkward silence answered me, telling me I was right. I snorted.

"You know how human kids are afraid of finding a bogeyman in their closet? Well, the Covenant of St. George is afraid of finding *us* in their closet. You don't want us to leave. You want us to get your people back."

"Do you think you can?" asked one of the dragons.

"I think we stand a better chance than almost anybody else you might call," I said. "And I think you can't be the ones who do it, because that would just put more of you in danger. You need humans. You need people the Covenant might hesitate to shoot. I hate to put it that way, but you know it's true."

The dragons turned to each other, muttering too low for me to hear for several seconds before they turned and looked levelly back at us. They weren't a hive mind. I knew they weren't a hive mind. In that moment, they managed to seem unified enough that they might as well have been.

"Fine," said the dragon who'd been speaking before. "We'll let you stay for now, but only because your granddaughter vouches for you, and you can do less damage where we can keep an eye on you. But you *will* be watched."

"Guessing that means we can't go out for another pizza, huh?" I asked.

The dragons ignored me as they filed out of the room, leaving the three humans alone.

Three humans, and one overwhelmingly loud psychic hum. I looked around as Thomas was turning to Sally.

"Taken?" he asked, voice low and dangerous.

There was a chair shoved into one corner where no chair belonged, too far from the table to be useful.

"I didn't see them," said Sally.

"I thought I taught you better than to be caught unawares."

"For a desolate desert environment, sure, but not here on Earth!"

"You'll need lessons in urban self-defense, then. Noted."

"And it was fine. Mary and Alice found me, and the yong didn't hurt me. I don't think they *wanted* to hurt me. They seemed . . . sad, mostly, like they were missing something they couldn't get back."

I moved closer to the chair, fighting the sudden urge to look away from it.

"Alice?" Thomas's voice was sharp with curiosity. "What are you looking at?"

"Well, unless I'm completely out of practice, which I'm pretty sure I'm not, I'm looking at one of our granddaughters who you have yet to meet," I said, making an effort to keep my voice as gentle as I could. "Sarah, would you like to stop screening yourself and meet your grandfather? He's been gone for a long time, but I bet he'd be really happy to meet you, wouldn't you, Thomas?"

"Sarah—oh, the Johrlac."

"Yes. Sarah." I kept watching the chair. "She's Kevin's wife's adopted sister, but age-wise, she's always been part of the grandchild swarm, and she's a granddaughter as far as I'm concerned. She's ours, and I love her very much."

"Um, boss?" Sally sounded dubious. "Alice is talking to the air."

"Yes."

"Why is Alice talking to the air?"

"Because I think Sarah is a little too overwhelmed to want to be beheld right now," I said, and sighed. "Sweetheart, I don't know why you're hiding—or when you got strong enough to hide this well, honestly, this is some grade-A hiding, I'm very impressed—but you can come out, I promise. No one here is going to be angry with you. I've missed you. A lot."

"Really?" The question was asked with heartbreaking hesitance as the air shimmered in the chair, and Sarah appeared. No—that makes it sound like she became visible as she entered the room, the way it worked with Mary. She had been there all along. She just hadn't been something we could see before that moment.

As always, she was skinny and pale, with long, dark hair and shockingly blue eyes, dressed in a sweater at least three sizes too large for her. It bunched around her waist, engulfed her hands, and generally threatened to swallow her completely. Her skirt was almost ankle-length, and she was wearing thick leggings underneath it. Compared to her, I was underdressed. Compared to her, *Thomas* was underdressed, and he had his sleeves buttoned to the wrist.

"You've really missed me, and you're not mad?"

Sally jumped. "How the fu— Where did she come from?"

I smiled. "Sarah, meet your newest . . . I genuinely have no idea what her relation to you is, and we're probably going to need a flowchart at this rate, but Thomas adopted her while he was lost in a murder dimension, and she's going to be sticking around. Her name's Sally. Sally, this is Sarah. She's a cuckoo."

"Hi," said Sarah, hesitantly. She stood, swaying a little, her hands still covered by the sleeves of her sweater. I opened my arms in invitation, and managed not to stagger as she flung herself into them, clinging to me tightly—careful, I noticed, not to touch even a centimeter of my skin. That was interesting.

One thing Johrlac and cuckoos have in common: their powers work better when they're making skin contact. Sarah had always been reluctant to touch people, but she'd never been this armored against the very possibility. It was like touching me was the worst thing she could imagine. Added to her ability to shield herself from me effectively while we were in the same room, it painted a slightly unnerving picture of her current situation.

"Sweetheart, are you all right?" I pushed Sarah out to arm's length, looking at her carefully. She'd lost weight since the last time I'd seen her, and there were dark shadows around her eyes; she hadn't been sleeping well. I frowned. "You need to eat something."

"Can that wait until after we find the missing dragons?" she asked, a little anxiously.

"I think it may have to," said Thomas. "Our hosts are very upset about the loss of their children, as well they should be. People who interfere with the young are the worst kind of predator, and if some of those taken were young males, they're in extreme danger."

"Verity already asked me to look for them," said Sarah. "Unfortunately, the Covenant equips their field operatives with anti-telepathy charms, and I can't track them. Wherever they've taken Cara and the children, it's a shielded location."

"Meaning you don't even know whether they're dead or alive," I concluded. I glanced to Sally. "Telepathy has limitations. It can be blocked."

"And every telepath has an effective range," Sarah added. "I used to be able to scan an area of about five square miles if I wasn't trying to look too closely and overwhelming myself. I can do more than that now, but I still can't punch through strong charms. Thankfully. I know it's selfish when there are kids in danger, but if I could push through charms, I'd never be able to sleep again."

"You need to sleep in warded rooms?" asked Thomas.

Sarah nodded. "Or I just pick up on the dreams of everyone around me, and that's not usually a good thing."

"What's your current range?" I asked.

Sarah glanced down at her feet and mumbled something. I frowned. "I didn't quite catch that. Try again?"

"I said, I can scan most of the tri-state area if I really try, and I've never picked up on a single Covenant agent." She glanced up again. "We know they're here, so they're all protected."

I didn't want to ask her how she'd expanded her range to cover that kind of distance, not in the presence of two people who might be her family, but were also relative strangers. So instead, I blinked slowly, then nodded. "Got it. You can't be much help, then."

"Not yet," she said. "I can keep my mind open in case they slip up now that they have the asshole dragon-slayer holy grail in their custody—they might get sloppy with their shielding, but it's unlikely that'll happen. It's good to see you, Grandma. It's nice to be near someone I can read who's not freaking out."

"I think my freaking-out days are mostly over," I said, putting a hand on Thomas's shoulder. "I found what I was looking for."

"I always hoped you would," she said gravely. Flicking her attention briefly to him, she added shyly, "Hi, Mr. Price. I know . . . I know you're not related to the Healy side of the family by blood, but—"

"I should hope not," said Thomas. "We've had several children, and that would be difficult to explain to them."

"—I still can't read you," she finished. "Your thoughts are even fuzzier than Grandma's. I know with her it's because of who her ancestors were. Why is it like that with you?"

"I have anti-telepathy charms built into my tattoos," he said. "They're not as effective at close range as the removable kind, but they do well enough for situations like this one."

"Oh," said Sarah, looking oddly disappointed. She swiveled back around to me. "You should hurry and find the missing kids. The dragons are really upset. If you don't find them soon, they're liable to make you leave, no matter what they said just now, and they'll make the rest of the family go, too. That would be bad."

"Yes, it would," I agreed, as she turned and walked out of the room without another word. I sighed, leaning against Thomas. "Okay, I guess it's time for us to pull a miracle out of our asses."

"Nothing new about that," he said, and kissed the top of my head.

"No, I guess not," I said.

Sixteen

"We make monsters whenever we disagree about how a limited resource should be spent. It's so much easier to kill a person whose personhood you've stolen away."

—Thomas Price

Manhattan, standing inside a former slaughterhouse filled with dragons, trying to figure out how to accomplish the impossible

SO: WE HAD LIMITED resources, including two people who were almost entirely out of synch with the present day, and myself, who had never bothered to become intimately acquainted with the way the modern world worked, since I'd had bigger things to worry about. Like finding a man who'd been thrown into another dimension by a cosmic force of being a giant asshole, and keeping myself from getting killed in the process.

Sarah was off the board, thanks to the telepathy limiters and whatever had happened to leave her so withdrawn. Normally I wouldn't say personal trauma was a good-enough reason for someone to stay benched when kids were in danger, but Sarah's a cuckoo. Pushing her when she doesn't feel stable enough to be in the field could have really bad consequences, for everybody.

I don't like treating my grandkids like they might be dangerous, but they could be, every single one of them. Even Artie, loath as he generally is to leave his room. We don't raise harmless children in this family. And maybe that's the way I *did* grow up to be my father. I didn't have much say in the way Laura brought up Kevin and Jane, but the expectation that they'd take after my mother had still traveled with me every time I'd come to visit during their childhoods. In my way, I gave them as little of a choice as my dad gave me. If they wanted my approval, they'd show me they were ready to survive in a world whose dangers I was all too intimately acquainted with.

Kevin had always been more enthusiastic about knife training and field work, had always been more eager to impress me and make sure I knew that he was still my son, even if he only saw me once or twice a year. Who would Jane have grown up to be, without the constant need to impress a mother who was more absence than attendance?

Could she have been happy?

So no, Sarah wasn't really on the table for this one. I didn't know how much field work Verity was feeling up for, with Olivia still so young. If Verity was anything like her own father, she'd have a much stronger parental instinct than I ever had, and she'd want to protect her child above everything else. But Dominic could still help us if she couldn't, and if he wasn't up for going into the field, he could stay behind and babysit. We wouldn't be going into this without *any* backup. Just with limited backup, which was nothing new, and would probably be more comfortable for Sally and Thomas, neither of whom were used to the current family dynamic.

As if I was. These people weren't quite strangers to me, but they were close enough that I needed to stop thinking of myself as being the one who had all the answers. I didn't. Thinking that way was only going to get people hurt.

The door creaked slightly as someone eased it open. All three of us turned to watch as Verity peeked around the edge, looking unaccountably relieved to find us standing there, considering our options, and not covered in blood or something.

"Sarah said you were going to go looking for the missing dragons," she said. "I wanted to check and see if there was anything you needed from me before you went."

That answered the question of whether or not she was feeling up for field work. As if she were the telepath, rather than Sarah, her lips drew downward in a frown and she stepped the rest of the way into the room, letting the door swing ease behind her.

"I'd go with you, but Livvy gets fussy when I'm out of her sight for too long," she said. "Mary says this is a normal developmental stage, and that she's better about it than some kids her age, since she has people around her all the time, but I still shouldn't go into an active combat situation with you. I'm sorry."

"Sweetheart, it's fine," I said. "Please don't feel bad about needing to stay here and take care of your child. It's understandable."

"But you went into the field when Dad was Livvy's age," she said, doggedly. "I should be able to do the same thing."

My stomach twisted, feeling uncomfortably as if it wanted to flip all the way over. I swallowed to hide my discomfort, glancing at Thomas.

"Your grandmother's situation was somewhat unique," he said, putting a hand on my shoulder, Sally between us, standing silent and watchful as a stone. "There's no obligation for any new parent to feel up to risking their lives for the lives of others."

"But if you don't find them, everything we've been working for falls apart," she protested. "The dragons are furious. They can see the logic of what you were saying—something about hairstyles?—but they still want someone to blame, and it's always easiest when you can shove the blame on someone outside your community. Outside your species is just a bonus. So they're willing to cut off all contact with humans over this, if it doesn't end the way we all want it to."

"You said there are three confirmed strike teams, with a fourth that may or may not be made up of members of the first three," I said. "You also said there were approximately twenty operatives that you knew of, in total. Which division makes the most sense, given those numbers?"

"Unless things have changed rather dramatically since my time, the smallest units the Covenant fields normally have three to five members," said Thomas. "Large enough that you can lose someone without losing the battle at hand, but also small enough that losing a team is unlikely to completely destroy a complex operation."

"Dominic says four teams is most likely," said Verity, uncomfortably. "He'd like to go with you, if you'd be willing to have him."

That explained her discomfort. I'd never been a big fan of Thomas going off to fight things without me, and the only reason it hadn't been more of an issue for us was that during the officially romantic portion of our relationship, he'd been confined to the house. Meaning he'd been the one who had to get comfortable with the idea of *me* running off into danger without him around to watch my back.

"We'd be glad to," said Thomas. "None of us is exactly a local, and it would be good to have someone who knows the city."

"Especially since not everyone shares your arboreal tendencies," I said, as warmly as I could manage. Verity mustered a smile. I returned it. "And it'll be nice for Thomas and me to spend some time getting to know our latest grandson."

"To be honest, I'm happy to get to know any of my grandchildren, born or married in," said Thomas, a little wryly. "I didn't expect I'd ever had the chance to meet any of you, and knowing your grandmother, there was more than half a chance your parents wouldn't have reached adulthood."

"Hey!" I protested.

Sally and Verity snickered, briefly united in mocking my questionable parenting skills. Thomas shrugged, unrepentant.

"I love you dearly, but in the time we had together, we both know I was the one who made sure Kevin had clean clothes and washed his hands, while you were the one who forgot that knives aren't appropriate toys for children," he said.

Verity looked between us with wide eyes. "Dad is starting to make so much more sense," she said.

I snorted.

"Sorry to interrupt this delightful look into the history of my new family, but weren't we supposed to be moving by now?" Sally folded her arms. "Honestly, with the way you people like to talk, it's a miracle you ever got around to *having* kids, much less selling your souls to the crossroads and winding up in horrible bottle dimensions."

"That's specific," said Verity.

"The mice will tell you all about it," I said. "Sally's right. We need to go. I know you're not coming, and I know Sarah's not coming, but is anyone else actually going to come along with us as backup?"

"The dragons are refusing," said Verity. "They don't trust you. They also don't want you looking for their children alone, so Istas and Ryan will be going with you."

"Istas . . . isn't that the waheela you used to work with?"

She nodded, looking pleased that I'd remembered. "Yup, and Ryan's her husband. He's a tanuki. They make it work."

"Okay. Cool." I pushed my hair back with one hand. "Where are we leaving from?"

"Come on. I'll show you." She turned to leave the room.

The rest of us followed.

Ever since she was a little kid, Verity had been drawn to the highest point in her environment. My grandparents used to joke about me pursuing an arboreal lifestyle, with as much time as they spent fishing me out of trees, but compared to her, I had always kept my feet firmly on the ground. If she had a life motto, it was probably "I can climb that."

It's normal for the Aeslin mice to play around with titles for a little while after a new baby is born to the family, since we can't really know what kind of person someone is going to be until they've had a little time to grow into themselves. Verity was dubbed the Arboreal Priestess by the time she turned three, and there has never, to the best of my knowledge, been any clerical question of changing that.

Taking all that into consideration, it probably shouldn't have been a surprise when Verity led us up three flights of stairs to the slaughterhouse roof, which had been partially converted into a rooftop garden, complete with herb beds, a pigeon coop, and several boxy things I thought were probably beehives. It managed to surprise me all the same. Sometimes the least surprising things manage to turn themselves around and become the most surprising of all.

Three people were already up there, waiting for us: Dominic, now wearing charcoal-gray leggings and a matching turtleneck, the Inuit woman I'd seen before, who had changed into a rose-pink-and-cherry-red confection of a dress, including matching shoes and parasol, pink-streaked black hair tied up in curled pigtails, and the man whose lap she'd been sitting on downstairs, whose clothing matched Dominic's. All three looked over at our approach, Dominic stepping forward to meet us.

"Are they ready?" he asked.

"I'd ask why you were so sure we'd be going, but that would just waste time, so instead I'm going to ask how we're supposed to get down from here," I said. "Even if I were big on parkour, which I'm not, Sally's had no training in jumping off buildings, and Thomas is out of practice."

"I assume you can all handle a ten-foot drop?" Verity gestured over the edge of the roof. "The nightclub next door belongs to venture capitalists who reinforced the hell out of the place in order to get away with violating noise ordinances on a nightly basis. I'm not really sure how they expected that to be cost-effective, but whatever, I'm not a rich twenty-something who made it big in tech. Anyway, jump down to there and you'll be fine. They won't hear you land, and if you cross to the back of the building, there's a fire escape that goes all the way to the ground on the block behind this one. Unless someone's there and looking up when you exit, they won't see you leave."

"Verity is trustworthy on the matter of exiting via overland routes," said Istas, almost serenely. "Her acquaintance with the ground is fleeting at best."

"We have roughly another four hours of daylight," said Dominic.

"Do you have any idea where these teams are based?" asked Thomas. "They won't all be clustered together. That would be bad operational security."

"There's one in Hoboken, on the other side of the river," said Dominic. "We think there's another in Brooklyn. The third is likely somewhere in Midtown. They may be based out of a hotel, or doing a long-term lease on one of the illegal sublets that people advertise online. But they won't bring a bunch of kidnapped children back to the place they're living and operating out of, they'll have secured a separate location or locations."

"The fact that you listed those three areas first tells me you think they have the children somewhere in the fourth," said Thomas. "Where would that be?"

Dominic actually looked faintly guilty before squaring his shoulders in an almost-military posture, turning to Thomas, and saying, "The East Village, sir. We've based our assumptions off verified activity and where it seems to be centered. There are too many incidents in that area to explain by assigning them to the other teams. It would make sense for the fourth team to be based there."

"We've both retired from the Covenant, son," said Thomas, voice gentle. "I'm not your superior. You don't need to hesitate before you speak to me, and you don't need me to approve of your ideas before they can be voiced. You know this city and we don't. We're following you into the field."

Dominic glanced to Verity, then Istas and Ryan, as if looking for confirmation. When all of them nodded, he returned his attention to Thomas, standing a little taller and a little less rigid at the same time. "We've spotted an agent we believe to be a woman named Margaret Healy with the team in the East Village. More than anything else, that makes me believe they're the central command. Margaret has been dispatched to New York before, and as you say, knowledge of the territory is essential if you want to succeed in your mission."

"Then we go to the East Village," I said. "Just show us how to get there."

"That, I will do," said Istas, and stepped up onto the edge of the building. Ryan hurried after her and actually jumped down first. She turned to face us and fell backward off the ledge a moment later, as nonchalantly as if she plummeted off buildings every day. Which maybe she did. I've never spent much social time with a waheela; I don't know what they do for fun.

Dominic was the next over the edge, pausing to kiss Verity on the cheek before he went. I followed him, getting a running start. I'm not necessarily afraid of falling, but I've always found it just a little easier if I'm moving quickly when it happens. Like making my own carnival ride, only you don't need a ticket and there's no safety rail.

Ryan was standing with Istas in his arms when I landed next to them, having apparently caught her before her impractical shoes could cause a problem. He set her on her feet as I straightened, and she turned a small, satisfied smile on me.

"It is a pleasure to finally meet you, Alice-Verity's-grandmother," she said, politely.

"Nice to meet you, too," I said, more wary than polite.

"We don't have many grandparents among my kind."

"No?"

"Istas, be nice," said Ryan.

Her smile became more of a snarl, showing me all of her strong, white, human-seeming teeth. "We eat them before they can become too much of a burden to the rest of us. So I lack Verity's sympathy for your role in her family."

Dominic started to protest. Istas raised a hand to quiet him. He stopped.

There was a soft thump as Thomas landed on the roof. I didn't allow myself to turn and look at him. Istas was a predator. A predator in a fluffy, lacy dress, but a predator all the same. Turning my back on her might be the last thing I ever did.

"I would like you to explain, please, why grandparents are necessary."

"We know things," I said, keeping my voice steady. "We've been around to learn more than someone younger might know. And sometimes we can be a little set in our ways, especially for people who are used to newer methods of doing things, but sometimes, the old way is the right way, because no one sees it coming. And because we're family."

Sally squeaked as she hit the roof, a small sound, quickly swallowed, but audible.

"Family needs family. It's not always about blood—Thomas and I aren't blood, and Sally isn't blood to either of us—but it's about knowing where you belong, and feeling like you'll be welcome there. Verity's our family. That means she needs us." I paused before venturing a guess: "I get the feeling Verity's your family, too, and that's why you're so concerned about whether or not we're good for her. I can't promise we'll always make her happy, but I can promise that we'll always love her, and that we're just here to help."

That seemed to satisfy Istas. She turned without another word, walking across the roof toward the promised fire escape. Ryan shot me a helpless, half-adoring look. The adoration was in no way for me.

"She can be a little intense sometimes, sorry about that," he said, and took off after her.

I waited until he was halfway across the roof before letting out a shaky breath and looking toward Dominic.

"That happen often?"

"No," he said, shaking his head. "Istas is the first waheela—the only waheela—I've had the pleasure of knowing. They're not found in Europe, and Covenant attempts at study and extermination have not historically ended very well."

"I wouldn't think so," said Thomas. To Sally, he added, "Waheela are therianthropes—natural shapeshifters. When it pleases her, our Miss Istas is likely to be somewhere between ten and twelve feet tall and capable of throwing motor vehicles, as well as resembling a hybrid of a dire wolf and a grizzly bear."

Sally blinked, looking momentarily nonplussed. Then she shrugged. "Okay," she said, like this was perfectly normal, and started across the roof after Ryan and Istas.

Thomas, Dominic, and I hurried to catch up.

"She takes things in stride for someone who appears to have quite a few holes in her education," commented Dominic.

"Sally was introduced to the cryptid world when she made a bargain with the crossroads which they couldn't refuse but also couldn't fulfill without going against an earlier bargain they had been holding to for over a century," said Thomas. "They hurled her into the prison dimension where they had placed me, leaving her surrounded by individuals we would class as cryptids here on Earth, but who she saw first as aliens, and later as people. I think that sink-or-swim approach to what it means to be a person is making it slightly easier for her to adjust."

"That, or she's going to have a screaming breakdown just as soon as we get back to Michigan," I said.

The fire escape was bare metal and probably violated half a dozen safety codes, most of them having to do with tetanus. I clomped down it after Ryan, Sally, and Istas, with Thomas and Dominic close behind me. Our feet echoed enough that it was difficult to believe no one could hear us inside the building, but no windows opened, and we made it to the ground without interruption. The alley smelled of slowly liquifying trash, stale beer, and old urine: the classic perfume of the city streets. Istas and Ryan were waiting next to a dumpster, and when I gave them a curious look, Ryan shrugged.

"The smell helps to cover our tracks."

"Not mine," said Istas. "Waheela leave no scent behind. Tracking our kind is a more difficult proposition than following a single human, or a tanuki. Although . . ." She looked at me and blinked slowly, a predator's assessing expression on her face. "Verity smells odd. Not quite of humankind, but close enough that I have always assumed it was within the normal deviance for your species. You smell much the same, but more strongly. Was your mother bred to something other than a human man, or was she something other than a human woman?"

"I'm really not sure how to answer that," I said, as the others reached us and saved me from the need to try. Dominic motioned for the rest of us to follow him, and led the way out of the alley to the other side of the block, where things were basically exactly the same. Oh, the businesses were different, but it was the same mixture of storefronts and street activity. We paused at the mouth of the alley to look around, making sure we weren't being followed, and I moved to the front of the group, away from the smell of trash. Which probably explained why Ryan and Istas were hanging back. As therianthropes, they had far more sensitive senses of smell than a bunch of humans, and the smell of trash was something they were accustomed to. It wasn't going to distract them the way it did me.

"Hey," I said, glancing at Dominic. "I thought alleys were rare in New York, outside of the movies. How . . . ?"

"The city as a whole, yes. The Meatpacking District, not as much. They used to dispose of animal corpses here, and it was easier if they could do it where no one was going to see."

"Charming," I said.

"This way." There was a subway stop halfway down the block. Dominic pointed at it and started walking, leaving the rest of us to follow. The subway is really the best way to get around New York. They built one of the most comprehensive public transit systems on the planet, and for all that New Yorkers seem to enjoy complaining about it more than they enjoy anything else, the wise ones understand that it's a gift beyond price. It gives them the freedom of an incredibly dense metro area, and even with the delays that seem to be innate to the system, it's still faster than taking a car.

The L train ran in a virtually straight line between where we were and where we were going, and both taking it and avoiding to keep ourselves from being followed would have been equally reasonable choices. So I wasn't overly surprised when Dominic led us down the stairs into the subway station.

I was a bit more confused when he slipped a twenty to the transit cop on duty and waved for the rest of us to follow him through a door marked DO NOT ENTER.

The hallway on the other side was the same industrial concrete as everything else in the New York subway but with exposed piping along the ceiling, bare bulbs lighting the area, and no smell of urine. No matter how much they clean the underground stations, pee runs downward, and what the humans don't manage to mark as their own, the rats will claim quickly enough. I blinked at him, raising an eyebrow, and waited for someone else to ask.

"Are we supposed to be back here?" asked Sally.

"No," said Istas. "If we were meant to be in this area, Dominic would not have given money to the policeman. That is called a 'bribe,' and sometimes they are used to gain access to places you are not meant to be."

Sally eyed her. "Okay, lady."

"I tell you only because you did not seem to know, and if you *did* know, you were asking the question for no reason, and might need to be bitten. I am making generous assumptions."

"No one's getting bitten," said Ryan hastily. "Istas, honey, sometimes humans have to ask really obvious questions out loud, or they feel like they don't understand what's going on and get fussy. We don't want our allies to be fussy when they're supposed to be helping us find the kids, remember?"

"I suppose," said Istas.

"These are the maintenance access corridors," said Dominic. "They parallel the subway line, and none of the cameras here work."

"You know that why?" Sally asked.

"Sometimes the local station workers want to smoke, and there's no smoking allowed in the station, so they come back here to do it," he said, starting to walk. As will normally happen when someone begins to walk away while still speaking, the rest of us followed him automatically. "So they disabled the cameras to keep from getting into trouble with the authorities. The door's usually locked unless there's an officer on duty, so they don't really have issues with crime in the corridors."

"How very . . . You know what? No." I shrugged. "It's a very human solution to the problem. A-plus, transit workers, thanks for the convenient underground passage."

"It's about a mile's walk to where we're going, and we'll get there almost as fast as we would have on the train," said Dominic.

He would have been right, too, if we hadn't run into a group of civic electricians when we were a little over halfway there. The corridor was dotted with junctions, other corridors connecting briefly before heading off to other parts of the subway system, and they came around one of those corners, toolboxes in hand and tool belts low on their hips, off to do their jobs. There were five of them. They stopped when they saw us, eyes going wide. Several of their mouths dropped open. I've seen more attractive sights, but since I wasn't sure whether they were about to call for help or not, I wasn't going to say anything. I settled for trying to look inoffensive.

I didn't imagine I did a very good job of it. Two heavily tattooed people, a woman in full goth Lolita gear, two men in tactical clothes, and Sally did not, on the whole, a deeply reassuring picture make. Or an inoffensive one. One of the men stepped forward, face drawing into an expression of posturing aggression, while another grabbed for his radio.

"Hey!" said the first, jabbing a finger toward Dominic. "You can't be down here!"

"Please, just don't tell anyone and let us pass." Dominic held his hands up in a gesture that was probably meant to be soothing. "We just want to get to Union Square. If you let us go, we'll go, and no one has to get hurt."

"Who said anything about anyone getting h— Hey, why is that lady taking her clothes off?"

I glanced back. Istas was in the process of undoing the many small buttons on her dress, peeling it down her torso to reveal a lacy black bra with little pink ribbons on it. She was an attractive woman. It was still somehow the least titillating striptease I had ever seen, maybe because I had a pretty good idea what was going to happen when she was done.

"Please," Dominic repeated. "You don't want to know what happens when she finishes getting naked."

"I like these shoes," said Istas. "I don't want to destroy them. Ryan, can you help me with the zipper?"

"These men didn't do anything wrong, sweetie," said Ryan, even as he moved behind her to begin easing her zipper down. "They really don't deserve this."

"Deserve what?" asked another of the men. The one who'd reached for his radio was standing silent and open-mouthed, apparently too stunned by what he was seeing to finish calling the authorities.

Thomas sighed heavily, rolling up his left sleeve and extending his arm like he was preparing to give blood. "I would rather not have spent the energy this close to what may be a rather nasty fight," he said. "But it seems better than allowing our fair lady waheela to have her way with you."

He pressed the first two fingers of his right hand to the image of a stylized poppy, murmuring something under his breath at the same time. For a moment, the air seemed to grow heavy with the scent of some unidentified flower—then the scent passed, and the men in front of us hit the ground, one by one, falling where they stood.

Behind me, Istas said, somewhat peevishly, "Oh. *Sorcery.* Ryan, help me zip back up?"

"We need to move," said Dominic, stepping forward and snagging the radio from the fallen electrician's hand. "These men were on an assignment for something, and someone's going to notice when they don't get it done or report back to their supervisors. Not much farther now."

"Have you never been caught before?" asked Thomas.

"No," he said. "There's miles of corridor down here, when you account for the whole system, and only so many electricians to go around. Normally, if I move fast and keep my head down, no one questions my presence."

I absolutely believed that Dominic used this passage on a regular basis without trouble, just as I believed that having me along had made the wild coincidence of running into someone all but inevitable. We needed to get me out of here, or more people would come along. That was just the way things worked.

Istas had re-secured her clothing to her satisfaction, and we started moving again. Sally glanced back at her as we walked, but didn't ask. After a few minutes of walking in silence, Istas took pity.

"When I change from human shape to my great-form, my clothing does not change with me. If I do not take the time to disrobe, I will destroy whatever I am wearing."

"So why wear anything but sweatpants and tank tops? You could just 'grr Hulk smash' your way through life, without worrying about buttons."

Istas made a small, horrified sound before replying, "Fashion is the greatest invention the humans have ever managed to pursue to perfection. It clearly demarcates the line between person and beast, it knows neither gender nor species, it is art and function and glory. Sweatpants? I would sooner return to the high tundra to feast on the bones of my ancestors than demean myself so."

Sally lifted her eyebrows. "That's . . . uh. That's a pretty hard line."

"Yes, well." Istas sniffed. "Properly fitted lingerie is worth the conviction."

"Istas really likes clothes," said Ryan. "She moved here from Canada so she could wear more of them, even."

"Simplistic but accurate," Istas agreed.

I kept walking, pushing away the urge to say something and make the situation even more awkward than it already was. Sally would have to learn that when you're dealing with nonhumans who can pass in human society, you can't assume they think the way a human in a similar situation would think. Even the ones who've all but completely assimilated—and no waheela who *hadn't* virtually assimilated into humanity would even have considered wearing those shoes.

The corridor ahead of us, which had seemed limitless up until this point, finally had a visible ending: a door, virtually identical to the one we'd come in through, marked OFFICIAL USE ONLY. Dominic picked up the pace slightly, and the rest of us matched him, as eager to get out of this subterranean warren as we were to get to the main part of our mission. We had to locate five hostile people we didn't know, most of whom none of us had ever seen before, in an area as large as Manhattan's East Village, with three people out of time, one human semilocal, and two therianthropes whose exact contributions to the goal—except for being absolutely terrifying—were as yet unclear.

So nothing too major.

Dominic motioned for the rest of us to wait as he reached the door and cautiously eased it open, peering out into the subway station on the other side. Apparently content with whatever it was he saw, he gestured for us to follow again as he pushed it all the way open and stepped out, into the station.

There was one transit officer standing a few feet away who gave us a curious look until Dominic walked over and slipped him a twenty-dollar bill. Istas was close behind, somehow managing to look as if she were looming over the officer even though she was considerably shorter than he was.

"You should refrain from staring," she said. "It's quite rude, and I do not appreciate it."

"Excuse my wife, she's just pissed about missing out on tickets for her favorite designer at Fashion Week," said Ryan pleasantly, taking Istas by the shoulders and steering her toward the stairs. If there'd been any question about whether they were married, it was answered by the way she allowed herself to be led away. A waheela doesn't do anything they don't want to do. It's sort of like trying to argue with a rhinoceros, only more likely to kill you.

"Sorry about that," said Dominic. "Thank you for your service." He took off after Ryan and Istas, and the rest of us followed, not saying anything until we reached street level.

Once we were there, Istas turned to Ryan and said, "He was staring at my chest. You should have permitted him to answer my challenge."

"Eating the police attracts attention, and we don't want to attract attention," said Ryan, voice almost mild.

"Where to now?" asked Sally.

Dominic looked around, stepping to the side so as not to block the exit, and said, "Now we find someplace where Ryan can shift down to something more useful."

"I find him perfectly useful in this form," said Istas. "His thumbs are very desirable when I want him to rub my feet, and we are incapable of mating in our more basic forms. But I will agree that human noses make for poor trackers."

"If he can pick up the scent of the missing kids, he'll be more than useful," I said, looking around. The street was unfamiliar—no real surprise there—and completely familiar at the same time. You've seen one city street, you've essentially seen them all.

That's applicable across dimensions, too. Once people reach the point of building large communities with civic infrastructure, certain elements become consistent. Which is not to say that Tokyo and Chicago are the same place, just that the base landscape remains similar enough to make them functionally the same environment. It's like forests. They come in flavors, and I'll never mistake another biome for my beloved Galway, but they're all forests, in the end.

"Alice?"

Thomas's voice snapped me out of my brief rumination. I glanced at him, lifting an eyebrow. He looked at me gravely.

"What were you thinking about?"

"Cities, mostly. They're all pretty much the same. If you can navigate one, you can navigate them all. Come on, if we don't know where we're going, we may as well walk until we find a place where Ryan can change." I started down the street, trying not to look as restless as I felt. For all that everything was familiar, it also had a certain rawness to it that left me anxious to be moving toward a goal.

"Yes," said Thomas, with near-surprising acceptance. "We may as well."

We ambled down the block, me temporarily in the lead, the others following behind. Only Dominic looked nervous about how exposed we were—I supposed there wasn't much concern about the rest of us actually being recognized before we could reach our goal.

We didn't find a safe place for Ryan to change on that block. We made our way to the next. Sally pulled up next to me and asked, in a low voice, "Is this really it? No plan? We don't have some grand strategy that's going to help us find the people we're looking for and make it all come out okay?"

"Dominic's planning to use Ryan as a sniffer dog, if that helps," I offered.

"Not really. That's not a *plan*."

"I thought I would wait and see what Alice decided to do," said Thomas. I looked at him, blinking. He smiled as he shrugged, a remarkable gentleness in his eyes. "We could do with a bit of that luck of yours."

Healy family luck: sometimes it's good, sometimes it's bad, but it's never, ever boring. Or, as it might be better called, Brown family luck, because I definitely got it from my mother. If you give me two doors to open, I'll always choose the one that leads to certain doom: two paths across a room, I'll pick the one with the hidden pit trap. Every single time. And then I'll survive them both, through some ridiculous combination of coincidence and one-in-a-million shots. Whatever it is, it's genetic, I know that much: both my kids have the same weird coincidence field. It extends to the grandkids, too. Where it stops, I don't know, but whatever something extra Mom brought to the family tree, it's gotten me in—and out of—trouble more times than I can count.

"It's not a switch I can flip, you know."

"I know. But when we most need you to be in the right place, you tend to wind up there." His eyes crinkled at the corners as his smile grew. "It would never have taken you so long to find me if there hadn't been someone yanking you in the wrong direction every chance he got. So go, follow your feet, and let the random coincidences that have kept you alive this long lead you."

"Okay," I said, rolling my shoulders in a shrug. It wasn't like anyone had a better idea. We still had no real intel or plan—and I was a little annoyed about that. Shouldn't Dominic have at least asked the shapeshifter who wouldn't be useful until he stopped looking like a human being to transform *before* we left the hidden passage in the subway? Amateurs. But picking a fight wasn't going to do us any good right now. So we walked.

We walked, and New York City closed around us like a fist, and that was exactly right. This was our world, where we should have been all along; this was where we could fit in. It might take us time, but eventually, it was going to be like we had never left, and that was going to be *wonderful*.

Thomas made a small, pleased sound. I stopped walking, snapped out of my brief reverie, and blinked at him. He smiled at me again. Was I ever going to get tired of seeing him outside in the sun, smiling at me? No. No, I was not. After the amount of time I'd spent trying to make this moment even remotely possible, I couldn't think of anything I wanted more.

Maybe to have it happen without a bunch of missing juvenile dragons and the Covenant of St. George in the mix, but there's wishful thinking and then there's being a little bit delusional, and I'd rather trend toward the former than the latter.

"You found me a bookstore," he said.

I blinked again, turning to see what he was looking at. We were standing outside a store, its wide glass windows crammed with books and its front overhung by a red awning. Carts packed full of discounted books had been pushed out in front, tempting customers.

"Good job, you found the Strand," said Ryan, sounding only a little bemused. "I don't think we're here to shop, though. We're supposed to be finding an alley."

"Do they have a public bathroom?" I asked.

"Yes," he said, sounding even more bemused.

"Great." I turned to Istas. "Can I have the ribbons from your pigtails?"

"Why?"

"I want to use them to rig a leash to put on him," I nodded toward Ryan. "If we go into the bathroom together and wait ten minutes, I can tie the ribbon around his neck and pretend that I'm one of those assholes who takes her dog everywhere she goes. I'm blonde. If I look confused, people tend to believe it."

"I want to be offended by the suggestion that we leash me, but it's not a bad one," said Ryan, slowly. "No security cameras in the bathrooms, either."

"And since we won't be shoplifting, if they ask to search my bag, they'll just find your clothes. Which is a little odd, but I don't think it's out of the ordinary for New York." It was a decent plan, if not a great one, and I tried to sound more confident about it than I felt.

Dominic sighed. "You know, standing out here and talking about going into the bookstore is not actually as effective as going *into* the bookstore. Shall we?"

"It's the beginning of a plan, if not the end of one, and we may as well go with it," said Thomas.

Dominic nodded, and as a group, we moved inside.

Seventeen

"I've always been lucky, since the start. There's people who'd say being found in a cardboard box isn't lucky, but I say that if I weren't lucky, no one would have found me."
—Frances Brown

The Strand Bookstore, trying hard to come up with a better plan, not really succeeding

THE DOOR OPENED ON a large room filled with shelves and tables, all groaning under the weight of more books than I'd seen outside of a library. Thomas nearly stumbled, his eyes gone wide behind his glasses, and I wondered, with a brief jolt of guilt, how long it had been since he'd *held* a book, much less seen such a massive assortment of them. There hadn't been time for him to get reacquainted with his library in Buckley before we'd been on our way out the door. For a man who loved books as much as he did, the last fifty years must have been hell.

Well. They'd been hell for both of us. I started scanning the aisles I could see, looking for a sign that might lead me to a public bathroom.

The aisles were a twisting maze of shelves and tables, giving me no clear sight lines on anything. I looked to my companions.

"Any of you been here before?"

"I have," said Istas, surprising me. "With Ryan." My surprise must have shown on my face, because her expression turned sour. "I *can* read. I like books on the history of fashion. And magazines."

"Big, glossy magazines full of pictures of shoes that make my feet hurt just thinking about them," said Ryan.

"Great. Then one of you can lead me to the bathroom." I leaned up to kiss Thomas on the cheek. "Don't get into any trouble before we get back."

"Does looking longingly at every book in this entire store count as getting into trouble?"

"Only if you get busted for shoplifting."

"As if." Sally rolled her eyes.

"True. You'd never get caught." I glanced to Dominic, who was watching the store entrance and what he could see of the street outside the window with concern. "Keep an eye on them?"

"Of course," he agreed.

I still didn't like letting Thomas out of my sight when I didn't have to. I wasn't sure when I'd be comfortable with that. Maybe never, and wouldn't that be fun? Jane already tried to psychoanalyze me every time I was in the same dimension long enough to come over for family dinner. She said that the fact that I'd gone running off into the unknown the second my husband disappeared proved I was seriously codependent, with possible attachment issues. I had tried suggesting she tell me something I didn't know, and all that did was kick off another massive family fight. Not my favorite way to spend Thanksgiving, no matter what my history may try to say.

So yeah, stepping away from him for a few minutes was probably a good idea, if only to remind me that I was *allowed* to step away from him, he'd still be here when I came back, this wasn't going to be the start of another fifty-year quest. Although, honestly, "I lost him in a bookstore" would be less traumatic for the both of us than what had actually happened.

Istas unwound the ribbons from her pigtails as she led us to the stairs, walking remarkably quickly on her ridiculous heels. "I know I can seem frivolous," she said, handing me the first of the ribbons. "It is a carefully cultivated impression."

"I can see where it would be helpful camouflage," I said. I'd practiced something similar, during the days in Buckley between my grandfather's death and my marriage, when I'd stopped caring about what any of the human residents of the town thought of me. I had Thomas and I had the ghosts and I had the Galway, and those had been all I needed. Maybe that would have changed as the kids got older, but I didn't think so. I knew myself pretty well. I'd still had a few illusions about myself in those days, and looking at the woman I was and the woman I'd been, I felt I could comfortably say that she would have been just fine if she'd never started pretending again.

But for those years, when I'd been doing my best to seem like a normal part of the community, I'd worn my hair in curls and my sleeves long, to cover the scars on my arms. I'd been careful to be seen in the right places, doing the right things—volunteering with the Friends of the Library after my shift was over, helping the ladies at the church take meals to the folks who lived at the outskirts of town. Good-girl things. It was easy enough to look at Istas, an apex predator dressed in ribbons and lace, and see her wearing the same mask.

"People are scared of you, huh?" I took the ribbon, wrapping it loosely around my wrist as she began unwinding the other.

Istas stepped onto the stairs. "People who have the sense to recognize me for what I am aren't scared of me," she said. "They're *terrified*, as well they should be. I am nature's perfect killing machine."

"Here I thought that was cats," said Ryan, in a tone that indicated a frequent joke, something with the edges of it worn smooth between them.

Istas looked at him with polite blankness. "It is also cats. More than one thing can be perfect, it's not a competition."

People were passing us on the stairs. None stopped to give us a second look. Our conversation, strange as it was, was really nothing all that unusual for New York City. Istas finished untying the second ribbon and handed it to me.

"I was born in the high tundra, where the wind and the snow own all that they touch, and any brief break in their attention is a trap designed to lure in the unwary," she said. "My kind eat our own, for nothing else is vast enough to fill our bellies or to satiate our hunger. And we eat others as well, when they come too close to us, or disturb us in our dens. We leave no scent when we pass, for we were made to hunt and haunt and never be seen unless we wish it. Any who know me for what I am should have the sense to quail in fear, and let me pass them by."

"That's my girl," said Ryan.

Istas looked at him fondly. We had reached the first landing, facing a second story as filled with books as the one below. People moved between them, browsing, and paid us no mind. Istas moved forward, and I followed.

"I am strange among my kind in that I can have this conversation without desiring to consume you for knowing too much of my truth, which is personal only to me, and not for anyone else to have," she said. "And because I wish to move in the warm world, to thaw and see things as they have the potential to be, I make myself over to seem as harmless as I can be. Plus, I enjoy it." She smiled toothily. "It is a brave and beautiful thing, to act for enjoyment alone in this world of complications and conflicts. Here is the bathroom."

She stopped, indicating a door. I stopped in turn, blinking at her, second ribbon still tangled through my fingers.

"That was . . . a lot. Thank you, Istas, for sharing something personal, and for answering my questions." Always be polite to the shapeshifting super predator. It's a simple rule of life, but a good one all the same.

Istas nodded, apparently pleased with my politeness.

"Abscond with my husband now, and return his clothing to me," she said, tone utterly mild. She turned to the nearest shelf of books, apparently fascinated with whatever subject they represented. I turned to Ryan, blinking.

He smiled a little as he shrugged. "She's always like this," he said.

"Great." I grabbed his wrist, dragging him with me into the women's bathroom. "Let's get moving."

The bathroom had three stalls, and the one farthest from the door was occupied when we arrived. I shoved Ryan into the first one with a quietly muttered "Strip" before taking up a position outside the stall door, trying to look nonchalant. Ryan said something I didn't quite catch about pushy blondes. I chose not to argue.

The sound of clothes being removed was mostly drowned out by the sound of the toilet in the last stall flushing, and a woman emerged.

She was a little taller than I was, with chestnut-brown hair pulled into a tight ponytail. If not for the familiar angle of her cheekbones, I might not have noticed her. See, the Covenant treats people like lines of livestock, arranging marriages to avoid genetic bottlenecking while also circling useful traits that they want those people to pass along to their children someday. It shouldn't work. That it does makes me wonder if they don't have a little something extra on their side, something that would explain why their carefully tended breeding lines still throw sorcerers like my husband every so often. But Covenant bloodlines produce people with similar talents, similar temperaments . . . similar appearances.

My mother looked a lot like me: petite, blonde, and very, very sweet, right until she decided it was time to stop with the sweetness. My grandmother was similar. I've always wondered if Mom and Dad didn't wind up together in part because of that old cliché where the sheltered boys are looking to marry their mothers. It would explain a few things, that's for sure.

What I have, that neither one of them had, that all five of my biological grandchildren have, are my grandfather's cheekbones. Apparently, that part of the Healy bone structure was bred in so completely that it kicks the crap out of all competing genes and asserts itself all over again. (Doesn't hurt that I went and married Thomas Price, a man with cheekbones that could be used to cut glass. Once, when Dad had been drinking, he said Thomas was so pointy that we already knew what he'd look like as a skeleton. He wasn't entirely right, but he wasn't entirely wrong, either.)

It's the one thing I've got in common with every other Healy I've ever seen a picture of. My father, my grandfather, my kids, even the aunt and uncle I never met, whose pictures I didn't find until after my grandparents were both dead, we've all had those cheekbones.

This woman had them, too.

She moved toward the sink, not seeming to pay me any attention, but I could tell by the reflection of her eyes in the mirror that she was watching me closely for any motion. I stayed where I was, doing a slightly better job than she was of looking nonchalant. She washed her hands, watching me the entire time, scenting the air with harsh soap.

I knocked my elbow against the stall door behind me. "Take your time in there, babe, the sink's busy," I said.

Ryan made a questioning sound.

"I know we have theater tickets, but we have plenty of time, and anyway, I hate to get there early. You know that." I tried to sound bored, like getting to the theater with more than five minutes to curtain was the worst inconvenience I could possibly imagine.

The woman was focusing a little more on her hands now, washing them meticulously. Finally, she straightened, ripped a sheet of paper towels off of the dispenser, and left the bathroom. I exhaled, tilting my head back until it was resting against the stall door.

"That was close."

"What was close?"

"Pretty sure I just saw one of my cousins. Pretty sure she got a good look at me, too. And if she's as smart as I suspect she'd have to be in order to get sent to New York with a Covenant team, she's going to put two and two together and figure out that I'm something she ought to worry about any minute now."

"Oh, that's just Margaret." Ryan cracked open the stall door long enough to shove a bundle of clothing at me. I took it, tucking it up under my arm, and he closed the door again. "If she's in the bookstore, that means we're in the right place. Good job."

"You're being awfully casual about 'We were just in a small bathroom with one exit and a known Covenant operative," I said, before taking another look around the room. "Scratch that. I think that's technically a window, even if Verity would have trouble squirming out of it, and that's an air vent. I could have gone through there if I'd had to, but I couldn't have taken you with me."

"Out of all the Covenant people in this city, Margaret's probably the best one for you to run into," said Ryan, and cracked the door open again, passing me his shoes. "She was with Dominic's original team. She thinks he's dead, and after the whammy Sarah put on her brain the first time she was here, she doesn't seem to be able to see him anymore. I've seen her looking straight at him without realizing he was even there. Since she's never met Istas or me, we're in the clear, and you're obviously new to her."

I decided not to point out the family resemblance. That plus "blonde" was likely to cause some issues, especially after Verity's little stunt on the dance show. There was no way she wasn't going to figure out that I was family, if she hadn't already. For all I knew, she was out there gathering the rest of her team.

One Covenant operative, I could take. A team of four or five, not as easily. I still might win, but there was a decent chance I'd get seriously hurt in the process, and I had to heal the ordinary way if that happened. Healing takes *time*. I'd been seriously injured a few times in my teens, and I hadn't enjoyed the recovery process. Signing up to do it again when I was trying to help Thomas and Sally get reacclimated and trying to acclimate myself just felt like a recipe for disaster.

So no soloing the field team, got it. I gave the vent another look. "Ryan? You still a biped?"

A strange chirping sound was his only answer. I opened the stall door, looking down at a perfectly ordinary tanuki, maybe a little larger than the average, but still small enough for me to lift. Looking at him, a new plan clicked together in my head, beautifully simple and perfectly straightforward, and a truly terrible idea. Which meant, of course, that it was the only logical way to go.

"Change of plans," I said. "We're going into the vents."

Ryan made a slightly more quizzical chirping sound.

"Margaret may be whammied not to recognize Dominic, but there's nothing stopping her from recognizing *me*, especially with as much as I look like my grandparents," I said. "She's going to realize I shouldn't have been here, and come looking. If we go into the vents, we can try and find the rest of her team. You're small enough like this

that you shouldn't have any problem." The first person to figure out
the scientific method by which therianthropes change their size so
dramatically is going to win some sort of an award. Of course, tanuki
can also turn themselves into stone at will, so it may take a while.
Their biology makes no sense. "I'm a little bigger, but I'm bendy." A
"little" bigger was a mild way of saying that I was larger than a small
carnivore that looked like it weighed forty pounds, tops, but Ryan
seemed to accept this, as he nodded and combed the whiskers on one
side of his muzzle with a paw.

The vent was in the wall above the sink. I put my hands on my hips
for a moment, looking up at it, then grasped the edges of the sink and
hoisted myself up, balancing on the edges of the basin. It groaned but
didn't snap off the wall; as long as I didn't do anything too enthusiastic, it would hold my weight, even if only briefly.

Briefly was all I intended to need.

Like most older vents, it was covered by a plain grate, screwed into
the wall with standard dome-head screws. I pulled a multitool out of
my pocket and got to work undoing them, tucking the first three into
the front of my bra for safekeeping and leaving the fourth in place to
keep the grate attached to the wall.

Problem: the grate had about an inch of additional metal on the
inside, presumably to keep people from doing exactly what I was doing. I let go of the edges and unscrewed the fourth screw before easing
the grate away from the wall, bending to set it in the gap between
faucet and mirror. It barely fit.

Well, we'd deal with that later. For the moment, I hopped down,
turning to Ryan, and asked, "Mind if I boost you up?"

He made a frankly adorable chirping noise and stood up on his
hind legs. I scooped him off the ground, resisting the urge to pet my
ally. It wasn't easy, and from the look on his semi-canine little face, he
knew it.

"Yeah, yeah, you're cute as hell," I grumbled, boosting myself back
onto the sink one-handed. It creaked slightly, protesting the additional weight of forty pounds of tanuki, and I hoisted him hastily
through the opening into the vent before bending to retrieve the grate.

"Sorry," I said, and slid it back into place, ramming the screws as
far into the holes as they would go without actually being screwed in
barely three seconds before the bathroom door burst open and the
woman I'd seen before rushed back in, two men on her heels.

She didn't look surprised to see me standing on the sink with my hands on the grate. "Figured you'd be looking for a coward's way out," she said. "Your kind always do. You going to come quietly?"

"I don't know what you're talking about," I said. So she thought I was taking it off, not putting it back on? Good. "This thing was rattling, I was trying to help the bookstore by getting it flush to the wall." I hopped down from the sink, landing with my knees bent to absorb the impact, keeping my eyes on her face the whole time. She watched me unblinking, as steady as a predator that knew it had finally locked in on its prey.

Protective coloration it was, then. Wouldn't be my first time. I straightened up, schooling my expression into one of complete innocence, and asked, "Didn't you hear it when you were in here before?"

"Where'd your friend go?"

"Huh?"

She nodded toward the bundle of clothing on the ground. I kept my expression steady, even as I was swearing inwardly. In my defense, I'd expected at least another ninety seconds to get the clothes out of sight before she came crashing through the door. Expectations can get you killed.

"That guy? I don't know," I said. "I went to pee, and he was gone when I came out of the stall. I was washing my hands when I heard the grate rattling."

"So he took off all his clothes and left the bathroom."

"Looks like it."

"We didn't see anyone leave the bathroom," said one of the men. "We'd have seen it if anyone had."

So why didn't Istas see you coming in? I shrugged. "I don't know what to tell you. I was on the toilet when he disappeared. Did you drop something when you were in here before?"

"Cut the crap," snapped Margaret. "I know it was you on television."

Oh. Well, that was a fun side effect of Sarah's mental whammy. Apparently, Margaret not being able to recognize Verity meant she thought I *was* Verity. Since I looked older than Verity for the first time her life, she probably wouldn't be too flattered by that, which was why there was no point in telling her. Instead, I could just modify my original plan a little, and let things roll as they would.

I stood up straighter, dropping the look of innocent bewilderment, and folded my arms across my chest. "So what are you going to do about it?"

One of the two men cracked his knuckles. The other drew a knife. Neither one of them looked like they had my best interests at heart, which was almost a good thing: I would have been disappointed in them if they'd suddenly decided to play nicely.

Then Margaret held up one hand in a clear stop gesture, and both men stopped moving. Interesting. From the way they were watching her, at least one of them didn't have a lot of respect for her, but they were doing what she told them to do.

"No," she said. "These damned traitors have knocked me down twice. They're not going to do it again. She's mine."

I love it when an opponent's pride lets them decide that one-on-one is the only way to handle things. It makes it so much easier on me. I shifted my stance, moving more of my weight onto my front leg, preparing to kick. I like kicking. I have strong legs, and unlike my punches, I don't telegraph what I'm going to do broadly enough to give people extra time to dodge. It's fun.

She surged forward, hands already raised to swing, and I responded by shifting the rest of my weight front, bringing up my rear foot and swinging it around in a vicious kick to her midsection. I hit solidly enough that I expected her to go staggering backward, and was only a little surprised when she grabbed me by the ankle instead, keeping my foot pinned against her side while she swung at me with her free hand.

It's even more fun when the people hit back. And when they give me free leverage, everything becomes a party. I pushed off the floor with my remaining foot, using the movement to bring my other leg up at the same time and locking them around her waist. It was a maneuver guaranteed to send me crashing to the floor, which it did only half a second later. I took the impact on my upper back, managing to keep my head from hitting until I was finished with my fall, having taken Margaret down with me. I tightened my legs, trying to roll her over.

Margaret responded by shrieking and punching me in the throat. That's always been one of my favorite tricks—the punching, not the screaming—and I would have been grudgingly impressed if I hadn't been trying to deal with the sudden struggle to breathe that followed her hit. I grabbed her head and rolled to the side, worrying less about flipping her onto her back than about slamming her head into the floor. She made a deep, bestial noise when I first slammed her head down. I took some satisfaction in this.

The two men who'd come in with her were watching us roll around on the floor, one looking disgusted, the other almost delighted, like seeing two women doing amateur wrestling in a bathroom was the best thing he could possibly have imagined.

Margaret was slightly larger than I was, which meant that once her head stopped spinning, she was able to roll me back onto the floor and get an arm across my throat, pushing down until I saw little black spots. That was an incapacitating move, not a killing one. I could feel at least three knives through her clothes, and she hadn't gone for any of them.

They wanted a captive. Well, I've been taken captive before, usually by worse than the Covenant, and I'd been planning on getting caught after I hoisted Ryan into the vent. I closed my eyes and went limp, making it seem like I'd passed out.

She kept pressing down for long enough that my masquerade almost became reality before she took the pressure off and pulled away, leaving me coughing but supposedly still unconscious on the floor.

"Get the propofol," she said, voice brisk. "I want her to stay out until we're ready to deal with her."

"And we're carrying an unconscious woman through the bookstore how?" asked one of the men. I couldn't tell them apart by voice alone.

"Employee exit," she said, briskly. "We can take the back hall down to one and go out the back. If anyone spots us, I'll pay them to look the other way."

"They may talk anyway," said the other man.

"And if they do, we'll come back and make them understand why they shouldn't have done that." She was starting to sound annoyed. "Give me the damn drugs, before I have to fracture her skull to keep her out!"

I made a mental note to start hitting again if she made any more noises that implied she'd be going with skull fractures as a solution. Thomas would forgive me for letting myself be captured in order to lead us to the missing kids. He might not be as pleased if I got a concussion for the cause, especially when the cause was currently "that half-assed plan I came up with in less than five minutes, without consulting anyone else."

The needle bit into the flesh of my neck, and my feigned unconsciousness transitioned smoothly into the real thing, carrying me along on a tide of peaceful nothingness. I didn't feel them scoop me off the bathroom floor and carry me out of the bathroom. I didn't feel them carry me down the hallway.

I didn't feel anything at all.

Eighteen

"You have to let people make their own mistakes. If you don't, they're never going to grow, and you're never going to get the chance to say I told you so."

—Enid Healy

Waking up in an unfamiliar place, still clothed, which is a nice change, but tied to a chair, which isn't

THE ROOM WAS DARK.

That wasn't much of a surprise—virtually every time I've been taken captive, I've woken up in a dark room, which is marginally better than the other popular option, "room lit by blinding floodlights, probably filled with the looming shadows of your captors"—but it was a bit of a relief. If they had me in a dark room, it meant they didn't want me to see where they were hiding, and they were at least ensconced enough to be prepared to take prisoners. And yeah, sometimes it's a good thing if your enemies have had time to dig in like ticks. Makes it easier to decapitate them when you dig them out.

The propofol had done its job, and they must have hit me with something else in the bargain; I had no idea how much time had passed between the bookstore and now. Judging by the knots on my wrists, ankles, and calves, it had been long enough for them to carry me out of the bookstore and to a secured location, put me down, and really take their time getting me tied up. Propofol was the best drug I knew of for knocking people out quickly, but it wore off in less than ten minutes when injected; it had to have taken longer than that for them to move me to wherever this was and tie me up. Okay, so say they were working with something that had been spiced up a little somehow. That might explain the lack of headache or pain at the injection site: if you're taking people captive instead of killing them, you'd want them to be cogent as soon as they woke up.

So, propofol, but not alone, even if they were still calling it that. Maybe fentanyl or some kind of benzodiazepine? Since I was waking up here and not back in the slaughterhouse with Thomas glaring at me and Sally saying I'd missed all the fun, I thought it was fair to say that whatever this was had a relatively short half-life, or they'd given me a lower dose than they'd intended to—another thing my weird form of coincidence has been known to influence, often to my detriment, since there have been times when I *wanted* the painkillers to last as long as the pain did, not cut out midway through whatever was going on. Whatever.

Call it at most somewhere between thirty and forty-five minutes. That was sufficient time for Ryan to have forced his way out of the vents, returned to bipedal form, and gone looking for the others. Say that took fifteen minutes . . .

All the scenarios I could run ended with "and the rest of my people will be here very, very soon," and that didn't leave me with long for my part in things.

"Hello?" I yelled, trying to sound at least a little querulous, like I wasn't sure what was going on, like they might have taken the wrong woman after all. I hadn't actually identified myself, just reacted to aggression with aggression, and that's a very New York thing to do, Price or not. But even the toughest New Yorker isn't going to be thrilled to be drugged in a bookstore bathroom and tied to a chair in a dark room. "Hello, is there anybody there?"

No answer came. I was starting to think I'd need to get to work freeing myself from the chair—it was going to have to happen anyway, might as well get started—when a rectangle of light appeared on one wall, violently bright in the darkness. I squinted my eyes shut and turned my face away from the opening door, making a small sound of protest. I hate this part.

"You're awake," said a voice I recognized as Margaret Healy. "Even sooner than I thought you'd be. You're a sturdy one, traitor. I'll have to put that in my notes."

"I don't know what you're talking about," I said, injecting a quaver into my voice.

One really nice thing about having been outside this dimension for so many years: if I'm not carrying my backpack, I don't have much on me. When they'd searched me, and I knew they'd searched me, they would have gotten an assortment of knives, none of which I was particularly emotionally attached to; a garrote that they might have mistaken for a simple loop of wire; my Metro card; a multitool; my wedding ring; and my mother's revolvers. Of those, the only things I needed to get back were the ring and the revolvers. The rest was utterly replaceable, and none of it could be used to identify me. My bluff wasn't going to work, but at least it might buy me a little time.

"You expect me to believe that?" She reached up, pulling a chain, and the ceiling light came on to illuminate the room.

It was small and boxy, with cement walls that seemed to be lightly sloped, like we were in the middle of a giant tube. Looking up, I couldn't find any corners where they hit the ceiling, just a smooth, continual blend. Definitely a tunnel of some sort. We were probably underground.

Well, wasn't that just dandy? New York has a lot of underground to be lost in. Between the subway and the currently active sewer system, you're already looking at miles, and that's before you start checking old blueprints for the stretches that have been sealed off and forgotten. New York has a thriving bogeyman community because of those tunnels, and some people say there are hide-behinds down there, too, although that one's more difficult to prove. If we were underground, this was going to be harder.

"I don't know what to expect you to believe," I said. "You attacked me in a bathroom! I was just minding my own business!"

"If you want to do this the hard way, we can absolutely do this the hard way."

She turned as if to leave the room. But she didn't turn off the light, and that was something of a relief. I don't have a problem with the dark, and I knew where the door was now, which would certainly make things easier. At the same time, I didn't really want to be stumbling around in the darkness if I didn't have to.

"Where are you going?" I asked, careful to whine.

She stopped. "Either you're one of the people we've been looking for, or you're not, and we've just abducted an innocent woman," she said, voice chillingly calm. "Either way, you have to know you're not leaving here alive. A little time to think about what that means should make you a lot more accommodating. You'll talk, when you get hungry enough, or when the ropes get tight enough. What you say *then* will be a lot more honest, and a lot more educational, than whatever it is you might decide to say *now*."

Margaret didn't turn around as she let herself out of the room, closing the door again behind her.

I let my head hang backward until I was looking at the ceiling, still squinting against the light. "Wow, Mom, thanks again for whatever awesome weirdness you brought to the gene pool," I said. "Between this lady and Dad, it's pretty clear that uncut Healy genetics really *suck.*"

That didn't explain Grandpa, but maybe he was the exception that proved the rule. The Covenant had to be keeping the family around for a reason. Whatever: it didn't really matter now. Either way, I needed to get out of this chair, and I didn't have any good way to cut these ropes. They hadn't been kind enough to leave me with a knife or a convenient length of exposed pipe. Instead, it was just me, and a chair, and an empty room.

When in doubt, improvise. I know how to take a hit, whether it's being delivered by a person or the floor. I also knew from the speed with which Margaret had come to check on me when I started yelling that the room wasn't soundproofed. I took a deep breath and began singing "The Wheels on the Bus" as loudly as I could.

No one came busting in to ask me to stop, which meant they were either ignoring me or out of earshot. I kept on singing, and when the song ran out, transitioned to "The Bog Down in the Valley-o." Still, no one came, and that song has been known to annoy dead people.

(I mean that literally. I once got Mary to threaten to go haunt someone else's house by singing it for too many repetitions in a row. It is a song with a powerful potential for driving people out of their minds.)

Still singing, I rocked back until I felt the front legs of the chair leave the floor. The fools really had left me *this* unsecured. They'd tied me up and they'd taken away my weapons, and assumed that would be good enough.

Too bad for them. Still singing, I pushed off against the floor as hard as I could, and kept singing as I toppled over backward. I stopped singing when the impact knocked the breath out of me, and resumed as I struggled to free myself from the wreckage of the chair. They just don't make chairs the way they used to.

I blame IKEA. Never tie a kidnapping victim to anything a college student can afford.

So now I wasn't tied to a chair, but I was still tied *up*, and sitting in the splintered wreckage of a chair wasn't that much of an improvement.

The chair legs were still attached pretty tightly to my own, which wasn't great either. I squirmed until I could reach them, then pulled the remains of the chair legs out of the loops around my ankles. This created space. Bending my right leg back at an uncomfortable angle, I was able to work my fingers into the slack I'd opened up and work the knot slowly free.

I straightened my leg out again, pins and needles already beginning to shoot from my ankle up to my knee as blood flow returned to the area that had been tied off, and repeated the process with my left leg. With both legs untied, I was able to maneuver myself first into a crouch, and then fully upright.

The room I was in was mostly featureless, with only the chair I'd destroyed and a few shelves around the edges. I was still wearing shoes, which was nice—I wouldn't have liked getting a splinter in the sole of my foot—and so I walked toward the shelves, looking for something that would give me a sharp-enough edge to work the rope against. The ropes on my ankles had been pretty standard hardware-store nylon, tough enough to tie a woman up, not tough enough to handle focused and continuous friction for a sustained period of time. I was assuming the rope on my wrists was the same. That kind of rope works mostly because skin gives way long before nylon does, which makes squirming out of them a very painful and potentially disabling activity. A good cutting edge, on the other hand, changes everything.

The shelves were mostly empty, which didn't help, since my hands were still tied behind me, and I couldn't get the knots to my mouth without dislocating both shoulders—not the best way to go into a potential fight. On the third shelf, though, I hit paydirt.

The shelf itself was empty, but the outside edge of one support was weathered enough to have developed the beginning of a rough cutting surface. It was speckled with rust, and I'd need a tetanus shot if I slipped and broke my skin, but it would do. I turned around and backed into it, beginning to saw away at the ropes holding my wrists together.

So far, my "get yourself taken captive and let the others find you and the abducted kids at the same time" plan was working great, except for the part where I didn't have any indication that I was in the same place as the missing dragons. And the part where there was no sign that the rest of my group was in the process of finding me. Honestly, that would have been a little unnerving, if I hadn't been locked in a small, mostly empty room: they could have been ten feet away and almost to my rescue.

The room wasn't soundproof. They couldn't be fighting right outside the door without my noticing. But everything else was still on the table.

With a final snapping sound, the ropes dropped away. I pulled my hands in front of me, rubbing my right wrist with my left hand to restore the circulation. Okay. So it had been an impulsive plan, and I could probably have taken more time to think it through. It'd been a while since I could rely on having backup when I was in the field. Not since Laura and I were in college together, really. I hadn't gone back to Buckley until my grandfather died, and Thomas had already been locked in his house by then, leaving me with no one to depend on.

Yeah. Relying on my team was going to take some getting used to, and I looked forward to getting better at it. I kept rubbing my wrists and resumed searching the room, stepping as quietly as I could near the door. The space was longer than it was wide, if I called the door one "end" of the room.

There was another door at the opposite end.

I paused when I found it, then tested the knob. It turned, which answered the question of whether or not I was going to head on through. The door swung open without a sound, which implied better structural maintenance than I'd been expecting from this place.

The room on the other side was completely dark, apart from the square of light cast by the open door. No windows, no lights, no way to break up the blackness.

I had recently been drugged, I didn't have any weapons, tools, or arcane foci with me, and I certainly didn't have any glucose gel. That made activating any of my dwindling supply of remaining tattoos a terrible idea. Sometimes terrible ideas are the best ones I have. I pressed two fingers to the inside of my left arm, seeking out the star I knew was tattooed there. It was the second in what had originally been a line of four; the first had already been discharged.

"Light, please," I said, voice low, and closed my eyes as a wave of dizziness swept over me.

Thomas says the reason he never suggested tattooing me when he'd still been house-bound and unable to keep me safe was one of practicality: I wasn't a sorcerer; my system wasn't built to carry and channel magic the way his was. And since I didn't have any power reserves for the spells tied to my tattoos to use, they found their fuel in other places. Sugars and electrolytes, mostly, which could leave me dizzy, off-balance, and even unconscious if I tried to pull off something really big without proper planning.

The man who'd actually proposed tattooing me had been an

honorary uncle at the time, and one of the few people I'd truly trusted to help me on my search for my missing husband. Look how that worked out. Naga is dead, killed by Thomas when we discovered that some of the mental conditioning Naga had been ordering on me had included an inability to pull the trigger if he was on the other end of the bullet, and when this batch of tattoos is used up, I'm not going to be getting any more. Which is probably for the best, considering what they do to me, but I'll be honest: I'm going to miss the ability to play all-purpose tool when working alone.

Good thing I don't have to work alone much anymore. I opened my eyes, shaking off the dizziness. Small light spells never hit that hard, which was a large part of why I was still standing. My skin was emitting a soft, continuous glow, making me about as subtle as a lightning bug during mating season, but lighting up the room in front of me enough to let me see that it wasn't a room at all. It was a short hallway, the walls closer in than the walls of the room I was currently in, ending at another door. I stepped inside, easing the door closed behind me. My loud singing and the sound of the chair smashing against the floor hadn't attracted any curious Covenant agents, but that wasn't something I could expect to last forever.

There's using your luck, and then there's depending on your luck. One of them is a tool; the other is a very elaborate means of committing suicide. I stepped carefully down the hall, watching the floor for signs of tripwires or pressure plates, and stopped when I reached the second door. Holding my breath to cut down on extraneous sounds, I pressed my ear against it.

Someone was crying.

Someone very young, if the timbre of their sniffles was anything to go by; they weren't wailing, but they were whimpering, a slow, steady stream of small, deeply unhappy noises. That settled it. I stepped back just enough to test the knob and, finding this one unlocked as well, opened the door.

The room on the other side was roughly the same size as the one where I'd been held, but looked smaller, thanks to the cages against the walls. They were the large, foldable kind sold by pet stores for short-term kenneling of aggressive dogs, each one big enough to hold a small child or a good-sized canine.

About half of them were occupied, three by golden-haired little girls in scruffy secondhand clothing—not a sign of neglect in dragon kids, since the urge to hoard gold kicks in so young that they would probably already have viewed buying anything nicer as a waste of money—and the other five by large reptiles about the size of Komodo dragons, if Komodo dragons came with wings. All eight of them looked at me warily, unsure how to react to the sight of a glowing human woman. The expressions of fear and dread on their little faces hurt.

The realization that they were all caged alone hurt even more. They'd been allowed to stay in the same room, but they'd been separated all the same, unable to pile together for comfort. Oh, I was going to take great pleasure in beating the living crap out of the people who'd taken them.

"It's all right," I said, holding up my hands as I stepped farther into the room. "Pris and William sent me."

Hopefully, invoking the names of the people I'd come to assume were the leaders of the local Nest would help, and it did, with a few of the kids. One of the girls stopped crying, and one of the little boys stopped mantling his wings, although he remained pressed against the side of the cage. I moved toward him first. He hissed, loud and angry.

"I can let you out, if you promise not to bite me," I said, kneeling. "Do you know where they took the woman who was with you? Cara, I think her name was?"

"No," sniffled one of the girls. "They put us in cages and they took her. They said we should get used to it, because we're just animals, and they wouldn't be doing us any favors if they acted like we were anything else." Her evident offense grew with each word, until she sounded more angry than scared. That was a good thing. I gave her an approving nod, then focused on the latch for the boy's cage.

The latches had been modified to keep them from being opened by captive children with clever fingers, but they were no match to an adult outside the cage with a background in lock-picking. In short order, I had the first cage open and moved away to let the little boy inside scurry free, not blocking him or moving to touch him in any way. He ran for the farthest corner and pressed himself there, hissing violently.

"It's okay, Kris," said one of the girls. "I think she's part of Miss Verity's family." She turned enormous blue eyes on me and asked, with a slight challenge in her voice, "Aren't you?"

"I am," I assured her. "My name's Alice. What's yours?"

"Ariel."

"It's nice to meet you, Ariel." I moved to her cage, repeating the process of getting it open. "I'm going to get you all out so you can take care of each other, and then I'm going to ask you to stay here while I go and find Miss Cara and make sure she's all right."

"And then we can go home?"

"As soon as it's safe."

Her face fell. "It's not ever going to be safe, Miss Alice. We're not people. We don't get to be safe."

"Oh, sweetie, never believe anyone who tells you that you're not a person. You're people, all of you, and you deserve to be safe. You're not *human* people, and I'm not so sure that's a bad thing, since it was human people who put you in these cages." I opened the door, and she crawled out on her hands and knees. I shifted to the side, making it easier for her to get out without accidentally brushing against me. Dragons generally aren't big on touching humans.

Ariel straightened once she was out of the cage, whirling to throw her arms around my neck in a brief hug. Dragons may not be big on touching humans, but scared children frequently are, and "child" came before "species" right now. I put a hand against her back as she hugged me, returning her embrace without trapping her, and silently vowed to kill anyone I had to in order to make sure this wasn't going to happen again.

Ariel pulled away and I let her go, moving on to the other cages. Very shortly, all the dragon children were free, and piling up in the corner as I had expected, becoming a tangle of limbs, tails, and wings. I straightened.

"I'll be back as soon as I can," I said. "If anyone comes in here while I'm gone, you have my permission and encouragement to bite them as hard as you can. Don't give them the chance to cage you again."

"Miss Cara says biting is wrong," said one of the other girls.

"And normally, Miss Cara is right about that," I said. "But right now, you're being held against your will, and that changes the rules enough to make biting just fine. You bite anyone who tries to put you into a cage, you got me?"

The children nodded in ragged chorus, and I nodded back.

"Good. I'll be back."

The only door into this room was the one I had arrived through. I walked back toward it, and several of the children moaned as they realized the light was going with me. I stopped, looking back at them.

"I'm sorry," I said. "I don't have any way to leave the light here with you, and it's not safe for you to come with me. Just pretend it's bedtime. Tell each other some nice stories, and get cozy, and I'll be back as soon as I can, I promise."

They muttered in discontent but made no further objections as I let myself out of the room, heading back the way I had come.

So: I was loose. I was unarmed. I knew where the children were. I knew that by now, Ryan had to be following our trail back to this location, which meant that I had backup on the way. Until then, I was in some sort of underground space with between three and five Covenant agents, none of whom realized who they actually had on their hands.

I smiled grimly as I made my way through the dark back to the room where I'd started.

Wasn't this going to be *fun*?

Nineteen

"I swear, if all children have as much sense of self-preservation as Healy children, it's a miracle anyone ever lives to adulthood."

—Mary Dunlavy

Opening the door between me and the rest of a Covenant team, ready for a fight

THE DOOR OPENED EASILY—APPARENTLY, these folks had been confident enough in their security (and their furniture) to think there was no point in locking me in. I slipped through into another hallway, this one lit with bare hanging bulbs very like the ones in the room where I'd been held. They could certainly do with investing in a better interior decorator. I'm several decades out of the mainstream, but even I know that "too creepy for the people in Amityville" is not a design aesthetic to emulate.

For all that I was still glowing—and would be until the spell ran its course—it was nice to have the lights on. The amount of light I can put off with a spell is nothing compared to good ambient lighting. I paid careful attention to my surroundings as I moved.

The walls were curved, like all the others had been, although when I looked back, there were actual hard angles in the wall around the door. I was still in the tunnel system, but this tunnel was at a right angle to the little offshoot where I'd been kept with the kids. The fact that they'd put us all that close to together there told me both that they hadn't been planning on another prisoner, and that they weren't very accustomed to taking prisoners at all. That would have been a good thing, if not for the fact that it meant they usually just killed people.

Corpses need a lot less in the way of operational security, unless they've been infected with something that parodies reanimation, or you have someone on your team with questionable ideas about scientific ethics and a lot of volts of electricity.

There were three doors, apart from the one I'd come through. I stopped to listen at each of them. The first had total silence on the other side. The second had a very soft sound that I couldn't quite make out, but didn't seem like anything I needed to worry about. The third had voices, raised enough to be in heated discussion, but not enough for me to make out a damn thing they were saying. I backed away. Door number two it was, then. When in doubt, always delay the open combat as long as possible.

Easing open the second door revealed a room much like the one where I'd been kept, absent the door at the back—this was a terminus, not a passthrough. There was a blonde woman tied to a chair at the center of the room, head bowed, weeping. She looked up as I stepped into the room, narrowing her eyes and glaring at me.

They hadn't bothered to gag her. I raised a hand, trying to signal her to silence. Maybe it was the fact that she didn't recognize me from the Covenant team, and maybe it was the part where I was still glowing—something evil monster-hunting assholes don't tend to do—but she didn't scream, only sniffled and continued to watch me warily as I closed the door behind myself and made my way across the room to her.

"Cara?" I asked, kneeling by her side.

When she nodded—a small, tightly controlled motion of her head, barely enough to make her hair shift positions—I began working on the knots holding her wrists. "I'm Alice. Verity's grandmother. I found the children. If you'll just let me untie you, I can tell you how to reach them."

"You're letting me go?"

"Of course I'm letting you go. I'm not in the business of torturing women for my own amusement." I finished untying her wrists and began unwrapping the rope, freeing her arms. It was a lot easier when I didn't have to smash the chair in the process. "The kids need someone with them. It's dark in there."

Cara wilted in her seat, making no effort to reach for her ankles. "It doesn't matter anyway. They know where we are now. They'll just keep coming."

"So we'll figure out how to move the rest of you. We'll—"

"We can't move William!" Cara clapped a hand over her mouth, eyes going wide as she realized that she had just shouted. She glanced anxiously at the door, clearly waiting for the Covenant to come to investigate the noise. I tensed, waiting for much the same. If they came in here, there'd be no way for me to hide. Not when I was lit up like a glowstick.

The door remained shut. No one came to see what the yelling was about. I untensed, just a little, and started untying her ankles.

"We can't move William and they know he exists, they know we have a husband, they know where we are, they know how to find us, they've been watching us for weeks—" Her voice was low and anxious, her words falling over each other like rocks tumbling in a landslide, each barely leaving room for the next.

"We'll find a way," I said. "If we have to, we'll find a way. My husband is an elemental sorcerer. Fire's his focus, but I'm sure he's done some work with stone. I know a Huldra who sings to the trees, but whose wife went to stone when she died. We have the resources. If we bring them all together, we can move your husband to safety—if that's even what has to happen. I was told they grabbed you while you were moving the kids. That doesn't mean they necessarily know where the entrance to the Nest is."

"It's only a matter of time."

"Not if we win." Cara glanced at me, eyes going wide again. I offered her what I hoped would come across as an encouraging smile. "This is a war. Us versus the Covenant. It was always going to *be* a war, because they were never going to let it be anything else. So we win. We beat them so badly they go back to Europe and never darken our doorsteps again. And we're going to win, Cara. We're going to make sure you and your children and your husband will all be safe."

Maybe I was making promises I couldn't keep. But I was going to do my best to keep them, no matter what, and that was really all I could do. If it turned out I couldn't keep my word, we'd probably all be dead, and she wouldn't exactly be in a position to blame me.

And ugh. That kind of thinking is why it's always been hard for me to make friends. I finished untying her ankles and straightened, offering her my hands.

After a pause that could easily be attributed to natural draconic reluctance to touch a human, she reached out and took them. I pulled her to her feet. She stumbled a little, ankles probably still sore, before reclaiming her hands and asking, in a soft voice, "Which way?"

"End of the corridor," I said, pointing. "There's a light on in that room. It leads to a dark hall, and if you walk straight down it to the end, there's another door. That's where they have the kids. They were keeping them in cages. The Covenant was keeping the kids in cages,

I mean. I let them out. There's no light, but at least they have each other." That suddenly didn't feel like enough, so I added, "They were all there. The number of kids in the room matches the information I'd been given."

Cara made a small gasping sound, somewhere between a bark of laughter and a sob, and slung her arms abruptly around my neck. No draconic reluctance here: just the deep relief of an adult caretaker hearing that her charges were safe. There was every chance one or more of those kids was literally hers, although even she might not know it; that's not how most dragons handle childrearing. They're more in the "put them all in a big pile, take on a maternal role to all of them at once" category.

I had to wonder whether reintroducing males to the mix had changed that at all. Were the dragons who had scaled sons more inclined to track maternity, even if only for the bragging rights? And that was a question for a later time, when I didn't have a dragon wrapped around my neck. A took a half-step backward. Cara seemed to remember herself and let me go, looking at me with aching hope in her eyes. Feeling suddenly awkward, I motioned toward the door. "We should probably get moving."

"Oh!" she said. "Yes. End of hall, door, end of hall, children."

She took off at something very close to a run. Unlike me, she had no shoes; her feet were almost soundless against the pavement. I followed a little more sedately, concerned about my boots making too much noise, and caught the first door before it could slam.

I wasn't fast enough to catch the second. She had already vanished into the room where I'd been kept by the time I reached the hallway, and the door swung shut while I was still reaching for it. I froze. There was no way they'd have missed that sound. And the first place they'd look would probably be in the room where they'd put the suspected Healy, meaning they'd run right into Cara.

I couldn't let that happen. I sighed instead, and turned to face the door where I'd heard voices before, counting down silently from ten.

I had barely reached six before the door flew open and Margaret spilled into the hall, followed by one of the men from the bathroom. I gave them a concerned look, shaking my head like they'd done something to direly disappoint me.

"You're not very good hosts," I said. "I'm absolutely *sure* I had my mother's guns when you knocked me out. I didn't say I was okay with bondage, and I'm *definitely* not okay with robbery."

Margaret gaped for a moment before recovering herself and saying harshly, "You're not supposed to be out here."

"I sort of got that from the way you tied me to a chair. Again, consent? Did you ever consider that maybe it was an important part of a new relationship? Because that was *not* the quality of either rope or hospitality to which I have become accustomed."

Her eyes narrowed. "You traitors think you run this continent."

What would Verity do in this situation? I tried to channel the spirit of my endlessly irreverent granddaughter, and decided she wouldn't take these people seriously in the slightest.

"No, sweetie, I *know* we run this continent." I lifted one hand, studying my fingernails with exaggerated care. As always, they were trashed. My last manicure was sometime in the 1990s. I looked back to Margaret, who was visibly reddening at the snub. I lowered my hand. "Y'all are the ones who put us here. You *gave* us this continent. And we don't do take-backs. So just give me my guns and get the fuck out of New York before this goes badly for you, okay?"

"You messed with my head the first time I fought you. You really think I'm giving you a weapon?"

Yeah, she definitely thought I was Verity. That probably wouldn't be as flattering to my granddaughter as it was to me, but Verity never needed to know about it.

"I think the weapon in question was mine to begin with," I said, reasonably enough.

"Peg, she's *glowing*," said one of the men. "How is she glowing?"

"They really don't teach you people anything before they send you out into the field to get yourself slaughtered by the first bigger dog to come trotting down the block, do they?" I was starting to feel a little bad for them. They were shifting their weight from foot to foot like they were afraid of the consequences if they made the first move. This wasn't Margaret's first rodeo. I was pretty sure it was theirs, and beating the crap out of them wasn't going to be enough of a challenge to make me feel better.

Field-tested or not, they'd been competent enough to capture an innocent woman and the children she was supposed to be shepherding, all for the crime of looking human when they actually weren't. I shifted my weight, finally falling into a fighting stance. No more of them seemed to be coming. It was just these three. Three on one isn't the best odds, but when it's one competent agent and two untested newcomers versus me, they get a whole hell of a lot better.

"We going to do this, or what?" I asked. "Because I have things I need to be doing, and the longer we stand here yapping, the harder it's going to be to finish them on a schedule."

With a shout that was half battle cry and half incoherent rage, Margaret charged for me, throwing a punch at my chest. I stuck out one arm as I pivoted to the side, clotheslining her and sending her crashing into the nearest wall, clutching her throat and choking. A good clothesline uses your opponent's momentum against them effectively enough to take them out of the fight, and Margaret had run right into that one. What *was* the Covenant teaching these kids, anyway? Any of my grandchildren would have dodged that by the time they were twelve, even Artie and Sarah, and they were mostly noncombatants.

Taking Margaret out hadn't removed her boys from the fight. The larger of the two lunged for me, clearly going for a grapple. I danced backward, evading his grasp, and tried to sweep his feet out from underneath him. This one, at least, had encountered the concept of dodging at some point, because he evaded the hit and delivered a knee to my midsection, doubling me over. The second man darted in, grabbing me by the hair.

That was fine. I've always had excellent core strength. I straightened as fast and hard as I could, using his grip on my hair as a guide for where I should slam my head. The sound it made when it impacted with his nose was as satisfying as it always was. There's something about the crunch of breaking cartilage that just *gets* me.

He reeled backward, losing his grip on me, and I whirled, grabbing his shoulders and holding him in place as I brought my knee up twice in quick succession: one hit to the belly, one to the balls. When I released him, he crumpled, moaning, to the floor, and I turned to the first man, smiling a bright, almost-feral smile.

He shied away, which may have been the first sensible thing he'd done since the bathroom. "Hi," I said, stalking toward him. My lip had split somewhere in the middle of that little tussle; I wiped the blood away with the back of my hand, but couldn't stop it from trickling into my teeth. That just made me smile wider, wanting to treat him to every last terrible drop of me. "You helped abduct me. I don't like being abducted."

His response was to dig something out of his pocket and brandish it at me. "Back, witch!"

Even if I'd been a sorcerer, I doubted there was any sort of talisman small enough to fit in a pocket that could have been used to ward me off. I still cocked my head, looking at the object in his hand. It looked like a rabbit's foot, albeit one wrapped in braided cord and adorned with a handful of charms. One of them, a glass disk with something liquid at its core, was recognizable as an anti-telepathy charm. The rest were mysteries to me.

He thrust it at me again, clearly expecting it to do something. And to be fair, it did. It pissed me off.

Snatching the thing out of his hand, I threw it on the ground and stepped down as hard as I could, grinding my heel over the glass disk until I heard a small but satisfying crunching sound. I looked up at his face, finding him staring at me with shock.

"Margaret's not in charge of the Covenant here in New York, is she?" I asked. I turned to Margaret, still gasping against the nearest wall. "You got demoted because you kept losing, and now you're mad about it, but they gave you the newbies. That's why we weren't sure whether there were three teams or four, and why there's no one else here. You're not supposed to be working independently. You went rogue and snatched some kids, and kept them secret because you wanted to deliver the dragons to your bosses to prove that you could still do the job."

She didn't have the air to answer me, but the glare she shot my way was more than answer enough.

"What the fuck ever." I threw up my hands and stalked past the one man I *hadn't* already incapacitated, heading into the room where they'd been holed up before Cara so unceremoniously alerted them to our presence.

It was a small room, very similar to the one where I'd woken up, only instead of a woman tied to a chair, it had a folding card table in the middle, complete with cards. They'd been playing a game at some point, recently enough that they hadn't cleaned up after themselves just yet. The shelves against the curving walls were more crowded, with a variety of objects I assumed were their kit. They should really have stopped to grab more of it before coming out into the hall.

"Um." That was the man whose little toy I'd taken. I glanced back over my shoulder at him. He was standing in the doorway, watching me warily. "Can you move away from that shelf, please, scary glowing lady?"

"Why?"

"That's . . . our stuff."

"You took my stuff." I reached for a shoebox, opening it to reveal my mother's guns. "But you didn't take it very far, so maybe I don't have to kill you."

He cringed. Some Covenant strike team. I lowered the box, giving him a critical look.

"Did they give you boys *any* training before they tossed you out into the field?"

"Ma'am, I'm a Bell," he said, halfway desperately. "I was never supposed to *be* in the field. They only sent me to New York because they'd heard rumors about a real dragon being found in the area, and they wanted a proper researcher to confirm the identification. I should never have been here."

"Tell you what, I'm feeling generous, since all my knives are here." A soft buzz had appeared at the back of my head, heralding the approach of a telepath who knew me. "Run. Run now, Mr. Bell, and maybe the people who are on their way here to retrieve me won't catch you."

He hesitated, and in that moment of hesitation, his face hardened, and he stood just a little straighter. "Thou shalt not suffer a witch to live," he said. "I know what your family does. You lead good Covenant men astray. I'm not doing *anything* you ask me to."

Out in the hall, I heard a door slam open, and the sound of shouting, followed by the roar of some unspeakably great beast. Sally was getting a real education into why everyone with any sense was afraid of the waheela. Something else snarled under Istas's roar. Oh, good. Ryan was here too.

"Too late," I said, gathering knives from the box and beginning to tuck them away in my clothing. "If you'd run when I told you to, I could probably have made a case for treating you as a hostile noncombatant. Now, I'm afraid, you're going to be firmly on the 'bad guys' list."

"*Alice!*" Thomas didn't sound panicked so much as, well, urgent, like he needed me to answer him *right now* or he was going to tip over some invisible edge into being genuinely concerned.

"That's my ride," I said, and walked toward the door where Bell still stood frozen, face a mask of terror. I nudged him out of the way. "Hang out here, smart guy, and you'll see what you just bought yourself in a minute."

The hallway was chaos. Istas, now in the massive wolf-bear shape she called her great-form, had Margaret by the middle and pinned against the wall. The woman was clearly too terrified to squirm, or to scream. She was staring at Istas, eyes huge in a colorless face, and the front of her jeans was suspiciously dark. I guess all the field training in the world doesn't teach you how to deal with being picked up and slammed into things by an angry waheela.

Sally and Ryan were over by the man I'd put on the floor, the one looming in his much, much larger bipedal tanuki form rather than the adorable woodland creature I'd shoved into a bookstore vent, the other crouched with a length of metal pipe she'd acquired somewhere pressed across the man's throat.

Dominic was ahead of all of them, standing in the doorway of the room where I'd been kept until I woke up, and Thomas was at the end of the hall, walking with calm, perfect deliberation. He had rolled up the sleeves of his shirt, the cuffs precisely folded into place, and the sight made me wince a little. I'd scared him more than I'd expected to.

"Alice," he said, shoulders slumping in visible relief as he caught sight of me. Then he tensed again. "Ryan told us what happened. What in the world would possess you to allow yourself to be taken?"

"They were coming," I said. "Either it was just me, or it was both of us. I didn't have time to get into the vent."

"You're not alone anymore." Somehow, he was standing right in front of me. I hadn't noticed either one of us moving. "You can't just run off into danger because you trust yourself to be good enough to wriggle out of it. You scared me half to death."

"I knew you'd find me, and I knew they weren't going to hurt me. At least not immediately." The first part was truer than the second, but that didn't matter just yet. "If coincidence arranged for Margaret showing up in the same bathroom, it wasn't going to let them be smart enough to put a bullet between my eyes."

"Alice . . ." He made my name half a moan, half a sigh. "I know you hate being told to be careful, and in truth, I hate to ask it of you. But I wish you'd try for my sake, if nothing else."

"I found Cara and the kids." Thomas's eyes widened. He didn't look surprised. He's known me long enough that surprise is no longer his first response when I say that something absolutely improbable has happened. "None of them are injured, although they're all shaken up a bit, and I wouldn't expect them to be very fond of humans for a while. These people are amateurs."

"Not what I would normally expect from a Covenant field team, but perhaps standards are slipping," he said gravely, and looked past me to where Bell still stood frozen in the doorway. He lifted an eyebrow. "You seem to have missed one."

"Nah. Didn't miss him. I tried to get him to run away, but you know how you Covenant boys are: stubborn to the last."

Thomas cracked a smile at that, looking briefly, almost unwillingly amused. "Yes, we do have classes on being stubborn."

The static of approaching telepath was getting stronger, becoming almost a crackle. I touched my temple, giving Thomas a curious look.

"*Someone*," he said, "seems to have broken the anti-telepathy charm on at least one of these charming individuals, and while parts of this hideout are well-shielded enough that she didn't find the dragons, she picked up on you as soon as you left those areas. Sarah can see the exposed individual now. She'll be just behind us. We were following your trail when Istas stopped and said we weren't alone. We turned around, and there was Sarah, walking along behind us. I don't know how she reached us so quickly."

"I have some ideas," I said. I might actually know more about true Johrlac than Thomas did, at this point, which was a little weird to think about. Not as weird as thinking about Sarah having reached even half that level of control over what her species was capable of, but something being weird has never been enough to render it untrue. "So she's coming?"

"She's coming. Sally? How's it coming with those charms?"

"You said to look for little glass disks, right? Well, we found one, on the dude. The lady's still holding out on us."

"Impressive, given that Istas has her against a wall. I don't know many people stubborn enough to act against their own best interests while a waheela has them pinned."

"She's a Healy," I said. "Not the same branch as me, thank God, but a Healy, and we breed for stubborn."

"Alice is right," said Thomas. "We'll be right there."

He offered his hand. I took it, and he tugged me along, away from the gaping Bell, over to where Istas was restraining Margaret. Sally was still keeping the other guy—we'd need a name for him eventually—pinned to the floor with her length of pipe, but both Ryan and Dominic had joined the cluster around my distant cousin, who was watching them with a mix of fear and defiance that would have been impressive even if she *hadn't* been pinned to the wall by something that looked like it had escaped from a Hammer horror production. Istas was snarling, showing her substantial teeth, and Margaret, despite having wet herself earlier, wasn't crying.

Ryan and Dominic were clearly trying to intimidate—not that they needed to bother with a waheela right there, although it was nice that they were still making the effort—but Dominic, as the only one with hands small enough to have searched her, was keeping those hands to himself. He looked relieved at my approach.

"We were friends, once," he said. "I would much prefer not to be the one to violate her person."

"I've never seen you before in my life," Margaret snapped.

That tracked with her believing I was Verity, after the way Sarah had scrambled her brain. "We were never friends," I said. "Istas, hold her still."

Istas growled, a sound I took as agreement, and I moved forward, briskly patting Margaret down. Nothing. My second search was more thorough, and peppered with occasional apologies as I had to fold bits of her clothing down or pull them aside in order to check them. Enemy combatants still deserve basic respect, even if they wouldn't extend the same to you. And since I had woken up fully clothed, I had to assume they'd been more polite about that sort of thing than most.

I found the anti-telepathy charm under the band of her bra, held in place by a pair of safety pins that I unclipped in order to pull the charm free. It was such a small thing. She glared at me like she thought looks could kill as I took it away.

Looks *can* kill, but only if the person doing the looking is a gorgon or related species. I dropped the charm to the tunnel floor, grinding it under my heel. "Dominic, go make sure Cara doesn't bring the kids out here just yet," I said. "I have the feeling they're not going to want to see what happens next."

What happened next was that another door opened, and Sarah stepped into the tunnel. She looked deeply sorry to be there, an expression of such profound regret on her face that it almost distracted from the fact that her eyes were solid white from side to side and glowing even more brightly than I was. Nothing could have distracted from the way her hair was rising from her shoulders, the ends of it floating languidly like she was underwater, even though she was as dry as the rest of us were.

"I can see all of them now," she said, voice gone distant. "You can let her go, Istas. She's not going anywhere."

I stepped reflexively closer to Thomas, who had positioned himself in front of Sally. This had to be even more terrifying for the two of them, who didn't know Sarah like I did, than it was for me.

"Hey, sweetie," I said, aware that I had taken on the tone usually reserved for addressing dangerous animals, but unsure of how to make myself stop. "How'd you get here so fast?"

"Everything is on a grid, and if you can see it, you can move through it as you need to," she said. "I needed to be here now."

"I . . . see," said Thomas.

Istas lowered Margaret slowly to her feet, taking her paw away from the woman's middle. Margaret didn't bolt. Margaret didn't move at all but remained exactly where she was, wobbling slightly, staring at the wall. I blinked, and glanced at the man Sally still had pinned against the floor. He had the same look on his face, and he wasn't moving either. Finally, I turned. Bell, too, had a vacant look in his eyes and was staring into nothing, not alarmed at all by the appearance of a white-eyed woman with floating hair.

"There are always frightened children in a city this size," said Sarah. "I wasn't there when the captives were taken and then they were placed behind wards where I couldn't find them. But once you escaped the wards, I could find *your* mind, and when you took the first charm away from your captors I could see where the others were being held. I can see them now. All of them."

Dominic emerged from the room at the end of the hall, a tiny blonde girl in his arms and Cara close behind him. She had one of the boys in her own arms, his wings half-open and wrapped around her in a leathery embrace. The rest of the children were behind them, looking warily around as they followed the adults to safety.

One of the little girls started to cry when she saw Margaret, and I wished I'd hit the woman harder when I had the chance. Hitting her now would have been like kicking a puppy, though. She didn't make any move to turn toward the sound, didn't react as Sarah advanced.

"They were acting alone, these three," Sarah said, voice still distant. "Margaret isn't in very good standing with the Covenant these days. They sent her back here to prove that she wasn't useless yet. Gave her two trainees to keep an eye on her, and left her here to do support work for the rest of them. She knows where all the other teams are, though—the actual teams. These three aren't supposed to go into the field, for fear that they'll do exactly what they just did: fuck up and reveal the rest of the Covenant presence in the area. She knows how to find them."

"Sarah—"

"You should go now," she said, voice never varying. "Take the children. Get them safely home. I'll come to join you soon."

"All right," I said, and stepped back, reaching for Thomas's hand. After a long beat, he took it, and I pulled him with me as I started for the door she'd arrived through, which I presumed would lead to the exit. Sally followed, Istas and Ryan behind her, and Dominic and the dragons brought up the rear.

The Covenant agents never moved as we all walked away, leaving them alone with my most dangerous grandchild.

But just before the door swung shut behind us, I heard Margaret start to scream.

Twenty

"Not all the choices we have are good ones. Sometimes the best outcome you can hope for is the one where you're still standing at the end."

—Juniper Campbell

Walking back through the subway maintenance tunnels to the slaughterhouse, leaving the Covenant behind

GETTING EIGHT CHILDREN, SEVERAL of whom didn't look even remotely human, from one side of Manhattan to the other was a herculean undertaking, one that wouldn't have been possible if Istas hadn't convinced the boys to submit to being carried in large dog carriers purchased from the nearest pet store after returning to her humanoid form.

"Yes, it is an insult to your dignity," she had said, calm and reasonable even when she had no business being, "and yes, you will be within your rights to set them on fire when we have returned to the Nest. But until then, we will need to travel with you, and this is the safest option for everyone involved."

None of the boys had mastered English yet, and their grumbles and mutters had been translated by their sisters, who seemed to find the whole situation more amusing than anything else.

Istas, who had recovered her clothing from the side tunnel where it had been hidden, had waited patiently until negotiations were concluded, and then gone to fetch the carriers.

Sarah would have told us if the information she got from Bell indicated more Covenant presence in this area, but we still chose to take the maintenance tunnels rather than the subway, preferring to remain at least somewhat out of sight. Five little boys in carriers meant one each for me, Dominic, Thomas, Ryan, and Istas. Cara had offered to carry one of them, but we needed her to keep hold of the girls, and so our motley little group proceeded onward, into the concrete embrace of the tunnels.

Dominic had needed to produce substantially more cash to get us through the door unseen this time, but it had worked, and so we moved on.

We walked in silence, and were roughly halfway back when the echoes around me shifted. I glanced to the side. Sarah was walking there, expression serene, looking as if she'd been with us all along.

"Everything good?" I asked.

"Yes," she said. "They don't remember anything about finding the dragons, or William's existence, or us. None of them will be suitable for field work again, sadly. Margaret's mind can't take another revision on this scale, and so she'll find herself becoming physically ill if she even thinks about another field assignment, to help make sure it won't be necessary."

"That's a little . . . uh, that's a little extreme, there, isn't it?"

"No." She turned wide blue eyes on me, blinking slowly. At least they weren't glowing anymore. "Killing them would have been the other option. Giving them a few small aversions is nothing compared to ending their lives. And you didn't have to see what they were planning for these children." She shuddered. "They don't remember those plans anymore, and they'll never plan anything like that again, for children of any sort. I'm not sure they'll even be able to eat meat unless they know the age of the animal before it reaches their plate. They will definitely be unable to eat eggs."

She didn't sound sorry about any of that. After thinking about it for a moment, I wasn't sure she actually needed to be.

"Well, thank you. I didn't want to have to kill them."

Sarah shrugged. "I didn't think you did." She sighed, then said, "Someone will have to go and take care of the real field teams."

"I've been thinking about that," I admitted. "Rose told us the anima mundi and the Queen of the Routewitches wanted us to come to New York, because there was a problem here that needed us to deal with it. We helped you find them, but you already have people who can fight. You know the city better than we do."

She was silent for a moment before she said, "You're better at killing than Verity is."

Her quiet admission didn't even sting. It was too accurate for that. "I'd have to be," I said. "I don't ever want her to get as comfortable with it as I am." There was a lot it was too late for me to do for my family. This, though . . . this wasn't too late. This was something I could still do. "You know where they are?"

"I can't track them. They still have anti-telepathy charms, and that keeps me out. But I know where they're based."

"Good enough." I hesitated before putting a hand on her shoulder, touching only sweater, no skin. "Sweetheart, I don't know what I missed, but you can read my mind. You know I love you."

"I do," she said, and smiled, small and shy and fleeting, before she glanced past me and her smile flickered out, replaced by renewed solemnity. "I'm making Grandpa nervous. I'm going to go walk with Dominic."

She sped up, leaving the rest of us to watch her go. I glanced at Thomas. "Sarah makes you nervous?"

"I never expected to find you close to a cuckoo."

"Oh, neither did I, believe me. I actually started a ruckus at Kevin's wedding—tried to deck the mother of the bride. It wasn't my finest hour." I grimaced, shifting the carrier from one hand to the other. The boy inside hissed in indignation. "Angela's great, though, and she was around for years before we acquired Sarah. Sarah's a good kid, and we all love her dearly, even if I don't really understand what's up with her these days. I think that's a story we're going to need to get first-hand, from her if at all possible. I've never met a cuckoo who could bend space the way the Johrlac can."

"Until, apparently, our adopted granddaughter."

"What can I say? All our kids are high achievers."

"You can say that you won't decide on a plan that involves using yourself as bait ever again."

I glanced at him. He was frowning, eyes fixed straight ahead, like he was afraid to even look at me. "I didn't mean to—"

"You have to get used to the idea that I'm here, Alice. And I'm going to *keep* being here, no matter what happens, and as long as I'm here, I'm going to worry about you. I'm going to want what's best for you. Being taken captive by the Covenant, with no backup? That's not best for you. Yes, it worked out this time. Luck runs out. It ran out for your mother. It's eventually going to run out for you."

His invoking my mother hurt. Even after all this time, part of me hated her for going into the woods and not coming back out, leaving me alone with a father who refused to understand me and grandparents who couldn't protect me from him.

"I didn't mean to scare you," I said, voice small.

"I know. If you'd meant to scare me, I'd probably be more angry and less upset. I know you've been risking yourself alone for fifty years. Please. I know it's going to be hard to adjust, but this isn't the first time, and I . . . I can't handle sitting back and watching you risk yourself like that."

"I'm always going to run into danger."

"I know." He smiled a little, still looking straight ahead. "I knew who you were when I bargained with the crossroads for your life, and when I kissed you for the first time, and when I married you. I'm not expecting you to change. I just want you to take me with you when you go charging wildly ahead. Please."

"I'll do my best."

This time, he *did* look at me, his smile wider now. "That's all I can really ask."

The end of the tunnel was approaching. Dominic opened the door and the rest of us filed out, back in the subway stop near the Nest. The transit officer who'd originally let us in was still there, and blinked when he saw how many additional people we'd acquired. Dominic slipped him several folded bills, and he stopped looking quite so interested in us. Money really does talk.

We made our way up to street level, still toting our carriers, looking like a weird cross between a school field trip and a dog-training class. At least nothing was on fire.

"Mary," said Sarah lightly, once we were on the sidewalk. "We're almost back."

Mary didn't appear. I wasn't sure Sarah had been asking her to. With the sort of telepathic range Sarah had now, she was probably just addressing our resident ghost babysitter so it wouldn't startle any of us when the Nest was waiting for our return.

Sure enough: Verity and Mary were outside the convenience store when we walked up, Mary holding Olivia against her hip. Olivia waved chubby fists and reached for Dominic as soon as she saw him, burbling away in the secret language of toddlers. He handed his carrier off to Verity before relieving Mary of his daughter, kissing Olivia on both cheeks before he looked to Verity and said, "It's done. May we go inside?"

"We've been waiting," she said, and stepped to the side, making space for the rest of us to pass.

We went in.

The dragons had been arguing for hours. No, it wasn't our fault the Covenant had taken the children: Sarah's accounting of what she'd seen in their minds verified that. No, the three agents we'd encountered so far wouldn't remember any of the day's events. They wouldn't remember us, or where they'd been, or anything about the Nest. Yes, we'd been key in getting the children back—without me breaking the charms, Sarah wouldn't have been able to find them, and now she knew what all the others currently in the city looked like. She wouldn't be able to distinguish them in a crowd, since her visual processing didn't work that way, but she could feed their images to Verity, and Verity could get some crime-scene sketches done.

Yes, we'd brought the boys back in carriers for their own safety, and yes, that particular insulting choice had been proposed by Istas, who wasn't human and thus couldn't be held against those of us who were. Around and around it went, as Sally, Thomas, and I watched, waiting to hear how quickly we were going to be expected to leave.

And the whole time, I was taking silent inventory of the weapons we had between the three of us, and what I could expect to steal from Verity's armory. Every hour that passed gave Thomas more time to tap fully into this dimension's pneuma, and left him better equipped to be a useful presence in combat. Sally . . . Sally was a bit of an unexplored area, since she'd never killed a human before, and I'd been hoping to wait a little longer before she had to start. Still, the kids were back, and seemingly none the worse for wear, which could only help our case.

Verity broke away from the argument, walking over to us. "I know it doesn't look it, but they're grateful, really," she said. "What you did today meant a lot to them, and to me. You didn't have to risk yourselves for people you don't know."

"Except that we kind of did, since that's why we're here," I said. Rose and I were going to have to talk about that. She might work for the anima mundi now, but we didn't, and I wasn't signing up to play errand girl and wetwork specialist for the living spirit of the world. I wanted to stay home and remember who I was when I wasn't running. That meant I needed time.

"I hate to ask you to do more . . ." She trailed off, looking quietly miserable.

"But you're going to," I said.

"I'm sorry."

"It's fine. I knew this was how things were going to go as soon as Sarah got the locations of the other three teams. Do you need us to take out all three? Because that's going to take a while, if you do."

"No." Her misery faded, replaced by an expression of grim determination. "Cara and Mary are going to take care of Liv while I head to Hoboken with Istas to take out the team there. Kitty's the most familiar with the part of Brooklyn where the second team is; she's heading over there with Ryan and Dominic. We were hoping you'd be willing to handle the third."

I looked to Thomas and Sally, raising an eyebrow, and waited.

"Those Covenant assholes messed with *kids*," said Sally. "That makes them worse than the crossroads, if you ask me. I'm in."

"The fact that you already see little dragons as kids tells me you're going to fit in with this family just fine," said Verity, smiling.

"It's best if we act quickly, before they realize something has happened to their absent trainees," said Thomas. "I would prefer a few more days to recover from our trip, but needs must. Of course we'll help."

And like that, we were committed. One more fight, and we could go home.

"We should try to hit them all at once, to keep them from coordinating too much of a response," I said. "And of course, we won't know whether they're there until we show up. They could be out running surveillance, or eating dinner, or having a meeting at one of the other safe houses. One of our teams could wind up facing all three of theirs."

"I know," admitted Verity. "Sarah will stay here to coordinate and keep tabs on everyone."

Something suddenly made sense. I blinked. "That's why you and Dominic are splitting up," I said. "So there's a family member with each team."

Verity nodded. "Yeah. Sarah doesn't project much anymore—too worried about melting someone's brain by mistake—but Mary can move between family members quickly enough to be almost as good in a game of telephone."

"Good," I said. "Do we have time to grab something to eat?" The light spell I'd used back in the sewer hadn't been enough to exhaust me, but my stomach was growling, and I had that sort of weightless feeling in my limbs that meant I needed to get food in me sooner than later.

"We probably don't want to move until after three o'clock," said Verity. "Between last call and dawn is the least populated you'll ever see Manhattan."

"So we've got a few hours?"

She nodded.

"Great." I turned to Sally. "You're finally going to get your pizza."
Her smile was the brightest I'd ever seen her wear.

This time, the pizza made it back to the slaughterhouse, possibly because Verity had asked a few of the dragons to go rather than letting us out alone again. I had looked at her with some amusement when she announced her intention to essentially order dragon delivery, but now here we were, me, Thomas, and Sally, sitting around a folding card table in our shared room, paper plates of melted cheese and hot grease in front of us, while the mice sang the praises of garlic knots and devoured their own portion of the spoils with wild abandon.

Sally's desire for pizza hadn't been born of a small appetite: she had put away her first slice even before I could finish handing out napkins, and was well into her fourth. I eyed her warily across the table.

"If you make yourself sick, you can't come with us to fight the Covenant field team," I cautioned.

"Why would anybody fight, ever, when they live in a world where there's pizza?" she asked, mouth full of pepperoni, cheese, and half-chewed dough.

"Fundamental disagreements about the nature of the world, generally," said Thomas. "The Covenant believes that if they ever share the pizza, it will run out, and no one will get to have it anymore."

Sally rolled her eyes and grabbed another garlic knot.

"Are you feeling better?" he asked, turning to me. "I'm not going to hover, but you were drugged and abducted, and then used one of your tattoos. I'm allowed to worry."

"It was a minor one," I assured him. To my own surprise, his concern was comforting rather than cloying. Maybe I was getting used to being someone people were concerned about.

"Is it always going to be like this?" asked Sally.

"Not usually," I said. "This has been an exciting day, even by my standards."

"Good." She took another slice of pizza. "When we get home, I'm going to sleep for a week. I'll wake up to eat, shower, and put on clean socks, and then it's back to bed."

"Sounds like a plan," I said, and it did. It really did.

I had a slice of pizza in my hand and we all had the rest of our lives ahead of us, and maybe this was going to work out after all. This was a world I could live with.

Twenty-one

"I don't care what you have to do, I don't care how you do it, but baby, promise that you'll always come back home to me."

—Alexander Healy

Midtown Manhattan, preparing to take on a Covenant field team

GETTING UPTOWN FROM THE slaughterhouse was rendered some-what easier by the fact that we now knew where we were actually going, rather than taking wild stabs in the dark and hoping we would hit something: according to Sarah, the Covenant field team was holed up in a residential building a few blocks from Times Square. That put them way too close to a lot of tourists for my comfort. It also meant they'd have trouble keeping track of everyone coming and going, since literally thousands of people would be doing it throughout the night. Sarah hadn't found any indications in the first team's minds that the others were paying any special attention to the Meatpacking District, so we didn't have to worry the Nest was under surveillance and that we might be seen leaving. After extensive discussion, we decided that if we headed uptown by three, even with fewer trains running, the subway would be safe enough to ride, and get us to Times Square in plenty of time for the planned pre-dawn strike. Once we got there and surrounded the building the Covenant occupied, we'd wait for Mary to pop over and give us the signal to move.

Kitty's team was taking the sewers—something that came naturally to the bogeymen, and that their allies had long since learned to deal with—while Cara and her van would be accompanying Verity's team into New Jersey. So it was after a short but much-needed nap and with our stomachs still full of pizza that Thomas, Sally, and I found ourselves on the subway heading uptown, bathed in stark industrial light and surrounded by the city that really did never sleep.

It was all so mundane and believable that it made me want to laugh. I would have, if not for the fact that Thomas was visibly struggling not to gawk at everything, while Sally looked once again like she was on the verge of a panic attack. I reached over and squeezed her knee with my free hand, earning myself an annoyed look, which I answered with a smile. She was growing on me. It wasn't her fault that Thomas didn't feel the need to protect her: despite our long history together, he'd had a lot more opportunity to see Sally at work in the field.

That was a sobering thought. But a good one, because it meant we had a lot of firsts still ahead of us, even after everything. A woman with electric green hair and tattooed roses twining up and down her arms got onto the train, giving Thomas's tattoos a frank look. He didn't seem to notice, leaning back in his seat and holding on to my hand for dear life.

"Nice ink," said the woman, after several minutes of noisy silence. "Who's your artist?"

"I do my own work, miss," said Thomas, as the train pulled into the station we'd been told to disembark at. We stood as a group, Thomas still holding my hand, Sally practically pressing herself against his other side. No one looked at us twice. In a population as diverse and chaotic as the New York subway, a blonde woman who cut her hair with a knife, a heavily tattooed man, and a younger Korean woman were basically normal.

"Okay," I said, once we were safely off the train. "This is where we split up, get up to street level, and circle the building. Everyone remember the directions Sarah gave us?"

"Not sure I could forget them after she yelled them inside my head," said Sally sourly.

"Telepathy is useful like that," I agreed.

Thomas squeezed my hand, then let me go.

It took everything I had not to grab for his hand. Even though I knew this was the plan, it ached a little to watch him step away from me. He'd separate from Sally a little farther on, while I took the nearest exit to the street. I watched them go, then stepped backward, heading for the exit I was supposed to take. Two flights of concrete steps took me to the street, passing through several fascinating bands of odor before I emerged. It was quieter than it had been earlier, but the occasional horn or shout echoed off the buildings, and everything smelled like a mixture of garbage, urine, hot dogs, and roasting peanuts that turned my stomach even as it made my mouth water.

New York City. There's no place on Earth quite like it.

No time to stand around getting my bearings or gaping like a tourist. I turned a single circle, checking the street signs, then started briskly forward, walking with speed and intent to match any local. Part of it was bravado, a concerted effort to avoid attracting notice. Part of it was Sarah's directions, which were just barely shy of an outright compulsion. I knew exactly where I needed to go, because she'd made sure of it: the route was clear and vivid in my mind, and following it was as natural as breathing.

It had been a little unnerving, the ease and power with which she'd slid that information into my thoughts. More unnerving, in its own special way, than watching her rip into the minds of the Covenant. I'd never seen her violating someone like that before: for all that I knew, what she'd done was entirely within the realm of what any cuckoo could do, if properly provoked by someone who hadn't inherited the slight veil of protection I'd received from my mother. But planting the directions in my brain . . .

Sarah had been in and out of my thoughts since she was a kid, shaky and anxious and unsure of her welcome. It had never been this *easy* before. We were attuned to each other, but this was the first time she'd been able to slide in like it was nothing, like the wind whistling through a keyhole. Whatever had changed with her, it was major, and it was starting to frighten me a little.

If it scared me, when I already loved her, how was it affecting Thomas?

I stopped, as abruptly as if I had a rope tied around my waist which had just snapped taut, and my thoughts stopped with the rest of me. I was here.

The building in front of me was perfectly normal for its surroundings, and I would never have given it a second look if I hadn't already known I needed to come here. I stepped back, giving it a more analytical look.

Based on the exterior, I was looking at six stories, with an inner and outer door at the entrance, at least two dozen windows, and two fire escapes, just on this side of the building. No telling how many there were in total, or whether there was a back entrance, or backyard or roof access to the buildings on either side. Hopefully, Thomas and Sally would be able to find out. Otherwise, if our targets got away from us in there, this could quickly turn into a ridiculous, impossible chase through Midtown.

I leaned against a wall, murmuring, "Mary, I'm in position."

It wasn't a surprise when my former babysitter walked around the corner and settled against the wall next to me. "So are the others," said Mary. "You're good to go."

I flashed her a furtive thumbs-up, aware that anyone who saw our exchange would probably assume drug deal, then pushed away from the wall. "Let everyone know," I said.

"On it."

Squaring my shoulders, I started across the street, scanning for signs of anyone paying attention to my approach. I didn't see any. As I approached the building door, I slid my hand into my pocket for my lockpicks. I didn't need them. Even as I was reaching for them, a young man stepped out, saw me coming, and paused to hold the door open for me. Being a nonthreatening young blonde comes with advantages as well as drawbacks sometimes. This was unremarkable; he wouldn't even remember it tomorrow, and I smiled at him as I stepped inside.

The hall was tiled in white linoleum, and the air smelled of boiled cabbage and floor cleaner. According to Sarah's directions, I needed to be on the third floor. The elevator would have been faster but more dangerous; elevators can jam, elevators can be stopped mid-trip, and most importantly, people can hear them coming. I followed the hall until I found the stairs, and slipped inside, climbing silently upward.

I was almost there when I heard footsteps above me and looked up to see Sally coming down the stairs in my direction. She stopped when she saw me, blinking in surprise. I motioned for her to stay silent, and she nodded, even though she didn't look particularly happy about it. Sure, I'd beaten her here, but barely, and we were both in. Call that a win.

I opened the fire door to the third-floor hallway, slipping through with one hand resting on the revolver at my hip, covered by my shirt but still easily accessible. Thomas caught the door before it could swing shut again, offering me a thin smile. It was my turn to blink.

I'd come in the front door. Sally had been coming down from a higher floor, having presumably used a rear fire escape to get there. There was only one stairway that I knew of. So how . . . ?

There would be time to worry about that later. According to Sarah, the door we wanted was only two down the hall. I pressed my back to the wall and started toward it, slow and easy, Thomas and Sally behind me. We'd agreed before leaving the slaughterhouse that I was the best suited for testing doors; if something happened to explode, my chances of missing the blast were better than anyone else's. Or at least, that was what I was trying very firmly to tell myself.

When I reached the door, I stopped, listening intently. If there was anyone inside, I couldn't hear them. I gestured for Sally and Thomas to stay back, then rapped my knuckles against the door, stepping back out of view almost before I was done.

Seconds ticked by, slow and heavy and almost alarmingly tense. I was on the verge of suggesting something more aggressive—nothing says "Hi, I'm here to kill you" like knocking a door off its hinges and chucking a grenade inside—when I heard the locks being undone and the door eased open a few inches. I couldn't see the person on the other side. I could tell from the caution with which the door had opened that they were at the very least trying to be careful; they had decent reason to suspect that trouble might be coming their way.

They didn't step into the hall or even stick their head past the threshold. That was probably good, from a personal safety standpoint; without cameras, it wasn't great from a security standpoint. A voice behind them asked a pointed question in Italian. The person at the door answered in German. The door began to close again.

That was the moment to move. I pivoted my weight on my left foot, smoothly putting myself in front of the not-yet-closed door, and raised my right foot to kick it open. The whole thing swung open with a satisfying crash, bouncing off the wall inside, and I stepped through, guns already drawn, to find myself facing a surprised-looking blond man in the nondescript clothing of a door-to-door missionary.

"Hi," I said blithely, as Thomas and Sally came in behind me. "I speak German."

Not well, but well enough to have caught the gist of what he was saying: that whoever knocked had probably run when they realized the forces of virtue were behind the door, keeping this city safe. Covenant talk if I'd ever heard it.

There was a noise from the room at the end of the hall. "Thomas?" I said tightly.

"Yes, dear." He stepped around the man, his empty hands by his sides, and started for the sound. The man tensed like he was going to reach for a weapon, and I made a soft tutting sound.

"Now, now, I wouldn't," I said. Sally eased the broken door closed behind us before sidestepping the man and going to join Thomas. "Are you all here?"

"Eyes on three," called Thomas.

"We have no valuables," said the man. He sounded unnervingly calm for someone who was being held at gunpoint by a strange woman who'd just broken into his apartment.

"Not here for your valuables," I said. He raised an eyebrow in silent inquiry. "Here to kill you so you'll stop harassing the local cryptids."

"Ah," he said. Now he sounded almost regretful, like he'd been hoping I'd have a different explanation for our presence. "Then may I assume you're human beings? Traitors to your own kind, choosing to side with the monsters in the great war of good against evil?"

"Kid, if there's good or evil here, the good side is the one that's not kidnapping children," I said, voice going flat. "Maybe this isn't where you try to appeal to my sense of species loyalty."

"Then why?"

"Because my family staked a claim to this continent and told you to stay out, and we don't like people messing with our things."

His face distorted in an instant, becoming a mask of disgust. "Healy," he spat.

"Price, these days," I said. "Has been for a while. But yeah, that's where we started, and we told you not to come back here, and you did what? You came back here. So we've come to make you go away."

I admit, I was halfway trying to bait him into attacking me. I've killed a lot of people, of a lot of different species, over the years. I've never been in the habit of cavalierly slaughtering humans. It shouldn't have felt any different. A person's a person, regardless of where they come from. But it *did* feel different, like killing humans who weren't fighting back would somehow make me the kind of traitor to my own species the Covenant wanted to paint me as.

Brains are weird.

"Ah," he said again. "So there's no negotiation, then?"

"Not so much."

"Noted." And with that he grabbed the edge of the half-filled folding bookshelf behind him—a shelf I had quickly scanned for weapons before dismissing—and pulled it off the wall, shoving it at me at the same time.

I could have fired, and I might even have hit him, but not getting hit by a piece of furniture seemed more immediately important. I dodged instead, losing my shot as he ran, still bent over, to the living room. I jumped over the fallen bookshelf and pursued, plunging into a scene of total chaos.

Sally and a woman with a mop of curly brown hair were backed into one corner next to a bunk bed, the woman swinging what looked like a hardwood club at Sally, while Sally parried with a pair of collapsible batons she'd taken from Verity's stash. Their expressions were equally grim, and they fought in total silence, ignoring the rest of the room.

That was probably for the best. Thomas had produced a handful of knives from somewhere, and was throwing them at a red-haired man who danced and weaved to avoid being hit, unable to get a solid shot lined up with his crossbow without holding still long enough to take a knife to the throat. As long as Thomas didn't run out of knives, they'd stay at a stalemate. The third person in the room was standing to one side, in front of the only visible interior door. It was the woman I'd heard speaking Italian before, short, lithe, and dark-haired, and apparently unarmed. Her eyes were even darker than her hair, full of shadows, and I realized with a start that she was the one who'd been supplying the anti-telepathy charms for the group; this was the witch they'd managed to talk into siding against her own kind.

Witches and sorcerers aren't cryptids, but they might as well be, for the way the Covenant goes after them. For a witch to side with the Covenant isn't as unusual as it should be: when the monsters that have been hunting you offer to stop if you'll just work for them, the temptation to go along with it is understandable, if unforgivable.

I could hear the man who'd tried to flatten me with the bookshelf moving around behind the door the witch was blocking. She was smiling distantly at me. It wasn't a warm expression. I aimed my revolver at her.

"I don't think so," she said, and began moving her hands through the air like she was weaving an invisible cat's-cradle, lips moving in sudden silence.

Umbramancer, then, and emboldened by the strengthening of the pneuma. I recognized those hand gestures from something Laura used to do, when I'd really been getting on her nerves. Laura would never have tried to throw that sort of working into a combat situation, wouldn't have trusted in her own ability to weave the air. Umbramancers aren't sorcerers, and the elements don't dance to their call. And for all that I knew that to be true, I could feel the noose of wind starting to settle around my throat, ready to choke off my breath.

I still had a few seconds, though, so rather than shooting her, I pulled out a knife of my own and flung it into her shoulder just as it started getting difficult for me to breathe.

She dropped her hands but didn't scream. I could be professionally impressed by that, even as I gasped for breath and pulled out more knives, advancing on her.

"You have to know you're going to lose," she said, Italian accent thick and words heavy with pain. "We have the numbers. We have the resources. You have monsters and misguided loyalties."

"You're working for people who wouldn't hesitate to kill you if you stopped being useful to them," I argued, readying another knife. "Which one of us is misguided here?"

"The one who let herself be distracted," she said, and smiled sweetly, dropping to the floor as the man she'd been buying time for reappeared in the doorway.

He had a gun now. Bully for him. The gun had a silencer, which probably explained why he thought he could get away with using it. People might not immediately call the police or come to investigate yelling and crashing, but a gunshot was a different story—not that they had been seemed that concerned about waking the neighbors to begin with. Sally was still tussling with her own opponent, both of them aiming blows at the soft parts of the other and parrying as swiftly as they could, while Thomas continued to distract the man with the crossbow. With the wounded witch on the floor, we knew where everyone was.

I just wasn't sure it was going to help.

"Who are you?" asked the man.

I pulled myself up straighter. "Alice Healy."

To my surprise, he smiled. "Not dead after all, are you? You people, you're like cockroaches. Unkillable."

"I'll take that as a compliment."

"Nothing's unkillable forever."

"If you weren't holding a gun on me, I'd think that was a threat," I said, sliding the knife in my hand back into my shirt and reaching around to my belt, for the one thing I always had on me, even when the people I was with would have been happier if I didn't. "Hey, honey?"

"Little busy, dear," said Thomas, a note of strain in his voice.

"That's cool. Remember how I dealt with Daddy's grave?"

Thomas didn't answer, but I knew he remembered. Some things you just don't forget. The man from the Covenant hadn't pulled the trigger yet, which meant he either wanted to keep us alive and talking for some reason, or was reluctant to escalate because he was worried about losing any of his own team. Luckily for this not turning into an indefinite stalemate, escalation is where I live.

The grenade came loose in my hand without any real resistance. It was a smaller modern one, oblong and designed for use in confined spaces like this apartment, but it would still pack a fairly decent punch. I hurled it past the Covenant operative in the door and hit the ground face-down while he was still blinking, trying to figure out why I was throwing things at him.

Thomas and Sally were both on the other side of the room, out of the range of the shrapnel blast, and I said a silent thanks for that in the half-second I had before the grenade went off and everything was smoke and light.

I counted to five to let the last of the shrapnel land, then bounced to my feet, surveilling the damage. The man with the gun was down, and his visible injuries were bad enough that I didn't expect him to get up again. The witch was lying on her back, face a bloodied ruin. I still paused to put a bullet in her chest, making sure she wasn't going to be a threat anymore. That covered my part of the problem.

I turned.

Sally's opponent was alive but on the floor, slumped against the wall, clutching her arm just below a wound from which blood ran freely. Thomas's . . . hadn't been so lucky. That man was flat on his back, knives protruding from his throat and eye socket. Thomas was standing over him, eyes wild, hands clenched. He didn't seem to have taken in the rest of the scene yet.

Which was a good thing, all told, since it meant the building wasn't on fire. But Sally . . .

Sally was lying on the floor with her arms outflung, and for a few horrible seconds I couldn't tell if she was unconscious or dead. There was a single gunshot wound high on the right side of her chest. The man I'd been facing must have fired as I was throwing the grenade. In the chaos of the explosion, I hadn't even heard the gun go off.

The woman who'd been fighting Sally saw me begin to move across the room. She glared, hatred and confusion in her eyes. "Why did you do this?" she demanded, voice barely above a croak. "We're trying to save humanity!"

"You kill innocent people and children. You're murderers," I snapped, dropping to my knees next to Sally.

Thomas caught the motion and turned, eyes still wild, to see me kneeling next to his adoptive daughter.

"Sally? Sally, hey." I reached for her throat, feeling for a pulse. The bullet had undoubtedly punctured a lung, but might have missed the heart. *Please*, I thought distantly, *please let it have missed.*

Behind me, I heard the woman who was still alive start to say some-thing else, only to stop mid-word in favor of screaming. I didn't need to look to know what the sudden smell of frying bacon meant, or that Thomas had reached the point of setting things on fire.

Sally had a pulse. It was faint and thready, but it was there. I took a deep breath, closing my eyes.

"Mary," I said. "I need you."

Twenty-two

"There is nothing more precious, nor more essential to preserve, than the life of a daughter."

—Jonathan Healy

St. Giles's, a cryptid hospital under Manhattan, waiting for news.

MARY HAD COME QUICKLY when called, and together, the three of us had been able to stop the bleeding and get Sally to street level, where Sarah had been waiting with a human cabbie who'd been under the star-struck impression that he was transporting a minor pop star to a secret rendezvous. He wouldn't be able to identify any of us later, had anyone been left alive to track him down and ask. I didn't remember calling Sarah. Maybe I hadn't needed to. Given how much broader her receptive range seemed to be these days, it was entirely possible that she'd just plucked the need out of the air.

And that was a concern for later, when I had the emotional energy to care about anything but getting Sally to help before she stopped breathing. The cabbie had dropped us off by a locked door, covered with a sliding steel grate. Mary looked at us, smiled reassuringly, then walked through to open it from the inside, allowing us to carry the still-unconscious Sally into the hallway on the other side. It was industrial and featureless, gray concrete and white linoleum, and we'd been roughly halfway along it when a pair of chupacabra had come loping out of the distance to relieve us, one carrying Sally around the nearest corner to a stretcher, the other escorting us to a surprisingly ordinary-looking registration desk.

Filling out paperwork never changes very much, and always takes too long. By the time we were done, Sally had been whisked away to an operating room, and we were being checked for injuries and hustled off for chest X-rays after Thomas mentioned the grenade to the doctor who examined us. After that, we were sent to the waiting area until there was news. It was all very mundane and ordinary, which just made it all the more terrifying.

I tried to take Thomas's hand, and flinched away. His skin was burning, almost hot enough to raise blisters. "Ow," I hissed, and stuck my finger in my mouth.

He turned to me, eyes bleak and haunted. "You knew we were clear of the blast before you threw the grenade," he said. "I may not always trust you with your own safety. I trust you with munitions."

"Thank you?" I said, not sure what else to say.

"But Alice . . . couldn't you see he had a gun?"

There was no good answer for that. Yes, I'd seen the gun: it had been aimed at me. Sally had been on the opposite side of the room, not remotely in the line of fire. He must have pulled the trigger as the grenade exploded, his aim going wild. He'd been looking at me. Sally shouldn't have been in danger. But there'd been a gun, and a bullet, and a finger on the trigger; once those things were in play someone was getting shot. That was the way it worked. My luck just meant it was rarely going to be me.

I'd been looking out for myself for fifty years. Thomas said he and Sally had my back now that we were all together. That meant I needed to figure out how to have theirs, or it wouldn't be safe for them to be around me. "Be careful" didn't only mean being careful about myself. It meant being careful with the people I loved.

All of that was too much for me to put into words, and so I leaned over, resting my cheek against his shoulder where the shirt covered his skin. Thomas slumped back in his chair, the heat that radiated off his skin slowly dying down, and we sat, alone, waiting.

Mary was gone, had been since we finished filling out the paper-work, off to check on the other two teams and how they were faring. It was just us, and it stayed that way until a man stepped into the room, dressed in blue hospital scrubs, scaly orange feet bare against the tile. That wasn't the most remarkable thing about him. No, that honor was reserved for the wide, white wings that grew from his shoulders, primary feathers long enough that they nearly brushed his ankles. He stopped in the doorway, looking at us.

"We don't normally treat humans here," he said, voice stiff and somehow awkward. "But it seems your family is determined to be the exception to our admissions policy. Your daughter was shot in the chest, as I'm sure you're aware. The bullet punctured her right lung and exited out the back. She's awake and well, if you would like to see her."

Thomas stood so quickly that he nearly knocked me over. "Please," he said.

"This way, then." The doctor turned, beckoning for us to follow, and walked away.

I followed. Honestly, I would have followed even if he hadn't wanted me to. Caladrius are rare enough in the modern world that the opportunity to spend time with one, even professionally, wasn't something I could pass up.

Now that we were in the hospital proper, it was much less brutalist, although no less industrial: the hall around us could have belonged to any hospital in the world. We even passed a few nurses and technicians. The only thing that made them stand out at all was that none of them were visibly human. This was not a human space.

I took Thomas's hand, relieved that his skin was cool enough to touch, and held on as we walked the rest of the way to Sally's room. The doctor stepped aside to let us go by. I smiled at him as we passed. "Thank you," I said.

"Just go as soon as you reasonably can," he said, uncomfortably. "We prefer not to have humans lingering on the premises."

Thomas didn't pause for conversation, plunging on ahead while I followed behind. The room was boxy, square, and white, remarkable only in its lack of windows; Sally was in the single bed, propped up on a pile of pillows, wearing an unfamiliar scrub top that was only halfway buttoned. I couldn't see any bandages, and she wasn't hooked to any machines.

Hearing us enter, she looked over and smiled, wearily. "Hey, boss," she said.

Thomas sagged with relief. "Sally," he said, and crossed to the bed to enfold her in an embrace.

I stayed where I was, smiling at the two of them. This was my family now. This was where I belonged. Oh, maybe not in an underground cryptid hospital, but in the room where these two people were, holding on to each other and not letting go. I turned back to the doctor.

"Thank you for the gift of your training and your gifts," I said, as formally as I could. "I know you risk discovery whenever you aid a human, and want to assure you that we pose no threat."

"Miss Dunlavy tells me the girl was injured taking out a Covenant team," he said.

"Yes. All going well, the other teams will be gone before morning."

"Good." He nodded, expression grave. "We've got deep roots in this city. I'd rather not sever them."

"I can believe it." I had so many questions, and this wasn't the time for any of them to be asked. I turned back to Thomas and Sally instead, watching them. The local Covenant threat was neutralized for the moment. We'd provided the additional firepower necessary to clear out the teams in the city, and now the war was well and truly on, as if it hadn't been before. Our cumulative scorched-earth approach would trigger a proportional response. The cryptid world might be exposed.

And maybe it was time for that. Nothing stays concealed forever. Not everything that's buried is dead. I'd call Rose, see if she agreed that our job here was done, and if she did, Apple could send us a ride home.

"You okay?" asked Mary, stepping up beside me.

"Yeah," I said. "I missed you."

"Missed you, too. What are you going to do now?"

"Well, first, I want to figure out how the world works and how to be a part of it again," I said. "But I won't be doing it alone, so that's all right."

"And I'll be here if you need me. I'm only ever a call away, and I'll always be your babysitter."

"I'm a little old for that, Mary."

"Maybe so, but you're who I was hired to watch, and you don't get away from me that easily." Mary laughed lightly, then continued, "And you're going to Portland sooner than later, right? You need to talk to Kevin and Jane. Like, *really* talk to them, not just say what you think they want to hear and run away again."

"We're going back to Buckley after this, and then we're heading to Vegas to get new IDs for Thomas and Sally," I said. "Then, yeah. Portland. We have a bunch of people we need to catch up on things. But we just got home, and then we had to head straight here. I think we're all still suffering from the dimensional-travel equivalent of jet lag, if I'm being completely honest."

"You are," said Sarah, walking up behind Mary. "You all are."

"See? Even the telepath agrees." I managed, barely, not to jump at Sarah's sudden appearance. I was used to the ghosts coming and going like distance was nothing. For Sarah to do it . . . that was going to be an adjustment. It was also eerie having her read me that easily after years of needing to make an effort. She clearly picked up on that thought, too, looking briefly sympathetic. I cleared my throat, focusing on Mary. "We're getting our bearings as fast as we can."

"Well, you did good here," said Mary. "The kids were *very* taken with the way you rescued them. And they're insisting on keeping the carriers."

I laughed at that. I couldn't help it. "Kids will be kids."

"Rose called while Sally was in surgery," said Mary. "Your ride will be here in about fifteen minutes."

"Is it always going to be like this?" asked Sally. "Running around like our asses are on fire, never holding still long enough to think?"

I smiled beatifically at my family—both old members and new ones, both familiar and less so—as I walked over to sit down on the edge of her bed and sling my arms around them both. Thomas smiled at me.

"I certainly hope so," I said. "It would mean everything was pretty much back to normal for us."

And for a moment, that felt like something we might someday actually achieve. We were, all of us, finally finding our way home.

Read on for
a brand-new InCryptid novella
by Seanan McGuire:

THE MYSTERIES OF
THE STOLEN GOD AND
WHERE HIS WAFFLES WENT

"For fuck's sake, Jimmy, you need to learn how to stand up for yourself. I won't always be here to do it for you."

—Sally Henderson

The kitchen of a large family compound in Portland, Oregon
Far too early in the morning for this kind of bullshit

JAMES

The sound of cheering drifted through the heating duct in the floor. It seemed impossibly loud, especially given that I knew the people doing the cheering were no more than a few inches tall. I groaned and rolled over, pulling my pillow down over my head. It didn't do nearly enough to block the sound. I groaned again. Hopefully they'd get tired soon and go back to whatever it was Aeslin mice did when they weren't waking me up before seven in the morning.

I am not what most people would call "an early riser." Other things that I am not include "a morning person" and "very friendly before noon." Sally used to give me hell for it when we were still young enough to walk to school together; she'd show up all pressed and ready to go, shoes shined and ribbons in her hair, and she'd find me rubbing the sleep out of my eyes, trying to toast my waffles by dropping them into the silverware drawer.

The silverware drawer is not a very effective toaster, in case you've ever wondered.

Most mornings I would wind up eating my breakfast still half-frozen as we hurried to beat the bell. It almost turned into a game as we got older: Sally trying to show up earlier and earlier in the hopes of making it through a quarter without any writeups for being tardy, me trying to make sure that no matter what time of the morning she arrived, I'd be in the exact same state of not-ready-yet.

I would have stopped if she'd ever gotten really *angry*, I swear I would have. She was my only real friend in those days, and the risk of making her throw up her hands and give up on me was something I wasn't willing to flirt with. Sally could have had a hundred friends if she'd wanted them: she was smart and pretty and good at the sort of social graces that the other kids expected, the little politics of the playground. She also had a vicious temper and a mean right hook, which is probably the only reason I survived school.

Unlike Sally, who learned early that since she was never going to fit in no matter what she did, that it was best not to stand out more than she had to, I was the sort of kid who walked through grade school with an invisible "punch me" sign taped to my back. I was smarter than the majority of our classmates—hell, I was smarter than *Sally*, but that just made me smart enough not to act superior to her. She was my best friend and my protector, and again, risking that wasn't something I was particularly interested in.

Everyone else, though . . . everyone else was fair game. I'd been the worst sort of smart kid, the kind who thought they needed to constantly remind everyone around them of how smart they were. I'd been so sure that we were going to find a way to get me out of New Gravesend, to let me go off to college in some far-off city where no one would remember what a jerk I'd been in high school, that I hadn't bothered to rein in any of my baser impulses.

And then Sally was gone, and everything had fallen apart, and I'd been trapped, friendless, in a town where my father basically ran things, and where an ancient bargain with the crossroads had seemed destined to consign me to a life of forced heterosexuality in order to uphold their promise to my long-dead ancestor: that there would always be a sorcerer in New Gravesend to protect the place.

Not that we'd been doing much protecting. I didn't even know what my ancestor had been expecting us to protect the town *from*, and since that was one of the things no one had bothered to write down, I was probably never *going* to know.

But that was all very long ago and far away, and the mice were still cheering as jubilantly as football fans who'd just been informed that their team was going all the way to the Super Bowl. I groaned again, pulling my head out from under the pillow and glaring at the vent. The temptation to yell down it for them to shut the hell up was strong. It wouldn't do any good. If the mice knew I was awake, they'd take that as an invitation to swarm my room and try to rope me into whatever ridiculous rodent event they were currently celebrating. I'd fallen afoul of that tendency a few times before I learned better, and I wasn't making that mistake again.

I grabbed my phone from the nightstand, swiping my finger across the screen to check the time. Not quite eight o'clock. Charming. At least it wasn't before seven this time, or—horror of horrors—before five. They'd only done that twice so far. The rest of the house tended to rise before I did, but even they had their limits, and rodent choirs at four thirty in the morning exceeded those limits.

Dropping the phone to my pillow, I rolled out of bed, grabbing a pair of sweatpants from the floor and yanking them on. Having my own bedroom was a luxury I hadn't been fully expecting when a strange girl who set things on fire with the power of her mind had informed me that I was her brother now and we were leaving. To be honest, I didn't know *what* I had been expecting, only that I needed to get out of New Gravesend, and I'd just watched her beat the living crap out of the crossroads, which made her my best chance at ever seeing Sally again.

That was four years and a lot of rodent rituals ago, and the idea that I might have considered arguing with her had become literally unthinkable somewhere in the middle of all that. And sure, it was only four years on the calendar, since I'd skipped almost a whole year in the middle by getting myself shunted to a parallel universe that was running according to a different clock, but—

But I was happy here, in Portland. Mice and all.

My name is James Price, originally James Smith. I'm from Maine, and now I live in Oregon, where I've been forcibly adopted by a family of professional cryptozoologists. Despite the way that sounds, I came pretty much willingly, and I like it here. My new family, such as it is, is a lot nicer than my old one. My dad was an asshole who hated basically everything about me, and my mother died a long time ago, leaving me alone with him. Here, I get siblings, both legal and honorary, parental figures who don't entirely suck, and an extended network of cousins and friends.

And the mice, of course. Mustn't forget about the mice. They certainly won't allow it.

Rubbing my face with one hand, I fished a sweatshirt out of the hamper and pulled it on, heading for the door. When all else fails, choose breakfast.

I opened the door and found myself confronted with chaos.

My room was on the second floor, along with most of the other bedrooms, and had pretty solid soundproofing in the walls—a necessity when your residents aren't always human, and sometimes have to deal with some pretty severe nightmares. So apart from the mice, nothing that was going on in the house had managed to reach me before I was ready to get up, and rarely had I been as impressed by that soundproofing as I was just then.

What sounded like everyone in the house was yelling. Not screaming: shouting to be heard above one another. Jane and Annie were the loudest, and I felt a small spark of pride at the fact that my adopted sister could out-shout so much of her family. Out-shouting even the quietest Price is an accomplishment. I could hear Evelyn and Kevin shouting under the two of them, along with Elsie and—more surprisingly—Artie, who didn't usually come to the house these days. I amended my assumption that everyone in the house was yelling. Sam wasn't. Sam was, if anything, unusually quiet.

I considered going back into my room, where the only noise I'd have to deal with would be the incessant cheering of the mice. I am not a morning person. I am also not an incurious person, and something that could cause this much chaos while setting the mice off was something I probably needed to know about. I took a deep breath, and started to descend the stairs.

Everybody was in the living room, for values of "everybody" that didn't include those members of the family who were currently out of the state, or either of the two ghosts who popped in and out according to their own schedules. In addition to the people I'd heard yelling before, and Sam, who I'd assumed would be there if Annie was, Jane's husband, Ted, was leaning against the wall with a cup of coffee in his hand. He raised it in greeting when I reached the bottom of the stairs, making him the only person to directly acknowledge my arrival.

"Morning, Jim," he said, voice warm.

I don't normally like being called Jim—or worse, Jimmy—but it's different when Ted does it. He manages to make shortening my given name sound like a secret for just the two of us to keep, the sort of innocent private joke that I used to have with my high school teachers. The ones who didn't resent the way I kept pissing off the rest of the kids.

I drifted toward him, not disrupting the ongoing argument in the slightest. It seemed to be the two households against each other, currently represented by Jane and Annie, who were shouting directly at one another. No chill here. Kevin, who looked like he hadn't slept in days, was trying to separate them, while Evelyn yelled for the both of them to calm down. Elsie was yelling at Annie for yelling at her mom, and Artie was just yelling random things, like he wanted to be included but wasn't sure precisely how that was supposed to happen.

He's been like that since we got home from our impromptu visit to the Dimension of Giant Bugs, bringing a bunch of cuckoo kids and a spider large enough to tell the square-cube law to go fuck itself as involuntary souvenirs. He got hurt right before we made the transit back, and while Sarah did her best to repair him, I'm not sure it worked quite right. I'm not sure it could have.

"What's going on, Ted?" I asked, looking at the mug in his hand with undisguised avarice.

"Family disagreement," he said. "There's more coffee in the kitchen. You'll need it. When they get like this, they can keep going for *hours.*"

"Got it, thanks," I said, and made for the kitchen.

Eventually someone was going to tell me why everyone was angry, and then maybe I could be angry too. In the meantime, there was coffee, and that was even better than inexplicable rage.

ACADIA

When a new Lineage of the Faith is born, the first tier of clergy must be Plucked from other Lines, or recruited from the Novices, many of whom are too young as yet to understand what is being asked of them. When the Precise Priestess did inform us that she had acquired for herself a Brother, who must carry his own Lineage, we were confronted with a question we had not asked since the Well-Groomed Priestess came before us with a new daughter, already old enough that many of her Truths had been lost to Time:

Was he to be Honored as a God, as if he had been with us since the day of his Birth, even as we would honor any other Brother to a Priestess named and known, or was he to be accepted at some lesser level within the pantheon? The Rites for acquiring a God or Priestess through mating were clear. The Rites of Adoption were less so, as they had been utilized only the once, and then only under a degree of threat which we would not care to experience again.

For lo, did the Well-Groomed Priestess not say unto us, "This Is Enid And She Is My Daughter Now, And Should You Choose To Disrespect Her, You Choose Also To Disrespect Me?"

But the Precise Priestess made no such declarations, only gave him unto us and commanded that we should Figure Our Shit Out, as she had Better Things To Do.

I was a dedicated novice then, chosen to serve as a member of her faithful and to recite her litanies into the open spaces of the Future. I, along with four of my number, was Called to serve the new line, for was it not that she had brought him forth, and was it not thus that his senior clergy should come from her ranks? Another four were drawn from the clergy of the Patient Priestess, as the last to be so Welcomed, and the rest from the novices who had been studying to pledge the Well-Groomed Priestess. So we had come together.

We are a new clergy, second only to those who now serve the Calculating Priestess, but newer in many ways, for she has been with us since her childhood, while the Stolen God came before us Already Grown, and so we learn his Mysteries only as he chooses to Share them with us. We may never know all that we desire to know of him, and that is sad, but it will not keep me from serving him with Honor and with Joy.

On the Day of Waffles, I was among those in the kitchen, awaiting his rising, even as the rest of the clergy sang a song of celebration in Honor of the New Mystery which had been in part unveiled to us. I sat near to the Toaster, groomed to Honor the lineage I served, a chunk of coffee cake clutched between my paws, nibbling at my own breakfast while I awaited the God's arrival.

When at last he came, I sat up as tall as I could, and with rapture, joined the choir of all those so gathered, greeting him as was only right and proper. "HAIL!" we cried, pulling the form of proper address from all we knew to be true, all we had known over our many years in service to the greater Faith.

"HAIL TO THE RISING OF THE STOLEN GOD!"

Wild cheering followed, ritual on the parts of the other clergies, relieved on the part of ours, for we must see his reaction when he was told of the night before, we must see if he could Understand.

He groaned and scrubbed at his face with one hand, setting his hair even farther askew than the night itself had managed. "Not yet, okay? I need at *least* a cup of coffee before I have to deal with rodent religion."

"At least" was not a number, but it was the beginnings of a Boundary, and we have had plenty of time to learn the ways of respecting Boundaries. We quieted our cheering, and those who were associated with clergies who took no specific interest in this new Mystery dispersed, carrying their breakfasts into the walls and thence to other parts of the house. The Observers to the Family Fight had already been chosen from among the most senior of the clergies involved, who could be trusted to listen calmly and recite what they had seen and heard without having missed any essential Parts. In seconds, the Stolen God was alone with his own clergy, six of us scattered among the cupboards and counters, all watching him.

He proceeded to the Machine of Coffee and prepared a mug, adding to it Hazelnut Milk and Honey before he wrapped his hands around it and blew upon the surface, then drank. The air grew slightly cooler as he did so. Like our beloved Precise Priestess, he is of the Line of Elements, but unlike her, or the God of Inconvenient Timing, he calls upon the Cold. We serve a mighty god, that he will never burn his lips upon his drink, nor scald his tongue upon his meat!

Leaning against the counter, he looked directly upon me—upon me, a simple member of his clergy—and asked, in a weary voice, "Do you know who threw the fox into the henhouse?"

My first impulse was to say I had no way of knowing, as the family has not kept chickens for food or eggs in many generations. But I have lived alongside them all my days, and am wiser than an untrained novice. Instead, I pushed my whiskers forward and asked, "Human idiom, yes?"

"Yes," he confirmed, and took another drink of coffee before looking at me more closely. "Acadia, right?"

Like all among the divine, the Stolen God is unable to speak our True Names, for they twist and bedevil the tongues of all large beings. Like the Precise Priestess who brought him before us, he has learned to tell us one from the next, and given us Names he can speak, with our permission, that he might know who he Addresses. It is an honor to be so Named, and I am Proud of the Name he has given me, which he says I share with one of the most beautiful places in the land of Maine, from whence he originally came.

"Yes," I squeaked, jubilantly. "You are truly Kind and Glorious to have Remembered me!"

"I remember you all the time," he said, and drank more of his coffee. It must be a magical brew, for it is reserved for the grown among the divinities, and never to be shared with mice, or with children. "Why is there a carnival going on in the vents?"

"Carnival?" I looked at him with polite confusion. "This is not the time of Carnival. We celebrate but one such festival, all apart from the place, which has been home and harbor now to three generations of the divine, and in whose name so many feasts are held."

He paused. "Actual Carnival? Like the Catholics?"

"I don't know what a Catholic is, but it is a great celebration, filled with joy and honor," I said gravely. "It lasts five days—"

"That sounds nice."

"—which is the time the Kindly Priestess lingered in her bed after her husband, the Cruelest God, struck her about the head and sent her falling to the floor. She never woke. Her child, the Well-Groomed Priestess, smuggled us from the home upon her mother's death, accepting at once the suit of the God of Hard Work and Sunshine, which she had previously Disdained, for did she not say, 'Better To Be Wed To A Carew Than Left Here With A Bastard'?" I preened my whiskers, momentarily overcome by the revelation of such a deep mystery. The Stolen God was forbidden none of the teachings, as he would one day take his Place in the Heavens among the very ones we spoke of, but still, to hear him invoke Carnival had been a shocking thing.

From the way he now stared at me, I was not the only one to feel the weight of the mystery I had released into the air. His mouth worked for a moment with no sound issuing forth before he put his coffee gingerly onto the counter and asked, "Are you telling me that . . . wait, wait, I've got this one, the Kindly Priestess, that was Elizabeth, wasn't it? The first member of the family to take care of you?"

He paused then, waiting for my nod.

"Are you telling me that Elizabeth's husband *killed* her, and so her daughter grabbed the colony and . . . what, ran to the first man who would have her? And you don't see anything wrong with that?"

"It is Forbidden to speak against the Teachings," I said, clutching my tail between my paws.

"So you don't get to have opinions?"

His distress was feeding into my own. "There are reasons we do not speak of Carnival outside the period of observance," I said. "I would not Presume . . ."

"Oh, please. Please presume."

I twisted my tail between my paws, the solidity of it, the warmth, and tried to find the words. He was a God, brought before us by a beloved Priestess, who had seen in him something of the familial even before he was accepted. He had come with her when she was

Returned to us, when we had feared she might be Lost Forever. And his place in the Heavens was assured.

I took a deep breath. "The Cruelest God has been cast from the Pantheon," I said. "Deicide is the greatest of Sins, and we could no more worship one who commits such an Act than we could break entirely with Faith. We do not teach his Mysteries. His clergy has been allowed to go silent, his Teachings forgotten."

The chapel of his divinity yet stood, rebuilt each time we had moved as a colony, constructed as a reminder that our gods were not, could not be, perfect. True, once he was cast out, he became no longer a god, and had never truly been. But the Kindly Priestess . . . her like would never come again, would not be seen within my lifetime or any other. She was the mother of all we had and all that we were, and she had erred by taking him for her mate, erred even to the point of her own destruction. We could not forget that—we were Aeslin, and Aeslin do not forget. But the chapel was a reminder that once, the greatest in our pantheon had acted in error; once, she had been wrong, and had died for her mistake. For that, and that alone, we would remember him forever.

But his chapel was a place of silence and shame, and no clergy walked there in his honor, and no rituals were recited in his name. Thus is the censure of the Aeslin.

"Then why don't you call him by his name?"

"Because," I said, with utter calm. "We have intentionally Forgotten it."

JAMES

I stared at the mouse, trying to reconcile what I'd been told was true about the colony with what she had just said. She looked utterly calm, no longer twisting her tail between her paws, watching me with unblinking eyes.

I needed more coffee before I could cope with this. Recovering my mug, I took a long, slow drink, then said, "I was told that Aeslin mice never forgot anything." That had been the first thing Annie said when we reached Portland and my meeting the mice went from a problem for the future to a problem for real damn soon now. Don't do anything embarrassing in front of the mice, or they will absolutely remember it forever, and probably develop a holiday around it. They seemed to enjoy celebrating people's worst moments a hell of a lot more than they enjoyed their best ones.

"We do not," Arcadia confirmed.

"But you just told me that you forgot his name."

"That is truth."

"How can both things be true?"

She took a deep breath. "An individual mouse, such as I, a lowly member of the clergy, is unable to forget anything I have experienced or heard spoken. These things are a part of me, indelible and immutable. This is truth. But the colony can choose, in times of great trial, to decree that knowledge be not preserved."

"Meaning . . . ?"

"Meaning that those who knew the Cruelest God in his life may well have known his single-name, to be spoken from one god or priestess unto another, but they were bid not to pass this knowing on to their children. Those who keep the Mysteries of the Kindly Priestess equally omitted those things which had been deemed Forgotten from their recitations." She flattened ears and whiskers both, visibly uncomfortable now. "Her catechisms leave out as much of him as they can while still retaining coherence. So it was decreed by our elders. He was Unworthy of our Recollection."

"Huh." I took another drink, mulling over what she was saying. It made sense, as much as anything that had to do with a colony of talking, intelligent, highly religious mice ever made *sense*. I sometimes felt like "sense" as a concept was banned in the Price household.

Speaking of the Prices, they were all still occupied with shouting at each other, leaving me to engage in acts of rodent theology before I'd had remotely enough coffee.

Joy.

"So this forgetting, it's a big deal among the mice?"

"Yes." She ran her paws through her whiskers, a gesture I had come to recognize as signaling discomfort with a topic. "A thing that is Forgotten runs the risk of being Lost, and that which is Lost cannot even be grieved. It is the greatest censure we possess, to declare that a thing be Forgotten."

"What happened to us when the cuckoos came, then—?"

Her head snapped up, eyes suddenly bright with something that verged on religious mania. "The Calculating Priestess acted according to her Nature, and meant no harm, or we would already have cast her from the pantheon and begun the process of Forgetting her. She trespassed against you, my God, and against the divinities of others, in a way that cannot be Forgiven. But she did not damage your clergy, and we exist to remember what you cannot. Nothing was Lost, only moved from one Book to Another."

"Sounds like you've been arguing this a lot, huh?"

"Her clergy fights near-daily with the others so impacted, including your own," squeaked Arcadia. "We will argue until the matter is settled, however long that may require, and Scripture will be Set."

"It's very complicated to be a mouse, huh?"

"Nowhere near so complicated as it is to be a God."

"I guess I can agree with that. Mice don't need fake IDs, and mice don't have to pay taxes." I finished my cup and reached again for the pot. "You didn't answer my question, though. Why is everyone throwing a big party, anyway? Annie normally warns me when a major celebration is coming up, and she didn't say anything last night."

"Ah!" She clasped her paws in front of her narrow rodent's chest and tilted her head back in apparent ecstasy, eyes rolling toward the ceiling. I didn't know enough about ordinary mice to know whether the thin edge of white that appeared at their bottoms was normal or another sign of Aeslin oddity, and I sure wasn't going to interrupt her rapture to ask. Not when it might be about to get me an actual answer.

"A Miracle has happened in this Kitchen!" she proclaimed, voice as ecstatic as her posture. "For lo, did not the Pilgrim Priestess appear before us, returned from her Endless Voyages, now brought near unto an End!"

"How does an endless voyage end?"

I might as well not have spoken. Her voice had taken on the cant that meant she was reciting scripture, and I could have stripped naked and performed a modern dance routine without disrupting her.

"For in her Company, absent so long, feared Lost, walked the God of Inconvenient Timing! Her Long Quest has Borne Fruit."

"Wait, *what*?" I stared at her. She sat back on her haunches, apparently pleased.

I'm a relatively new addition to the family—their first non-romantic adult adoptee in quite some time, assuming they've ever had one before—and even I know about Grandma Alice and her endless search for her husband, Thomas, the aforementioned God of Inconvenient Timing. I know more about her as a person than I do about him; she likes grenades, bakes cookies, and apparently comes by the house a couple of times a year under normal circumstances, whatever those are. If normal circumstances exist, I haven't experienced them since I joined the family. I met her once, when we stopped off in

Michigan on our way to Oregon from Maine, and she'd taken off basically as soon as Annie told her what had happened to the crossroads, vanishing into another dimension.

After my own experiences with dimensional travel, which had been less than pleasant, I wasn't sure there was any possible way the woman could still be considered sane. But that was a conversation for another time. Here and now, I was trying to coax something coherent out of a mouse without triggering another digression into horrifying family history.

I don't know much about Thomas, but I know two things, absolutely: first, that he made a deal with the crossroads to save Alice's life, which was why he'd been missing for all this time, and second, that he was a sorcerer. Annie and I had been using his notes on his own powers to train ourselves, if "Here, you try to freeze me while I'm actively trying to set myself on fire" could really be considered training, and not just a really complicated game of *Jackass*.

If he was back, that could change everything. Everything. And it explained a lot about the yelling people in the other room, since Jane hated her mother, and no one in the current family had really known Thomas. The stories I'd heard, which were confusing, and surprisingly contradictory for a family that externalized and cared for its collective memory, said that he'd been taken while Alice was pregnant with Jane, and Kevin was very young. He probably didn't have any conscious memories of his father.

So someone who caused chaos just by existing had dropped in to cause chaos on purpose, and now everyone was going to be agitated for the rest of the day. That, plus the return of a previously lost mouse god, explained a lot. I poured more coffee into my mug, doctoring it appropriately before I returned my attention to the mouse.

"Cool. So everyone's mad because Grandma came home and brought the dead guy who isn't actually dead. Any chance the shouting inside the vents is going to die down any time soon?"

Gravely, she shook her head.

"That's what I was afraid of. Anything else I really need to know?"

"They came, they spoke to the God of Decisions Made in Necessity, and they departed again, to finish what Must Be Done." Acadia ran her paws through her whiskers. "And the Sally opened the freezer and removed Food That Had Been Entailed, and instructed that we should, lo, 'Tell James Sally Ate His Waffles.'"

I dropped my coffee cup.

ACADIA

The Stolen God stood frozen, his eyes wide and his face pale as he stared at me. His throat pulsed as he swallowed, but he did not otherwise move. The drinking vessel which had been clutched in his hands lay in fragments at his feet, and soon the more daring among the novices would begin to snatch up the shards, to whisk them away as potential holy relics.

My chest wanted to swell with pride, for I was clearly standing on the cusp of a Revelation, some great and holy Mystery about to unfold for my eyes to chart and chronicle. The retention of this moment depended upon my attention. It was a great Honor, and an even greater Responsibility. I had never been the first to witness a Mystery before. To think that I, so young among the priesthood, barely better than a novice, should witness a Mystery!

But I pushed the pride away. The Stolen God might not know us well enough to recognize it for what it was, might see no shame in my reaction, but his eyes were keen and his connections clever: he might realize I was taking Joy in his evident Distress. Such a thing might set him against his own clergy, and a clergy opposed is a clergy excluded. So much could be lost to us if I reacted Poorly.

Still he stood, unmoving, unspeaking, barely seeming even to breathe. The yelling of the family in the next room had changed timbre when the cup smashed to the floor, and footsteps approached us.

"James?" The Precise Priestess appeared in the doorway, a male of her clergy with whom I had once mated riding on her shoulder in place of pride, his paws clutching a long lock of her hair. She looked upon the Stolen God with sisterly concern, as befit their relationship, and I was glad to know them both. "Everything okay in here?"

The Stolen God did not react. The Precise Priestess came farther into the room, eyes going first to the mess on the floor, and then to me, the only mouse close enough and still enough to have been in conversation with the Stolen God when he discovered his Dismay. "You," she said. "What did you *say* to him?"

"Nothing that should have Alarmed him so!" I protested. The wrath of the Precise Priestess is a thing to be feared. "Did he not ask, Why Is Everyone Throwing A Big Party, Anyway? And did I not reply with the truth of the day's events, the Arrival and the Departure of the Pilgrim Priestess and the God of Inconvenient Timing, and the Theft of the Stolen God's Waffles?"

"What? Waffles? Dad didn't mention waffles. Tell me about the waffles."

I ran my paws anxiously through my whiskers. "I was not present. I know only the catechism of the moment, and not the details that may not have been included. Shall I summon one who Witnessed?"

"Please." She put a hand on the shoulder of the Stolen God, curling her fingers to hold him tight. "Breathe, James. Keep breathing. Whatever's wrong, we'll figure it out."

He made a noise, small and pained, and spun to put his arms around her, holding her tightly. She began to stroke his hair, saying nothing, and watched me.

I did not want to go. This was a Mystery Unfolding, and it was my duty as a member of his clergy to witness it. But I had been given a Command, and I was no senior priest, to deny such a thing. Speed must be my answer. I flattened my ears and bowed my head, and bolted from the counter into the hole that had been cut for us, throwing myself into the maze of tunnels and climbing paths that riddled the walls of the house.

Our colony's current home was constructed for us at the order of the God of Decisions Made in Necessity, and he did Decree that the walls should be built to Accommodate our needs. Some of the first tunnels were laid by his hands, built into the very structure of the House. Others have been opened since then by our Builders, all guided by the Keeper of the Plan, a senior member of the God's clergy who reads the runes of the original blueprints and tells us where safety can be found. No colony ever, since the beginning of all records, has had such a safe and glorious system of movement! Why, we can travel from one end of the house to the other in an instant, all unseen!

I ran, and others passed me in the tunnels, and some gestured for me to stop, indicated that they would like to speak with me, but onward I ran, one ear flattened to signal that I followed a Command, and none moved to prevent my passage. When I emerged into the highest point of the house, it was to behold our City, a Metropolis within an Attic, the finest that had ever been in all the world. This time, I did permit my chest to puff with pride, as it always must when a member of the colony beholds our home.

The space, which was vast almost beyond comprehension, would only have been a Very Large Room to human eyes, for they are built at Such a Scale as to demand more resources from the world, and had been divided into the necessary components of a world.

Central were the temples, chapels, and schools, where we could observe the religion which shaped our lives. In the next ring lay the trade schools, for those few not called to the clergy to learn the art of weaving, or stitching, or construction, and the libraries, where all knowledge is recorded, to be sure that a chance loss of a member of the clergy does not mean the more upsetting loss of a piece of the litany. Grief is transitory. When a member of the colony dies, they are lost to us forever, save in the record of their experiences, which remains to keep and comfort us.

Some heretics have suggested, on occasion, that we should rather worship ourselves, for the record is of our doing, the mysteries are of our codification. They are brought to the highest points of the city to behold all that has been given to us, and asked if the colony would exist to worship anyone at all in the absence of our gods. Could the colony alone provide such peace, such prosperity? It could not, and so our worship is not misplaced.

Most who speak such blasphemies recant, once reminded of why we are as we are, why we live as we live. Those who do not are cast forth, and none has ever once returned. The world is a harsh place for something so small and civilized as a mouse.

My moment of awe concluded, I ran forward into the street, heading for the Temple of the Stolen God. It was as yet the newest of our structures, consisting only of the nave, chapel, and sanctuary, but it would grow with time, as our numbers increased and our mysteries grew equally in number. Members of the colony not engaged in their own worships turned to watch me go, and some children chased me along the length of the schoolyard, exclaiming at my raiment, which was still novel enough to excite their interests. I paused long enough to wave to them before ducking into the chapel.

As I had hoped, the rest of the clergy were gathered there, reciting and reviewing our new Mysteries. They stopped upon my arrival, mindful of the placc I had been set to hold, and the elder of our priests stepped forward, whiskers a wide fan of respectful interest.

"Initiate," she said. "What word do you carry?"

Oh, the temptation to recite all that had transpired was heavy and deep in my bones, the urge to share threatening to burst free! But of such strength is an elder one day made, and so I forced it aside, and bowed my head, and said, "Elder. The Precise Priestess has requested the presence of one who witnessed the Theft with their own eyes."

"One among the undecided has pledged to us in the aftermath of the holy event," she said, whiskers returning to a neutral place. "He was Overcome with Rapture, and seeks to serve Our God with devotion."

What a fortunate novice, to have had his path so Cleanly Charted by witnessing a Mystery! I paused to groom my own whiskers, almost overcome with joy for the newest member of our clergy, then returned my eyes to the elder.

"He has been Requested, and I must Oblige," I said. "Where can he be Found?"

"In the sanctuary, meditating on the night's events," she said. "Go, and fetch him forth to glory in the new wisdom of the Stolen God. For is it not said, 'Annie, I Know This Seemed Like A Good Idea In Idaho, But Are You Sure Your Folks Are In The Market For Another Kid'?"

The rest of the clergy cheered with joy at the repetition of the holy words, and I ran on.

JAMES

I clung to Annie for what felt like years but couldn't have been all that long, since the people in the living room were still shouting when I finally relaxed my grip and stepped away from her, nearly putting my foot in the still-hot pool of coffee on the floor.

"Sorry," I said. "I don't know what came over me. it's been an odd morning." I wasn't crying. I was dimly, distantly proud of that, even as I suspected it might be shock, and that the tears, when they came, would be cataclysmic.

"You want to tell me what happened?"

My mouth worked for a moment, no sound coming out, and I was suddenly reminded of trying desperately to tell my ninth-grade family life education teacher that her breezy assumption that no one in her class would need information about "deviant homosexual lifestyles" to keep themselves safe and healthy was incorrect, because I was in the room. No sound had come out then, either, and she had eventually put her hand on my shoulder, looked into my eyes, and informed me that God had a plan and would send me the right wife when the time came.

Sally and I had filed the paperwork to start our school's first GSA the next day, but the feeling of shame had remained, the memory that when it mattered, I had been entirely unable to speak.

The thought of Sally smacking me in the arm and telling me that I was braver than I thought I was snapped me out of my silence, and I moved away from Annie, toward the closet where the cleaning supplies were kept.

"Not really," I said.

"You're going to have to tell me eventually, or the mice will do it for you," she pointed out. No secrets in the Price household, not from the mice, and not from each other. Annie was an impressively terrifying woman, and I sometimes thought the most impressive thing about her was that she'd started setting fires in her sleep and somehow managed to keep her parents from finding out. That, and not the violation of the laws of thermodynamics, was the truly impossible thing about her.

"Maybe." I opened the closet, pulling out the wet broom—not a mop, and distinguished from the dry broom in that it had a strip of painter's tape around the handle and was intended for use in cleaning up the inevitable wet messes that needed to be swept up before they could be wiped dry—and a dustpan. It was a soothingly mundane activity. Spills happened all the time. Spills didn't have anything to do with missing grandparents or impossible girls who couldn't possibly be *here*, coincidences like that didn't *happen*, not to me, and so the girl who'd been with them, the girl who'd stolen my waffles, she couldn't be—she couldn't be—

My hands clenched on the broomstick, so tight that half my knuckles popped and the other half just ached from the tension of it all. Then Annie was there again, easing the broom out of my grasp, pushing me gently backward.

"Maybe you should put some ice on that, killer," she said. "It's cool if you don't want to talk to me yet, even though you have to know I'll find out eventually, but that doesn't mean you get to hurt yourself. That's not allowed."

"It's not?"

"Nope." She began sweeping up the shattered remains of my coffee mug, sloshing most of the coffee into the dustpan alongside the shards of ceramic. "I know you've always been an only child, so that has been a little bit of an adjustment for you, but no one gets to hurt my brother but me."

"Is that how this works?" A thread of amusement was beginning to work its way through my anxiety. Annie was good at that. If distracting people were a viable career, she could probably have pursued a degree.

"Yeah. Your siblings get to torture you, and you get to torture your siblings, but you don't get to torture yourself."

"Like you can pick your nose, and you can pick your friends—"

"But you can't pick your friends' nose," she concluded. "Just like that. So stop hurting my brother, before I'm forced to kick your ass."

"Having siblings is surprisingly violent."

"Surprising, no, violent, yes." She finished sweeping up the mess and walked the dustpan over to the wet trash. Back in Maine, we had one trash can, and everything went into it. Convincing my dad that separating out the recycling would have been a good idea had been a nonstarter, and I'd given up the fight long before Annie had rolled into my life.

Here, they not only had separate cans for wet and dry trash, they had two different recycle bins—one for glass and metal, the other for plastic and paper, and sometimes Jane grumbled about how we really needed to split those up and go to four, which would have Evelyn remind her, always with utter politeness, that she had her own kitchen in which she could have a hundred recycle bins if she wanted, while Evelyn's kitchen needed to retain room for things like "appliances" and "food." Since no one ever seemed very upset about this argument, I had to assume it had been going on for years and would probably outlive us all.

There were also two bins for scraps, one to go into the compost bin, the other to go into the bloodworm tubs. Bloodworms lived naturally in wet earth, and were usually found in swamps and wetlands, and their blood was like catnip for a wide range of cryptid species. After leaving Buckley, the family had started breeding them for bait purposes, and so they occupied five twenty-seven-gallon tubs in the garage and got all the household meat and dairy leftovers.

Annie had confessed, almost ashamed, that when she was a kid, she used to give the bloodworms ice cream on her birthday, figuring that everyone deserved a treat. "I'd still be doing it, but it turns out bloodworms are lactose intolerant. A few cheese scraps is fine, a whole gallon of ice cream is not. And you do *not* want to be around a flatulent bloodworm colony."

She moved to the sink, rinsing the coffee stains off the dustpan and propping it up to dry before tearing off a few paper towels. "Are you feeling any better?"

"I'm trying," I admitted.

"You ready to tell me what happened?"

"I am not."

"Okay. Just checking." She crouched down to wipe the remaining coffee off the floor, keeping an eye on me as she did. "You realize you're on the countdown before Sam notices I've been gone more than five minutes and just 'happens' to come wandering in here to check on me."

"How much longer are you going to put up with that?"

"I don't know. When it stops being cute and starts being annoying."

She shrugged. "I figure he's earned a little neurotic hovering, after everything."

I sighed. "I guess you're not wrong. It would still be driving me absolutely out of my mind."

"Yeah, but you grew up with an expectation of privacy. I did not. My childhood prepared me for a traumatized boyfriend who doesn't like it when I'm in a different room."

I reached for a fresh mug, making a noncommittal noise. She wasn't wrong: Sam had been through a lot. We all had, really, but in some ways, Annie and I had gotten off lightly. For us, our little pan-dimensional adventure had been a few days of trauma and screaming, followed by a crash landing back in our home reality. For everyone who hadn't been with us, well . . .

Some of them had been here in Portland when Sarah ripped a hole in reality and Annie, Artie, and I had followed her through, vanishing in an instant. Others had been elsewhere, either as close as the fence line—Sam—or as far away as Australia—Alex and Shelby. They hadn't been given an opportunity to react.

We'd reappeared in Iowa, only to vanish again, this time taking an entire college campus with us. That would have been bad enough if time had been running at the same rate between dimensions, if we'd been gone and completely out of contact for a few days—something that really didn't happen to Prices, since they had phones and allies and their small but reliable network of ghost aunts, who would normally make sure that nothing short of dying would keep a Price from checking in. But no, time couldn't be that accommodating.

We'd been gone for a few days . . . for us. We'd been gone for a solid year for the rest of the world, meaning that our return to Ames with an entire college campus had been even more dramatic and upsetting than originally anticipated. People had mourned. People had moved on. Construction for several new structures had begun, all of which had been summarily smashed flat when we'd dropped the university on top of them. We'd disrupted a lot of plans rather severely, first by disappearing, later by coming back.

At the time, if you'd asked me, I would have said that Sarah and Artie had an understanding of sorts, one that might not be as formal as "dating" but which definitely encompassed "in some sort of complicated relationship that would have been weird even if it hadn't been between two nonhuman intelligences." I'd been tragically single, as always—Sally used to say a boy could tattoo "James Smith, I like your ass, will you take me to the prom?" across his forehead, and I still wouldn't be sure that he was into me—and Annie had been with Sam. Who hadn't made the dimensional crossing with us.

He would have been absolutely within his rights to decide that disappearing into an alternate dimension for a year was a really complicated method of breaking up with him. Instead, he'd spent the entire year of our absence working with the rest of the family—dead aunts included—to find a way to bring us home, or at least to confirm that we were still out there somewhere to be found. For that year, everyone in the family had been a little closer to understanding Alice than they normally were, and then we'd come back, battered and bruised and completely unaware of how long it had been for everybody else.

And Sam had been waiting.

Since we'd come home, it had become a rare thing to find Annie in any room without him, apart from the bathroom and the barn we used for our makeshift "sorcery lessons," and he would usually walk her to both those places. I thought it was cloying and a little invasive. Annie thought it was sweet, or at least she said she thought it was sweet, and not being one of the family telepaths, I had to take her word for it.

"I'd like it if my life had prepared me to have a boyfriend at all," I said, glumly.

Annie paused. "You're just trying to distract me from asking more questions about the waffles," she accused.

"Maybe. Is it working?"

"Yes, but only because you've refused to seriously talk about your dating prospects up until this point." She looked at me levelly. "Dirty pool to bring it up now, James Price. Dirty pool indeed."

"Any rope when you're falling." I shrugged, pouring coffee into my mug. "Besides, it's not like I have a lot of opportunities to meet people, much less start dating them. There's the whole 'Sometimes things freeze solid when I touch them' aspect—which, I know you and Sam play your kinky little games with heat, and don't think I wish I didn't know that, but cold is a *lot* less sexy when you're not expecting it—and then there's the 'I never *go* anywhere' part of things. You moved me cross-country and I don't *know* anyone here."

"As opposed to that bustling social circle you had back in New Gravesend. Pour me one of those."

"For my sins, I must watch you torture innocent coffee," I said, and took out a second cup.

"Your sins are many and great," said Annie, straightening to throw away her paper towels and get the mini marshmallows down from a cabinet.

"This great?"

"Greater. Now please, continue telling me why it's my fault you can't get a boyfriend."

"Well, one, you're my sister now, and you're kind of terrifying." I filled her cup and handed it over, only grimacing a little as she topped it off with a generous serving of mini marshmallows. Her crimes against coffee may never be forgiven. "So there's that."

"It's true, I am skilled in the area of frightening off boys," she said, grabbing a spoon and giving her coffee a stir. "I did it for myself, pretty consistently, for years. Still not sure what I did differently with Sam."

"Sam's not human."

"Yeah, that probably helped. Our specific flavor of weird flies a little bit better with people who aren't defaulting to thinking the world both makes sense and belongs to them. Huh. Maybe that's part of why the boys never wanted to hang around when they saw me coming." She took a long drink of coffee. "Sounds like they're starting to wind down out there. You want to tell me what happened before they all come in here looking for something to eat?"

"Not really." I pushed my hair back with one hand. "I was talking to Acadia—she's one of the priests who's least likely to freak out because I'm paying attention to her—and she said that when your grandparents showed up last night, they had someone else with them. Someone she called 'the Sally.'"

"Oh," said Annie, eyes widening in apparent understanding.

"And apparently 'the Sally' left a message for me." I sighed. "She said to tell James that Sally took his waffles."

The mice remaining in the kitchen cheered.

ACADIA

The novice—formerly undecided, now Called—was where I had been told to find him, still draped in the beige and white of the clergy-to-be, with only the first small gleaming beads of his station-to-come affixed to his sleeves and collar. He was bent over the book of the teachings of the Stolen God when I entered, and looked up at the scratching of my claws against the floor. Seeing my raiment, he straightened, flattening his ears and fanning his whiskers in show of respect.

"Priest," he said, bowing his head. "I am Honored by your Presence."

"I am told you have come to join our number," I said, more briskly than I intended, but I was on a mission from the Precise Priestess, and had little time for niceties. "I am told you Witnessed the coming of the Pilgrim Priestess, the God of Inconvenient timing, and the Sally?"

"Yes," he squeaked, nerves splintering his voice into a shrill crack.

"Fortunate, to Witness such a Moment, such a Mystery!" I exalted. "Now come. The Precise Priestess has asked to speak with one who Witnessed."

He stepped nervously forward, ears still flattened. "I have never . . . never spoken to the Precise Priestess. I have heard—"

"She is not cruel to the Faithful," I said, reassuringly. "And was she not the one who went into the Wilderness and returned with the Stolen God, not mate nor child, but sibling stolen from the wide world? She will be kind to you. She wishes only to hear what you have Witnessed, to receive the details of the moment that she might better understand them."

Still he hesitated.

Hesitation was allowed; only refusal was forbidden. Still, I didn't want to leave the divine waiting, and so I cajoled, "If we are Swift, and the news we carry is Welcome, there may be Cheese and Cake."

No Aeslin has ever been born who could resist the allure of cheese and cake. His ears came up and his whiskers relaxed. "It counts as my required time in contemplation if I am attending upon our God, does it not?"

"Of course it does," I said. "What truer Devotional could there be than serving as His memory of a moment which he was not present to behold with his own eyes? Come. They are waiting for us."

I ran back the way I had come, and he followed close behind me, the two of us plunging past the senior clergy without pause and out into the streets, paved with buttons and with pennies from the pockets of our divinities, worn smooth and gentle upon the paws of pedestrians. Still we ran without pausing, until we reached the tunnel's entrance and plunged through, racing down, down, down into the darkness, into the depths of the house.

When we at last emerged into the kitchen, the Stolen God and the Precise Priestess were yet there, awaiting our arrival. The Stolen God had a fresh cup of coffee, which was good; the divinities are calmer, by and large, when they have something to sip at as we speak to them. The Precise Priestess had a cup as well, and the bag of marshmallows was open on the counter. How I yearned to dive into its sugary depths, and how firmly it had been forbidden. So instead, we took up place beside the toaster, and I squeaked for their attention, as the initiate beside me clutched his tail in his hands and tried not to pant with nerves.

"Good, you're back," said the Precise Priestess, as the Stolen God went very still beside her. "Is this the one who witnessed?"

"I am," squeaked the initiate, nerves still shattering his voice. Then he winced, and said, "Your Divinity. I am, Your Divinity. I am sorry, I mean no Offense."

"Oh, he's young," she said, with evident sympathy. "First time talking directly to a member of the family, hey, kid?"

He squeaked wordless affirmation, as she elbowed the Stolen God lightly in the side.

"He's wearing your colors. This one's yours."

The Stolen God looked upon us with interest, focus intent. "Are you new?"

The initiate nodded, silent with awe.

"I can't pronounce your real name. I'm sorry. If there's something you'd like to be called, I can absolutely use that name for you, or I can give you one that I can use. Which would you prefer?"

The initiate, whose name I had not bothered to learn in advance of his meeting our mutual God, looked as if he might pass out from the sheer ecstasy of the moment. He stood, quivering, in silence, until I reached over and tweaked his tail, startling him. He flinched away from me, then looked to the God, squeaking a desperate, "Please! If I might have the Gift of a Name, it would be an Honor!"

The Stolen God glanced to the Precise Priestess, as if seeking her counsel. She laughed.

"He's an initiate," she said. "Look at that cloak. I bet he was undecided before he saw your waffles get stolen, and now he's part of your clergy. Initiates are jumpy. They're not used to speaking directly to the family. Not like a Priest, or even a fully initiated novice. You learn to tell the differences between the tiers. After a while, it's second nature. Just be gentle with this one. He's not used to us yet."

The Stolen God nodded his understanding, then looked again to the initiate. "Your friend there, I called her Acadia, because it's the prettiest park in the state I'm from," he said. "I always liked Camden, too. Would you be willing to let me call you Camden when I need to address you directly, or ask the other mice to send you to see me?"

The initiate—Camden—nodded, ears going flat. He hugged himself, and I knew this moment would be replaying in his heart for the rest of his life. So it went, for those who served the divine. We all had our private catechisms, the things which mattered more to us than to the collective memory.

"Nice to meet you, Camden," said the Stolen God.

"I am Honored," Camden managed, voice only cracking a little.

"Now that we're through the pleasantries, can you please tell us what you saw last night?" The Precise Priestess's words were polite. Her tone was not.

The newly dubbed Camden picked up on her intonation as easily as I did. He twisted his tail between his paws as he looked to the Stolen God, took a breath, and began his recitation:

"It was two hours and seventeen minutes past the Striking of Midnight when a Hole did Open in the Membrane of the World, and Three Humans did Appear . . ."

JAMES

Sally.

The little mouse in the virtually unornamented cloak had described Sally so perfectly that a police sketch artist could probably have drawn her. He had described her, and when he'd shifted his stance to repeat the words she'd spoken—actually spoken, in this house, in this *kitchen*, while I'd been asleep less than fifty feet away—he'd managed to look like her, despite being a mouse and not a human being. He *sounded* like her.

Sally was alive. My Sally was alive, and somehow, she'd ended up with Annie's grandparents, and they were planning to come back here, and when they did, we'd be together again. Me and Sally, the way it was supposed to be, without New Gravesend to pen us in and tie us to an endless succession of parental expectations and molds we were never going to fit. Sally.

Camden had finished speaking and looked at us expectantly as he said, "And thus is the Mystery Revealed."

A general cheer went up from all the other mice in the room, who had quieted to pay attention to his story. Annie smiled at him.

"That was very well told, and we thank you," she said. "The Stolen God is a bit overcome right now, by the return of his friend, but he'll thank you too, when he's able."

I nodded vigorously. The lump in my throat was so large that I could barely swallow, much less speak. The mice, Camden and Acadia both, continued to look at me with wide, expectant eyes. I glanced at Annie. If they were expecting some great show of gratitude or wise proclamation, they were going to be waiting for a while.

She met my eye and winked, then set her coffee down on the counter. "A story so well told deserves a reward," she said. "Who wants cheese and cake?"

I would have sworn there were fewer than two dozen mice in the kitchen. The cheer they sent up was still loud enough to border on deafening, and continued as she turned to open the fridge and extracted half a sheet cake from the top shelf. "This was meant to be tonight's celebration," she said, removing the foil. "I'll have to get someone to drive me to the store before dinner. But they've earned it."

She set the cake on the counter next to her coffee. The mice watched, ears and whiskers vibrating with eagerness, still cheering. She didn't pull out a knife. Instead, she opened a drawer and removed a Tupperware container of pre-cut cheese cubes. "Gouda and cheddar today," she announced, popping off the lid and putting the container down next to the cake. Then she retrieved her coffee and stepped back.

"Go for it," she said.

The mice descended. Not just the mice that had already been in the kitchen: more boiled out of the holes in the walls and up the sides of the counter, appearing like magic from every crack and cranny. I swallowed, and found that I could speak, as long as I didn't try to talk about Sally.

"How many mice *are* there?" I asked.

"No one knows for sure," said Annie. "A few hundred, at the very least. Not enough of them. Their whole population is in this house, or as good as. If we ever stopped taking care of the colony, they'd go extinct inside of a decade."

"It's not easy out there for a mouse."

"No, it's not." She looked at me. "You ready to go join the fight already in progress in the living room?"

"Not sure what I have to fight about, but I know I don't particularly want to be alone right now, so I may as well."

Annie took my arm and led me with her out of the kitchen, leaving the mice and their ceremonial feast behind. I knew that the next person to go in there would find the cake tray and the Tupperware both spotlessly clean, although they'd still wash the Tupperware before they put it back into the rotation. The mice were tidy. The dishes still had to be done.

Sam was waiting in the hall between the living room and kitchen, trying to look casual about it. Annie smiled at him as we passed, toasting him with her coffee mug. He looked at her arm linked through mine, grumbled something about humans needing more hands, and turned to follow us to the living room.

"Not everyone's lucky enough to have a prehensile tail, asshole," said Annie.

Sam laughed, and this was normal, this was right, this was what my life was like now. This was what the world was supposed to be. Add Sally and it would be . . . perfect. It would be *perfect*. And maybe that was why I felt like I was going to cry, throw up, and have a panic attack, all at the same time. Guys like me don't get *perfect*. We never have. We get sorcery we don't know how to use and fathers who pay the bills but don't know how to deal with us, and mothers who die too soon.

If Sally was coming back, something else was going to leave me. That was just the way things worked. There was no way anything else was going to happen. And maybe that made sense. Maybe things had been too good for too long. Even with the year missing in the middle, because that had been a kind of perfect, too—a year for any trail my father might have tried to follow, if he'd decided to care enough, to go cold, a year for "James Price" to replace "James Smith" in all the official databases, even a year for the two versions of me to age apart. James Price was physically a year younger than James Smith would have been, if he'd still existed.

We stepped into the suddenly silent living room, and I stopped wallowing in my thoughts to blink at the somewhat bewildering sight of all four senior Prices staring at us. Elsie and Artie had taken a seat on one of the couches off to the side, a full cushion open between them, so that there was no risk they might accidentally touch each other. They'd been like that since Artie got out of the hospital, keeping their distance, never making contact. It was odd, but it was such a small oddity that it barely stood out against everything else.

Annie nodded briskly to her parents and pulled me with her over to one of the other couches, where she pushed me down before perching on the arm. Sam hesitated for a moment, looking put out that she hadn't left the arm for him, then hopped smoothly onto the back of the couch and wrapped his tail around her waist. She squeaked, less surprise than acknowledgement, and shifted her position enough to lean against his legs.

If they weren't so sickeningly cute, it would be very easy to hate their little codependency floor show. As it was, I still considered hatred occasionally, usually right after someone reminded me that I had no idea how to get a date in Portland, or anywhere else.

"Why are all the mice celebrating?" asked Kevin, finally.

"Oh, I gave them their cheese and cake early, as thanks for sending one of the initiates down to tell us everything about what happened last night." Annie made that statement sound perfectly reasonable, even though we all knew it wasn't. She took a slurping drink of coffee, punctuating her reply.

"I was there," said Kevin. "I could have answered any questions."

"You were kinda busy, Dad, and you couldn't have, because what we were asking about wasn't important enough to you."

Kevin looked confused for a moment. Then he glanced at me, and his expression cleared. "The girl who took Jimmy's waffles," he said.

"Sally," said Annie. "But yes. Sally took James's waffles without asking, and you know he has a thing about people touching his food—"

"Which doesn't make a lot of sense, since you've said he was an only child when you found him," interjected Evie.

"—but not everything makes sense, and he's allowed to want us to keep our hands off of his waffles," Annie continued. "We were asking about her. One of James's priests went to fetch an initiate who'd witnessed the whole thing and get them to give us all the details before they could be codified into proper ritual."

"Smart," said Kevin. "Did you find out what you needed to know?"

Annie turned to face me, and raised an eyebrow. "I think we did," she said, and stopped, clearly waiting.

I swallowed. If ever there was a time when I needed to be brave enough to speak up in front of the entire waiting family, this was it. I looked down at my coffee. If I couldn't choose the coward's way out in silence, I'd do it by finding something else to focus on.

"I can't be absolutely sure without seeing her myself, but based on what she did while she was here, and what the mice had to say about her, the woman in the kitchen with . . ." I hesitated, stumbling over what I was supposed to call them. They weren't my grandparents yet, even by adoption; I figured they got the choice to decide what I was to them when they came home for good. ". . . with Annie's grandparents was my friend Sally from New Gravesend."

"Wait, wait," said Elsie. "You mean the one who got swallowed by the crossroads?"

"That would be the one," said Annie cheerfully, when it had become clear that I wasn't going to answer. "Guess she wound up wherever it is they've been keeping Grandpa."

"That's great news!" Elsie paused. "Isn't that great news? James?"

"Sally was my friend when I didn't have anybody else," I said, still looking at my coffee. "She was the only person who didn't think there was something wrong with me because I liked to turn in my homework on time, or because I listened to our teachers, or because I solved puzzles for fun. And then we got older, and she didn't freak out when I started freezing things, or get upset when I told her I liked boys."

Sally in the sunlight slanting through the windows of our crappy little cardboard fort, three refrigerator boxes and a bunch of plywood we'd stolen from behind a dumpster, laughing and saying, "Well, at least one of us does," after I'd made the biggest and most terrifying admission of my life so far. Then she'd punched me in the shoulder and told me not to worry so much, I was stuck with her until one or both of us was dead and gone.

Sally in the dress she'd worn when her parents not-so-subtly convinced me to invite her to prom. She'd been fine with it, since none of the girls in our class had been willing to face the social consequences of going stag, or with another girl, even though we weren't going to be the only people attending as friends. I'd been planning to go by myself—the cost of attending as a single male wasn't the same as the cost of attending as a single female, socially speaking—and spending time with Sally had never been a hardship. Plus it pissed my dad off. He *hated* that my best friend was a girl. He hated the fact that she wasn't white even more. And most of all, he hated the fact that because police chief was an elected position, he couldn't be open about why he hated her so much.

Sally in the library, cheeks red with anger, telling me to get over myself and stop acting like I didn't have any options, telling me to start planning for my future like I was going to have one, telling me again and again that she was going to get me out of our shitty little town. She'd been reading my mother's journals, and she was absolutely sure she'd figured out a way to fix everything.

And I'd let her. Recollection turned to acid in my throat, scarring and charring me as I struggled to swallow it. Annie's hand settled on my shoulder, pressing down firmly enough to let me know that she'd seen my expression turn.

"Hey," she said, voice soft. "You know that wasn't your fault. None of this is your fault."

I took one hand off my mug to reach up and clutch her fingers.

On the other side of the room, Elsie made a scoffing noise. "Are you seriously sitting there telling him it's not his fault he's gay, like there's something wrong with being gay? Because there's nothing *wrong* with being gay."

"No, I'm sitting here telling him it's not his fault that his best friend tried to go to the crossroads *on his behalf* and got herself cold-cased into another dimension," said Annie, rather more hotly. "You know me better than that, Els."

"Sorry," said Elsie. "But you know how it sounded."

"Fuck you," said Annie, tone turning pleasant.

"Girls," said Jane, a sharp edge to the word. It was what I thought of as her Mom voice, and it made me ache a little. My own mother had died before I'd been old enough to remember what it sounded like when she used that tone on me. "Stop picking on each other."

"Sorry, Mom," said Elsie. "You've just got us all on edge with your yelling."

"You'd be yelling too, if people were acting like your least favorite person in the world suddenly coming back was a good thing," said Jane. "You should have called us immediately, Kev. We should all have been involved in the decision to tell them they were allowed to come back here."

"This isn't your house, Jane," said Kevin. It was clear that this was ground they'd been over before, probably several times since the fight started. "It would have been inappropriate of me to extend the hospitality of *your* house, but this isn't your house. You don't live here."

"You've always said this house was open to me, if I ever needed to come home."

"If," said Kevin. "In the future. You don't live here *now*."

"And I never will, if *that woman* is going to be here. It's her or it's me. You can't have us both."

"At least your mom's alive."

Everyone turned to look at me with wide, startled eyes, and I realized that I had been the one to speak. Oops. I finally raised my head, finishing my coffee in one long drink before setting the mug on the coffee table and shrugging Annie's hand off my shoulder. Jane narrowed her eyes.

"You don't know the history there," she said. "You don't know what she *did*. I have every right to be angry."

"I think I know the history as well as your own kids do, with maybe a little less opinion coloring the facts," I said. "I've had access to the same histories, and the same clergy. Your mother was pregnant when the crossroads took your father, and she did exactly what I would expect any member of this family to do: she took off looking for him as soon as you were born and stable enough to survive without her."

"She *left* us," said Jane. "No one else in this family has ever run out on our children, and it's insulting that you think we would."

I looked at her calmly. "She left because she thought she could fix everything if she just did it on her own. I've watched Annie do the same thing. I watched Artie do it, too."

"And look what it cost him!" Jane waved her hands, indicating Artie.

He was staring at the ceiling, seeming to ignore the whole conversation, like it was no more relevant to him than the shadows in the corner of the room. He'd snap out of it in a minute and return to the present day, but those stretches of absence were getting more and more common, and no one was quite sure what they meant. I suspected that the brute-force reprogramming job Sarah had done to restore his memory and a facsimile of his original personality was starting to break down, but with Sarah in New York pretending she didn't know any of us, that was hard to prove one way or the other.

"Everything," said Kevin. "It cost him everything, because that's what it always costs when we have to sacrifice ourselves for the sake of someone else. I know you're mad at Mom, Janey. You have every right to be. But being mad at her doesn't mean the rest of us don't get to have a relationship with her if that's what we want to do."

"How can you forgive her after what she did?"

"I didn't say I had forgiven her," said Kevin. "Maybe it's because I was old enough to miss Dad when he was taken from us, but I've always been able to understand why she did what she did, even if I wanted her to be with us more than I wanted her to be looking for him. Aunt Laura was the best not-a-mom I could have asked for. She took great care of us, and I loved growing up in the carnival. So did you, you know."

"That's not the *point*."

"Then what *is* the point, Jane?"

"She left us! We were her children, and she left us. She could have decided to stay. I told Ted on our honeymoon that if we ever had kids, I'd stay with them before following him into some unknown dimension."

"That's true," said Ted. "She did. Killed the mood a bit. Here she is, wearing this piece of red lace that I can't in good conscience call a garment—a scrap, maybe, if I'm feeling generous—and kneeling over me, telling me that if I ever get into the kind of trouble that people don't usually bounce back from, she won't come to save me."

"Dad!" objected Elsie.

"What? Child, you're Lilu, and you exist. You have to be aware that your parents have had sex."

Artie made a vague humming sound. We all looked at him.

"But fair enough," allowed Ted. "No more unwanted details, all right?"

"*Thank* you," said Elsie.

"Yes, thank you," said Jane.

"You started it," said Ted.

I stood. This had all the hallmarks of an argument that had been going on since before I was born, and would probably continue until long after I was gone. Annie watched me go but didn't shift from her place on the arm of the couch.

"I'm going to my room," I announced, before anyone could ask or offer to go with me. "I'll see you all at lunch."

And with that, I proceeded up the stairs.

ACADIA

Oh! What glory, what delight, what rare and unbelievable honor! To witness not only a Mystery, but a Revelation! I joined the swarm around the cheese, grabbing a portion for the elder priests, twice the size of what I would have been allowed for myself, and showed my teeth to the one novice who attempted to dispute my claim. She backed away, head bowed in submission, and I fled for the hole behind the toaster, cheese clutched close, Camden following behind with the cake he had secured while I was elsewhere.

The senior among the priesthood do not leave the temples often, are needed to see to the spiritual health and journeys of their congregations, and so it is the first duty of the juniors among our ranks to bring them what we are offered, and ensure that when the colony feasts, they feast with us.

The run should have seemed longer, with my front paws burdened so. Those whose sole duty it is to gather for the priests often wear clever packs which allow them to run properly while also carrying far more than I could carry on my own. But I was so full of elation that I ran with twice the speed, and close behind me, Camden did the same.

I might never learn his original name now. Those of us fortunate enough to serve divinities who see fit to name us in their Honor often forsake the names we bore before as too much useless weight to carry. What need for the mouse I was, when I could be Acadia now, in service to the Stolen God?

The Polychromatic Priestess worries, sometimes, that we subsume our own desires to the divinities and forget the strength of our own nonhuman intelligence. We have tried to make her understand that we forget nothing unless we do so with intention, and even then, we save the shadows, enough so that no one should go seeking a mystery where none exists. We serve because it is the Aeslin way. We choose the paths we follow, the divinities we cry to, and should we desire another way, another life, there is always the path of schism.

True, none who walk it return to the colony, for the world is large and we are small, but nothing binds us here save our own custom and culture, and our personal desires. So let me be Acadia, and let him be Camden, and let us find joy in our service to creatures vast enough and powerful enough to protect us. One day we would have mates and families, if we so desired them, and they would be safe because of the world we built for them.

What else could we possibly desire?

We reached the attic and emerged into the revel which always accompanied an offering of cheese and cake, the fastest of the scouts already delivering packets of precious communion to the schools and hospitals, for the very young and very old to enjoy. I have heard them, the gods, making light of the speed with which we strip the plates, the voraciousness with which we address the offerings. For lo, did the Thoughtful Priestess not say, It's All Right To Slow Down, I Swear We're Not Going To Stop Feeding You? And she was correct, for when any of us eats alone, we do so at our own pace, feasting and fulfilling our needs without rushing. When something is intended for the colony, however, we must act quickly, and as one.

It is an act of Service, and we are made better for performing it.

Together, Camden and I ran along the streets, past the celebrating throngs, past the children with their frosting-dipped whiskers and paws full of cheese crumbs, until we reached the chapel and ran inside.

The elder priest who had set me onto Camden's trail was yet there, head bowed in contemplation, and looked up as we entered, taking quick measure of the prizes in our paws. "You have gathered well," she said, and I preened under her approval. "But have you remembered to gather for yourselves?"

Camden and I looked at one another in shock. In our excitement at having been the cause of an offering—the first such made in the name of the Stolen God, for his adoption feast did not count—we had gathered only our duty to the temple, and not a morsel to hold back.

"No, Elder," I squeaked. "We have been Fed on the Regard of the Divine, and sought to fill your belly before our own."

"You are Young," she said, not approvingly—not disapprovingly, either, but with a sort of recognition that told me we were not among the first to make this error, nor would we be the last. "Hunger is a constant companion, but not yet a Burden. It will weigh you down more heavily as you age, as the heat runs from your limbs and all that remains is the burning ember of your faith. Do not feed me."

"Elder?"

"Do not," she repeated. "I will go to the central chapel, and eat with all the others among the clergy who have no novices dedicated to caring for them—I am an Elder, but not so old as all of that, and I have the Humility to eat at a communal table."

We both stared at her. She fanned her whiskers forward and spread her paws.

"Go to the sanctuary, and share a holy meal between the two of you, in honor of this good day, which followed such a momentous and glorious night. Come to know each other better, for it seems the two of you will be building blocks of the clergy that is to come."

Camden and I exchanged a look. It is not uncommon for the elders to encourage mating within the junior members of the clergy, to bring forth the next generation of the faithful. So long as she did not explicitly order us to breed, however, she had asked no more of us than was her right as our elder, and obedience is a well-honed instinct in those of us who have survived this long.

"We thank you for your generosity, Elder," I said, and bowed, and the two of us scampered for the sanctuary with our burdens.

Once there, Camden spread his cake out across the table provided for just such meals, and I did the same with my cheese. "We have just met," he said, somewhat uncomfortably.

"Yes," I said. "I do not wish to mate with you."

He relaxed. I could find no insult in that, for I would have done the same had the conversation provided me the same assurance. "Nor I with you."

"Perhaps when we know each other better?"

Best to know now if he had a sweetheart in another liturgical line, that I could ask the Elder to leave us from her plans for theocratic expansion.

"Perhaps," he agreed. "Yesterday, I was not sure I would ever be Called. I am not prepared to be Called and Mated in a single day's time!"

"I can see that. I am the eldest of nineteen. My parents are sworn to the service of the Thoughtful Priestess, and are ranked among the elders in her service. They thought I would follow their path, or perhaps swear myself to the Arboreal Priestess." I shuddered. "I have never cared for heights. Neither of them would have been suitable for me to dedicate my life to."

Camden laughed. "Parents see ideals in place of individuals at times. My parents serve the God of Scales and Silence."

"And you did not swear to him directly?"

"No. As you see no appeal in heights, I find no comfort in creatures which may eat me and I am not allowed to defend myself against. But I felt no strong Calling to any other clergy, and so have lingered among the undecided far longer than my peers. They all pledged seasons ago, and have settled well into the places that were Meant for them, while I stand barely at a beginning. There has been no time for courtships, nor to consider pups. How could I provide for them, without a priest's portion?"

"There are places outside the church," I said.

"To hunt and gather and craft is no shame nor sin, save in the eyes of my parents, who would cast me from our family line for remaining Uncalled when they raised me better than that," he said, some bitterness in his voice.

I worried my lip between my teeth. "You will be well suited to the service of the Stolen God," I said, finally. "For lo, did he not say, 'I Was Never Going To Be The Man My Father Wanted, So I May As Well Be Someone I Actually Like'? Here, you can be whomever you desire. If you would like to be a spiritual guide to the mice who build our places of worship, you can. Or if you would prefer to teach the paths of the faith to the pups who come to us in search of knowledge, you can do that as well. We will not demand any single path of you, nor will any pups you have be required to follow the outlines of a life that they do not desire."

Camden's whiskers drooped as he seated himself at the table. "You tempt me so. Are you a true priest, or a phantom sent to lure me astray?"

"I believe myself a priest, for I have been schooled in the ways of the Precise Priestess, and completed my liturgical training before I was Called to serve the Stolen God," I said. "She would not care either for the idea that we serve her out of anything but true desire. Your faith is strong. Your calling may be weak, but there will always be a place for you here."

"Then sit, and celebrate the feast with me."

"I am honored," I said, and sat.

The ritual thus completed, we looked at each other and then at the food, with pleasure. We had believed ourselves to be gathering for an elder, and so had taken the choicest morsels, the tenderest flakes of cheese, the thickest swipes of frosting. It seemed near to a sin that we should enjoy these things ourselves, but as we had been ordered to do so by an elder, it was not a sin. It was a sacrament.

Conversation died as we filled our bellies with the blessings of the divine. When we were finished, every crumb consumed, conversation rose from the grave as Camden said, haltingly, "I think I have found my faith. I think I can serve here, as is expected of me, as my family line would desire."

"Then the halls of the Stolen God are fortunate to have you," I said, serenely.

"How are you sure in your place?"

"I completed my liturgical training, as I have already told you, in the name of the Precise Priestess. I was not with her when she stole our current God from his original dwelling place, as none of us were," and that gap in the histories would ache and burn for my entire generation and well beyond it. We had her accounting, and the accountings of the Stolen God and the Large Monkey Man, but as today has well illustrated, sometimes the accountings of divinities forsake details of true importance. There would always be pieces missing from her story, and from his, and should the Large Monkey Man one day ascend to godhood, as many among the clergy expected, from his as well. "I had long awaited her return, and when at last it came, I found that she had become Strange to me in her long absence. But the new god by her side . . ."

I trailed off, searching for the words, the taste of frosting in my mouth, the comforting weight of a successful meal in my stomach. Finally, I sighed. "The new god looked as lost as I felt in those moments. Everything was new to him. We were overwhelming in our joys, as we have not been to one among the divine in many, many years. He was strange and different, and he was Family, so decreed in absence of the colony, deified already. He needed clergy. I cannot say I was Called, but I can absolutely say I was Swayed. My faith never faded, merely changed allegiances. I have no regrets. The Stolen God has named me, and knows me on sight. In his service, I can thrive. I will be an elder someday, and my future pups will grow well fed and knowing that they have a place in the clergy of their choice. It is a great gift I will give to them."

Camden nodded. "You think the elders would not object if I wanted to leave the clergy and become a carpenter?"

"Do you believe in the divinity of the family?"

"Yes," he said, without hesitation. "They did not create the Aeslin, or the world, but they have made a safe haven for us in a place that does not privilege our lives. They have cared for us and protected us when they could easily have sent us out into the wilds to wander and die as have the splinter colonies. They give us far more than we could ever give to them, and so they must be gods, for only the gods could be so infallible in their grace and generosity."

"Then if you truly believe, why would the elders see fit to question the form of your devotion? The priesthood is not for every mouse. It is a difficult life, full of study and of necessary, unending dangers. Only the hunters risk a failure to return home with any more frequency, and for them, the rewards are tangible and clear." Those hunters who fell in the act of leaving the safety of house and colony to acquire fresh meat for our tables and delicacies beyond those provided by the gods died knowing that their families would be well provisioned until the end of their children's generation. It was the price of their form of service, and one which the colony paid gladly.

Priests were almost as likely to die, especially those who had served well enough to become favored of the gods themselves, and their families suffered more for their absence. Oh, it was *claimed* that the family of a fallen priest would still receive the honors due to them as family of a living clergy member, but it was more often the case that they were forgotten, bit by bit, pushed to the side of the congregation until another could be provided to replace the fallen one.

"I like to work with my paws," admitted Camden, voice quiet.

"You serve the church by serving the church," I said. "Build our walls tall and beautiful, or set the panes of stained glass that will one day be needed to tell all who venture here that this is a place of worship and value, or plant the seeds, stitch the raiments, tend the pups. Even become a calligrapher and transcribe the holy words as they are spoken, only do so with faith and with joy. The gods do not ask more of us than we are suited to provide."

Camden bowed his head and flattened his whiskers in clear thought. I held my silence and let him have his moment. They teach us early, in our schooling for the priesthood, that epiphany can no more be rushed or compelled than a mystery can: when we see one approaching, it is our duty to sit back and allow it to approach, to give it the space it will require to thrive, and not force the moment. I could see his epiphany tugging at the edges of his ears, like a pup insistent for a treat or a trip to the park between lessons. He would turn his thoughts toward it, or he would not, and that was his decision, not anything of mine.

Finally, after the silence had grown longer than anyone outside the Aeslin would have believed possible for one of our kind, he raised his head and looked at me, eyes clear and bright.

"If I may chart any course I desire without shaming my family or my line of worship, then I shall be a priest," he said. "I will learn the catechisms and the liturgical recitations, and I will take my vows with honor, pride, and belief. This is where I am meant."

"Then I shall be your peer, your confidant and your companion, and your student when the arc of our time together is correct," I said, making no effort to hide the jubilation in my heart. "We shall grow in faith and fellowship together, and we will craft of this church a fine place of worship worthy of any pantheon the world has ever known. All we ever needed was to be sure."

"I witnessed a Mystery unfolding last night," said Camden, with what sounded like new awe in his voice, as if he had just realized the importance of the moment. If he had still been grappling, even a little, with the question of his future in the clergy, perhaps that was the case. Perhaps he hadn't been certain it was a true Mystery until this very instant. Oh, what joy, to see him fulfilled so! What joy, what blessing!

"You did," I agreed. "Would you care to recite it for me?"

"You have already heard the recitation this day."

"Yes, but for my own benefit, and I did not Witness with my own eyes. I would very much like to hear it again. Properly."

Camden rose, clearing his throat, and assumed a neutral position, not yet speaking for any of the gods in specific. That would come as the recitation unfolded.

All would be revealed.

Taking a deep breath, he began: "It was two hours and seventeen minutes past the Striking of Midnight when a Hole did Open in the Membrane of the World, and Three Humans did Appear . . ."

JAMES

No one followed me to my room. I didn't know whether to be relieved about that or annoyed that they'd let me go off to be miserable alone. I settled for flinging myself onto the bed and staring dolefully up at the ceiling, which was painted a cheery shade of dandelion yellow which Elsie assured me was soothing and promoted good sleep. And hell, maybe she was right. I'd definitely been sleeping better in Portland than I ever had in New Gravesend. I mostly attributed that to the absence of my father, but maybe it was the bedroom paint job. Hard to tell without moving to one of the other open rooms, and I liked this one, mice in the vents and all.

Not that the mice were making any noise at the moment. Their grand celebration seemed to have finally drawn to a close, or maybe been short-circuited by the early offering of cheese and cake; the room was quiet except for the soft buzz of the air purifier in the corner, which had been annoying at first but now provided a soothing white noise that I probably wouldn't have been able to sleep without. This was my space. This was my home, and these people were my family, and they were going to keep me forever, because honestly, I was pretty sure they were all too scared of Annie to tell her otherwise. Also, she beat the crap out of the *crossroads*. If she wanted to come back from her time-travel roadtrip adventure with a talking monkey boyfriend and a queer new brother, okay. They could be fine with that.

And they *were* fine with that, was the weird thing. Kevin had invited me into his study shortly after Annie brought me home, when I'd still been carrying myself like a possibly unwanted guest, and asked if I wanted to help him shelve his books for a few hours. No "I hope I'm not imposing," no "You're a guest but," just "Annie gets bored easily and Alex has been off in Ohio for a while now, things are getting out of hand, can you help me out?" It was like he'd figured out just by watching me that I was an old-books-and-library-sciences kind of person.

I'd agreed, too intimidated by Antimony's father and all too aware of his ability to kick me out when I was across the country from everything I'd ever known, with no way to get back to New Gravesend. And would I even have tried to go back if he'd said it had been nice, but my welcome was worn out and I had to leave? I hadn't known then, half-frozen with fear and still trying to put books back where they belonged. I still didn't know now.

New Gravesend was behind me. James Smith didn't exist anymore. I wasn't sure whether he was legally dead or whether he'd been written out of the world through some aggressive trick of computer wizardry—normally I want to know everything, but in this specific situation, it seemed better not to ask—but I did know that his life didn't fit me anymore. The thought of trying to put it back on was like trying to wiggle into the jeans I'd worn in fifth grade: comfortable once, worn thin in the places where I'd needed them to be, but now much too small, and better left for someone else. That wasn't my life. This was my life.

That day, in Kevin's study, was the first time I'd realized I actually wanted to stay. I wasn't just being swept up in the chaotic energy that Annie seemed to radiate around herself: I wasn't playing along out of fear that she'd set me on fire if I stopped. I was so unused to the feeling of people *wanting* me, and so accustomed to being constantly tensed against judgment or discovery, that relaxation had felt like exhaustion for a long time. I'd frozen in the middle of putting a book onto the shelf, staring off into space until a chuckle broke my fugue, and I turned to see Kevin watching me.

"It's all right, son," he'd said, voice surprisingly kind. Maybe it shouldn't have been a surprise. Everything I'd experienced so far told me that he was more likely to be kind than cruel. But in the moment, it had been an utter shock. I'd frozen again, unable to respond, unable to turn any farther.

"Let me guess." He plucked the book from my nerveless fingers and turned it over to check the spine before sliding it onto the shelf, exactly where it belonged. "You think we're tolerating you until Annie—who is not what I would call a model of dependability and reliability and consistency—gets tired of you and we throw you out on your icy backside. Is that about right?"

It had almost been a relief, to hear it put so plainly, to have my fears out in the open air, where they could hurt me but not surprise me. They didn't have that power anymore, not once they were out in the open for everyone to see.

Somehow, I had managed to nod. I still hadn't been able to speak, and the temperature in the room had begun inching steadily downward. Kevin would notice soon. He had to notice, and then he'd lose his temper, just like my father did every time I did something "unnatural" or that he didn't like—

"You look at your ID recently?" When I still hadn't moved or said anything, Kevin had sighed, and smiled, and said, "Tells me you're a Price. We took you in—or, in Annie's case, just plain took you. You're ours now. You may not have been born to this bloodline, but you belong to it whether you like it or not. You're worried about us getting tired of you. What you should be worried about is us forgetting that you haven't always been here and expecting more of you than you're willing to give. We're never making you leave, James. This family is weird and loud and messy and imperfect and *yours*, and you belong here, and we're not letting you go unless that's really what you want. So breathe, and stop freezing the room while I can still feel my toes."

He had finally taken his hand off my shoulder then, and we'd spent the rest of the afternoon shelving books, and while he'd never be my father, I thought I might be able to think of him as a dad eventually. I'd never quite had one of those before.

It was a good memory. I revisited it often, and somewhere in the middle of revisiting it this time, it slid seamlessly into a dream, becoming gold-tinted and hazy, then filled with singing flowers and butterflies the size of dinner plates, which flitted from place to place, humming the whole time. I watched them, afraid to reach out, since I knew the touch of my hands would freeze their wings in an instant. Better for all of us to hang back, watching the scene without changing it.

Someone knocking lightly but insistently on my bedroom door dragged me out of the dream, and I opened my eyes on a room now filled with afternoon light. I had, apparently, slept all the way through the morning. Well, that was just great. So much for being productive today. I sat up, wiping my eyes with the back of my hand.

The knocking continued. "Ugh," I said. "Annie, come in."

"How'd you know it was me?" She opened the door and stuck her head around the edge, eyeing me critically. "You look like hell."

"Anyone else would have realized I wasn't answering for a reason and gone away to let me sleep."

"You wouldn't know what to do with yourself if I suddenly developed manners." She came into the room, sitting down on the foot of my bed. "Brrr, it's like an icebox in here. Bad dreams?"

"Confusing ones."

"Why are you so upset? I thought you'd be relieved to know that Sally isn't dead."

"I am! I am . . . I just . . . What if she doesn't like me anymore? For a long time, she was the only person who liked me at all, and then she went away, and what if she's back and she doesn't *want* me?" I knew how pathetic I sounded, but I couldn't seem to stop. "What if she blames me for whatever happened to her? What if she hates me now?"

"Then she's a lot less intelligent than you've always painted her to be, and to hell with her," said Annie bluntly. "She wants to be awful to my brother, she can eat a sack of live leeches and choke."

"Annie!"

"What? You care about her, so I'm willing to give her a shot, but I *love* you. You're my brother. I'm not going to sit back and let her hurt you, and I'm not going to let you worry yourself sick about whether she's going to want to, either. Whatever's coming is coming, whether you worry about it or not. You've always said Sally was smart and tough and loyal. So try to believe that she still is. The mice said Grandma and the others would be coming back. You just try to be in the best shape you can be for when they get here."

I looked at her. She shrugged. I leaned over and hugged her, fiercely.

"Hey," she said. "What's that for?"

"You helped me solve the mystery of where my waffles went and why the mice were making so much noise," I said, letting her go. "And you're my sister. For that, you get a hug."

I didn't have waffles, and I didn't have Sally, yet, but I had a home and a family and a place to call my own.

That was maybe even better.

Price Family Field Guide
to the Cryptids of North America
Updated and Expanded Edition

Aeslin mice (Apodemus sapiens). Sapient, rodent-like cryptids which present as near-identical to non-cryptid field mice. Aeslin mice crave religion, and will attach themselves to "divine figures" selected virtually at random when a new colony is created. They possess perfect recall; each colony maintains a detailed oral history going back to its inception. Origins unknown.

Basilisk (Procompsognathus basilisk). Venomous, feathered saurians approximately the size of a large chicken. This would be bad enough, but thanks to a quirk of evolution, the gaze of a basilisk causes petrification, turning living flesh to stone. Basilisks are not native to North America, but were imported as game animals. By idiots.

Bogeyman (Vestiarium sapiens). The thing in your closet is probably a very pleasant individual who simply has issues with direct sunlight. Probably. Bogeymen are close relatives of the human race; they just happen to be almost purely nocturnal, with excellent night vision, and a fondness for enclosed spaces. They rarely grab the ankles of small children, unless it's funny.

Chupacabra (Chupacabra sapiens). True to folklore, chupacabra are blood-suckers, with stomachs that do not handle solids well. They are also therianthrope shapeshifters, capable of transforming themselves into human form, which explains why they have never been captured. When cornered, most chupacabra will assume their bipedal shape in self-defense. A surprising number of chupacabra are involved in ballroom dance.

Dragon (Draconem sapiens). Dragons are essentially winged, fire-breathing dinosaurs the size of Greyhound buses. At least, the males are. The females are attractive humanoids who can blend seamlessly into a crowd of supermodels, and outnumber the males twenty to one. Females are capable of parthenogenic reproduction and can sustain their population for centuries without outside help. All dragons, male and female, require gold to live, and collect it constantly.

Ghoul (Herophilus sapiens). The ghoul is an obligate carnivore, incapable of digesting any but the simplest vegetable solids, and prefers humans because of their wide selection of dietary nutrients. Most ghouls are carrion eaters. Ghouls can be easily identified by their teeth, which will be shed and replaced repeatedly over the course of a lifetime.

Hidebehind (Aphanes apokryphos). We don't really know much about the hidebehinds: no one's ever seen them. They're excellent illusionists, and we think they're bipeds, which means they're probably mammals. Probably.

Huldra (Hulder sapiens). While the Huldrafolk are technically divided into three distinct subspecies, the most is known about *Hulder sapiens skogsfrun*, the Huldra of the trees. These hollow-backed hematophages can pass for human when they have to, but prefer to avoid humanity, living in secluded villages throughout Scandinavia. Individual Huldra can live for hundreds of years when left to their own devices. They aren't innately friendly, but aren't hostile unless threatened.

Jackalope (Parcervus antelope). Essentially large jackrabbits with antelope antlers, the jackalope is a staple of the American West, and stuffed examples can be found in junk shops and kitschy restaurants all across the country. Most of the taxidermy is fake. Some, however, is not. The jackalope was once extremely common, and has been shot, stuffed, and harried to near-extinction. They're relatively harmless, and they taste great.

Johrlac (Johrlac psychidolos). Colloquially known as "cuckoos," the Johrlac are telepathic ambush predators. They appear human, but are internally very different, being cold-blooded and possessing a decentralized circulatory system. This quirk of biology means they can be

shot repeatedly in the chest without being killed. Extremely dangerous. All Johrlac are interested in mathematics, sometimes to the point
of obsession. Origins unknown; possibly insectile in nature.

Laidly worm (Draconem laidly). Very little is known about these
close relatives of the dragons. They present similar but presumably
not identical sexual dimorphism; no currently living males have been
located.

Lamia (Python lamia). Semi-hominid cryptids with the upper bodies
of humans and the lower bodies of snakes. Lamia are members of
order Synapsedia, the mammal-like reptiles, and are considered responsible for many of the "great snake" sightings of legend. The sightings not attributed to actual great snakes, that is.

Lesser gorgon (Gorgos euryale). One of three known subspecies of
gorgon, the lesser gorgon's gaze causes short-term paralysis followed
by death in anything under five pounds. The bite of the snakes atop
their heads will cause paralysis followed by death in anything smaller
than an elephant if not treated with the appropriate antivenin. Lesser
gorgons tend to be very polite, especially to people who like snakes.

Lilu (Lilu sapiens). Due to the striking dissimilarity of their abilities,
male and female Lilu are often treated as two individual species: incubi and succubi. Incubi are empathic; succubi are persuasive telepaths. Both exude strong pheromones inspiring feelings of attraction
and lust in the opposite sex. This can be a problem for incubi like our
cousin Artie, who mostly wants to be left alone, or succubi like our
cousin Elsie, who gets very tired of men hitting on her while she's trying to flirt with their girlfriends.

Madhura (Homo madhurata). Humanoid cryptids with an affinity for
sugar in all forms. Vegetarian. Their presence slows the decay of organic matter, and is usually viewed as lucky by everyone except the
local dentist. Madhura are very family-oriented, and are rarely found
living on their own. Originally from the Indian subcontinent.

Manananggal (Tanggal geminus). If the manananggal is proof of anything, it is that Nature abhors a logical classification system. We're
reasonably sure the manananggal are mammals; everything else is
anyone's guess. They're hermaphroditic and capable of splitting their

upper and lower bodies, although they are a single entity, and killing the lower half kills the upper half as well. They prefer fetal tissue, or the flesh of newborn infants. They are also venomous, as we have recently discovered. Do not engage if you can help it.

Oread (Nymphae silica). Humanoid cryptids with the approximate skin density of granite. Their actual biological composition is unknown, as no one has ever been able to successfully dissect one. Oreads are extremely strong, and can be dangerous when angered. They seem to have evolved independently across the globe; their common name is from the Greek.

Sasquatch (Gigantopithecus sesquac). These massive native denizens of North America have learned to embrace depilatories and mail-order shoe catalogs. A surprising number make their living as Bigfoot hunters (Bigfeet and Sasquatches are close relatives, and enjoy tormenting each other). They are predominantly vegetarian, and enjoy Canadian television.

Tanuki (Nyctereutes sapiens). Therianthrope shapeshifters from Japan, the tanuki are critically endangered due to the efforts of the Covenant. Despite this, they remain friendly, helpful people, with a naturally gregarious nature which makes it virtually impossible for them to avoid human settlements. Tanuki possess three primary forms—human, raccoon dog, and big-ass scary monster. Pray you never see the third form of the tanuki.

Ukupani (Ukupani sapiens). Aquatic therianthropes native to the warm waters of the Pacific Islands, the Ukupani were believed for centuries to be an all-male species, until Thomas Price sat down with several local fishermen and determined that the abnormally large great white sharks that were often found near Ukupani males were, in actuality, Ukupani females. Female Ukupani can't shapeshift, but can eat people. Happily. They are as intelligent as their shapeshifting mates, because smart sharks is exactly what the ocean needed.

Wadjet (Naja wadjet). Once worshipped as gods, the male wadjet resembles an enormous cobra, capable of reaching seventeen feet in length when fully mature, while the female wadjet resembles an attractive human female. Wadjet pair-bond young, and must spend extended amounts of time together before puberty in order to become immune to one another's venom and be able to successfully mate as adults.

Waheela (Waheela sapiens). Therianthrope shapeshifters from the upper portion of North America, the waheela are a solitary race, usually claiming large swaths of territory and defending it to the death from others of their species. Waheela mating season is best described with the term "bloodbath." Waheela transform into something that looks like a dire bear on steroids. They're usually not hostile, but it's best not to push it.

Yong (Draconem alta aqua). The so-called "Korean dragon" shares many qualities with their European relatives. The species demonstrates extreme sexual dimorphism; the males are great serpents, some easily exceeding eighty feet in length, with no wings, but possessing powerful forelimbs with which to catch and keep their prey. The females, meanwhile, appear to be attractive human women of Korean descent, capable of blending easily into a human population. Unlike European dragons, their health is dependent on quartz rather than gold, making it somewhat easier for them to form and maintain their Nests (called "Clutches").

PLAYLIST:

ACKNOWLEDGMENTS:

We have made it past *Spelunking Through Hell* and into the semi-charted waters on the other side of the book that started it all. Alice and Thomas are back together again, at long last, and now, for the first time, they have to learn what that actually looks like—and whether they can live with each other without someone winding up buried in the woods. It's going to be an adventure, no matter how it shakes out, and I'm so glad to be moving into this phase of the Price-Healy family's journey—and to have you all along with me. Your readership means the world, it truly does.

I remain a resident of Seattle, and remain steadfast in my determination to stay put for as long as humanly possible. I like where I live, I like my house and my social circle and my cats and my stuff. So I think I'm good. As I write this, we're still in the middle of a global pandemic, and that makes me even less likely to roam. I hope you're all okay with the decision not to include COVID-19 in the InCryptid setting. There was just no logical way to make it work, and unlike the real world, fictional realities do need to hang together narratively. Even ones as ridiculous as this.

2022 saw a bit more travel on my part, as I attended both the World Science Fiction Convention in Chicago (I won two Hugos! I had a five-hour panic attack! On the balance of things, I'll still call it a good convention, albeit an exhausting one) and the San Diego Comic Convention in, well, San Diego. I was fortunate enough to avoid infection in both locations, and am very glad to have gone.

It's gratitude time! First and foremost, thanks must be offered to my agent, Diana Fox, without whose tireless efforts in the face of personal adversity this book might never have been finished, much less beaten into a publishable shape. Diana went above and beyond what can be expected of an agent, and I am grateful every day that she was willing to put in the effort to make this book as good as it could possibly be.

Thanks to Chris Mangum, who maintains the code for my website, while Tara O'Shea manages the graphics. The words are all on me, which is why the site is so often out of date. Something's gotta give, and it's usually going to be me! Thanks to Terri Ash, who has joined the team as my new personal assistant—if you email through the website I just mentioned, she's the one who'll send your mail on to me. She's essential, and I am very glad she's here.

Thanks to the team at DAW, and to our new team at Astra, where I hope we will have many long and happy years.

Cat update (I know you all live for these): Thomas is a fine senior gentleman now, and while he has a touch of arthritis, his sweaters help to keep him warm, and I've set up cat stairs all over the house so he can still come and go as he pleases. Megara remains roughly as intelligent as bread mold, and is very happy as she is—this is not a cat burdened by the weight of a prodigious intellect! Elsie is healthy, fine, and very opinionated, and would like me to stop writing this and pet her. Tinkerbell is a snotty little diva who knows exactly how pretty she is, and Verity would like to speak to the manager. Of life. (If that all seems familiar, it's because it is. The cats are stable, which is wonderful.)

And now, gratitude in earnest. Thank you to everyone who reads, reviews, and helps to keep this series going; to Kate, for sharing an Airbnb and keeping me sane, as she always does; to Phil, who knows what he did; to Shawn, for being the best brother a girl could possibly want; to Chris Mangum, for being here even when it's inconvenient; to Whitney Johnson, for doing a friendship on a regular basis; to Manda Cherry, for a heated car seat and a wonderful friendship; to Michelle Dockrey, for my fabulous new pin board; and to my dearest Amy McNally, for everything. Thanks to the members of all four of my current ongoing D&D games. And to you: thank you, so much, for reading.

Any errors in this book are my own. The errors that aren't here are the ones that all these people helped me fix. I appreciate it so much.

Let's go home.